SOUL SWITCH

BILL HIATT

Edited by
GEORGE DONNELLY
Cover designed by
PETER O'CONNOR

For all of those who have done whatever it took to rescue someone they loved

ABDUCTION

THE DOOR BURST open so suddenly that DL jumped despite himself. Max raced in as if he had been shot out of a cannon. His hair looked as if he had been standing in a wind tunnel, and his eyes were wide with panic. He seemed jarringly out of place in the sedate Victorian interior of the house he had inherited from his grandmother. Posed against the intricately patterned floral wallpaper and the red and gold brocade curtains, he looked like an involuntary time traveler desperate to return to his own era.

"She's missing!" he yelled, grabbing DL by the shoulders. "Someone's taken her!"

"Calm down," said DL. "Who's missing?"

"Adreanna! She called me half-hysterical, saying someone was after her. When I got to her dorm room, she wasn't there."

"That's...odd," DL conceded. "What did her roommate have to say?"

"She wasn't there, either. The furniture has been knocked around—and there's blood on the carpet."

DL frowned. "What did the campus police say?"

"I haven't called them yet. There were...also signs of violent magic. Just standing in there made me feel a little crazy."

"Are you sure? You're the only sorcerer in the area, aren't you? Well, the only living one, anyway."

"I'm the only one we know about. This could be someone who has been hiding, or it could be a new arrival. Come to campus with me and help me check out the room."

"I'll help any way I can, but shouldn't you also get another spellcaster?"

Max slumped a little, and a hurt look flickered across his eyes. "You don't think I can handle this?"

"I've seen you go toe-to-toe with vampires—before you knew you had magic," said DL. "You can handle pretty much anything. We don't know who or what we're dealing with, though. I just thought we could find Adreanna faster if someone like Morfesa helped out."

"I tried contacting Morfesa, but I got no response. She told me that, depending on what's happening in Tír na nÓg, she might not be able to come right away. DL, we should go now."

"Don't be too hasty," whispered a voice in DL's head. Judging by Max's expression, he heard it, too.

A few months ago, Max's ghost grandmother, Maeve, would have frightened DL, but he was used to her making herself known from time to time by now. She was just another symptom of how crazy his life had become.

"I can't let something happen to Adreanna," said Max, one foot literally out the door.

"You need to have some kind of plan. You also need to have protections in place in case there really is a hostile sorcerer around." Maeve hardly ever wasted energy to make herself visible, but DL noticed a little flicker in the corner. As he watched, a translucent human form materialized. It flickered like a candle flame, but Maeve's stern and disapproving expression was clear enough.

Max looked as if impatience would cause his head to explode. Nonetheless, Maeve did have a point. He fumbled together some general protections against sorcery, wards that looked like rainbows folding around them. DL was no expert, but even he could tell they were a little uneven. Maeve had a number of critical things to say about his technique.

"Perhaps it would be best to wait for Morfesa."

"But Adreanna is in danger now, and Morfesa might not be able to come for hours," said Max. "We have to start searching for her."

The front door slammed shut. The magic that kept Maeve earthbound didn't allow her to do much outside the house that had once been hers, but she could still manipulate the magic that kept it secure from intruders—or, in this case, kept a panicky grandson safe from himself.

"I'm not a little kid," said Max. "You can't tell me what to do."

"Yet I am," said the ghost. *"When your studies with Morfesa and me have advanced enough that you can counter my magic, I'll stop interfering."*

Max looked imploringly at DL, who felt torn. Maeve had some grounds to be concerned about a semi-trained sorcerer running headlong into an unknown magical threat. On the other hand, DL knew what it was like for the woman he loved to be in danger.

"Maeve, you and I both know I can rip that door right off the hinges if I have to." More softly he added, "I'll make sure nothing happens to him."

"You're formidable in a physical fight," Maeve conceded, *"but there is magic in the world that could beat you easily. Have you forgotten how quickly those enchanted bullets tore through you faster than you could heal?"*

"Have it your way," said DL His inner dragon was never far from the surface these days. It came roaring out of the cave in his mind. He felt his strength surge far beyond what an adrenaline rush would produce and reached toward the door.

"Think twice about that. Your vampire lover slumbers in my cellar, and I could make her situation very uncomfortable."

DL hesitated. He doubted Maeve would really hurt Ekaterina, who had risked her own life to save Max's not very long ago. However, the house did have numerous protections against vampires, spells that Maeve kept in abeyance—but could activate at the drop of a hat if she felt like it.

"Enough of these threats!" shouted Max. "Ekaterina is as much a friend as DL is. If you hurt her, you'll get a rude reminder that I own this house now. I'll have bulldozers here tomorrow. How'd you like that?"

DL could feel Max's and Maeve's emotions crackling around him as if their nervous energy were bursting out of them and charging the air. "How about a compromise? Max and I will check out Adreanna's dorm room and see how much we can tell from it. We won't do anything else until Morfesa can join us."

After a long pause, Maeve said, *"Both of you must swear a solemn oath to me not to take action without appropriate backup."*

Both Max and DL swore the oath. DL could tell Maeve was just saving face, though. Had she wanted to be sure, she could have bound Max at least with magic to force him to live up to his oath. She didn't do that, presumably because she knew Max would refuse, and they'd all be back to square one.

Once Maeve released the door, Max went through it so fast he almost tripped going down the front steps. DL got out just before the door slammed loudly enough to make the neighbor's dog bark.

Max tripped on his way down the steps. He dropped his keys trying to get the car door open. DL wished he could cast a calming spell over him, but Max was the one with the magic. As Maeve never tired of pointing out, DL was the muscle—as if he were just a pile of meat, a sidekick to the heroic Max.

"She gets more difficult by the day," said Max as he and DL got into Max's Prius.

"She means well," said DL, though he felt his muscles tighten as he said it.

Max made a tense attempt to grin. "I know. This is one of those days when I want to find a good exorcist, though."

"Much as I hate to say it, she does have a point about being cautious."

Max scowled. "You're not going to start treating me like a kid, too, are you?" He pressed the dashboard a couple of time before realizing he was missing the power button.

"No—but you and I are both amateurs as far as the supernatural is concerned. Just a few months ago, you didn't even know about your magical heritage, and I had no idea I was some kind of Korean proto-dragon. We're both still learning how things work. It's not unreasonable to watch our step."

Instead of responding, Max pulled out of the driveway. Normally, he was a careful driver, but he accelerated to twenty miles over the speed limit before they reached the end of the block.

"We don't want to get pulled over," said DL. Max, trembling with impatience, could look suspicious to a traffic cop. Someone who didn't know Max could easily think he was high on some illegal stimulant—even without DL's draconic senses to detect the accelerated heart rate; rapid, shallow breathing; and muscular tension. Only in a combat situation had DL ever seen Max in such an agitated condition before.

Max greeted DL's warning with more silence, but he did slow down to the speed limit. DL relaxed just a little.

Max might not be the only one who would attract suspicion if they were stopped. Though the attempt to frame DL for murder had failed, he'd never been happy with the cover story concocted to explain away some of the weird goings-on a few months back. He couldn't be sure everyone in the police department bought it. Anyone who didn't might recognize him. It wasn't just that Eau Claire, Wisconsin had a small Asian population. That he looked like a bodybuilder made him more conspicuous. A lot of cops had seen his picture and might recognize him. That could lead to more questions. He and Max didn't have time for questions right now—and there were too many they couldn't answer.

Max drove on in silence, his cold and forbidding aura a sharp contrast to the bright sunlight and trees swaying in the gentle breeze on both sides of the road.

DL put a hand on his arm. "It'll be OK. We'll get her back."

"I hope so." Max kept his eyes on the road. His knuckles were white from gripping the wheel so hard. His breathing quickened when they reached the University of Wisconsin campus.

"Where're we going to park?" asked Max. He had a permit for the Phillips Hall lot—but Adreanna's dorm was Oak Ridge Hall on the other side of the campus.

"Never mind," he said. "I'll fix it." He picked up his permit and stared at it for a moment. It blurred and became an Oak Ridge permit. The illusion was so strong even DL's draconic sight couldn't penetrate it.

"What if somebody—" began DL.

"We don't have time to run across campus. Anyway, what are odds someone who knows me sees us get out?"

Max might look like a bundle of nerves ready to explode at any moment, but his voice was surprisingly calm and even. He mind was not just made up—it was set in concrete.

The lot had plenty of space. Max jumped out of the car as soon as he'd turned the engine off, but he surprised DL by not running in the direction of the red brick dorm. Instead, he glanced around furtively, muttered something in Old Welsh, and made a couple of quick hand motions. DL saw a magic field clear as glass envelop Max and him.

"See, I'm being cautious," muttered Max. "Now we're invisible to anyone except each other."

"Good move, but don't let it make you careless. Didn't you tell me any decent sorcerer can see through invisibility?"

Max looked at DL closely. "Are you trying to talk me out of rescuing Adreanna? Because if you are—"

"Chill, dude. You know me well enough to know I would never tell you that. Let's just make sure we're smart about what we do."

"I'll be the soul of caution," he said. He ran toward the dorm, almost colliding with a couple of students going out, and went through the door without looking to see if anyone was watching. Max might be invisible, but someone could certainly see the door opening and closing by itself—and wonder.

DL sighed and jogged after him, afraid he would vanish into the dorm—particularly problematic since DL had no idea what Adreanna's room number was.

Max had at least enough self-control to wait for DL. As soon as they were together again, though, the young sorcerer raced over to the stairs and bounded up them. His heavy footfalls echoed in the stairwell, and DL realized Max had forgotten to make them inaudible.

Max was mature for his age, as well as very intelligent, but adrenaline was making him stupid.

Max exited the stairs on the second floor and loped down the west wing hallway. The floor was carpeted, but the pounding of his feet was still unmistakable. DL was surprised people weren't sticking their heads out to see what was happening.

Adreanna's door was slightly ajar. Max pushed in before DL could stop him, leaving prints for the campus police to find. Of course, he was Adreanna's boyfriend, so his prints would likely be all over the room, anyway. DL reminded himself to avoid touching anything with bare hands.

Once in the room, Max assumed a more businesslike demeanor, though the darkness of his aura revealed that his anxiety hadn't lessened. DL could see immediately why Max had panicked. A couple of chairs had been knocked over, what appeared to be Adreanna's cell phone was lying on the ground, and there was a suspicious- looking red stain on the carpet.

DL awakened his dragon again and sniffed. "That's human blood," he said.

"I know," said Max. "I checked with magic when I first got here. Speaking of, you see what I mean about magic residue?"

DL's eyes narrowed. "Yeah. I'm not experienced enough to tell what kind of magic, but I can definitely see traces of something beyond whatever you did in here." Angry red flecks like bloody dust floated in the air and spotted some of the furniture.

"To me, it looks like…an effort to violently subdue someone. See why I'm sure this is a kidnapping?"

"You're right. You better try Morfesa again and see if you can reach her."

"In a minute. Let's see if we can track Adreanna before the scent gets cold."

Max performed what DL thought was a locator spell, using the blood as an anchor. Tiny tendrils of magic rose from the blood and stretched out in all directions, searching for Adreanna. DL sniffed around the room and out into the hallway. He could catch Adreanna's scent, but the trail was older than the blood. There was no sign of a trail exiting the room after the blood had been shed. Nor was there any blood trail in the hall, though Adreanna would have to have been bleeding by the time her abductor left with her.

He walked back into the room as quickly and quietly as he could. "There's no sign Adreanna left the room once she got here. Either someone flew her out the window, or they took her out by portal."

Max raised an eyebrow. "You can tell all that from scent?"

DL shrugged. "Ekaterina's been using heightened senses for centuries. She helped me train."

"Lucky for me she did," said Max. He checked the window. "It's locked. Unless somebody went to a lot of trouble to camouflage the fact that they used the window, I'd say flying is out of the question."

DL squinted as he scanned the air in the room. "Those little silver flecks over there. I can barely see them. They look like portal residue, though, right?"

Max nodded his head. "First break we've had. Someone had been sloppy when they exited. I might be able to follow the trail left by the portal."

"Wait a minute!" DL said, alarm bells going off in his head. "I thought you hadn't mastered portals yet."

"I haven't," admitted Max. "They take a lot of skill and practice. However, jumping through the remains of a portal someone else created is easier—if we can do it before the traces fade away. After that, we're stuck. My locator spell got nowhere, which either means someone is blocking it or that Adreanna is not in this world anymore."

"If you're working up to telling me we have to do this before Morfesa can get here—"

"I'm afraid that's exactly what I'm doing," said Max, his words edged with steel. "The traces are already almost gone now. Another few minutes, and there'll be nothing left."

"Max, this whole situation has *trap* written all over it. A nonmagical human gets kidnapped by someone with magic for no apparent reason. Then the kidnapper leaves a portal trail—which you told me just the other day no competent sorcerer ever does—as if inviting us to follow."

Max chewed his lower lip a little and looked into DL's eyes.

"If it were Ekaterina at the other end of that portal trail, you'd follow it without a second thought—and I'd be right behind you. I'd crawl halfway around the world over broken glass to help you."

DL sighed. Max could be a drama king at times. However, DL had no doubt that the kid would always have his back.

"This better work out well, or your grandmother will skin both of us alive."

"Well, look at this way," said Max. "If this is a trap, my grandmother is going to be the least of our worries."

If that was supposed to be a joke, DL wasn't laughing.

"If I can manage to follow that recent portal to wherever it leads, I can…prop it open, I guess you'd say. I can keep it from vanishing completely, then use it to get back. See, the plan isn't as risky as you thought."

Max's body was stiff with tension as he strove to pry open the earlier portal. The faint traces stirred, sped up like dust in the wind, and resolved themselves into a silver swirl big enough to walk through. Max and DL stepped through the argent doorway into the unknown.

MISFITS

"ARE WE…UPSIDE DOWN?" asked DL.

"No," said Max, wrinkling his forehead. "Something is wrong, though. I think it's just appearance."

"Let's hope," said DL. The ground beneath their feet was sky-blue. The sky was dark brown, like the roof of a cave. The effect was enough to stir up even the most deeply repressed acrophobia.

DL sniffed. The air smelled like soil, though at least he didn't feel he was breathing dirt. "Is this world safe for us?"

Max nodded. "I'm not sensing or seeing any immediate threat."

DL knelt down and sniffed at the ground, which smelled like fresh air.

"Can you pick up Adreanna's scent?" asked Max.

"No such luck," said DL, looking quickly around. The landscape was more or less unvarying, though here and there were patches of ground that looked like clouds. In the distance stood patches of trees with green, veined trunks and brown, barklike leaves.

Max closed his eyes. His face tensed with concentration. Thin tendrils of magic reached out from the sorcerer in all directions.

"I can't sense any sign of her either," said Max. "This is bad. I don't know if her abductor moved her far from here at tremendous speed or just portal-hopped her to another world. Either way—"

"Welcome!" shouted someone from behind them. The voice sounded too happy, almost manic. Then there was a soft thud, as if someone who had been flying had just landed right behind them.

DL and Max both spun around. DL braced himself for a possible attack and let his inner dragon get very close to the surface. Both paused, though, at the sight of the faerie who was smiling broadly at them.

Only a few months before, they'd fought side by side with faerie leaders like Gwynn ap Nudd and Coventina, the original Lady of the Lake, so DL thought the newcomer might be a potential ally. Maybe Morfesa, unable to come herself, had sent someone to help.

"Your greeting cheers our heart, friend," said Max, bowing slightly. "I fear we are lost. Can you tell us where we are?"

"I'm not sure of the name of the place myself," said the stranger. "I find it suits me well, though." He fidgeted as he spoke, and his words tumbled out rapidly.

The faeries DL and Max had met before were invariably good-looking. This one could have been called handsome, but his dark hair was wild, as if he had never heard of a comb. His eyes darted back and forth, and his general manner was unsettling. The more DL looked at that smile, the more disquieting it became. It might not be phony, but there was something off about it.

"I am Max of—"

"Oh, I know well who you are," interrupted the faerie. Then he giggled as if he were in on some joke from which DL and Max had been deliberately excluded.

"Then you have us at a disadvantage," said Max. "May we know to whom we have the honor of speaking?"

The faerie giggled again. "Know you not your own kinsman? Is not your grandmother Maeve Murphy, a descendant of Maeve, faerie queen of Connacht?"

"So I have been told," said Max.

"I am distant kin to Maeve, and therefore I am kin to you as well. Perhaps you have heard of me. I am the Amadan Dubh."

Max froze as if the stranger had just announced he was a serial killer.

DL would have liked to know what was up. After DL had used his blood to heal Max, the two of them had some ability to communicate mentally, but Max was so tense that he didn't respond when DL tried to ask who the Amadan Dubh was.

"Forgive me, kinsman, but we must be on our way," said Max, taking a step back and bowing again. "We are on a most urgent mission."

"To save the girl?" asked Dubh.

"What do you know of the girl?" asked Max, his voice cracking.

"There's no need to save her. She's my guest." Dubh's grin remained plastered on his face, giving him the appearance of the villain in a clown horror movie.

"What do you mean, guest?" asked Max, his tone far less polite than it had been. "We found blood in her room."

"An unfortunate misunderstanding. She didn't want to be my guest at first."

DL braced himself to lunge at Dubh. Faeries were fast, but his inner dragon could make him just as fast.

"Stop!" yelled Max. "Stay away from him!"

"Ah, so you have heard of me," said Dubh, his smile getting even bigger. "That will make things so much easier."

"I could take him," muttered DL.

"The wizardling knows why you can't. One touch from me can drive a person mad or even paralyze him—permanently. We wouldn't want that, now would we?"

"What do you want?" asked Max. His voice was cold as a sword in the Arctic.

"Right down to business," said Dubh, flashing them a mocking smile. "And here we were having such a nice chat. Well, as you wish.

"I won't bore you with the various wrongs I have suffered over the centuries. Faerie society never understood me. In one way or another, the rulers all sought order. I, on the other hand, sought chaos. So much more invigorating! Eventually, I realized that I would need to create my own world if I wanted to live as I pleased.

"Alas, creating a world is not as easy as it sounds. My early attempts failed for lack of power. I finally managed to obtain a tool that might have given me enough power to do the job: the lyre of Orpheus. I'm quite a good musician, if I do say so myself." He pulled out small reed pipes and played a few notes to demonstrate. The melody was subtly wrong. DL and Max both winced.

"I won't favor you with any more of my playing. I'm afraid that, too, can drive a man mad if he fails to appreciate its finer points. In any case, the lyre amplified my own magic considerably. Unfortunately, it was stolen from me, and I was imprisoned. I only recently managed to break free."

"And you want us to retrieve the lyre for you?" asked Max.

Dubh laughed maniacally. "No, of course not. I know you and lizard boy lack the strength to do that, for the lyre is well-guarded by powerful forces. You do, however, have access to something that in my hands could give me enough magic that I would no longer need the lyre: Merlin's grimoire."

"I don't have that," said Max. He was a smoother liar than DL expected.

Dubh giggled. "Yes, Morfesa keeps it with her in Falias. Did you think I hadn't done my research? Still, you have access during your training, do you not? When you have it in your hands, grab it and run. You already know the book is more than just a compilation of spells. Green as you are, with it in your hands, Morfesa won't be able to stop you, especially if you catch her by surprise.

"Deliver the book to me, and I will deliver the girl to you. Simple, easy."

"Except that Morfesa will—" began Max.

"I know, I know, she'll try to prevent you from making off with the book, even though it is yours, a gift from the spirit of Merlin himself. She'll figure out someone is forcing you to take it. Likely, she'll bring in the other druids of Tír na nÓg, the Tuatha de Danaan, and, given the time, a dozen or so other faerie armies.

"Leave them to me. I'm good at hiding. Even with Merlin's book, I'd be no match for the united forces of the faeries—but they'll never find me."

"If you know that much about the grimoire, you must know it also has…a mind of its own," said Max. "It will only open for Merlin or for someone who has Merlin's blessing."

Dubh giggled. "You think I'm so easily tricked. I know as well as you do that, as the current owner of the book, you could grant me the ability to open it.

"What is it to be? Adreanna or the book? Which one do you value more?"

DL didn't want Max to have to face that kind of choice. Fighting Dubh was certainly dangerous, but it might be possible if DL could catch the faerie by surprise.

Dubh's attention was focused on Max, who looked frozen. DL threw himself in the direction of the faerie. With DL only inches away, the faerie flew into the air as if he were rocket-powered. He looked down and laughed in a way that would have made a psychologist shudder.

"As if I didn't see that coming! I can see I need to give you time to reflect."

Drawing on his draconic strength, DL leaped inhumanly high and grabbed Dubh's ankle, then let gravity do the rest. The faerie could fly, but he couldn't carry all two hundred pounds of DL. He squirmed and thrashed furiously as the ground loomed beneath them.

DL managed to flip their positions so that Dubh hit first with a resounding thud. DL landed on top of him with a satisfying crunch and pinned his arms to the ground.

Max wove a magic suppression spell that looked like liquid gauze around Dubh. He also locked the faerie's arms in place so that DL could get off him.

"Let me go!" Dubh yelled, twisting against the spells in which he was netted. "You can't hold me for long, wizardling, and when I'm free, you and the human lizard will both be dead."

"If you kill us, you'll never get the book," said Max, smirking.

"Then I'll make you wish you were dead," said Dubh, though he sounded more whiney than menacing.

"Here's what's going to happen instead," said DL—who did sound menacing. "You're going to take us to Adreanna, and if she's unharmed, we'll let you go. If she isn't, or if you refuse to take us, I'll kill you with my bare hands." Just to make sure Dubh got the point, DL let his inner dragon peer out through his eyes. Dubh looked satisfyingly horrified, and a shudder ran through his helpless body.

"I'm a faerie royal. If you kill me, Queen Maeve will avenge me." Dubh's eyes darted back and forth as if he were expecting the cavalry to come charging over the nearest hill. The shudder had now become continuous.

"You're a fugitive," said Max. "Not only that, but you've meddled yet again in the human world. Your own kin would thank us if we killed you. However, just to be on the safe side, we won't kill you. We'll hand you over to the faerie authorities and let them decide what to do with you. They *might* let you live—in prison forever."

"What about a different deal?" asked Dubh. "I don't need the book forever, just long enough to make my world. Give me the book, I'll give you the girl unharmed. After that, I'll return the book as soon as my world is complete. I'll take an oath, and you can impose a *geas* on me to ensure I fulfill all the terms. That's fair, isn't it?"

"I don't trust what you might do while you have the book," said Max. "Why should I? You kidnapped someone I care about."

"Enough talk," said DL. "Tell us where Adreanna is, or I start ripping you apart." He felt fangs and claws yearning to break loose. Dubh's eyes widened.

"You…you think I didn't…I didn't plan for this? Any pain I suffer will be shared by the girl. If she loses her connection with me, she will die."

Dubh's skin had gone chalk white, and his shaking was more or less continuous. Did fear make him more likely to tell the truth or more likely to lie?

DL looked at Max for confirmation. The young sorcerer squinted at Dubh.

"There is complex magic around him—too complex for me to be sure."

DL couldn't interpret the overlaid auras he saw around Dubh, either. Looking at all the minute twists and turns was like listening to Dubh's jarring music.

"If they're connected, couldn't we find her by following that connection?" asked DL.

"In theory," said Max. "The bond itself—if there is one—isn't visible. It could take a lot of probing to trace it."

"I don't want to hurt her. I only took her to get your attention." Dubh was shaking a little less. "You, of all people, should understand what I've gone through, why I need my own world. You're both as much misfits as I am."

"Lizard boy, how do you suppose your dragon kin view you after you sacrificed your Yeouiju to reanimate your *vampire* lover? If I were you, I wouldn't wander into a dragon realm to find out.

"And you, wizardling, the mere student to whom Merlin inexplicably gifted his grimoire, what of you? You may be envied for that—but if you think you will ever be respected, think again.

"Oh, let us not forget Lizard Boy's vampire. Most of the supernatural community suspects her goodness of being some kind of act, and her vampire kin hate her for making such a claim in the first place.

"I'm a misfit, an outcast—but at least I have the wit to realize it."

"You're just trying to get in our heads," said DL.

"Tis easy to get inside your heads," said Dubh. "There's so much extra space there."

"Here's the deal." Max put up a restraining hand to deter DL from taking a swing at Dubh. "Surrender Adreanna unharmed, or face eternity in prison—at best. You can taunt us as much as you want. It will not change the reality of the situation."

Dubh managed a somewhat hardier laugh. "Take me to the faerie rulers then. Go ahead!"

Max glanced back at the remains of the portal that they had used to follow Dubh. At some point while he and DL had been focused on the faerie, the spell keeping it from closing completely had failed, and their only way home had faded away.

Had Dubh done enough research to know that Max couldn't open portals on his own yet? Had he just been listening in on the conversation before he made his appearance? Either way, DL and Max were trapped now.

"The book for Adreanna—and a way home. Seems like a fair deal to me."

"It would be less risky to figure out how to cut your bond with Adreanna and then kill you," said Max.

DL restrained himself from looking in Max's direction. Was his friend bluffing?

Max raised a grayish barrier between them and Dubh. "We need to talk without Dubh eavesdropping."

The faerie gave another spasmodic jerk at his magical restraints and started screaming for no apparent reason. The barrier became a little grayer, and the sound of his screaming faded away.

"I can't really risk meddling with a spell I don't understand," said Max. "I can't give Dubh the book, either."

"Why not just call Morfesa?" asked DL.

Max held up his right hand. A silver ring glistened on one of his fingers. "This ring lets me call out to her across the boundary between planes of existence, but it only works between Earth and Tír na nÓg. Where we are now, it's just a metal band."

"Can you…oh, I don't know. Change its settings or something?"

"It's tricky enough to communicate between planes. It's even harder to adjust an object like this once the magic has been forged. Morfesa could probably do it, but I haven't learned how yet. Anyway, even if I could reach her, she's probably never been here, which means she can't open a portal to wherever this is."

DL closed his eyes. "We must be too far away for my blood bond with Ekaterina to do us any good, either."

"Yeah, it figures this place isn't close enough to Earth from a magical perspective for such ties to function. Dubh may be crazy, but he picked a good spot to lure us."

"You're sure you can't open a portal?" asked DL.

"I'll give it a try eventually, but let's not forget the reason we came in the first place. I don't want to leave without Adreanna. Who knows what kind of a horrible place Dubh has her imprisoned? And think about how frightened she must be."

"Yeah, finding her is the first priority. Can you use magic to get the location out of Dubh?"

Max frowned. "From what Morfesa's told me about him, the insanity may be just a way to trick people. He's outwitted faerie rulers more than once. Anyway, mind control's always tough, and Dubh is a faerie with centuries of experience at resisting it. We aren't the first people who needed information that he refused to give up."

DL scowled. "So we can't find Adreanna, and even if we could, we can't get her—or ourselves—back home. I bet no one else can find us either."

"Not easily," Max said. "There is an infinite number of planes of existence, and my guess is Dubh hides here because no one from the faerie realms except him has ever found it. Morfesa has told me about many places, but none that looks even remotely like this."

DL raised an eyebrow. "If it's so remote, how could he have found it? He couldn't open a portal to someplace he'd never been any more than Morfesa could, right?"

Max frowned. "In theory, it's possible to visualize the *kind* of place you want to be and open a portal based on your vision—in Dubh's case, a world far more chaotic than any of the faerie realms. However, that requires far greater power than opening a regular portal, and it's risky as hell. That's why it's called a wild portal. The caster might end up in a place that meets the literal requirements of his vision but is dangerous in some other way he didn't anticipate. Let's say a sorcerer wanted to visit a world with a purple sky for some reason and managed to reach one— only to discover that whatever was making the sky purple was also instantly poisonous. There's no way to visualize every possible problem.

"Anyway, I assume that's what Dubh did to reach here, but knowing that doesn't help. Even if I could reach Morfesa from here, and even if she were willing to try opening a wild portal, without knowing exactly what Dubh visualized to get here, there's little chance she'd open a portal to here. Strange as it may seem, there could be many worlds with reversed earth and sky color. And even if she somehow beat the odds and opened a portal to the right one, it might not be anywhere near where we are. Who knows how long it might take to find us?"

"We've been in tougher spots before," said DL, trying to sound more confident than he felt. They'd never been in another world with no way back.

Max looked in Dubh's direction, and his eyes widened. "I shouldn't have muted him. He's sung his way out of my spells."

Sure enough, Dubh was on his feet, playing frenetically on his pipes, stopping only to sing. They couldn't hear any of it, though.

Max tried to bind him again, but this time the faerie was ready for him. The spells swirled around him but couldn't get a grip.

"He'll figure out we can't hear him any time now and try to strip that spell away," said Max. He was sweating and looked pale. "Then it won't be long before he can drive us mad."

"The protective spells—" began DL.

"Won't hold for very long against him. He's powerful, and the music amplifies his magic."

DL knew what he had to do. He drew strength and speed from his inner dragon and charged Dubh. The moment he passed through the sound barrier Max had put up, the discordant music assailed his senses, but the dragon also made him tough enough to bear it for the few seconds it would take him to close the gap between them.

Dubh stopped playing and raised his hands, which were gloved in a glow that was hard to look at. The faerie was ready to hit him with madness or paralysis, maybe even both. DL dived low, almost as if he were trying to slide into home plate. Dubh flew straight up. DL, committed to hitting at almost ground level, couldn't jump up fast enough to grab the faerie this time.

"You'll take my deal—eventually," Dubh yelled down at them. He laughed and flew away, until only his mocking echo remained.

DL looked helplessly after him and cursed. "Max, can you follow him?"

"Sorry," said Max, coming up behind him. "I can levitate, and I can float a little, but I could never keep up with a natural flier like a faerie. He's already far beyond my reach. That might be a blessing in disguise, though."

"How do you figure that? We're trapped here, and we have no way to find Adreanna."

"The only way to get help from Dubh would be to agree to his terms. Do you want to trust a lunatic like Dubh with the power to make a new world?"

"No way!" said DL.

"Well, neither do I. He'd be as likely to destroy our world by accident—and then laugh about it. With him gone, we can look for Adreanna in peace.

"At some point, Morfesa is going to answer my call and discover I'm missing. She'll consult a seer, figure out where I am, and find a way to get us back. If we're reunited with Adreanna by then, Dubh will have no more leverage on us."

"You just said there was no way for Morfesa to get us back."

"No way I know of," said Max. "Morfesa has the experience of centuries and the wisdom of the Tuatha de Danaan to draw on. It may take time, but she can do it."

DL figured having a sequence like the one Max described actually work was about as probable as someone creating lasting peace in the Middle East by the time they returned. He didn't have a better idea to offer, though, so there was no point in trying to crush Max's optimism.

Long-range locator spells still didn't turn up any sign of Adreanna, but Max wasn't daunted.

"Dubh could be masking her presence somehow. We'll just have to look for her the old-fashioned way. I bet she's somewhere nearby. Dubh would have expected me to demand to see her and make sure she was all right before agreeing to his deal."

They walked slowly across the unsettling landscape. Max searched through magic, looking both for Adreanna and for "holes" in his scans that might suggest concealment spells. DL used his draconic sight, hearing, and smell to search for more physical clues. Between them, they made an effective team—but after several hours, they had found no sign of her.

They did, however, find someone else.

"People are approaching our position," said Max.

"I'm getting an unfamiliar scent—humanoid, but not quite human. Lots of them, right?"

"I'd say twenty. What do we do now?"

"Run like hell?" DL wasn't really expecting Max to take his advice, but that was his first impulse.

"I can't be sure they're hostile. This is a highly magical world. They might have the power to find someone in it much faster than we can."

"Or they might decide we look like dinner. Seeming more or less human doesn't mean they are human."

The advancing natives looked somewhat like Hollywood cavemen, but with one important difference: their physical appearance was inverted in much the same way as the landscape was. They appeared to be wearing human skin, and their own skin looked like furry animal hide. All of them were armed with long spears, also inverted (stone shafts and wooden tips). They did not at first seem hostile, but when they caught sight of DL and Max, they broke into a run. DL had to resist the impulse to grab Max, who clearly wanted to meet the natives, and carry him away, running at full dragon speed.

"Welcome, strangers!" yelled one of them in a deep and resonant voice.

"They speak English?" asked DL.

"It's some kind of translation spell. I can feel it in the air," said Max.

The group reached spear-throwing range but didn't try to attack. They spread out to encircle DL and Max. Though their manner was friendly enough, DL began to feel claustrophobic.

The tallest among them stepped forward. His skin robe was covered with symbols DL had never seen before, but they did remind him of a magician's costume. Instead of a spear, this native carried what looked a lot like a sorcerer's staff. It gleamed like crystal but had a large wooden ball at the top.

"Strangers, we have never seen your like before. How did you come here?"

"Through a portal from another world," said Max. "We did not mean any trespass. We are just looking for a friend who has been lost."

"Another world?" asked the leader.

Max tried to explain the concept, but he got nowhere. "Excuse me," he said at last. "I fear I'm just confusing you. Let's just say we came from a different place. Perhaps you can help us find her."

The leader sniffed at Max. "You have command of natural forces?"

"Not perhaps here as well as in my…place, but yes, I have some ability to manipulate nature."

The leader turned to DL. "Your smell is strange to me. You are special in your home place?"

"I wouldn't say special. More like…unusual."

"Unusual? In other words, rare?"

"I guess you could say that," said DL. Dubh's insult about misfits still bothered him.

The leader smiled broadly. "That is excellent Each of you is special, and you are welcome indeed.

"You will be the perfect sacrifices to our god."

HUMAN SACRIFICES

"What…what do you mean by sacrifices?" asked Max.

"I do not know what the custom is in your…place, but here we usually use fire," replied the leader. "Our god seems to like sacrifices better when there is much screaming."

There was a time for diplomacy, but DL figured this wasn't it. The leader's magic looked strong, but he didn't seem physically formidable, so DL threw himself at him with every ounce of strength he could muster. The leader fell, letting go of the crystal staff in the process. DL moved to follow up, but magic gripped his limbs, holding him in place.

None of these native could take him in a physical fight—but all of them had magic, not just the leader. He struggled as hard as he could, but, judging from the strength of his bonds, some of the spear carriers had united against him in a restraining spell, and he lacked the strength to break it. The remaining ones had their spears aimed right at Max's heart.

Max's fists were clenched, and magic crackled around him like static electricity. The spear carriers poised to throw. DL yelled, "We surrender," hoping the kid would take the hint. He looked puzzled but stopped trying to use magic. They restrained him as tightly as they had DL.

The leader glared at Max and DL as he dusted himself off. "What is the meaning of this breach of tradition? It is not permitted to assault a staff holder in this way. Were you not so perfect for a sacrifice, you would be severely punished."

"It is not our custom to sacrifice people to our god," said Max, his voice surprisingly even.

The leader may have raised an eyebrow. His face was so furry that it was hard to tell.

"What an uncivilized place you must come from! It amazes me that your god will tolerate such insolence. And you! Why would you want to turn down such an honor?"

"We believe that our God requires service from us. He does *not* require us to sacrifice others."

"I have never heard of such a thing. Your god must be very weak by now from the lack of sacrifice. If he opposes the practice, I would have thought he would protect you. Only his weakness could explain why he has not rescued you."

"Weakness?" thundered a voice from the brown heavens. "I am not weak!"

A lightning bolt struck the ground nearby, and the spear carriers jumped. A gigantic figure that looked a lot like the white-bearded and white-robed God from Michelangelo's *Creation of Adam* materialized where the lightning had struck, and the spear carriers froze. His expression was more like an image of the last judgment, though—wrathful and implacable.

"Release my followers!" The voice was loud enough to shake the ground.

DL had a hard time imagining the intruder actually was God—but at this point, he'd take help anywhere he could find it.

The staff holder squinted at him. "You do not look like a god to me. Let us see if you truly have a god's power." He waved his staff, which shot a beam of brownish light in the direction of the apparition, who dodged rather than letting the beam strike him.

"Feel my wrath!" shouted the figure, and lightning flashed and crackled all around them. Undaunted, the leader fired another beam, and this one struck the supposed god.

"Ouch!" cried the alleged deity.

"Begone!" yelled the leader, firing again. The figure dodged, and the beam missed him by inches.

DL strained against the spell holding him in place, but he still couldn't move much.

Their defender clearly wasn't God, and the natives knew it. Even DL noticed that the ground seemed unaffected by the lightning strikes. Illusions!

The leader kept up his attack, filling the air with so much magic that the breeze twisted as if it were trying to blow in different directions at the same time. DL was surprised he could still breathe.

Max's eyes were closed, and his face tightened in concentration. DL tried to reach along their blood bond to lend him strength, but the connection felt frayed and shrunken, unsuited for the stress DL was putting on it.

The fake god continued to dodge, but more slowly. Sooner or later the leader would injure him enough to bring him down, and then the charade would end. DL threw every ounce of dragon strength he could muster into an effort to rip free of the imprisoning spell. He couldn't move an inch.

A wild idea occurred to him. To save Ekaterina's life, he had imbued her with the power of his Yeouiju. Merlin had told him that in some ways she now *was* his Yeouiju. Could the bond between Yeouiju and dragon be strong enough to work across worlds? He'd never tried before, but he'd never faced a life-or-death situation that required him to.

He reached out, not through the blood bond with Ekaterina but through the Yeouiju.

"Speak to Ekaterina as you once spoke to me," he told it. *"Let her know where we are."* He concentrated as hard as he could on that message, repeating it over and over. He longed for even a slight hint of connection, but he felt nothing. His words could be getting lost somewhere in the vast space separating him from Ekaterina. He couldn't even be sure that the Yeouiju could hear him anymore. Maybe in saving Ekaterina, it had lost whatever sentience it had possessed. Merlin could have been wrong about it.

Of course, even if Ekaterina got the message, she had no way to reach them, but perhaps Morfesa could if the Yeouiju connection really worked. Max had called to her what must have been hours ago.

DL reached out to Max through their blood bond. *"Max, I may have a way to communicate with our world, through the Yeouiju, but I'm not sure what's left of it is strong enough. Can you find some way of boosting its signal?"*

Max didn't answer directly, but DL felt a surge of power crackling through him. He did what he could to channel it into the Yeouiju, which was still unresponsive.

As the bogus god weaved back and forth in a desperate effort to avoid getting blasted with the leader's magic, DL noticed something in his hands—reed pipes.

The Amadan Dubh was the one trying to rescue them!

Even as he flew around frenetically, he began to play on his pipes. The sound was jarring, but this time, at least, its insanity-producing tune wasn't directed at DL and Max. The spear carriers shook, wild-eyed, though the leader remained calm.

DL tested the magical restraints and found he had a little more wiggle room. If Dubh could keep up the music just a little longer, he might weaken them enough for DL to escape.

One of the brown rays hit Dubh, and this time he screamed, a sound even more jarring than his music.

He kept playing through the pain, but the music was different. The notes tore at the very world around them. Reality blurred.

"Max, what's happening?" he yelled. The natives were too preoccupied holding onto their own sanity to care what he and Max were doing.

"Dubh's music is disrupting the magic that holds this world together!" Max yelled back.

"He's that powerful?"

"I think only the immediate area is affected. The balance was very delicate, though. Dubh could do a lot of damage."

"Who is this Dubh?" demanded the leader, waving his staff.

"Better release us before you find out," said DL, trying his best to sound menacing.

The colors around him flashed frantically. Sometimes the sky looked as blue as in DL's world. Other times it was green or gold. The ground looked like a rainbow half the time.

The spear carriers dropped their weapons and screamed in weird unison with the music. Dubh's God illusion was shredding, revealing more and more of the faerie underneath it, but his playing never faltered.

"*DL,*" whispered a voice in his head. Ekaterina!

"*You got my message!*"

"*I felt it in my blood. I felt it in my heart. Stay focused on me. Morfesa is trying to figure out how to use the Yeouiju connection to open a portal to wherever you are. Maeve is helping her as much as she can.*"

"*They're working together?*" asked DL. "*I never thought I'd see the day.*"

The leader's magic blasts shifted colors with psychedelic haste, and their reach was falling short of Dubh, who now clearly had the upper hand.

"*DL, can you hear me?*" asked Max. "*I'm trying to link us up.*"

"*I can hear you fine—and, thanks to that power boost, I managed to link with Ekaterina. We may be getting rescued soon!*"

"*It's a good thing! Dubh is making this place as unstable as he is.*"

"*Morfesa can't get a portal open.*" Ekaterina's thoughts were barely audible. The warring magics in the air must have been whipping up a ton of static. "*She needs someone on this end who's been to that world to make her spell work.*"

"*Does that mean we're stuck?*"

"*No, but the only way she can think of to get you and Max back is risky.*"

"*It can't be any riskier than staying here. What does she have to do?*"

"*She wants to try to draw your spirit here, sort of like astral projection. If she can do that, you'll be close enough for her to use your experience with the place to open a portal to it.*"

"*So, what's the risk?*" DL asked. He already had a pretty good idea what it might be.

"*Even exploiting the Yeouiju connection between you and me, Morfesa is having a hard time maintaining contact. It's possible she could lose her grip on your spirit somewhere in between that world and this one. It might…take time for your spirit to find its way back to your body. It's…DL, it's even possible your body could die before your spirit can return.*"

"DL!" Max's thoughts were like a shout in comparison to Ekaterina's whisper. *"If we aren't getting rescued right now, we've got to move. Somewhere, just beyond the chaos, I'm sensing off-the-charts power. I think whoever—whatever—is the god of these people is coming."*

DL tested the bonds again. The spell that had once felt like steel was now more like spaghetti. He could definitely break free. However, when he looked around him, both earth and sky had become one undifferentiated, strobing rainbow. Just looking at it made him nauseated. He couldn't imagine trying to run away from Dubh or the natives in an environment like this. Whoever won the magical duel, Max and DL would definitely be running away from someone.

"Ekaterina, tell Morfesa to do whatever she needs to do. There's no choice."

Ekaterina didn't respond, but DL felt a wrenching sensation, as if the world had turned sideways. Darkness engulfed him, and a weird sensation halfway between falling and flying made him dizzy. How long that continued, he couldn't tell. He wanted to let Max know what was up, but their connection had shriveled down to a tiny hole through which his thoughts could no longer flow. He could at least feel Ekaterina's presence somewhere, but he couldn't communicate with her, either.

He found himself in the Eau Claire house as abruptly as if he'd changed channels on a TV. Reality shifting so rapidly disoriented him for a few seconds. It was also disquieting to be hovering, ghostlike, above the floor. He had to remind himself that only his spirit was here; his body was still in another world.

"He's here!" said a familiar voice. DL looked over and saw Maeve standing in the corner. He couldn't normally see the ghost this clearly—but then they weren't normally on the same wavelength. When she did manifest enough to be visible, she often favored appearing as her younger self, but this time she was in her more grandmotherly form. The concern on her face was plain.

"Yes, I can see him," said Morfesa. She looked grim, and the green glow from her staff was so intense it washed out everything about her except the green of her piercing eyes. Her red hair faded to dull brown, and her light skin darkened to sickly green. She reminded DL so much of Dubh's nightmare world that it was hard to look at her.

It was much easier for him to look at Ekaterina, though her even paler skin was also green in the reflected light. On her, the green light looked more emerald than sickly. Centuries of suffering had failed to grind away the modellike beauty of her features, the youthful exuberance of her expression, or the warmth of her smile. He had found his first real love later than some people, but the wait had been worth it.

DL could feel someone else in his mind, no doubt Morfesa. At the same time, he caught flickers of what was still going on in that faraway place. The leader still stood, but Dubh had reduced the space all around him to chaos.

A portal flickered to life but collapsed again. Morfesa's expression shifted from grim to pained. She made another attempt, which lasted a few seconds later before blowing out like a candle in the wind.

"DL, can you help me? The Yeouiju power could give me the strength to do what I must, but I cannot fully access it. Can you try?"

"I didn't even know before today that I could still communicate with it, but I'll do what I can."

Morfesa was holding hands with Ekaterina, but physical contact wasn't enough.

"Can you feel the druid reaching for your power? Let her use it. I'm going to die otherwise."

As with his attempt to send a message, the Yeouiju didn't answer him. Maybe it couldn't. However, a portal swirled into being and did not immediately collapse.

"Morfesa! Put me back in my body so I can step through the portal."

She took so long to respond that DL panicked despite himself. Finally, she thought, *"If I do that right now, the portal could collapse. Can Max carry you through?"*

Under other circumstances, DL would have laughed. Max wouldn't have been able to lift his own body weight, let alone carry DL's.

"I doubt it. What about levitation?"

"Whether that will work in such a magically charged atmosphere I don't know."

DL reached out across the minimal link his soul still maintained with his body. He couldn't tell what was going on anymore, and he couldn't move his arms or legs, but he did manage to say Max's name.

A burst of rainbow light shot through the portal, which shuddered.

"DL, Max needs to get both of you through now, and I can't make contact with him," thought Morfesa. *"Can you?"*

"Trying," thought DL.

"Max." He was pretty sure he was only whispering. The kid would never be able to hear him over Dubh's racket.

"I'll go through and get them," said Ekaterina.

"It's day over there," said Morfesa. "There could be the equivalent of sunlight. You might not make it."

Another burst of rainbows came close to rending the portal.

"What choice do we have?" asked Ekaterina.

"If you let go of my hand, the portal could collapse," said Morfesa. "I'm not sure…I could restore it."

By now the druid's face was twisted so much with pain that it was hard to imagine how she was still standing. Whatever she was doing wasn't coming naturally to her. It was something she had to bend her magic out of shape to accomplish.

"I'll go," said Maeve.

"What good would that do?" asked Morfesa. "You couldn't carry DL through."

"I could at least—"

The portal flickered momentarily, then stabilized again. Morfesa cried out. Apparently tired of explaining herself to the druid, Maeve tried to dive through the portal but bounced back.

"I can…I can only manage one-way travel now," muttered Morfesa.

"Max!" DL thought maybe he had managed more than a whisper, but his connection to his body was so thin now that he couldn't be sure of anything.

"I got you, buddy." The thought was barely perceptible, but DL recognized it as Max.

"I broke the last of the binding spells, and I'm splitting my consciousness so that I can move your body over to the portal. I'll be coming through in—"

DL lost the connection.

Twisted psychedelic rainbows filled his vision, though whether because they had exploded through the portal or whether he was seeing through his body's eyes, he couldn't tell.

Then all was darkness.

IDENTITY CRISES

A HAND TOUCHED HIS CHEEK. Ekaterina? But this hand was warm.

DL forced one eye open. It was Morfesa, not Ekaterina, who was leaning over him.

"Max, you're awake!" the druid said. She looked happy, but her face, which normally showed no sign of the hundreds of years she had lived, was pale and unhealthy.

"I'm...not Max." He had to force the words out. "You OK?"

The voice sounded a little higher than his own. It sounded like Max's.

"What's...what's happening?"

Morfesa stared at him, her expression shifting rapidly from happiness to horror.

"Something's not right," DL heard his own voice say.

He pushed himself up enough to look around the room. He saw himself lying some distance away, with Ekaterina bending over him. She looked at Morfesa, who didn't say anything.

"We need to get this mess fixed!" Maeve thought.

"What could have happened?" muttered Morfesa.

DL looked down at himself. He was wearing Max's clothes, and his muscles seemed to have melted away.

"That should be obvious to someone of your experience," thought Maeve. *"Their souls are in the wrong bodies!"*

"That can't be," said Morfesa. "It's impossible."

A faint image of Maeve appeared right next to the druid. *"It's as plain as the nose on your face. This is DL, right here. You can't see that?"*

"My magical senses are a little scrambled," said Morfesa. "Still—"

"I know this isn't common, but it's true. I can see DL under Max's skin." The ghost drifted over to where DL's body lay. *"And this is Max here, underneath DL's."*

Ekaterina jumped as if stung by a wasp. "Max, I'm sorry I kissed you. I thought you were DL."

DL's body sat up. A goofy looking grin was on its face. "You don't hear me complaining, do you?"

The voice was DL's, but the tone was Max's

Were they really body-switched, or had Dubh driven DL insane?

"I need a mirror," DL muttered. Morfesa stared at him as if he had suddenly turned purple and seemed not to hear him, but Ekaterina quickly brought him a hand mirror.

Max's face stared back at him.

"How do we fix this?" asked DL.

Max lumbered over in DL's body and helped him up. "First, we need to figure out what caused this. Morfesa, any theories?"

"I...I don't know." DL had never seen the druid look so lost before, not even in life-threatening emergencies.

Morfesa looked back and forth between them.

"She's in shock," Maeve suggested.

"She probably needs rest," said Max. "Having to work out a new way to open a portal under such strange circumstances must have been draining."

"We have to fix this," said DL, trying not to sound panicked.

Ekaterina pulled him into the cold comfort of her arms. "We will. I'm sure we will. I agree with Maeve, though. Morfesa needs to rest first. I felt some of what she went through, and Max was right—it wasn't easy."

"I could use rest," Morfesa agreed. Ekaterina gently helped her upstairs to one of the guest bedrooms. DL wanted to protest, but Ekaterina was probably right. The druid was barely capable of managing the stairs. It was ridiculous to think she was up to solving a complicated magical problem.

"Didn't I tell you not to do anything rash?" Maeve asked Max. *"Plunging into an unknown world on your own is rash!"*

"I couldn't just let Adreanna be kidnapped and not do anything about it," said Max.

"Since she's not with you, you didn't successfully do anything about it, anyway. All you did was risk your life—and DL's."

Max looked at DL as if the truth had suddenly hit him like a sledge-hammer. "Man, this is all my fault! I'm so sorry."

"You didn't force me to do anything," said DL. "Remember, just being my friend nearly got you killed a few months ago. At worst, we're even."

"The fact remains you could both have died for nothing."

"They're both brave young men who don't need a lecture right now," said Ekaterina as she came back down the stairs. "Perhaps it would be a better use of your time to start brainstorming with Max about how to reverse this body switch."

"Don't you suppose I would have shared my ideas already if I had any? I've never heard or even read of something like this happening."

Max sighed. "I guess we'll just have to wait for Morfesa. My magical training hasn't covered anything like this. All I know is that it's very diffi-cult to force something like this to happen, let alone have it happen by accident. The soul has a natural affinity for its own body. It takes tremen-dous energy to pull it out. Keeping it out should require even more. Maybe if we stay close together, our souls will revert naturally to our own bodies."

"Do you really think so?" asked DL. He had never been bothered by the sound of Max's voice before, but having to speak in that voice grated on him.

"Well, I don't." Maeve's mental whisper was even more grating to DL than Max's voice. *"I felt something of what Morfesa went through. The world you foolishly stumbled into was much more highly magical than Earth. Things that would have been impossible here might well be able to happen there. Then there was the conflict*

between the Amadan Dubh and the some of the inhabitants of that world, correct?"

"Yeah, the atmosphere ended up very magically charged," said Max. "Toward the end, I had a hard time casting because of all the accumulated magical energy."

Dubh by himself brings chaos. Dubh on a world much more supportive of magic than this one, locked in combat with powerful native sorcerers? There's no telling what the consequences of that might be.

"In other words, we're in bad shape," said DL.

We'll get this sorted out, but I fear it will take time.

"What about Adreanna?" asked Max. "Who knows what she's going through? We need to rescue her as fast as possible."

You are not going to put yourself in danger again! snapped Maeve. The temperature in the room dropped several degrees.

"Neither you nor DL are in any condition to rescue someone else right now," added Ekaterina more gently.

"Don't rub it in," said DL, looking down at the scrawny arms on his current body.

Max hesitated, glancing uncomfortably at DL.

"DL might not be up for combat right now, but I am."

"Let's see if you are," said Ekaterina. She lunged at Max and knocked him over with a single push.

"I wasn't ready!" Max protested. "I didn't have time to awaken DL's inner dragon."

"All right, go ahead then," said Ekaterina.

Max closed his eyes for a minute, then opened them again. Despite the impressively manly body he was now in, he looked like a lost little boy more than anything else.

"I don't know how to call upon the dragon," he said.

Not as ready as you thought, eh? Maeve's mocking laughter echoed in their heads.

"I couldn't do it on cue at first," said DL. "Originally, the dragon woke up when I was upset or in danger. It took a little practice for me to tap into that strength at will."

"This is a different situation," said Ekaterina. "None of us know how the draconic part of you operates, DL. Maybe it isn't just about your body. It could be body and mind together—in which case Max couldn't draw on the dragon. You couldn't either."

"I still have DL's physical strength," said Max, flexing his arm muscles a little to demonstrate.

"Again, don't rub it in," said DL.

"Sorry, I'm just pointing out that I wouldn't be useless in a fight."

"The body is indeed magnificent," said Ekaterina. "But no human body is up to fighting a vampire, for instance. There are beings out there far stronger than vampires."

"Ah, but I have magic," said Max.

"Saying you have magic is like a teenager with a learner's permit saying he's a race car driver." Maeve laughed again. Max looked stricken. Her expression softened, and she added, *"You've made good progress for someone just starting to learn, but you aren't yet ready to fight Dubh on your own."*

"I guess not," Max said, "but I can't just abandon Adreanna to her fate. What about Merlin? Maybe he'd help us out again."

"It was an incredible stroke of luck I found his spirit last time," thought Maeve. *"Finding him again would be like winning the lottery three times in a row. Besides, he's probably reincarnated by now. He made it pretty clear that's what he wanted to do. It makes more sense to wait for Morfesa to rest up. If she can't solve the problem, she can easily bring help."*

"Adreanna could be dead by then," said Max. "We need help now!"

"If it makes you feel better, I'll do a little exploring and see if Merlin is still around. Don't get your hopes up, though. Oh, before I go, I'll give you the ability to control the protective spells on the house, just in case something unforeseen comes up."

DL felt the sudden jolt as Maeve vanished. "I'll never get used to that."

"Well, now that she's gone, we can get down to business," said the Amadan Dubh, peeking up from behind the sofa.

"You…you can't be here!" said Max, raising his hands as if to cast a spell.

"Relax," said Dubh. "I will do none of you any harm." He giggled. "I don't think the house would let me even if I wanted to."

"How did you get in?" asked Max.

"Through the same portal you used. Invisibly, of course. I assume your ghostly grandmother had to lower the defenses to let that self-righteous druid's magic get through. So much excess magic came through with me that I was able to hide within it. The ghost never noticed me."

"You've obviously studied the house's protective magic since you got here," said Max. "Didn't you realize you can't cast any spells or even leave without my grandmother's explicit permission. You just trapped yourself."

"Ah, I got confused by that musclebound body. I forgot you were the smart one."

"Hey!" said DL, bracing to throw himself at the annoying faerie, then remembering it would do him little good.

"However, you have erred in one respect," said Dubh as if DL hadn't spoken. "I don't seem able to cast a spell, but the house isn't preventing me from using my innate abilities—which means my touch can still madden or paralyze if I will it. That should be power enough to force you to do as I wish."

"The house will prevent that," said Max.

"Are you sure of that? Sure enough to stake your sanity on it?"

"As for being trapped here, surely, you must have the power to release me, which you will do—if you wish to see the young lady alive."

"That's all you want now?" asked Max.

"Of course, Merlin's grimoire would also still be part of the deal," said Dubh. "As much as you've inconvenienced me, I ought to ask for far more than that. However, I can be generous to those who deserve it.

"Lady Vampire, do not think to attack me," the faerie said. "I can see you contemplating it. You could easily overpower me without my magic, but you could never get me to reveal how the girl could be rescued."

Ekaterina was on him in a second, pinning him against the wall and staring into his eyes. Instead of acting frightened, Dubh giggled.

"Your mind control doesn't work on me. Crazy I may be, but not weak-willed."

Ekaterina let her fangs show. "I might have to drain enough blood to weaken you first. Faerie blood is quite tasty, or so I hear."

For the first time, Dubh looked worried. "You would not—at least, not in front of your lover."

Dubh got a hand far enough up to touch Ekarterina's wrist. The vampire staggered backward as if she had been struck in the head by a brick.

"Ah, the house doesn't seem to care what happens to you," said Dubh, looking at her with a widening smile on his face.

DL saw red. He threw himself at the faerie, tripped over his own feet and hit the floor with a resounding thud.

"What is the expression you humans use?" asked Dubh. "Oh, yes. I bet that worked much better in your head."

Max shot a small burst of energy in Dubh's direction, but the faerie easily dodged the attack.

"Wizardling, you should know that flying is another innate ability. The house doesn't prevent me from doing that, either."

Max lunged at Dubh, but, as unused to his new body as DL was to his, the young sorcerer looked more as if he were stumbling than charging. The faerie had no difficulty dodging his clumsy swing and flying up to the ceiling. He lay flat against it, just out of reach.

"You're all so tired," said Dubh in a mock-concerned tone. "Wouldn't it be better to rest and listen to me?"

"No!" roared Max. DL knew from the sound that Max had managed to awaken the dragon. The sorcerer jumped at Dubh, reached for him, missed, and put his hand through the ceiling. Moving out of reach again, Dubh laughed merrily.

"Your granny will be cross with you when she returns."

Max jumped again, this time missing Dubh by less than an inch and avoiding another collision with the ceiling.

"Practice makes perfect," said Dubh. He turned and flew up the stairs, leaving his grating laughter echoing behind him.

Max would have run after him, but Ekaterina, somewhat recovered, stepped in front of him. "We need a plan. We could be chasing Dubh around for hours otherwise, and—Max, your hand!"

Max glanced down and screamed. The hand he had been so close to grabbing Dubh with had become a green-scaled, four-fingered claw.

"What's…what's happening?" he asked. His eyes widened in horror.

"Stay calm," said Ekaterina. She hugged Max "DL?"

"This never happened to me," said DL. "I could sometimes feel and even see magical extensions of my human body, like a dragon superimposed over it, but they never manifested physically, well, except for the one time I became a dragon."

"But you could only do that through the full power of the Yeouiju, which Max doesn't have."

"It's getting worse!" said Max, waving his arm. The scales extended half an inch further up his arm.

"That bastard Dubh must be doing something," said DL.

"No, no, the house should prevent that," Max insisted.

"Then it must be your emotions doing it somehow," said Ekaterina. "DL, your inner dragon reacted to your state of mind in the beginning, right?"

"Yeah, that's right. Calm down, buddy. That may solve the problem."

"How can I calm down? I'm turning into a giant lizard!"

The scales had traveled another half an inch.

"This isn't right," said Ekaterina, shaking her head. "Even if he's upset, how is he able to transform his body like that?"

"What's happening?" Morfesa came unsteadily down the stairs. Her skin was unusually pale, but her eyes were more alert than before.

"You shouldn't be—" began Ekaterina.

"From the look of things, I have no choice," said the druid. She looked at Max's arm, and her eyes widened. "Max, what have you done to yourself?"

"I don't…don't know."

"Dubh somehow came back with them through the portal. Max was trying to capture him, and this happened," said Ekaterina.

"The Amadan Dubh is in this house?" asked Morfesa, looking even more horrified.

"The house's defenses are holding. He can't do magic," said DL. "Uh, well, his touch did do something to Ekaterina."

"DL, watch for him," said Morfesa. "I'll try to discern what is happening to Max."

She carefully examined his arm, on which the scales had advanced almost to the shoulder.

"I can see the dragon force I have noticed in DL before, but I also see something else. Max, it's your own magic."

"I'm doing this myself?" asked Max.

Morfesa frowned. "The dragon power needs a Yeouiju to manifest fully, yes?"

"Yeah," said DL, eyes fixed on the stairs.

"I wish I knew more of the lore of Eastern dragons," said Morfesa. "I can only guess, but DL's transformation from imugi to full dragon was interrupted before it was complete. From what little I do know, such a thing has never happened before. What if the imugi body longs to complete that transformation? What if it found Max's magic within itself and is trying to use that to complete the process?"

"How do we stop that?" asked Max. The scales were nearly to his shoulder.

"Alas, I cannot say. Even if I knew, I am nearly exhausted. I must take you at once to Tír na nÓg."

Morfesa tried to open a portal, but after three attempts, she gave up.

"I'm too weak. I will try summoning my fellow druids instead. They may not be able to get here right away. Max, while I reach out to them, try to stay calm and see if you can get control of this transformation."

"What do you think I've been doing?" asked Max. He closed his eyes, though, and his face tightened so much that it almost looked like a mask.

"I just don't know how," he said, sounding desperate.

"DL, you've had some experience," said Ekaterina. "Can you tell him what to do?"

"My experience was one actual transformation, remember? Anyway, I don't know how to describe what I did."

Morfesa's eyes opened, and she looked straight at Ekaterina, whom she normally did her best to ignore. "Yet the idea has merit. Right now, DL and Max are in each other's bodies. Each soul still has an affinity for its own body, though. That effect is amplified by the fact that Max's body was once healed by DL's blood. Maybe DL can't explain what to do, but Max might be able to pick up enough of DL's thoughts to at least know how this kind of transformation should feel. That might be enough to reverse it."

"Do you really think so?" asked Max. His teeth started to become fangs. All of his arm visible below the shirt sleeve was now scaled.

"Physical contact might help," said Morfesa.

DL put a hand on Max's shoulder.

"I'm not feeling anything," said Max.

"Closer contact might do it. Embrace each other."

DL raised an eyebrow. Max awkwardly threw his arms around him.

"Still nothing," said Max. "And this is weird."

"You know each other well enough it shouldn't be that weird," said Ekaterina. "Maybe you aren't close enough together." She reached around them and pressed them together, creating a group hug.

"I…I'm getting something," said Max. "I don't think it's just DL, though. It's as if there are two voices in my head."

"I recognize that other voice," said DL. "It's the Yeouiju that's talking to us, though I can't make out what it's saying."

Morfesa's eyes widened. "We just learned the energy from it created an unusual link between DL and Ekaterina, but this is different—an actual intelligence that persisted beyond the destruction of the physical form that contained it! Even I can feel it now."

Max's eyes closed as if he were in a trance, and his face looked much more relaxed than during his previous effort. His scales, claws, and fangs began to fade.

As the reversion ended, Ekaterina staggered backward and almost fell. DL broke away from Max and put his arms around her.

"What's wrong?"

"I don't know. I feel…oh, I don't know. Weak, I suppose."

"How are you feeling?" Morfesa asked Max.

"More like my old self…well, more like I felt when I first got caught in DL's body, anyway." He looked at his scaleless arm and smiled. Then he looked in Ekaterina's direction. "How about you?"

"Still a little weak, but I don't think it's anything to worry about."

"I'm not so sure." DL maneuvered her toward the couch. "I could understand your being affected by the Amadan Dubh's touch, but this is different. The Yeouiju must have been speaking through you, but why would that have made you weaker?"

"Magic twisted from its original form and purpose can react in unexpected ways," said Morfesa. "The Yeouiju was originally a sphere, was it not? When you asked it how to save Ekaterina, it told you to break the sphere, and its energy passed into her, replacing the force that would normally animate a vampire.

"The problem is that the Yeouiju was never meant to be used that way. It had two purposes only: to enable an imugi to transform into a full dragon, and to provide a power source for that dragon. I know not from whence it came, but its creator may not have even heard of vampires and certainly didn't intend it to power one."

"It worked, though. It saved Ekaterina's life," said DL.

"It did preserve her existence," said Morfesa slowly. "But at the cost of being unable to fulfill its natural purpose. It has a mind of sorts, and that mind survived the destruction of the sphere. What must it think of its current situation?"

"I don't like where this is going," said DL. "After all this time, and after all the good Ekaterina has done, you're still throwing her vampirism in her face? She's saved lives—yours, for one."

"I meant no offense," said Morfesa. "I do not question her personal virtue. Nature is what it is, though. It has a balance. From what little we know, Eastern dragons are part of that balance. Vampires are not part of that balance, but a perversion of it. The Yeouiju obviously can power Ekaterina, but it does not truly know what it's doing, or so I believe. That's why she weakened when it tried to perform its normal function. Perhaps it cannot both animate her and help Max get control of a transformation that was running amuck."

"Isn't that kind of a moot point?" asked Max. "I'm back to normal now."

"But do you have any idea what caused the problem in the first place?"

Max shrugged. "It must have had something to do with exerting myself to stop Dubh."

"Which means it could happen at any time there is a threat," the druid said. "Unlike DL, you don't have the instinctive control. The Yeouiju can help you, but only at the expense of the vampire."

"I'll be fine," said Ekaterina.

"Perhaps, but we can't take the chance," said DL. "Max, we're going to have to bench you until you get back into your own body. That way you won't exert yourself enough to awaken the inner dragon, and the Yeouiju won't need to intervene."

"You know I won't do anything to hurt Ekaterina, but we need to think about Adreanna. I can stay out of action until I'm cured, but someone needs to rescue her."

"Maybe you can be put back in your own body quickly," said Ekaterina.

"There is no way to know," said Morfesa.

"Then I have to do something," said Max. "I'll search for Adreanna without taking Ekaterina with me. That way the Yeouiju won't intervene."

"We have no idea where Adreanna is," said Morfesa. "Even were we to find out, there is no possibility of your going alone to rescue her. DL's body is powerful, yes, but you do not yet know how to invoke that power without risking another unwanted transformation. As for your own magic, you show promise, but you have only had a little training. There are any number of menaces you wouldn't be a match for."

"Are you ready to bargain now?" asked Dubh as he flitted quickly down the stairs.

Morfesa glared at him, but DL could barely see any of her normal magical aura. She was too tired to attack the faerie.

"Yes," said Max.

"What?" asked the druid, staring wide-eyed at Max. "You would seek a deal with this…this…"

"Faerie royal of the line of Connacht…or so I assume you meant to say," said Dubh, smirking.

"Fugitive, thief, rascal—" the druid began.

"Those will do as well," said Dubh. "Call me what you will, you will not find the girl without my help. The book is a small price to pay, surely."

"The book? Merlin's grimoire? I forbid it!" Morfesa looked at Max with a sternness normally reserved for Ekaterina or Maeve.

"He only wants to borrow it," said Max. "We could make the agreement magically binding, right?"

"Of course," said Dubh, making a little bow in Max's direction.

"Such a creature as Dubh can't be trusted with something that powerful for even one minute!" said Morfesa. "The last time he got hold of a powerful artifact, he nearly destroyed one of the faerie isles west of Ireland."

"Some would say I improved upon it." Dubh sneered at Morfesa. "In any case, I wasn't talking to you. Max, what's it to be—the girl or the book? And we already played this game once, my Lady Vampire. Don't be foolish enough to attack me again."

Ekaterina had been trying to maneuver her way behind Dubh. She stopped, but she glared at him in a way that would have sent many people screaming in the opposite direction.

"The book," said Max. "You can work magic now."

Maeve must have given Max more power over the house's protective spells than DL realized. With a wave of his hand, the faerie trickster opened a portal and flew through it. Max ran toward the portal.

"Stop!" yelled Morfesa, but Max ignored her. Ekaterina tried to tackle him, but he sped up just enough to elude her grasp. As soon as he plunged through, the portal snapped shut with a silver flash.

Morfesa looked as if she might faint. DL moved in her direction, but she waved him off.

"I'm all right," she said. "It is Max about whom we need to worry now. I fear we will never see him again."

BETWEEN A ROCK AND A TRICKSTER

MAX FLOATED UNCOMFORTABLY above snow-covered mountains. The wind was blowing hard, tearing at him like knives of ice.

The Amadan Dubh laughed wildly, like a little kid at an amusement park. He flew higher, dragging Max with him.

"It's such a treat to get out of that stuffy house, don't you think?" the faerie asked, smiling a little too broadly to look entirely sane.

"Where…where are we?"

"This place is called Elphame."

"Ah, I've heard of it," said Max, trying not to sound frightened. "It's the realm of the Scottish faeries, right?"

"It is, but we mustn't stay more than a few minutes. The faeries here took a beating not so long ago, and their might is not what it once was. Still, even they will notice me if I linger too long, perhaps get ideas about trying to collect the bounty on me."

Dubh sped up, towing Max behind him. They were moving so fast the wind chill factor alone was freezing Max, but he couldn't concentrate well enough to try to conjure some heat. The faerie, seemingly unaffected by the temperature, just kept speeding up as if trying to outrun the wind.

Just when Max's hands became numb enough to make him worry

about frostbite, Dubh slowed his hectic pace and looked back. "Enjoying yourself?"

"I'm freezing!" shouted Max. He was afraid he might sound whiney, but since he was speaking in DL's deeper voice, his statement came out more like a demand for warmth than as a petty complaint.

"All you had to do was ask," said Dubh, warming Max with one wave of his hand.

"You aren't keeping Adreanna here, are you?" asked Max. "She'd freeze to death in minutes."

"Do I look like an idiot?" asked Dubh. "What kind of a kidnapper would I be if I just left my hostage to die? She is nowhere near here. If you must know, she's in another world entirely."

"Then what are we doing here?"

"The druid might borrow your trick and try to follow us through the remnants of my portal. I doubt she has the energy, but I'm taking no chances. Besides, this place is the only way I've yet discovered to get us to our true destination."

"Which is?"

"Why are young people always so impatient?" asked Dubh. "Can you not just enjoy the scenery for a while?"

"I didn't come with you to enjoy the scenery!" snapped Max. "The book you want is in Tír na nÓg."

"So it is," agreed Dubh. "However, I can't exactly just walk into a realm where I am a wanted man. I need to prepare first."

"I can retrieve it and bring it to you," said Max.

"It's not that I don't trust you," said Dubh. "It's just that I don't— trust you. You could be thinking of betraying me to the Tuatha de Danann. Perhaps you expect them to torture from me the whereabouts of your Adreanna. No, I'm not letting you wander off on your own until our business is finished."

"Let's get on with it, then," said Max.

"First we need to go a little farther. Follow me!"

Dubh flitted off again. Max had no choice but to follow—especially considering Dubh was still dragging him along by magic.

Dubh finally landed next to what looked like a fixed portal hidden from view by two large, gray rock outcroppings. In sharp contrast to their snowy surroundings, bright, warm sunlight shined through the portal.

Dubh clapped his hands in delight. "You are in for a treat. As far as I know, no one in Elphame or the other faerie realms remembers this portal anymore. It has fairly strong concealment spells on it, and it is far from any of the places where the Scottish faeries dwell."

"Then how did you find it?"

"When one is on the run, one finds a great many things," said Dubh.

Of course, traveling with Dubh through a portal no one else knew about sounded like a surefire way to get lost again, but Max had to take the chance. Anyway, Dubh yanked him through before he had a chance to respond.

Max blinked when the full sunlight hit him. When his eyes recovered, he was astounded by how much different this land was from Elphame. Instead of being freezing cold, this place was mild as a warm spring day. Instead of being filled with imposing mountains, it was decorated with grassy hills. Indeed, grass and flowers were everywhere, much as they were in Tír na nÓg.

"Where are we?" asked Max, but much less irritably than before.

"It is always questions with you," said Dubh, but Max couldn't tell whether the faerie was annoyed or just pretending to be. He didn't seem to be in any hurry to move, despite his earlier frantic pace.

"This is Álfheim, home of the Ljósálfar, or light elves. At one time some of them settled in Elphame, which is where the place got its name —but that was long ago, and the light elves have forgotten the portal just as much as the faeries have. The opening on this side is out in the open, but just as concealed by spells as the opening on the other."

"Álfheim is Norse, right? But I thought the Norse gods—"

"Were inaccessible?" Dubh laughed shrilly enough to crack the nearby ice. "For the most part, yes. That killjoy God so many of you mortals insist on worshipping did at some point bar the old gods from the mortal world and barred mortals from the various planes of existence where the other gods dwell. Claimed those gods were really his creation, if you can believe such nonsense, and were not fulfilling their purpose in the way he intended. They made Earth much more interesting than it is now, if you ask me, but that made no difference to God. The egomaniac

was obsessed with being the only one. The Celtic gods escaped an absolute ban only by renouncing all claim to divinity and becoming faeries.
Even at that, the spineless cowards have largely cut themselves off from
mortals to avoid being banned from them—as if that made any sense
at all!"

Max was tempted to point out that Dubh was hardly in a position to
criticize other beings' egos or their lack of sense, but he didn't want to
take a chance on the faerie's erratic temper. "Then why is the portal still
there?"

"Free will, of all things. Apparently, there are loopholes that allow
really persistent mortals to reach the old gods. In the Norse case, this
fixed portal must be the loophole. It would indeed take a determined
mortal to find it, though. Even a faerie as powerful as I almost missed it."

"What do you need in Álfheim?" asked Max, staring at the beautiful
landscape. If not for Adreanna's imprisonment and Dubh's heinous
nature, this could be a wonderful place to explore.

"Oh, this isn't our final destination," said Dubh. "At least, what you
see right now isn't."

Before Max could ask another question, Dubh's magic pulled him
along so fast the scenery blurred. They rose high into the air, then dived
straight down so fast that Max visualized his brain smashing like a melon
against the ground.

He missed that fate by inches, plunging instead into a deep, dark
hole that seemed to extend forever. When at last they stopped, he was
shaky, dizzy, and nauseated.

"What…what did you do that for? Are you trying to kill me?"

"Not yet," said Dubh cheerily. "I spotted some light elves in the
distance and didn't want them to see us. In any case, this is our
final stop."

Max looked around him, but there wasn't much to see. They were in
some kind of cavern, but the ceiling was claustrophobically low, the air
was cold, though not quite as much as that of Elphame, and the few
torches didn't do an adequate job of lighting the place. Sick as he was
feeling, Max managed to cast a spell to enable him to see in the dark. He
immediately wished he hadn't.

He and Dubh were surrounded by people so dark-skinned that they could have been made out of shadows. Even with magically enhanced vision, it was hard for him to make out their features. He could see their eyes because of their reddish glow, but even that was so slight he hadn't noticed it before.

They were hostile. Waves of hatred poured over him. There was nowhere to run to and no way to fight back.

"These are friends…well, friends of mine, anyway," said Dubh "You they aren't so partial to, but I have an understanding with them. They are the Dökkálfar—dark elves—but every bit as powerful as their shiny, above-ground kin. Luckily for me, they are not strangled by the same moral constraints that bind the light elves."

Dubh spoke to the army of strangers in what sounded like Old Norse. Max had picked up a little of the language from his studies with his grandmother. That, combined with a translation spell, enabled him to get a general idea of what they were saying.

Dubh addressed the one who seemed to be radiating the most intense hatred. "Have you brought the item I asked for?"

The dark elf gestured, and one of his men brought forward what looked like a belt. An instinctive shudder went through Max's borrowed body as he realized it was made of dragon skin. The belt buckle was highly polished black silver set with a stone that changed colors with dizzying speed.

"Ah, as good as your word! Let us see how this works."

Dubh strapped the belt around his waist and fastened it. He became a shifting mass of color that matched the belt's gem. When the light show faded, Max was staring at himself—at his original body, not the one he was currently wearing.

Max knew enough about the magic involved in shapeshifting to know that there were different ways to achieve that result. Dubh's new form could have been an illusion, but if so, Max couldn't see through it, no matter how hard he tried.

"It's an actual change of shape," said Dubh in Max's voice. "A good likeness, is it not? The dark elf magic, unfamiliar to the faeries, will mask my own presence better than I could alone. It still won't hold up under close inspection by someone who knows you and knows magic, but it should suffice for what I have in mind."

"And what is that?" asked Max, though he already knew.

"This way I don't have to take the risk you might betray me. I can pick up the book for myself."

"You could have done that without me," said Max, wondering what Dubh was really up to.

"That I could. I know well, though, that the book will only respond to a few people—and you're one of them. This transformation is probably not good enough to fool it. I will bring it back here, and you will give me your blessing. Then I can use it. Then—and only then—will you get your precious Adreanna back."

"And what of us?" asked the dark elf leader. "What of your bargain with us?" This voice was sandpaper on stone.

"I will do what I have pledged. With the power of the book amplifying my considerable talents, I can lead you to victory against the light elves."

"That wasn't part of our deal!" Max yelled. "You said you wanted to create your own world—"

"And so I shall."

"But you didn't say you also wanted the book to start a war!"

Dubh adopted a mock-indulgent voice as if he were speaking to a little kid. "Now, Max, don't make this difficult for yourself. I didn't lie to you. I just didn't tell you the whole truth. When you refused me at first, I had to turn to my dark elf friends for help, and as you know, help always comes at a cost.

"What do you care how many elves die? It's not as if you've ever met any of them—or ever will. I'm not sure there'll be many light elves left after we get finished with them. What of it? You'll have what you want."

"I won't let you do this!"

Dubh's mocking laughter echoed in the cavern. "Let me? You have no choice if you ever want to see Adreanna again—or even leave this cave yourself, for that matter."

Dubh giggled. "That's what you mortals call Plan B. Your curious moral notions might cause you to refuse me. There are those who care about you, though. Morfesa may be an old bat at heart, but I can see she would not willingly let you be torn to shreds by my friends. Even if you don't give me what I want, she will."

Max opened his mouth, but Dubh shut it with a wave of his hand. "Further conversation would serve no purpose. Friends, put your new prisoner to sleep for me. He's been more trouble than he's worth, so follow your own inclination about his dreams."

Max tried to fight off the mental assault, but the combined weight of so many sorcerers felt like Mount Everest resting on his head. It wasn't long before nightmares engulfed him, tearing at his mind with claws fashioned from his deepest fears. He swore he wouldn't give Dubh the satisfaction of screaming, and he didn't—for two minutes.

FINDING MAX IN A COSMIC HAYSTACK

"HOW COULD HE HAVE DONE THIS?" said Morfesa, shaking her head. "Instead of having one hostage, Dubh now has two."

"Perhaps Dubh will get more than he bargained for," said DL.

"I have the highest respect for Max's abilities as a sorcerer," said the druid. "However, he isn't remotely ready to face someone as powerful as a faerie royal with hundreds of years of experience."

"What are you talking about? Max is standing right there," said Maeve, just returned from her Merlin hunt.

"Look more closely," said DL. "It's me, DL, but I'm in Max's body."

"What?" The ghost escalated from her usual whisper to a shout. *"Morfesa, how could you have allowed this to happen?"*

"Allowed?" said Morfesa in a voice that could have frozen boiling water. "I didn't allow anything. Dubh managed to get into this house using the same portal I opened for Max and DL, but he was trapped here by the protection spells. Unfortunately, he tricked Max into leaving with him. *Someone* seems to have given Max total control over all the spells connected with the house."

"Are you suggesting this is my fault?" asked Maeve. The room became so cold that DL could see his own breath.

"No, I suppose not," said Morfesa. "You couldn't have predicted Max would do something like this. Of course, you might have set a better example. Max should know that bargaining with someone like Dubh can never come out well—any more than a druid trying to hang on to life, when her time to die has come, can never come out well."

"This bickering isn't helping us get Max back," said Ekaterina.

"Speaking of bad examples—" began Morfesa.

"Enough!" snapped DL. "I thought we had gotten past this months ago. I know you consider the existence of vampires a violation of the balance of things, but Ekaterina didn't choose to be one. As for Maeve, that argument is between you and her. Save it for later. Right now, we should be focusing on rescuing Max."

"Exactly!" said Maeve. *"Let's focus on getting Max away from the Amadan Dubh."*

In less urgent circumstances, DL would have chuckled over how Maeve conveniently forgot she had started the argument in the first place. Morfesa hesitated for a moment. She looked as if she wanted to point out Maeve's abrupt pivot.

"No one is more interested in getting Max back than I am," she said slowly. "The trick right now is going to be finding him.

"Dubh's already shown he's familiar with at least one plane of existence none of us have even heard of. There could be others. Tracking someone who isn't in this world is difficult enough. Tracking someone who could be shifting from one unknown world to another? That would be nearly impossible—if not for the unique connection among Max, DL, and Ekaterina."

"You mean because Max and DL are in each other's bodies? Or are you talking about the blood bonds?"

"We discovered some other things while you were gone," said Morfesa. "The Yeouiju we thought DL had destroyed to...revive Ekaterina somehow still exists in some form inside of her—an intelligent form. It communicates with her and with DL—and I would suppose with Max as well now. It was that contact, even across planes, that made possible getting Max back in the first place."

"Well? Are you getting any communication from Max now?"

"Nothing direct," said Ekaterina. "I keep feeling as if he's out there somewhere, but I get no sense of where yet."

"That could be good news," said DL. "If Max were in trouble, he'd surely call for help."

"If he knows he can," said Morfesa. "You were still in your own body and were the one who called out the last time.

"However, we have one thing working in our favor. We may not know where Max is right now, but we know where he will be. He agreed to trade Merlin's grimoire for Adreanna. Dubh can't get at it without him. That means Max will have to go to my home in Tír na nÓg to fetch it. Given Dubh's legendary impatience, he will send Max there as soon as possible."

"Then what are we waiting for? We need to get to Tír na nÓg at once!"

"You can't go," said Morfesa. "Regardless of what I think, a druid who deliberately became an earthbound spirit would not be welcomed. Besides, you could do little once we left this house."

"I could let her draw on my strength," said DL. "That's worked before."

"With your dragon body, yes," said Morfesa. "Have you forgotten you aren't in it at the moment?"

A portal swirled to life behind Morfesa, and from it stepped Esras, one of her fellow druids. Like her, he wore glowing white robes and carried a staff that throbbed greenly with the power of nature. He was a little taller than she and looked about the same age—late thirties or early forties. However, his muscles suggested he was more athletic than the average guy at that age. He'd really been around for hundreds of years, but his appearance betrayed no hint of that.

"I heard your call and came as quickly as I could," said Esras. "How can I help?"

"I have much to tell you, but I lack the time now to relate the whole story. Suffice it to say that Max has been tricked by the Amadan Dubh into giving him Merlin's grimoire. We must stop the bringer of madness and oblivion at all costs."

Esras frowned. "Grave news indeed! We must return at once to Tír na nÓg. Are you ready? Wait! Max is right here. I don't understand."

"I'm DL in Max's body." He had the feeling he would be tired of explaining that pretty soon.

"Strange tidings!" said Esras, staring at DL. "You are coming with us, then?"

"Only I am coming," said Morfesa as she picked up her own staff. Its much duller green reflected her exhausted state.

"What?" asked DL. "Ekaterina and I need to come. The bonds—"

"Would be very important if we needed to find Max, but if all goes well, we will find him as he comes to take the book.

"Besides," she added, raising a hand to forestall further protests. "Ekaterina would be no more welcome than Maeve is, and it is daylight in Tír na nÓg. A vampire could never survive there."

"I wouldn't want to place Ekaterina in danger, but at least I—"

"You shouldn't go," said Morfesa, though her voice sounded a little less stern than it had been. "You aren't used to this body. Did you not trip over your own feet not so long ago? Even if you were, it isn't a warrior's body as your own is. If we had to fight Dubh, you'd just be in the way. Esras, we should go now."

The other druid looked confused. He met DL's eyes. "We will come back with Max soon. Worry not." His expression didn't do much to reinforce his reassuring words, but DL was too shocked to argue anymore. He nodded slightly, and Morfesa practically dragged Esras through the portal, which closed once they were through.

"Much as I try to put up with that woman for Max's sake, she really is insufferable," said Maeve.

"She means well," said Ekaterina. "Every time I think she's accepted me, though, she finds another excuse to remind me my very existence is an affront to nature."

"We fought side by side in Teren de Vampiri. You'd think that would mean something."

"Since none of us can follow them, I guess there's no point in dwelling on it. I'm pretty tired from the way in which Morfesa got us back. I think I'll lie down for a while," said DL.

DL turned and headed for the stairs. Ekaterina caught up with him halfway up and put a cold hand on his shoulder.

"DL, what's wrong?"

"You mean aside from Max being kidnapped and me losing my body?" he asked without a trace of his usual humor.

"That's not all that's wrong, though, is it?" she put her arms around him.

"Nothing except what you know about."

"You do remember I can tell from your heartbeat whether you're telling me the truth or not?" she asked.

"If every woman had that power, men would be in big trouble." It was a typical DL joke, but he delivered it without even the hint of a smile or any change in tone. His normal deadpan expression was never that complete.

"Seriously, tell me the truth." She spoke gently but firmly. He was not going to be able to divert her this time.

"It just hit me when Morfesa said it. I'm useless now. I can't do a thing to help Max or myself."

They reached the second story—a good thing too, since Ekaterina was hugging him so hard he would have had difficulty walking much farther.

"How can you even say something like that?" she asked.

"Before I could have made a difference in a fight against Dubh. Now I'd just be in the way, a bystander everyone else would have to worry about protecting."

She kissed him tenderly. "Did you think of Max that way in the fights we had a few months ago?"

"Actually, yes, at least in the beginning. Once Max discovered he had magic, things were a little different. But I don't have Max's magic. I don't have his brains.

"Suppose this body swap can't be reversed. He could step right into my life. If I tried to do the same, I'd make a mess out of his college classes and probably have to drop out."

"You are far more intelligent than you give yourself credit for," said Ekaterina. "Anyway, there is at least one aspect of your life where Max couldn't do as well as you."

DL pulled away from her a little. "Wouldn't he? He has the looks, he has the body—and he's always had the brains. Are you so sure he couldn't end up being your lover?"

Ekaterina stared at him as if he had just announced he was a Martian. "Do you really give me so little credit? You think appearance is all I care about?"

"Of course not, but Max is a good person, too. He's courageous—we've both seen that. This whole Adreanna thing proves he'll do anything for the woman he loves."

"As would you," said Ekaterina. "You did save my life, remember? And you didn't know what using the Yeouiju's power to save me would do. It could have killed you."

"So Max and I are both good guys. He's now the more studly good guy—and don't tell me that's meaningless. Suppose Max and I had both been in that bar the night you met me. Suppose he was in my body, and I was in his. Was there even one chance in a billion you would have gone home with me instead of him?"

Ekaterina was no longer hugging him. "I had no idea your sense of self-worth was tied so completely to physical things. Yes, when I saw you I was impressed by how handsome you were, how manly. I sensed what turned out to be the sleeping dragon inside you. But I also sensed what kind of person you were, even under all those layers of lone-wolf posturing."

She hugged him again, this time hard enough to crack his ribs. "I love you, DL—your mind, your heart, your soul. I doubt this swap is permanent, but if it is, I'll be with you, not your body. I'll make love with you right now if you like, just to prove it's you I want to be with—whatever your form."

"You will do no such thing!" snapped Maeve. The air around them chilled noticeably.

"Eavesdrop much?" asked DL.

"I...I was worried about you, that's all."

"Worried you'd miss something is more like it."

"Don't be so suspicious. In any case, you can't make love in Max's body. That just isn't right."

"I guess it would be kind of weird," admitted DL. "But if this is permanent—"

"It isn't. The soul has a natural affinity for its own body, remember? Once we get you Max in the same place, it won't be hard to—"

Ekaterina closed her eyes and staggered backward, almost falling.

"What's wrong?" asked DL.

"It's…it's…Max. He's in trouble. Not only that, but he's not in Tír na nÓg."

"Can you tell where he is?"

"I'm trying, but the more I concentrate, the more painful the bond becomes. He's in more or less total darkness, but that's not the real problem. His mind is being bombarded by horrible images. I…I can't even describe them without trembling."

"Is Dubh trying to drive him insane?" asked Maeve. *"What would be the point of that?"*

"I don't know, but I sense he's losing his grip on reality."

"Can you talk to him through the link?"

"He doesn't seem to be aware of me," she said. "Perhaps if we tried together."

They held each other, and she trembled, but DL couldn't feel the Yeouiju the way he could in his own body. Trying his hardest, he heard Max in his head like a distant scream.

Ekaterina's own scream jolted him, but he held on to her. "What's happening?"

"I…I can't stand it. It's too horrible!"

Coming from a vampire who'd lived for centuries, that was really saying something. DL tried to hold onto her, but she slumped to the ground.

He had seen her near death, even dead, but he had never seen her like this.

"What's happening?" Maeve's presence brushed very close to DL.

Ekaterina had squeezed her eyes shut, but now she opened them and stared wild-eyed at DL.

"He isn't going to survive this! We have to rescue him—now!"

DRAGON IN THE DARK

MAX'S EYES flew open as if someone had just jolted him with electricity.

He was still shaking, but as long as he was awake, the nightmares couldn't torture him anymore—at least, he hoped they couldn't. The reality of being in total darkness, his arms and legs connected to a cold stone wall by heavy chains, was bad enough.

It took him only a few seconds to realize that being awake didn't keep what he'd already seen in his nightmares from haunting him. What if some of them were premonitions of the future? The idea clung to him like spider webs.

Discovering he had magic had been an adrenaline rush at first, and it had helped build his self-confidence. Now, with the supernatural intruding on his life almost to the point of squeezing it out of existence, magic was less rush and much more like being crushed. He came close to wishing that DL wasn't an imugi, that they'd never become friends, that he'd never uncovered his own talent for sorcery.

"Get your act together," he told himself. Whining wasn't a good strategy, and if there was one thing he needed right now, it was a decent plan.

His jailers seemed to not be paying much attention to him. If they had known he was awake, certainly they would have plunged him back into nightmare-ridden sleep. Maybe their carelessness would give him an opening to escape.

Who was he kidding? Even if he hadn't been chained to a wall, he had no idea where he was, except that he was underground. He might have been able to use magic to check for possible escape routes, but it seemed inconceivable that the dark elves would have left any unguarded exits, and their collective magic, even if he only encountered a small group of them, could certainly overcome his own.

On the other hand, he had somehow broken the sleep spell a mob of them had placed on him. If he could figure out how, that might give him a clue about escaping.

He felt tingly, a reminder that he was in DL's body. The elves may not have realized that there was draconic power behind his human façade. That must have enabled him to break the spell. What else might he be able to accomplish?

He was about to awaken the dragon and pull his chains out of the wall when he remembered the feeling of scales creeping up his arms. Then, he had help to avoid becoming a man-sized lizard. This time, he was alone. Evoking the dragon within might cause a similar change or some other undesirable side-effect.

Max knew where he was—well, at least what plane of existence he was in and what world he was on. Could he communicate with Ekaterina in the same way DL had?

He concentrated so hard he gave himself a headache, but he felt no connection. Maybe DL's mind and body had to be together to pull off that particular trick.

He kept trying, though. He didn't have any other options except invoking what draconic might he had and attempting to break out by brute force.

"*Master?*" a tiny voice in his head whispered.

"*I'm not your master exactly, but I am in his body. That body is imprisoned. Can you help in some way?*"

"*I am broken.*" The mental voice was toneless but conveyed a feeling of deep sorrow. "*I do not know what has happened to me.*"

"*You were in a sphere, right?*" Max got the mental equivalent of a head nod. "*Then your…master asked you how to save Ekaterina.*"

"*I know not who that is.*"

"*The woman who was dead.*"

"*There was one who was dead, yes. She had not truly been alive for a long time, but my master demanded that what animation she had be returned to her.*

"*I had no skill at such a thing, but he wanted it, and his wish is my command, so I tried. There was one of great power nearby who helped. My master cracked the sphere, and I flowed into the woman. In some ways, I became the woman, but I was still separate in others.*

"*I longed to fulfill my purpose, but I had become enough part of the woman that I could not. I slumbered for a time. Then I was awakened and felt odd forces, powers I had never before experienced, all around me. Yet I was not truly in the place I felt. I was still with the woman, who was in another place.*"

Max felt sorrow again, this time more like a sledgehammer hit than the relatively gentle touch he had gotten before.

"*I am not here either. I am still with the woman, far, far from here.*

"*I should be with my master always, yet part of him is with the woman, and part of him is here. He is split as I am. He is broken, too.*"

The sorrow was getting as hard to take as the nightmares. Max knew from what DL had told him that the Yeouiju could communicate and therefore had to be able to think in some way, but neither of them had known how emotional the Yeouiju was. They had thought of it as an object, but clearly, it was far more than that.

"We seek to mend him, but we cannot while his body is trapped here. Can you communicate with the part of you that is within the woman?"

"*I did before, but now I am not sure. Everything is different.*"

"If you cannot do that, can you help me to free this body?"

"*If the body shed its human semblance and became a dragon, it could easily free itself. My power is supposed to aid in the maintenance of that draconic form, but the part of me that is here is but a shadow.*"

Max had to admit that made sense. The piece of the Yeouiju with him was only part of the link the Yeouiju had with DL.

"*Can you feel the chains that bind my…the body's hand and feet. Could the strength of the body be enough to break them without having to become a dragon?"*

"The body has strength above the human norm, but the chain is strong. I do not think it powerful enough to break the chain."

The Yeouiju was putting Max into a corner from which there was only one escape.

"I have magic of my own. Can you help me use it to increase the body's strength enough to break the chains?"

"The types of power are not the same, but perhaps they could be made to work together. My master's body wants it."

That was exactly what Max was afraid of, but he had little choice.

"Teach me how to do it."

Max had no idea how long the process took. It seemed like hours, but in the unchanging darkness, he had no way to know. He might have tried to find out through magic, but he needed to keep his attention fixed on what the Yeouiju was telling him. Its understanding of reality was completely different from his own. Even concepts like the difference between mind and body were alien to it. On the other hand, it had ways of distinguishing among different kinds of magical energy that were alien to him. The process was a lot like trying to learn physics from someone with a completely different language and background.

Once Max learned what the Yeouiju could tell him about how to channel his magic into the muscles of DL's body, the young sorcerer tried his best. The body's arms felt as if they could lift a giant. The legs felt as if they could run ten back-to-back marathons.

Max strained against the shackles with all his might. Nothing happened. He kept pulling until his muscles burned, and the bones protested. Still nothing. He might conceivably break those bonds through hours of exertion, but he wasn't sure he had hours. The Amadan Dubh could be back any time.

"Wait a minute! The body can expand into a full-sized dragon if it has the power. Can it also shrink?"

"Dragons can transform back and forth to human form. They have no natural smaller form, but there would be nothing that prevented your magic from reducing the body's size."

Max should have expected this—another good news/bad news situation. Celtic sorcerers and druids learned shapeshifting as a matter of course, but Max's studies hadn't advanced that far yet, and he was hesitant to try doing something like that on his own.

A large part of getting magic to work was visualizing the desired outcome with absolute precision, and Max was already tired. He had to try, though, so he used all the mind-clearing techniques he had been taught. Imagining himself in a quiet place in the heart of a forest had always worked before. This time, Max found himself imagining dark elves lurking in the shadows.

He didn't reach an ideal mental state, but he had to attempt a spell, anyway.

Morfesa and Maeve had told him that there were many kinds of magic, each with its own feel. Because everyone's mind was different, everyone experienced each of these varieties differently. For Max, most spells felt like bringing himself into harmony with the universe, then coaxing it in a different direction. The spells he used most he could cast almost automatically because his mind remembered what was supposed to happen. In a case like this, though, he needed to move much more slowly.

Since this was a body spell, Max let his mind flow into every cell. He felt his own breathing, his blood pumping through his veins, his neurons firing in his brain. Once he was aware of his body's current state, he visualized the change he wanted. He saw his body shrinking slightly as clearly as if he were watching a high definition video. He chanted quietly as he fed magic gently into his body to make the mental video a reality.

The shackles were suddenly looser on his wrists and ankles. After another try, he was able to slip out of them.

Getting the body back to its original size proved to be a little trickier because of how tired Max was. All he had to do was reverse what he had just done. Even so, it took several minutes before his sluggish magic flowed through the body thoroughly enough to expand it. He was more familiar with spells to see in the dark, so shifting his magic into his eyes and adapting them to give him a view like night vision goggles only took another two minutes.

Unfortunately, he'd expended as much energy as he could for a while. He knew something about Celtic power-sharing, but the fragment of the Yeouiju that was with him lacked the kind of power he would need.

He was free of the chains, but that was all. He could be hundreds of miles underground, with no obvious way of getting out.

Come to think of it, though, he did have one power source.

"Can I tap the draconic strength of this body to fuel my magic? I need to do one more thing."

The Yeouiju sounded dumbfounded. It was used to feeding energy to a dragon's body, not the other way around.

"Will you not need the body's strength for possible combat?"

"Yes, but I just need to borrow a little for the magic. I need to create a light source strong enough to fend off the dark elves."

The Yeouiju was familiar with the ideas of good and evil and knew that some evil creatures could not endure sunlight. Neither it nor Max had any idea to what extent the dark elves were vulnerable to a light attack, but to Max it made sense that beings that lived in the darkness all the time could at the very least be blinded.

He hated to stake his life on a guess, but he'd been doing that for hours. What was one more gamble at this point?

Somewhat reluctantly, the Yeouiju told him enough about how it sent power to the body to help him make an educated guess of how to drain power from the body. As with his other efforts, this one took time, but he finally managed to surround himself in a reasonable approximation of sunlight without weakening the body too much.

Of course, he would need to keep drawing on it, or the light would weaken over time. If he didn't reach the surface before he ran his meat battery down too far, he was going to be in trouble.

Who was he kidding? He'd be in trouble no matter what happened.

UNEXPECTED ENCOUNTER AT TÍR NA NÓG

THE DAY WAS SUNNY, the breeze was cool, and every plant pulsed with the intense emerald shade of unbridled nature. Morfesa, consumed by the urgency of the moment, didn't notice any of it.

"Hurry along, Esras! We can't afford to miss Max's arrival. We may not have such an easy chance to recover him again."

"I'm moving as fast as I can. I'm missing the energy I had to donate to get you moving again," said Esras, hurrying along behind her as fast as he could. "I still say you should have sent word ahead, It would have been easy enough for someone else to keep watch before we got here."

"Both Semias and Uiscias are on urgent missions, and Max is too bright not to notice one of the Tuatha de Danann showing up in Falias for no particular reason. I don't know what Dubh may have threatened him with or what kind of *geas* he may have put on him, but we don't want him to panic and flee back to the Faerie Fool before we can catch him. This is better—but we must hurry."

When they reached the top of the hill, the city of Falias spread out before them, its whites and golds contrasting with the surrounding green. Even at this distance, the faint music and sounds of celebration reached them.

"At least nothing looks amiss," said Esras.

"Looks can be deceiving," said Morfesa. "Still, it is a comfort to see the alarm hasn't been sounded. It would have if Max had attempted to remove the grimoire from the city without me present."

They passed quickly through the outer gates. Morfesa was effectively ruler of the place, and Esras was also well-known to the guards.

"My lady," said the guard captain, "something most unusual happened just a few minutes ago. "Your pupil, Max, showed up. I had not thought he had learned how to open portals yet. I was surprised to see him here alone."

"He is not here of his own free will. Alert all the guards and seal the city."

"At once, my lady."

"How did the guards know it was Max?" asked Esras. "Isn't he still in another body at the moment?"

"He probably cast a convincing illusion so that he could get in without having to answer too many questions," said Morfesa. "Speaking of which, we aren't too late, but very close," said Morfesa. With a wave of her hand, she opened a portal, which in a couple of steps brought her and Esras into her workroom in the palace. They almost ran right into Max, who did indeed look like his normal self.

"Fear not!" said Morfesa. "We will save you from whatever that horrible troll in a faerie's body has threatened you with."

Max turned pale at the sight of them and attempted an awkward smile. "I...I...he said he'd kill my parents. I've already worked out a way to stop him, though. I remember Merlin's book has some great protection spells. All we need to do is get back to my world and cast them."

Morfesa stared at him for a moment. "I should have known you wouldn't panic. Yes, if that were what he threatened you with, using the grimoire would be an excellent way to defang his evil.

"Before we go, however, I must ask you one thing. There is strange magic on you that doesn't feel like Dubh's. What is it?"

Max frowned. "It must be residue from that weird world we followed Dubh into. I sensed some kinds of magic I've never felt before. By the time we left, the fight between Dubh and the natives was so intense that we're lucky we survived. It's not surprising I must have picked up some of the side-spray. Dubh asked about it, too.

"Can we go, please? I don't want to take a chance with my parents' lives."

"Of course. Where's the book?"

"Still in the chest over there. I'm so nervous I couldn't make the protective spell respond to me."

Morfesa raised an eyebrow. "It should have let you open it with no problem. I'll renew your permissions when we have time."

Morfesa lifted the lid of the chest and pulled out an ancient volume about the size of *Webster's Unabridged Dictionary*. It glowed white hot with raw magical energy.

"Can I see that for a minute?" asked Max, arms extended. "I want to double-check the spell while you get the portal open."

"Surely," said Morfesa, passing the book to him. "That reminds me that I just had the captain of the guard initiate a lockdown. I need to countermand that order so we can open a portal from here. Much faster that way."

She closed her eyes and concentrated for a moment, then opened them again. "The protective spells have been adjusted."

Max giggled in a way totally unlike him. With a swing of his arm, a portal burst open at his command.

"You've learned—" started Morfesa, pleasantly surprised by Max's progress.

"That isn't Max!" shouted Esras, raising his staff and firing a forest green bolt of natural energy straight at the imposter. The fake Max leaped out of the way, then tossed the book through the portal in one quick throw.

"Retrieve the book! I'll take care of this fraud," yelled Esras, firing again. Morfesa dived through the portal and found herself surrounded by snow and ice, buffeted by freezing winds. The book was nowhere to be seen.

Dubh hadn't had time to cast a spell that would have kept the book moving. Yet Morfesa sensed it traveling rapidly away from her. Concentrating as hard as she could, she saw through the invisibility of a fleeing faerie. Dubh had an accomplice. From a distance, it looked like the Leanhaum-Shee, the evil seductress who could give men poetic inspiration, but only at the cost of the lives. She was as much an outlaw as

Dubh, but at least her signature spells would have no effect on Morfesa.

"Leanhaum-Shee, give back what you have stolen!"

The Leanhaum-Shee looked back at her and sneered. Her face looked beautiful, but Morfesa could see the blood of the men she had drained was what colored her cheeks and lips. The outlaw turned and dashed toward a nearby mountain.

Dubh's accomplice had an uncomfortably large lead, but Morfesa took a moment to tether herself to Esras. By the look of things, this was Elphame, a suspect land at best, and Dubh could have other allies nearby. If nothing else, Esras might need to follow her after he had taken care of Dubh.

The connection between her and Esras firmed, and Morfesa raced as fast as she could after the Leanhaum-Shee, who had already vanished behind the mountain.

She could no longer sense the book. Had Dubh's partner in crime taken a portal elsewhere? Morfesa hadn't felt one open.

Then she felt it—a fixed portal, largely obscured by boulders and by concealment spells. She noticed it only because she had been tracking the Leanhaum-Shee, who must just have jumped through it.

Morfesa followed her through the portal into a much warmer and sunnier land, more or less like Tír na nÓg. The Leanhaum-Shee was flying now, so she had to as well, even though she could ill afford the magic.

The faerie thief dived straight into a cave that led steeply downward into the ground. Morfesa had to follow, even though that meant plunging straight into almost absolute darkness. She had little time to examine her surroundings, but her ability to sense magic told her she was surrounded by a daunting array of caves and tunnels. There was enough magic glimmering in the walls to enable her to navigate, so she didn't bother to adapt her eyes to see in the dark. The Leanhaum-Shee was too far ahead for vision to be of much use, anyway. She had to track Dubh's ally using the book's magic as her guide.

After a short time, she felt the book stop moving and speeded up to close the gap. She had expected to face the Leanhaum-Shee, but the thief must have dropped the book and fled. It lay on the floor, its magic providing the only illumination for the large cavern.

The Leanhaum-Shee could have kept running. She had a big lead. Why had she abandoned her prize so easily?

Morfesa stepped toward the book cautiously. Her fatigue settled on her like a shroud. Her ability to sense magic was getting foggier. She could still see Merlin's grimoire, but the magic in the walls was reduced to blurry flickers. She'd rely on the tether to Esras to get back.

The book was at her feet. She bent down to pick it up—and shadowy hands reached out of the magic that had concealed them. They grabbed her roughly. Hostile magic struck her like a tidal wave, crushing her feeble resistance and forcing her toward unconsciousness.

A burst of sunlight darted along the tether and cut through the darkness. Had Esras sent it? Her captors screamed and covered their eyes, losing their physical grip on her. They slumped as if they were losing consciousness, and their psychic attack faded like night retreating from the first light of dawn.

Her would-be assailants had to be Dökkálfar—dark elves from the Norse plane—though Morfesa had not encountered one in centuries and had no idea there was still a way from Elphame to the lower reaches of Álfheim, where the dark elves dwelled.

Esras's burst faded, and the dark elves revived with alarming speed. Grabbing her staff, Morfesa scraped together what little magic she had left to surround herself in sunlight. Once she had Merlin's grimoire in her grasp, she could use its power to revive herself.

Where was the book? It had gotten kicked aside in the struggle. Why couldn't she see it?

"Morfesa!" yelled Esras from two worlds away. He sounded as if he were in trouble, but she couldn't leave without recovering the book. She looked around for it frantically, but in the glow she had conjured, it was no longer as easy to spot, and she dared not lower the light for fear the dark elves would charge again.

Panpipes played discordantly on the other side of the portal.

Dubh had escaped from Tír na nÓg. Even worse, he had gotten his portal closed, cutting her off from Esras. He seemed to be taking his time reaching the portal to Álfheim, but even at a leisurely pace, Morfesa had only minutes at most.

"Where is the book?" she asked the huddled and shuddering mass of dark elves all around her. "Give it to me, or I will make the light even more intense."

"Do as you will," said a shaky voice from somewhere in the mass. "The light can blind and weaken us, but it cannot kill us."

She squinted at them. She was not used to their kind, but she was used to determining the state of living beings. The light seemed to have robbed them of their capacity to do magic, and they were rapidly moving from frightened to dormant.

Somewhere under that heap of bodies was the book, but there was too much residual magic in the air for her to sense it very easily. Nor would digging through them be practical.

She reached out, knowing the book would come to her if it could. There was a commotion near the far end of the cave—the book trying to dig itself out from the piled elves, no doubt. She walked in that direction. Sure enough, she could now feel the book.

Dubh came hurtling down into the cavern at lightning speed. He struck her like a war hammer, knocking her to the cold stone floor. She struggled to hold onto the sunlight, which flickered dangerously.

Instead of landing on top of her, Dubh had fallen backward, stunned at least as much as she was. By the time he got back up, she had scrambled to her feet as well.

"Well, what have we here? Another guest for my dark elf friends?"

"Don't be so smug," said Morfesa. "You're looking tired, Dubh, and your 'friends' are of no use to you so long as I can keep them in sunlight.
"

"You look as weary as I, and you'll find this place is inimical to sunlight," said Dubh, smirking. "Its nature is opposed to it. It may not have reacted at first because your magic is different from that of the light elves, but are you not feeling its weigh upon you by now?"

Morfesa wasn't about to give him the satisfaction of admitting it, but she was beginning to feel pressure, and the light had begun to waver.

"Now who is looking more tired?" asked Dubh, grinning broadly. "You have not long before the light fails. You could abandon the book, I suppose. Oh, but I'm probably still strong enough to block your way until the darkness returns." He positioned himself between her and the tunnel that was her only exit. "Even if I weren't, the dark elves enabled me and my good friend, the Leanhaum-Shee, to find our way in and out. Without their aid, you could never navigate this maze of tunnels well enough to reach the surface."

"What do you want?" asked Morfesa. She longed to beat him to a pulp with her staff, but she was far too weak.

"Merlin's grimoire, of course, but that I already have. You are free to go if you leave me to enjoy it in peace."

"Never!" yelled Morfesa. She chanced blasting him with her magic, but the effort of sustaining the sunlight while doing something else became too much for her, and the light faded.

"Going, going, gone!" shrieked Dubh.

The Faerie Fool's laughter echoed in the cave, but it did not completely drown out the rustling of the revived dark elves.

VISITING THE DRAGON KING

"I COULD REACH you from another plane of existence. Why is reaching Max so much harder?" asked DL. "We've been at this for hours, and all I've gotten is a headache. I just don't understand."

"I think the tie between you and your Yeouiju is the primary one," said Ekaterina. "The bond you have with Max from healing him with your dragon blood is secondary and not as strong."

"But he's in my body. Shouldn't that count for something?"

"I suppose, but perhaps the fact that your body is in one place and your soul is in another confuses the Yeouiju."

"What we need is someone who knows about such things," said Maeve. She'd been unusually quiet for so long that both of them jumped a little when they felt her in their heads.

"If only we knew someone like that," said DL.

"None of our faerie contacts know much about Korean lore," said Ekaterina. "I tried to reach that practitioner of the Way I met in New Jersey, but I haven't been able to. The only other option I can think of would be for you to travel to South Korea. Chances are it would be easier to attract the attention of some of the resident supernatural beings from there than it is from here."

"There's no time for a long trip," said Maeve, more sadly than critically. *"We need an answer much faster than that."*

"Come to think of it, DL, maybe we know someone. You told me you've spoken to the Yeoiuju, right?"

"Once when it helped me to save you, and again today when I asked it to get a message to you," said DL. "It only answered the first time, though."

"The first time you asked a question, didn't you?"

"I wonder if it's really that simple," said DL. "I'd feel like an idiot if it was."

"No doubt that's not a new experience for you," said Maeve, though without the usual mental sneer that accompanied her more sarcastic remarks.

DL closed his eyes and tried to focus.

"Yeouiju, can you answer a question for me?" Not exactly the height of eloquence, but it should get the job done if the Yeoiju was still capable of responding.

"I do not know," the Yeouiju replied. The words entered his mind softly and slowly, as if the Yeouiju was considering what to say.

"You hear that?" DL asked Ekaterina.

"Loud and clear. See if you can get somewhere."

"Does your ability to answer depend on the question?"

"Yes, for there are many things I do not know, and the circumstances are strange. Part of you is here, part of you is elsewhere, and I am within the woman next to one part of you. I am confused."

"You gave the woman life. Do you remember?"

"I reanimated her flesh. Life I could not give her, for she had not possessed it for a long, long time."

"Ask about Max," said Maeve impatiently.

"My friend Max is with my body. Can you enable me to communicate with him?"

"He is far, and the act of splitting you I do not understand. I fear I cannot establish direct communication for you. Nor can I communicate directly myself. Only the part of me that is with your friend can communicate with him. Perhaps with more study, I could make contact. Now I cannot."

"Can you communicate with someone else, someone who might be able to help?"

"Normally, I could send a message to Yong-Wang, the Dragon King, but in my present state, I do not know."

"That sounds promising," said Ekaterina.

"Would you please try?" asked DL.

"You are my master. I will do what I can."

Minutes ticked away as the Yeouiju struggled to make contact. Just as DL thought he could bear the tension no longer, the Yeouiju said, *"The Dragon King will grant you an audience."*

"Excellent! What do I need to do?"

"Sleep," replied the Yeouiju.

The drowsiness hit DL so fast he barely had time to sit down on the couch before he passed out.

He had gotten used to traveling by portal, but this journey was different. He was doing astral projection again, but the trip was slower than before. He had an impression of passing through a tunnel, though he couldn't get a real fix on the tunnel's appearance.

His movement slowed, and muted light surrounded him. As it brightened, he could tell he was under the sea, or at least in some realm that looked like it. Even though only his mind was present, he could feel the cold water as if it surrounded his physical body.

A large form loomed in front of him. Blurry at first, it gradually became more distinct.

The Dragon King was huge, far bigger than DL had been the one time he'd achieved full dragon form. His scales were iridescent blue with a blue-green border that blended with his reddish underbelly. Even in the relatively subdued light, all three colors sparkled.

His face was somewhere between human and lizard. It was scaled and shaped roughly like a lizard's, but his nose looked somewhat human, and he had a white beard and spiky white eyebrows. From the top of his head sprouted two coral horns. As odd as the combination sounded, the overall effect was majestic. DL felt compelled to bow—if only he had a body to bow with.

"So, you are the one who has been such a disruption to dragonkind," said Yong-Wang. His voice was booming, but not threatening.

"I don't know what you mean."

Yong-Wang's large white eyes stared in disbelief.

"Surely that cannot be so! Why would an imugi choose to live with humans instead of with his own kind? How could an imugi deliberately infuse dead flesh with the power of his Yeouiju?"

"Your majesty, it's not that simple. My parents abandoned me—"

"Impossible!" interrupted the dragon. "Parents of our kind never abandon their children."

"All I know is I was left in a human hospital on the day I was born. I grew up in foster care and had no idea I was anything other than a regular guy. I only discovered my draconic heritage a few months ago."

"That might serve as a partial excuse," replied Yong-Wang. "However, it does not explain your misuse of your Yeouiju. I doubt anything could satisfactorily explain such a breach."

"You have to understand the circumstances." If DL had had a body at that moment, he would have been sweating. "The 'dead flesh' you refer to is Ekaterina, a woman who became undead through no fault of her own."

"I have heard tales of Westerners who became 'undead,' as you say, in an effort to avoid death," said the king. "Is not this Ekaterina such a one? Does she not feed on the living to sustain herself?"

"Not at all," DL insisted. "Her uncle transformed her as an experiment. She was given no choice. As for living on others, she…she does drink blood, but she is careful not to take enough to harm anyone."

"How does she know no one is harmed? I have heard such beings are generally savage. More often than not they drain their victims dry in one frantic feast."

"Ekaterina is the exception. She prayed to God for help during her transformation. Maybe that has something to do with it. She'd be the first to admit the hunger is hard to resist, but she manages. I've known her for months, and she's never injured someone in her feeding, let alone killed someone."

"I find that hard to believe," said the dragon. "Even if it were true, how did your Yeouiju come to reside within her?"

DL fought to keep from getting choked up. "She…she had been killed. I asked the Yeouiju how to save her, and it told me what to do."

The dragon's expression was hard to read, but it was a safe bet the king was not pleased by the impulsive actions of his subject. It was hard to be sure, though, because he stared at DL without speaking for a long period of time, as if he couldn't quite decide what to do with him.

"You must be aware that the undead are an affront against nature. Your sacrifice of your own Yeouiju is equally an affront. In the first case, someone has tried to increase her potential at the expense of others. In the second case, someone has wasted his potential. Neither situation is tolerable."

"I told you Ekaterina—"

"I heard you the first time," said the dragon. "Let us say I believe she was not transformed by choice. Even so, her existence is not natural. That you would have tried to extend it by using the power entrusted to you—"

"Majesty, I mean no offense, but I did what I had to do. Any man would do the same to save the woman he loved."

"Loved?" asked Yong-Wang, raising a spiky eyebrow. "You love an animated corpse?"

The Dragon King was even harder to deal with than a druid.

"It's not like that. She has a personality just like anyone else. She's a good person. She's risked her own life to save the lives of others. Most of the living can't even say that."

"It is perhaps easier to risk one's life when it isn't real," said the dragon, gazing at DL the way a parent would look at a kid who's just said something incredibly stupid.

DL was fighting hard to control his temper. "I wish that you could meet her, get to know her. If you really knew her—"

"It would not change my opinion in the slightest," the Dragon King said. "You have come for my help if I understand your poor, fractured Yeouiju correctly. Well, you may have it—as soon as I have extracted the Yeouiju from this Ekaterina and restored things to the way they should be."

"No! I will not let you kill her!"

"*Let?*" asked the dragon, booming a little more loudly. "What makes you think you can allow or disallow my actions? I am your king. It is your job to obey me, not mine to obey you."

"*My king?*" said DL, realizing he was losing his temper but no longer able to rein it in. "Where exactly were you, my king, when I was abandoned? Where were you when I was rattling around in foster care? How about when my life was being threatened multiple times by vampires and sorcerers? Where were you? Nowhere to be found!"

"Silence!" roared the Dragon King. "For this insolence, I should expel you from our kind, let you become one of the humans you prefer to your own people, and see how well you like that!"

DL had to admit being a regular guy had its drawbacks. On the other hand, having draconic powers meant little if he lost Ekaterina to retain them.

"I was a regular human for more than twenty years, and it wasn't so bad."

The Dragon King's eyes bulged with surprise. "Do you truly care so little about your heritage?"

"I care about it—but just not more than the woman I love, not more than my friends."

"So be it," said Yong-Wang raising his right claw. DL could feel power surging all around him and wondered if he had screwed up bigtime. He meant it when he placed other people ahead of his ties to the dragons—but how much help could he be to those people if he lost his powers at this particular moment?

Abruptly, the energy around him faded, and the Dragon King looked even more surprised than before. "Your body is missing?"

"My friend Max and I became switched accidentally, and Max was kidnapped by an evil faerie. That's why I came to you for help to begin with."

"With your identity scrambled in this way, I cannot make you human as you seem to wish so badly."

"Majesty, forgive my earlier outburst. Concern about my friends has made me more impatient and angry than I should be. I don't really want to sever myself from my heritage—but really I have two. Imugis are normally raised by their parents, aren't they?

"They are," agreed the dragon.

"But I wasn't raised that way. I was raised as a human. You don't want me to reject my dragon heritage. Can you understand why I wouldn't want to reject my human one, either? I beg you to take a closer look at my situation before passing judgment on me."

"Humility becomes you more than arrogance," said the dragon. "I still doubt that any amount of study, no matter how intense, will change my mind about your unnatural intermingling with humankind. However, it is true your situation is novel. Perhaps I too was overly impatient. Tell me how you were torn from your body."

DL explained what happened as well as he could. He tried to be brief, but the king kept asking for more details. When he had finally told the story to Yong-Wang's satisfaction, the dragon's expression changed. It took DL a few seconds to realize that he was smiling.

"I do not condone your earlier defiance, but I admit your life is even more unusual than I imagined. It is the mission of dragons to maintain the natural order of things—and in that area, I might well find fault with you. However, it is also our mission to help humanity, and in that respect, you might merit some praise. If what you say is true, you plunged yourself into peril trying to rescue a woman you hardly knew."

"I didn't realize how much peril would be involved," said DL.

"Even so, you did not evade it when it came your way. I will take time to study your life, just as you asked.

"You came for some other help, however. Something about the body switch?"

"Yes, that's the problem. I know some other people with supernatural powers, but no one seems to know how to switch Max and me back. Even if they did, the fact that his mind and my body are somewhere we can't find would probably prevent them from doing anything to help."

The dragon sighed. "I might be able to help, but you are right—I can do nothing if we do not have your body, and I cannot immediately locate it. I discovered that when I sought to make you human. The Yeouiju should be able to tell me, but it is unable to do so."

"Yes, we figured that out ourselves. Isn't there some other way to locate it?"

"Eventually," said the dragon. "No piece of information about any of our kind is ever completely out of my reach. However, it may take time to find your body. When I have discovered the truth, I will share it with you."

"Thank you," said DL. "I couldn't think of who else to turn to."

For a moment, the Dragon King seemed to be looking right through DL. Then he looked directly at him. "How different things might have been if you had been raised as an imugi. Farewell for now."

The Dragon King and the seascape faded rapidly. DL opened his eyes. He was back in Max's body.

UNEXPECTED COMPANION

DL BARELY HAD time to catch his breath. Ekaterina hovered over him, and Esras had arrived and was staring at him. His friends leaning over him made DL feel like Dorothy in the last scene of *The Wizard of Oz* —except that her adventure ended at that point. His promised to be more like a thirty-mile crawl over molten lava than a joyous homecoming.

Esras's story only heightened DL's sense of looming disaster.

"We need to find Max and Morfesa—right away," said DL. "Where might Dubh be holding them?"

"I wish it were just Dubh we had to worry about. He used strange magic to appear as Max. When Morfesa went through a portal he had opened, she tried to tether herself to me, and I felt the same kind of magic where she was. It took me a while, but I recognized that magic from one of my youthful adventures. It is the magic of the Dökkálfar, dark elves you would call them."

"That doesn't sound good," said DL.

"Oh, it isn't, for their hearts are evil. I have no doubt they made a bargain with Dubh, one which could potentially unbalance Álfheim, and perhaps the other Norse realms as well. Echoes of that chaos will be felt on Earth and beyond. Add to that whatever efforts Dubh makes to create his own world, and the damage he can do to the universe is immeasurable."

"You can get us to this Álfheim?" asked Ekaterina.

Esras looked uncomfortable. "The Norse realms are mostly inaccessible. I didn't get enough detail through my link with Morfesa to know exactly how she got there. Fortunately, I do know a way in. However, at least part of that way will be in sunlight. I fear you cannot come, Lady Vampire."

"Surely the two of you will not be sufficient to defeat Dubh and his dark elf allies." DL wasn't sure if Maeve was lobbying for Ekaterina or wanted to go herself.

"We're more like an advance party," Esras said. "We will scout the route I have in mind to make sure there are no obstacles." He held up his hand to show a ring that throbbed with a dull green light. "This ring allows me to leave a magic trail, so that the assembling army can follow us.

"As you can imagine, the abduction of one of the four druids of Tír na nÓg angered the Irish faerie rulers as few things could. A great force is being assembled at Falias to hunt down Dubh and bring him to justice. When the army is ready, it will follow my trail straight to him. Waiting for it to assemble to start scouting would lose too much precious time."

"If this is just a scouting mission, why take DL?" asked Ekaterina.

DL tensed up. "Because I'm useless?"

"You know I didn't mean that—" began Ekaterina.

"And indeed you are not," said Esras. "I can explore faster if you are with me. Even if Dubh is still with the dark elves, their realm is vast. Your soul's connection to its own body could provide invaluable guidance."

"As could the Yeouiju within me," Ekaterina pointed out. "It too is connected to DL's mind and body."

Ekaterina jumped a little when the Yeouiju joined the conversation. *"I should definitely go, for my place is with my master. That part of him is in another world is torture for me."*

Ekaterina repeated the words to Esras, who couldn't hear them as she and DL could. His frown deepened.

"I can appreciate the advantages of having you come with us, but devising a way to keep you safe from sunlight would take more time than we have. Minutes we could spare, but hours or days? Dubh will surely have pried his way into the grimoire by then."

"Maybe this is simpler than you think," said DL. "The Yeouiju resurrected her even though it didn't know what a vampire was. Protecting her from the sun seems simpler. Yeouiju, can you protect Ekaterina—the woman in whom you reside—from the sun?"

The Yeouiju didn't answer, but a mist rose around Ekaterina, completely engulfing her. Esras stared wide-eyed at the instant cloud.

"Will that work?" asked DL.

"Amazing!" said Esras, running his hand through the mist. "It looks like ordinary mist, but there does seem to be magic in it that might work. Lady Vampire, may I test the protection?"

"Fire away," said Ekaterina.

Esras raised his staff, whose glow shifted from emerald green to pale gold. Gradually, he drew more and more sunlight from the staff, until every corner of the room was bright as high noon—except where the mist wrapped around Ekaterina.

"When are you going to start?" Ekaterina asked.

The Druid's eyes widened. "Amazing!" The room is in full daylight, and she can't see or feel any of it. Can you see at all?" he asked her.

"Clear as night," she said.

"The Yeouiju is supposed to be able to control the weather," said DL. "I guess even in these…unusual circumstances, it can manage a mist."

"That doesn't surprise me," said Esras. "Sun-resistant mist is a little more of a trick, though. Lady Vampire, you do realize there are still dangers. A high enough wind might dissipate that cloud around you, or the Yeouiju could lose power for some reason. If either of those conditions occurred while you were in the sun, you'd be destroyed."

"I don't like the sound of that," said DL.

"I'm going, and that's that," said Ekaterina. "If something goes wrong, you'll need me, and you'll need me to help find your body regardless."

"Even if the Yeouiju can keep up the mist at all times, it may draw unwanted attention. Ekaterina could pass for human normally. She will not be able to with mist wrapped around her like that," said Esras.

"Yeouiju, can you keep the mist protection up but make it possible for people to see me?" asked Ekaterina.

"See you?"

"Make me visible."

"But you are visible."

Without his body, DL had no inner dragon—but he could feel some part of it lingering within him, attached to his soul rather than his body. Straining enough to give himself a headache, DL conjured up what draconic vision he could and looked at Ekaterina. If he stared long enough, he could see her through the mist. No wonder the Yeouiju was confused.

"You are aware of what she looks like under the mist. Humans and some other beings may not be. Can you keep the mist protective but make it less visible to humans?"

"I will try."

Esras reduced the sunlight to an early dawn level for the test. The mist twisted around repeatedly. It cycled through the colors of the rainbow.

"Changing color isn't making it any easier to see through," said DL. "Can you make it colorless?"

The best the Yeouiju could do was make an almost invisible mist that nonetheless gave Ekaterina's skin and eyes a blue tinge.

"Well, now you don't look like some kind of phantom," said Esras. "More like a large pixie."

"Is that a problem?" asked Ekaterina.

"Pixies and faeries have often warred with each other in the past, but that was long ago, and anyway the Norse races we might encounter have nothing against pixies."

DL still didn't like the idea of Ekaterina risking herself, but he knew her better than to think she could be convinced not to go. Esras's stiff posture and tense expression suggested he wasn't entirely happy with the situation, but he didn't seem inclined to forbid her from accompanying them, either.

"Speaking of preparing for the possibility that things might go wrong, I have something for you, Lord Dragon," said Esras. Reaching behind the couch, he lifted an enormous spear that looked familiar.

"I've never trained with a spear," said DL.

"Remember, this is the Spear of Lugh," Esras said. "All you have to do is throw it in the right general direction, and it will do the rest. Max's father wielded it in the battle against the Collector, despite all his protests about not being able to use it."

DL took the spear in his hands. It vibrated at his touch.

"See? In battle, you will find it hard to restrain from leaping into action. Even throwing it is just a formality. I hope we don't have to fight, but in the event we should, at least you will be armed."

"Well then, let's get on with it," said Maeve.

"I don't suppose it would do me any good to point out that it may be dangerous for you to travel with us," said Esras. "This is not like the trip to Teren di Vampiri, where you became stronger. We go to a place with its own realm of the dead, and there is the possibility that you might be drawn to it and get trapped there."

"No, it wouldn't do you any good. This is my grandson we're talking about. Whatever little help I can give to this quest I intend to give."

Esras sighed and gave her an it's-your-funeral kind of glance.

"As I mentioned before, I don't know how Dubh managed to get into a Norse realm. As with most of the domains of beings once worshipped as gods, getting in and out is tricky, and the way is different for each one. Fortunately, as a younger man, I was quite adventurous, and I got it into my head to visit the Ljósálfar, the light elves. Unfortunately, the common paths had all closed by the time I had that notion. It took me many months of research, but eventually, I discovered I could gain access through certain ancient places that had been sacred to the Norse.

"In a place called Gamla Uppsala in Sweden, there are three burial mounds in which ancient kings were interred. More important for our purposes, each of these mounds was a place of worship for a different Norse god and thus can serve as a gateway to one of the nine worlds of the Norse plane.

"The mound of Odin is said to lead to Asgard and that of Thor to

Svartálfaheim, where live the duergars who forged his mighty hammer, but I didn't try either.

"Instead, I made use of the third mound, sacred to Freyr. Though he came from Vanaheim and ended up dwelling in Asgard, he was also king of Alfheim, the home of the light elves—and, deep underground, the dark ones as well."

"So we can use his mound to reach the place where Dubh has his hostages and the book?" asked Ekaterina.

"If we are fast enough," said Esras. "Having been there, I can open a portal. It will be morning in Sweden, and there may be people about, so I will cloak us in invisibility and inaudibility first. Once we arrive, there is a short ritual to perform, and then we should be in Álfheim fairly quickly." He turned to Ekaterina. "It will be very bright there. It is not too late to change your mind."

"I will trust in the Yeouiju," said Ekaterina.

The whole idea still made DL's heartache, but he knew there was nothing he could say to persuade her to change her mind. He couldn't blame her. Had their positions been reversed, he would have insisted on going.

Esras had no trouble making them invisible. Opening a portal was not hard for him, either. Hundreds of years of practice showed in his confident movements.

They stepped through into a green countryside lit by midmorning sun, though the wind was chilly. DL looked nervously at Ekaterina, who took his hand.

"I'm fine," she said. "Focus on the mission."

Esras led them unhesitantly to one of three large mounds. The grass was browning a little, but otherwise, the mounds looked unremarkable. However, there were enough people exploring in the area to make their invisibility a good thing. DL would have hated to explain why he was carrying a spear or why there was a blue woman at his side.

"Can you see the sunlight?" he asked Ekaterina.

"I'd like to—if it didn't burn my eyes out—but just as at Max's place, I'm seeing as if it were nighttime."

"I can feel something," said Maeve.

"Yes, this is a place of power," agreed Esras. "It's subtle, though. One has to know it's here to notice it."

The druid tensed, and he looked around quickly.

"Something nearby is not so subtle. There is evil here."

DL looked around and saw nothing at first. Then he noticed a boy walking—no, more like staggering—toward them. He stuck out among the nearby tourists and sightseers like the proverbial sore thumb.

Everyone else looked European, but the boy was clearly Asian. Everyone else looked well-fed and well-dressed. The boy was emaciated and was clothed in ill-fitting rags, made even more incongruous by the sword belt he wore around his waist and the scabbard hanging from it. No one except DL and his friends noticed him, though he was incredibly conspicuous. Not only that, but it was clear he could see them.

"Help me," he whispered. "Help me."

"Stay back!" shouted Esras, waving his staff, which glowed angrily.

"He's just a boy," said Ekaterina.

"Dark magic surrounds him," said Esras. "As for being a boy, that may just be an illusion. I can't clearly perceive him through that cloud of magic."

"I'm under a spell," whispered the boy, who fell to his knees right next to DL. "I was torn from my home and thrown into this place, and I was cursed."

"What kind of curse?" asked DL, reaching for the boy.

"Don't touch him!" commanded Esras. "Even if he is cursed rather than being the source of the evil, the curse may be infectious."

"I can't get anyone to see me or hear me. I've had no food except scraps from the garbage, no place to stay, no one to talk to."

"How long have you been like this?" asked Ekaterina.

"I don't know. Months, maybe."

"How did you get cursed?" asked Esras. "Such powerful curses are rare on Earth these days."

The boy patted the scabbard. "I stole this from a powerful user of magic. He is the one who cursed me."

"Enough questions!" said Ekaterina. "The boy is cold. Can't you see him shivering? Warm him up at least, Esras."

The druid grudgingly swung his staff in the direction of the boy, who looked frightened and backed away.

"He won't hurt you," said Ekaterina, reaching for the boy. He looked at her and became even more frightened.

"You…you're dead!" he whispered, trying to scramble away from her.

"Strange curse," said Esras. "It allows us to see him, and it allows him to see us as we are. Why would anyone cursing you do that, boy?"

"I don't…I don't know, sir. I know a little magic myself, so perhaps that is how I can see you as you are. You may be able to see me because the one who cursed me did not expect anyone with magic to stumble across me. Maybe the curse only keeps ordinary people from seeing me."

"All very convenient," muttered the druid.

"Can't you see he's just a frightened boy, not some evil sorcerer?" asked Ekaterina. What is your name, boy?"

"My name was taken from me by the curse as well. Now I am called Chubang Doen—Outcast."

"We must find you a better name, some clothes, and something to eat," said Ekaterina.

She tried to move closer to Outcast, but he backed away.

"Kid, she isn't exactly dead, and she means you no harm." Outcast looked at DL, but the boy didn't look reassured.

"There's something wrong with you!"

"Long story there," said DL, trying to smile. "We'll help you if you let us."

"There is no time!" protested Esras. "Besides, for all we know, he could be some kind of distraction sent by Dubh to slow us down. I still can't tell if he's a real boy or not."

"How long would it take to send him back by portal to the Eau Claire house?" asked Ekaterina. "We can figure out his status after we've done what we came to do."

"It would take some time to adjust the protective spells enough to let someone as soaked in dark magic as he is in," said Maeve. *"For once, I think I have to agree with a druid. That's time we don't have."*

"How about Tír na nÓg?" suggested DL.

"No one there will be any more eager to receive this little pile of dark magic than I am, especially during preparations for war."

"Let me come with you," said Outcast. "I'll be good."

"We go to war ourselves, child," said Esras, sounding slightly more compassionate than before. "We cannot take you into battle."

"The one thing the curse gave me was the ability to hide real well," Outcast said. "Watch!"

He disappeared completely.

"I can't even sense him," said Maeve.

"Nor I," admitted Esras. "But it doesn't make sense someone would curse him with an extra ability."

"He didn't," said Outcast, reappearing. "I was already good at hiding. I couldn't break the curse, but I found a way to twist it just enough to make me really hard to find, at least for a while."

"May I speak to you for a moment?" Esras glared at DL and Ekaterina. His tone was more like a command than a request. Taking the hint, they moved a little bit away from Outcast, though Ekaterina kept glancing back at him.

"There is no chance this Outcast is a human boy," said Esras.

"How can you be so sure?" asked DL.

"Because his story makes no sense. Human children who have magic potential typically don't start developing it until puberty. Even partially human children with a large supernatural heritage don't. Yet this boy who appears to be ten at the most has enough power to make changes in such a complicated curse. Does that seem reasonable to you?"

"No," admitted DL. "Still, I'd hate to just leave him here. What if we're wrong? How much more suffering would we put him through in that case?"

"I see the wisdom in not taking him with us now, but I also agree with DL," said Ekaterina. "I'm not willing to risk just leaving him here if there's even a small chance he's telling the truth. You've said yourself you can't really tell what he is, Esras. What if he's exceptionally precocious? What if he's from some other world? Then he wouldn't technically be human, but he might still be telling the truth about what happened to him. There are many possibilities."

"I suggest telling him we'll come back for him. Once Max and

Morfesa are rescued, and the book is restored to us, we can take the time to investigate his claims more thoroughly."

Esras sighed. "I suppose it wouldn't hurt to take a second look when we have time."

Ekaterina walked over to Outcast, who still cringed away from her.

"We go into a place of great danger now. If we took you with us, you could be far worse off than you are here."

"Please," he said, reaching toward her with both hands despite his fear. "Please!"

"We can't take you right now, but we will come back for you as soon as we can."

"Do you promise?" asked Outcast, looking from one of them to the other. "Do you all promise?"

Esras nodded reluctantly, DL much more vigorously.

"What about her?" asked Outcast, pointing in the air.

"You can see me?" asked Maeve. *"My, what a clever boy you are! Yes, I promise as well."*

"Stay close to this area," said Ekaterina. "We'll be coming back to one of these hills nearby."

"I will," Outcast replied, though he looked so pathetic that DL and Ekaterina both hesitated. Leaving him here all alone was hard.

"We need to move along now," said Esras. "The sooner we finish our scouting, the sooner we can get back."

When they reached the approximate top of the mound, which was big enough to be a natural hill, Esras chanted a little in Old Norse, then waited. After several minutes, he chanted again, and a golden doorway opened before them.

DL looked around nervously again, but Esras just laughed. "Only we can see it." The druid ushered them through, and the door closed and vanished as soon as they were through.

Álfheim's sunlight was more intense than Sweden's, though it somehow managed to not be blinding. Its landscape was green without any hint of brownness. It was not fall here, but some kind of perpetual spring. The trees were even taller and leafier than in Sweden, the grass lusher, the sky bluer. The area around the mounds in Gamla Uppsala still had a fair amount of forest, but here there was no sign of civilization aside from the occasional distant castle spire, just one massive wilderness stretching out in all directions, broken sometimes by a meadow or a lake.

They were standing on a hill higher than the mound had been, but because of the taller trees, they couldn't see very far in any direction.

"How do we go about finding Dubh here?' asked DL.

"We need to—" began Esras. He froze. Without a single rustling of a leaf or snapping branch, a large number of light elves, most of them carrying bows, surged from between the trees, surrounding them.

DL had expected from the name that the elves would probably be luminous. He hadn't counted on them glowing quite so intensely. All faeries had a little glow to them if one looked closely, but these elves were like miniature humanoid suns. Only the brightness of the surrounding light kept them from being overwhelming.

DL had also expected them to be singing happily or something like that. He had not expected their angry looks or the sunbeam arrows that were pointing at his heart and those of all his friends.

"Who are you?" demanded the tallest elf in the group. "Why have you come here?"

"We are seeking a fugitive who has invaded your realm with two or more hostages from ours and a powerful magical artifact which we believe he means to use against you," said Esras.

"Most noble of you," said the lead elf in an angry tone. "Why undermine such noble intentions by bringing a dead creature into our midst?'

"I'm getting tired of this," mumbled DL.

"You think you're getting tired of it? Imagine how I feel," Ekaterina muttered.

"The woman to whom you refer is noble despite her…unusual existence," said Esras.

"You have two such," said the elf leader. "The animated corpse and the ghost—half your party. "No, wait! There is another, something covered in the stench of dark magic. We cannot see him, but we can feel him."

Esras was usually far more light-hearted than Morfesa, but now he looked angrier than DL had ever seen him. "The last one you described is not with us; he came through without our knowledge. Outcast, show yourself!"

Esras's stern command produced no result, and the archers' fingers shifted slightly on their bows, as if they itched to shoot.

"Outcast, please make yourself visible," said DL gently. "No one will hurt you."

"We make no such promise," said the elf leader.

"Do you want him to appear to you or not?" asked DL more angrily than he had intended. "He's just a little boy. The dark magic you sense is a curse placed on him by somebody else, not anything he did himself."

"We don't know that," said Esras.

The leader looked back and forth between DL and Esras, disbelief etched on his bright face. "You do not even all tell the same story. How are we to trust you?"

"Outcast, please," said Ekaterina. "You need to make yourself visible, or we will never be able to complete our mission. We have friends who may die. You wouldn't want that, would you?"

Outcast revealed himself, but very slowly. First, he was just a shadow, then a flat image in black and white, then a little boy, shaking so visibly that DL wanted to give him a hug.

The elf leader looked at him skeptically. "He appears to be a human child, but all that magic around him prevents me from telling with certainty."

"Send him back to our world," said Esras. "We never meant to bring him here."

"Please, no!" said Outcast, dropping to the ground and grabbing Esras's knees before the druid could move out of the way. "Please don't send me back! I've been alone for so long. I just can't stand it anymore."

"The least risky course for us would be to send all of you back together," said the leader, his eyes fixed on Outcast. "We would be rid of you, and the boy would not be alone."

"Our presence here serves you as well as us," said Esras. "A faerie seeks great power through an alliance with the dark elves. If he succeeds, we think he intends to give them the means to defeat you."

The elf leader laughed loudly, and the sound echoed all around them. "How much power could he possibly have? Enough to keep the sun from shining? That's what it would take to give the dark elves a victory.

"Since the birth of our two races, we have been weakened by darkness, and our underground enemies have been weakened by light. They cannot enter our realm without being rendered helpless, nor can we enter theirs for exactly the same reason. No magic can alter reality at such a basic level."

DL didn't know that much about magic. Really, he only knew bits and pieces he'd picked up in conversation with Max and others or from watching magic done, but it occurred to him the elf leader might have been thinking too literally. Sure, nothing Dubh did could wipe the sun from the sky. What if he could shield the dark elves from its effects, though? After all, Ekaterina was shielded, and she still seemed fine.

As if in response to his thought, clouds started to roll in and cover the sun.

"We are under attack!" yelled the leader. Most of the archers lowered their weapons and joined hands. As shadows touched them, their glow faded, but enough of them were still in the sun to merge their individual light into a great burst that lanced upward and struck the clouds. Grayness and shimmering light warred within them. The light prevailed—but just barely.

"This has never happened before," said the elf leader, looking at the sky as if he expected the sun to disappear completely at any moment.

"This is the work of the very fugitive we have come here to seek," said Esras. "I fear you will see worse if you do not allow us to complete our search."

"How would you do this search?" asked the leader. "If the one you seek is truly an ally of the dark elves, he will be in the tunnels beneath our feet. You could never venture there and hope to live. As for magic, it would fail you."

"It may be that your magic does not work below ground, but mine might," said Esras. "It is not as light-dependent as yours seems to be. In any case, what do you have to lose?"

"That would depend upon what you intend to do when you find him."

"With your permission, I would summon an army from Tír na nÓg to defeat the fugitive and his dark elf allies."

The leader's eyes widened. "If such a thing were possible, it would truly be a blessing to us. However, I cannot give an army permission to enter our territory. That approval would have to come from Freyr himself."

"The army would take time to arrive, and it will not come until I have found the one we seek. If you do me the favor of submitting my request to Freyr, perhaps he will give his consent quickly."

"I know not how fast I may procure his approval, but I will make the attempt," said the leader. He hurried off. His men lowered their arrows but did not follow him.

"Not much trust yet," mumbled DL.

"Elves and faeries have a long and complicated history," said Esras quietly as he pressed his palms on the ground. "The fact that there has been little communication between the two groups for centuries has not improved the situation. Ah, there is much magic below us, but I do think I can find Dubh if I have enough time. You and Ekaterina can work on finding Max. Now that we are so close, perhaps the Yeouiju can sense DL's body more easily."

The ground shook enough to rattle DL's teeth. Even the elves, who moved as if their every step were choreographed, couldn't keep their footing.

"Do you have earthquakes often here?" Esras asked the watching elves.

"We never have earthquakes," one of them answered.

It looked as if Dubh wasn't going to give them the time they needed to find him.

FINDING THE SURFACE

MAX'S WALK through the cavernous tunnels had rapidly become a trudge. At least he didn't have to fight; he produced more than enough sunlight to keep the dark elves away, though he did hear occasional rustling coming from somewhere. Maintaining the sunlight was more draining than he had expected, though. Something about the atmosphere in the caves must have been resistant to it. It might be a blessing in disguise that he was drawing on DL's draconic body to power it. Whatever anti-sunlight spells existed down here would have been fashioned by someone who had never encountered an Eastern dragon.

Unfortunately, the caves—or tunnels, if the dark elves had dug them in the first place—weren't laid out in any logical way, at least not one he could discern. Seemingly promising routes dead-ended with annoying frequency, forcing him to backtrack. He pressed his hands to the wall and tried to map a route to the surface by magic, but he seemed able to perceive only the tunnels closest to him. The layout must be too vast for him to scan all at once—either that, or his fatigue was limiting him even more than he thought.

His head throbbed. The sensation was faint, more like the ghost of a headache, but it was constant. Pulling at the chains before he'd figure out a magical way to escape had left him with sore muscles. The body's draconic nature caused actual muscle pulls to heal quickly, but it didn't prevent fatigue.

Every so often, the tunnel walls and floor throbbed more than his head did. He had visions of a tunnel cave-in burying him alive, but the vibrations never rose above a barely discernible shaking. It was more like the marching of a distant army than an earthquake shockwave.

Contemplating this world's seismic activity was not going to get him out. His best bet was to find sunlight. He tried reaching straight up through the rock with his mind, but he never felt the sun's reassuring warmth. Was it in permanent eclipse?

His own artificial sunlight looked paler, but even at full intensity, it still left too many shadows. It was easy to imagine every rustle was an army of rats huddled just outside the light, waiting to catch him by surprise and gnaw his skin off.

"I'm an idiot," he muttered to himself. He'd been so obsessed with finding a way out that he'd forgotten to spread his mind out enough to sense nearby life forms. It didn't take much energy to do that, and he could stop imagining rats, giant spiders, or anything else his imagination could dream up.

A quick scan calmed his fears about wildlife. He did feel the cold presence of dark elves like specks of blackness deeper than ordinary darkness, but they weren't following him. As far as he could tell, they were moving about on other business as if the presence of an escaped prisoner from another world was an everyday occurrence.

Why were they being so casual? He observed them flit around like bats for a while. If there was a pattern to their movements, it escaped him.

Could they sense him the way he sensed them? If nothing else, the sunlight would be easy for them to track, and he lacked enough spare magic to conceal it.

Max smiled to himself. They weren't doing anything to conceal themselves, either. If he could spread his mind out far enough to see how they were distributed in the tunnels, he could find the elusive exit. The dark elves couldn't get too close to it without being exposed to sunlight. Any area without dark elves would be a possibility.

He tried to extend his reach, but he stopped when the walls and floor started to vibrate with less subtlety than they had before. He pressed his hands against the tunnel walls, and the stone shifted slightly beneath his fingers. He could also hear a distant rumbling.

Letting his mind seep as deeply into the stone as it would go, he felt the presence of weak but pervasive magic he should have detected before. Was the rock alive? The constant pulsing reminded him of a faint heartbeat. No, the rock itself remained lifeless. What he was feeling was the humming of the magic as it twined in and out of the rock like tree roots. Trees were patient, though, taking years to crack their way through. This magic sparked through like lightning.

Was it a response to his presence? The magic had an ancient feel as if it had fused with the stone centuries ago.

Looking at it from the inside, he understood its purpose. It was what had kept him from mapping the tunnels. The magic made them change constantly. They were writhing like snakes in the darkness, elusive and deadly. The dark elves' seemingly random movements were designed to navigate the changing landscape. Someone like Max could wander here until he starved and never get an inch closer to the surface.

No wonder Dubh hadn't set guards on him!

No Norse myth had described anything like this. In all those centuries following the last contact between the old Norse gods and human beings, the dark elves must have made improvements to their security system. Who knew what other unpleasant surprises he might encounter?

Not that it mattered. This one surprise ended any real hope he had of escape. Even on a good day, his magic wasn't yet strong enough to blast through solid rock—and this wasn't a good day.

"Not My Master, I have news," said the part of the Yeouiju linked to DL's body.

"What is it?"

"I feel the presence of my other parts nearby."

Max's heart skipped a beat. *"How close are they?"*

"I cannot tell the distance exactly, but close enough for me to feel them."

"Can they feel you? Can you get a message out?"

"I have tried. I think I succeeded."

"Max? Are you all right?" Max wanted to jump up and down. That was DL—and he was close. He could feel his presence.

"Physically, yes. I'm trapped, though. The tunnels keep changing so that I can't reach the surface."

Max felt the tunnel shifting again. As far as he could tell, the tunnels were rearranging themselves again, but he felt claustrophobic. Were the tunnels limited in how much they moved? Could the one he was in crush him if it felt like it? He couldn't wait to be free of them.

Pushing back the static created by the ambient magic, Max tightened the link with DL so that they could communicate more rapidly. Words could be thought faster than they could be spoken. Raw thoughts not formed into words traveled even faster. DL was able to bring Max up to speed in seconds that way.

Max wasn't used to such fast communication, though, and his headache began to feel less like a mental itch and more like a nail being pounded into his forehead. The joy of knowing DL, Ekaterina, and Esras were nearby was outweighed by the realization that Dubh had Morfesa. Max shuddered despite himself. It sounded as if Dubh had access to Merlin's grimoire—and Morfesa would not have given that to him easily. She could be in pain. She could be dying. Max had to get out of these damned tunnels!

"Wait! Esras is pretty sure he's pinpointed Morfesa," thought DL. *"She's alive—and she's in the tunnels. Dubh's probably with her."*

"In which case, the book is probably down here with them. Can you talk me back to where she is? The tunnels don't want me to reach the surface, but they might not stop me from moving toward Morfesa."

DL didn't respond right away. The contortions of the tunnels weighed on Max's mind more the longer he was in them. He felt as if all those tons of rock were resting right on top of his skull.

"Esras is pretty sure there's nothing you could do to stop Dubh now. You'd need to be closer to Ekaterina to draw on the power of the Yeouiju, and even fully charged, you might not be able to beat him as long as he holds Merlin's book.

"We have cavalry coming—if we can get this Freyr guy to let them in. Esras says sit tight until then."

The idea of trapped in a maze of tunnels until Freyr made a decision was about as appealing to Max as being buried alive. *"Wait! I have an idea."*

"As long as it doesn't involve you risking your life, I'm all ears."

"If I could get back together with you guys, we'd be better off, right? More able to use the Yeouiju."

"Yeah, but from what you say, there's no easy way to do that."

"How close am I to the surface and to you?"

For a moment, Max was alone in the tunnel again. Was his head throbbing in harmony with the magic?

"Pretty close," thought DL.

"If the Yeouiju really has magic the dark elves haven't anticipated, can Esras tap into it? Use it to freeze the tunnel walls in my area, so they don't keep moving?"

Despite the distracting rumbling of rock scraping against rock, Max could hear his own breathing, and he imagined he could hear his own heartbeat. It too sounded as if it were gradually adopting the rhythm of the rocks.

"He's acting like it's a pretty tall order," thought DL. *"While we're waiting for Freyr, there's really not much else for him to do right now, though, so he's going to give it a try."*

Max couldn't avoid listening to the ever-shifting tunnels as Esras worked. Was he just more aware of them, or were they getting progressively louder?

"Brace yourself," thought DL. The tunnel sound became as raspy as cogs in a machine grinding against each other the wrong way. The stone beneath his feet vibrated hard enough to make him clutch at the wall for support. A grinding sensation like bones breaking forced him to pull back the part of his mind that he had sent into the stone.

"Given enough time, Esras tells me he could probably do it, but getting together with the Yeouiju is more complicated than he anticipated. He needs more power and doesn't know how to get the Yeouiju to yield more. Perhaps if we can get you to the surface somehow—"

"Or get you all down here. How about some variation on that trick Morfesa used to open a portal into that world Dubh got us stuck in?"

"Esras said that was too—"

"You're not listening. I'm not talking about facing Dubh alone. I'm

talking about you, Esras, and Ekaterina coming down here to help. Sunlight is enough to overpower his dark elf friends. With all of us together, and the Yeouji able to yield more power, we might beat him, right?"

"Yeah—but wouldn't we have to pull your mind up here for Morfesa's strategy to work? That didn't work so well last time."

"Perhaps the connection would be tight enough without any astral projection. When Morfesa did it, we were on a different plane of existence and fighting a ton of static. This time, we're in the same plane, on the same world, and relatively close together. That plus the connections among us should make it possible for Esras to use my knowledge of this place without my mind having to move at all."

DL had to confer with Esras again. Max tried to shut out the tunnel magic, but it felt even more insistent. Before, it had felt impersonal, detached. Now it felt angry. Magic that was complex enough, particularly old magic, could develop a kind of sentience. Were the tunnels pondering how to get revenge?

"Esras isn't crazy about the idea. However, we still haven't heard from Freyr. Your plan, risky as it is, may be the only way to keep Dubh from doing something we can't readily undo. He'd already tried once to block the sun, and he just tried again."

DL flashed Max his memory of Dubh's latest attack. A large number of light elves were on hand, and they worked their magic together as if they had been working as a team for centuries. That didn't prevent Dubh from spreading enough clouds to half cover the sun before bursts of light magic ripped the cloud cover away. The elves were shaking by the time their golden light had banished the grayness of Dubh's magic. The fear in their eyes made clear how close they had come to disaster.

"Dubh is getting better at using Merlin's grimoire to amplify his spells," thought Max. *"How soon can Esras get you guys down here?"*

"He isn't sure what Morfesa did. He's going to try to get the Yeouiju to talk him through it. Hang in there for a while."

If Max was learning anything from these experiences, it was that he had very little patience, and these long waits were wearing it thin. Unfortunately, he didn't have any choice but to wait. The feeling that the ceiling was going to collapse on him didn't help. He felt some reassuring tingles from Esras that kept him from panicking. The druid would—

A rock fell at Max's feet. Looking up, he could see cracks that he hadn't noticed before.

Another rock fell.

Max tried to conjure up enough protective shielding to keep the ceiling in place. His headache felt like a railroad spike through the forehead, and he almost passed out. He wasn't just scraping the bottom of the barrel for magical energy—he had scraped right through it.

A portal started to open but collapsed. The connection had snapped when he nearly lost consciousness.

"What's happening down there?" asked DL.

"The tunnel is getting ready to collapse." Max tried to sound as if he weren't in a blind panic, but, linked as they were, there was no way DL could miss such a strong emotion.

"Hang in there. Esras almost has it."

A third rock hit the tunnel floor with an echoing thud. Dust tickled Max's lungs, making him cough. He resisted the temptation to use any more magic.

A portal swirled to life right in front of him. Through it stepped DL, Esras, and a blue Ekaterina.

"You made it!" said Max. He tried not to sound like a little kid on Christmas morning.

"Barely," said an especially pale Esras.

"Are you OK?" asked Max.

Esras managed a smile. "I will be. This roundabout way of opening a portal is exhausting. Fortunately, the trip out will be simpler."

"Uh, ceiling," said DL, pointing upward. The cracks had gotten bigger.

Esras held up his staff. His hands shook, and the knuckles that gripped the staff were white, but a warm brown glow flowed from it into the tunnel's ceiling.

"The magic that shifts the tunnels was damaged by my effort to stop it," said Esras. "I can't easily repair it, but it won't collapse that rapidly. We should be all right once we move out of this particular tunnel."

"And Dubh?" asked Max.

"Still in the same place." Esras pointed to a small, flickering light behind him. "The Will-o'-the-wisp over there will lead us through the tunnels to Dubh's lair. Morfesa is still with him. Should I take over providing the sunlight?"

"I'll be OK," replied Max. "I've been expending too much magic too quickly, but if the light is all I have to manage for a while, I should be able to sustain it."

Something brushed against Max.

"Who's there?" he asked. DL and Ekaterina looked around, stood back to back and took a defensive stance. Max had to suppress a snicker at how awkward DL looked trying to do that in Max's body.

Esras looked more angry than suspicious. "I think I know who it is. Outcast, show yourself!"

The boy slowly became visible. He was pressed against one of the tunnel walls, shaking and looking fearfully at Esras.

"Stop acting!" snapped the druid. "If you were really that afraid of me, you might actually do what I said. I told you not to come with us."

"I…I was afraid," said Outcast. "I was afraid to separate from you. You're the only way I could ever get back."

"There's plenty more to be afraid of down here," said Esras, waving his staff.

"There's no point in scolding the boy now," said Ekaterina, stepping between him and Esras. "Anyway, if we fail down here, the surface isn't likely to be any safer than these tunnels."

"Will you feel the same when he plunges a stake through your heart?" asked the druid.

"We don't have time to keep arguing about this," said DL. "If Outcast did pose some kind of danger, he could have attacked us when we first met. Are we going to get moving, or what?"

Esras glared at him but reluctantly gestured to the wisp, which led the way through the twisting maze of tunnels. There didn't seem to be any movement. The druid, DL, and Ekaterina kept looking from side to side. Outcast followed their example.

It wasn't long before Outcast started to cry. Ekaterina picked him up and carried him, murmuring soothing words. Despite his earlier fear of her, he stopped crying pretty quickly.

Occasionally, dark elves crossed their paths, but they hardly ever saw them, and when they did, it was from a great distance. As long as they had light, they had little to fear from Dubh's allies.

"When we get to Dubh, how much can the Yeouiju help?" asked Max.

"More now that the three of us are close together," said DL. "Not as much as we'd like, though. It can't fuel my body's transformation to dragon form, for instance."

"It might do better if we had your souls in the right bodies," said Esras. "It's unfortunate we have no time to get that sorted out."

"Even so, the biggest obstacle is that its power is mostly inside of me, keeping me alive," said Ekaterina. "I never thought about that before all this trouble, but it could do much more in its natural state."

"Even if all it does is keep you alive, that's more than enough for me," said DL, putting his arm around her.

"I can't help but feel a little guilty," said Ekaterina.

"Blame the Collector," said DL. "He's the one who killed you in the first place. If you're worrying about Dubh, don't. We'll beat him."

Max looked at Esras, who wasn't joining the conversation. It was clear the druid wasn't so sure.

"How will you know when Freyr gives his consent for the army to come?" asked Max.

"I won't," said the druid, raising his bare hand. "I left my signal ring with the light elf leader and told him how to use it. He will send the message when the time comes—if it comes."

"Why wouldn't it?" asked DL. "Isn't Freyr going to be happy to get help?"

Esras sighed. "If only it were that simple. Unfortunately, there was a lot of bad blood between elves and faeries during the years when travel between the Norse worlds and places like Tír na nÓg and Annwn was easier. At one point there was even a war between the Scottish faeries and a group of light elves who tried to colonize—or invade, depending on your point of view—Elphame. The faeries weren't eager to share their land, and eventually, they won. Their victory was quite bloody. No doubt, the light elves remember it as a massacre.

"In recent times, there's been hardly any contact at all between faeries and elves. There were no new conflicts, but no way to bring the old hatreds to an end. Instead, I'm sure they've festered and deepened. Freyr might not trust a faerie army to put down aggression by the dark elves. Indeed, he's just as likely to see us as their secret allies."

"That's why you're doing this, isn't it?" asked Max. "Going along with my idea, I mean."

"Yes, because it may be the only way we have a chance of getting the book back," Esras admitted.

"Is…is this dangerous?" asked Outcast.

"We could all end up dead," said Esras. He didn't give the boy a second glance.

"Obviously, you've never raised children," said Ekaterina, glaring at Esras and drawing the whimpering Outcast closer to her.

"I know how to act with children," replied Esras. "I don't know what you're holding, but I know it isn't a child."

"Well, until Outcast does something that proves he isn't a child, I say we play it safe and treat him like one," said DL.

Esras kept walking forward without looking at DL. The tunnel echoed with their footsteps. Everybody had to pick up their pace to keep from losing sight of the determined druid and his Will-o'-the-wisp.

"I don't get it," said DL. "He wasn't anything like this when we fought the Collector."

"Try to cut him a little slack," said Max. "He's worried about Morfesa."

"So are you, but you're doing it without treating a little boy like dirt. If you ask me, Esras is the one who's not acting like what he's supposed to be. Maybe he's the fake."

"I'm afraid," said Outcast, pulling even closer to Ekaterina.

"We all are," said DL, "but everything will be OK."

Esras gestured for quiet. They must be getting close. Would being quiet do any good, though? Surely the dark elves could sense their approach a mile away.

A loud thud echoed behind them. The group turned. Solid stone blocked their exist.

"Everything's not going to be OK," whined Outcast. A single tear slid down his cheek.

LIKE RATS IN A TRAP

"THEY SHOULDN'T KNOW we're here," said Esras. "I've been masking our presence as well as I could."

"I bet the sunlight is something that can't be masked," said Max. "We obviously don't have the element of surprise, but we still have to try, don't we?"

Esras nodded. "There's no choice if we want to keep Dubh from running amuck. Stay together, and stay alert." The druid turned and resumed his man-with-a-mission pace. The others hurried to keep up.

DL looked around suspiciously. Why not just seal off the way ahead to keep them from reaching Dubh? Unfortunately, the answer was obvious.

The dark elves intended to kill them.

They turned a corner and found themselves at the entrance to an enormous cavern. The place was so full of magic that, even without using his dragon senses, it felt as if he were bathing in a sea of sparks. Esras had already raised what protection he could, but was it like using paper to hold off a charging lion?

Max was staggering more than walking. They were still linked closely enough for DL to feel fatigue eating away at him like a flood eroding a river bank.

"You OK, man?"

Max glanced at him with the expression of a man holding on by his fingernails. "I'm fine." His knees came close to buckling. DL reached for Max, who waved him off.

They stepped into the cavern. It was filled with dark elves, as if the entire underground population had gathered in this one place. Volleys of arrows struck at the barrier Esras had established, dented it, came close to breaking through. The druid's face, grim with concentration and damp with sweat, betrayed how much of a toll the attack was already taking on him.

Max tried to spread his sunlight into the massive chamber in front of them. The light flickered, and he staggered. Tremors ran across his face. His eyes were unfocused.

DL grabbed him in time to keep him from falling, but the sunlight shrank to the size of a candle flame—not enough to deter the dark elves. The thudding sound of their arrows striking Esras's magic gave DL chest pains as if those shafts were piercing his heart.

"Yeouiju, can you help us?" DL asked. He didn't get an immediate response. The dark elf arrows kept up their relentless barrage. Esras's shielding crackled as the druid struggled to keep it together. A few arrows made it partway through. One sailed past

The Spear of Lugh pulsed at his side. DL had forgotten all about it. He gave it a feeble toss—Max really needed to start working out. The spear flew as if it had been cast by Hercules. DL watched its fiery path as it ripped into one of the elves near the front and just kept going. Elven flesh was no obstacle to it as it pierced one after the other.

Against a smaller force, the spear would have prevailed immediately. Against the army facing them, its effect was surprisingly small. Despite the carnage and disruption caused by its attack, it did not break the morale of the elves who were not immediately affected. Instead, they shot arrows even faster. The spear would eventually work its way through all of them—but not before they had broken the shield of Esras and satisfied the deadly thirst of their own arrows.

DL looked back at Ekaterina, who was still holding the trembling Outcast. The child stared at the rain of arrows as if he could see his own doom.

"Kid!" DL couldn't bring himself to call him Outcast. "Kid! You said the sword was magic. What does it do?"

Outcast looked at him as if he no longer understood English. Taking the risk the stolen weapon wouldn't curse him just for touching it, DL pulled the sword from its scabbard.

"It is magic," muttered Max. He sounded barely conscious. "Strong…"

"It is the sword of Haemosu," said the Yeouiju. Its usually emotionless voice sounded amazed.

Esras moaned, and his outstretched arms shook. The sound of arrows striking the now-flickering barrier was like bullets striking metal. The whole cave echoed with the noise.

"It is Yongwanggeom, the Sword of Dragon's Light."

"What does it do?" DL almost shouted. The light part sounded hopeful, but the sword was dead metal in his hand.

"Think about light," said the Yeouiju

DL couldn't concentrate. Had he seen a momentary gleam? He couldn't tell.

Max reached over and touched the blade. Writing in Korean script glowed momentarily, then died again.

Ekaterina gently put Outcast down. She crouched low, bracing to charge the dark elves under their arrow fire.

"Don't!" said DL. "You don't stand a chance against a force that size."

"None of us stand a chance if I don't try. Once Esras can't sustain his protective spell any longer, those archers can take all of us down in about a minute."

DL felt as if his heart was going to explode. He was about to see Ekaterina die.

"Max!" The sorcerer looked at him with vacant eyes.

"Max! Focus! If this sword has something to do with dragons, I think we need to concentrate on it together. You've got the body; I've got the soul. Maybe the sword needs both—"

"Maybe it needs all of us," said Ekaterina. "Most of the Yeouiju's power is inside me."

Esras sagged for a moment, then straightened. His body was shaking.

All three of them put their hands on the hilt at the same time. The

Korean writing blazed again, and this time it didn't fade. Instead, it flared across the entire sword, becoming brighter each second, until it was a miniature sun.

DL wasn't blinded. Max didn't seem to be, either. Ekaterina had to turn away, though. Even the mist that had shielded her from full daylight wasn't enough to protect her from the sword's power. Fortunately, its radiance persisted even after she let go.

The light was bright enough that the archers, distant as they were, stopped firing. A few of them cried out.

"If we can get the sword closer to them, we can defeat them," said Ekaterina.

DL's first impulse was to grab the sword himself and charge. In the battle against the Collector, he'd wielded Nuada's sword, the sword of light, without any trouble.

Of course, then he'd had his own body. Normal long swords didn't weigh much more than three and a half pounds, but it was hard to hold one straight out for very long if you weren't used to it—and Max's body wasn't. The muscles in his right arm started to burn almost immediately.

"Dude, you're going to start working out whether you like it or not," DL muttered. He tried getting Max to take the sword, but his friend was barely conscious, and the hilt just slipped through his fingers.

"I'll take it," said Ekaterina. The mist around her had turned almost black as the Yeouiju tried to compensate for the sword's radiance.

"It's too dangerous," said DL, trying to see her through her protection. "The sword's way stronger than ordinary daylight."

Arrows hit the protective spell again. The elves might not be able to see what they were shooting at, but enough arrows were flying that some of them were bound to hit as soon as the shield went down.

Ekaterina grabbed the sword from DL and ran forward with it. He'd have had a hard time stopping her in his own body. In Max's, there was no chance. She raced forward at faster-than-human speeds. She passed beyond the protective spell, and the dark elves stopped shooting. They fell back, yelling in pain.

"She's lying," said Outcast, who had gotten up and walked over to where DL and Max were.

"What do you mean?" asked DL. He kept his eyes on Ekaterina, but she was moving so fast that she was almost out of sight.

"She's burning. I can feel it."

DL didn't ask how Outcast could feel that. He just started running. Outcast followed him more slowly. Max staggered along behind. Esras, looking less pained now that there was less pressure on his shield, joined them as they passed by.

The cavern where the dark elves had assembled looked even larger once DL was inside it. He could see it much more clearly in the magically intense daylight.

The dark elves close enough to see all lay unconscious on the cavern floor, their faces twisting as if they were having an agonizing nightmare. DL couldn't see the Spear of Lugh, but occasional screams echoed through the cavern as it continued to find fresh victims. It was more insatiable for blood than a typical vampire.

Ekaterina's pace had slowed. Was her sword hand smoking? In all that mist, it was hard to tell.

It wasn't hard to tell that, although the dark elves were down for the count, the biggest threat remained.

So far away that DL could just barely see him, the Amadan Dubh was wildly playing his pan pipes and surrounded by a cloud of magic so intense even mortal eyes could see it. DL couldn't see Merlin's grimoire at that distance, but he had no doubt it was open right in front of the faerie.

Unlike the dark elves, Dubh wasn't slowed by the flood of sunlight. If anything, he picked up his pace.

Around the frantic faerie, darkness swirled. DL started to run in his direction. The darkness spread and deepened. It touched and grayed the edge of the sword's light. With the added power of Merlin's grimoire, Dubh might just succeed in blocking that light completely.

DL was already out of breath, but he was still much farther away from Dubh than Ekaterina. He tried to speed up. His chest was burning. The others were even farther behind him.

Ekaterina continued to move toward Dubh, but even she was slowing down. There wasn't any doubt now—her sword hand was smoking. Despite that, she continued to grip the hilt.

"Yeouiju, can you stop Ekaterina from burning?" DL asked. He got no answer. Ekaterina's rapid movement away from him and Max must have disrupted communication among the Yeouiju.

A wave of blackness surged toward the vampire, completely obliterating her surroundings. The glow from the sword prevented it from closing around her, but dark elves started to rustle nearby as soon as its light could no longer reach them.

DL and the others were still relatively far from Ekaterina. If that flood of darkness washed over them, they would be surrounded by dark elves in no time.

Sure enough, the darkness kept its hold on Ekaterina but reached tentacles out to grab them and engulf them. The tentacles would have them in less than a minute.

DL realized what he had to do.

"Return!" he thought as hard as he could, not knowing if it would work.

In seconds the Spear of Lugh, bloody but undamaged, was in his hand again. Thinking about Dubh, he tossed the pulsing shaft in the faerie's general direction.

He thought he heard a distant scream, though that might have been wishful thinking—until the darkness shuddered and dissipated.

Unfortunately, the wound wasn't fatal. A faraway portal flashed, and the spear returned to his hand too quickly. Dubh had managed to escape.

At least DL had achieved his most urgent goal. With the darkness spell broken, the revived dark elves again screamed and fell. They were back to unconsciousness in seconds. That left no obstacle between DL and Ekaterina. He raced in her direction despite his aching leg muscles and pounding heart.

He reached her, and she dropped the sword. DL grabbed her and pulled her as far as possible away from the radiant blade. The mist subsided back to its earlier blue-tinged invisibility, and he hugged her as hard as he could.

As they embraced, he reached down and touched her sword hand. He could feel the uneven texture of burned flesh and blisters.

"What have you done to yourself?" he whispered.

"What I needed to do. What you would have done in my place." She pressed even closer to him, and he could feel her trembling.

DL looked over at Esras. "Ekaterina needs healing." The druid still looked shaky. DL immediately regretted saying anything, but he couldn't just leave her injured so badly without trying to do something.

Esras looked back as if his eyes were having trouble focusing. "I…I'd like to help, but vampires are physically completely different from humans. If I had time to study—"

"It's all right," said Ekaterina. "I can heal myself. I may need a little blood, though."

"You only need to ask," said DL, baring his throat.

"Actually, the blood from your original body would be better," said Ekaterina, glancing in Max's direction. Seeing DL's downcast expression, she brushed her good hand through his hair. "Don't feel bad about that."

"I'm not. It's just that, uh, for us the sharing of blood has always seemed more intimate."

"I love you, remember, not Max—regardless of who's in what body. And I've taken blood from many men before you. You are the only one with whom I have been truly intimate. The sharing of blood doesn't have to mean anything."

"I promise I won't try to seduce her with my incredible charm." Max winked.

DL managed a grin despite how down he was feeling. "Nerd!"

"Dropout!" Max laughed. It occurred to DL that none of them had laughed in hours.

Max didn't laugh long, though. His happy expression morphed into a frown so fast DL didn't notice at first.

"Wait a minute!"

"Don't worry—you won't need a condom for this," said DL

"No, I'm serious. I'd have expected my grandmother to interfere in that blood conversation. After she didn't, I realized I can't feel her presence anymore. She's gone!"

"It has been a while since she said anything," agreed DL. "Not since we got here."

"It is as I feared," said Esras. "When she entered the Norse plane, she became subject to its rules."

"You mean she's in Valhalla?" asked Max.

"No, Valhalla is reserved for those who died in combat, remember? Maeve would have passed on to Helheim, the gloomy abode of Hel. The Norse feared her as an embodiment of death without honor."

"You mean Maeve's gone to Hell?" asked DL.

"Helheim is not as terrible as Hell," said Esras. "It is, however, far grimmer than Valhalla. I doubt Maeve will be happy there."

"I doubt Valhalla would have pleased her, either," said Ekaterina. "She anchored herself to her house so that she could protect her family. She didn't do it to end up in a Norse afterlife, not even a pleasant one."

"We have to save her!" Max looked around frantically. "How do we get to Helheim?"

Esras put a hand on Max's shoulder. "It isn't as easy as that. None of us could get in. Only the dead may go there. Even Ekaterina probably couldn't get in. The Norse tradition says nothing of vampires, but it does say the dead cannot pass on while their bodies remain."

"Surely the former Norse gods will help us." Max was beginning to sound a little desperate.

"We can always ask," said Esras. "However, even they hardly ever journey to Helheim. The place may not be like the Christian Hell, but its ruler is formidable. I don't know if even they can force Hel to let go of a soul she has taken in accordance with the normal rules of this plane."

DL had been in a lot of desperate situations with Max, but he'd never seen the kid look as hopeless as he did now.

"We just keep losing people," Max muttered. "We lost Adreanna. We lost Morfesa. Now we've lost Maeve."

"We won the battle, though," said Outcast, looking from one of them to the other as if hoping for even a crumb of encouragement.

"I fear we won the battle only to lose the war," said Esras. "Dubh must be wounded, but not badly enough to prevent his escape—with Merlin's grimoire. Now we don't even know where he is."

Outcast sank to the floor like a deflating balloon.

THE QUEST AT THE CROSSROADS

"Dubh, uh, I don't think he can leave," said Max. "He made a deal with the dark elves and hasn't fulfilled it yet." It hurt DL's heart to see Max struggle to get the words out.

"That's true," said Esras. "That may be the one thing we have going for us. We need to get back to the surface and see if the army has been let through yet."

"We're sure Dubh isn't still underground?" asked Ekaterina.

"I feel only the residue of the spells he cast during the battle. The likelihood is he hasn't been working with Merlin's book long enough to know how to mask it effectively. If he's learned already, we won't be able to find him down here, anyway."

"We're also in no shape to take on another attack by dark elves," said DL. "All of us except Ekaterina are exhausted, and she's wounded."

"Alas, that is also true," said Esras. "It would be best for us to leave as rapidly as we can. Max, get the sword. I'm sure we're going to need it."

Ekaterina picked up Outcast somewhat awkwardly because of having to work one-handed. She didn't complain, though.

"I'm more than ever convinced that can't be a real child," Esras whispered to Max and DL. "That he could have stolen such a powerful weapon on his own is impossible to believe."

"But he gave that powerful weapon to us," Max pointed out. "If he means us harm, he has an odd way of showing it."

Esras looked away and busied himself with getting a portal open. He managed, though it took an uncomfortably long time.

When they stepped out of the portal, a large group of light elves was milling around nearby. The elves stopped and looked at them suspiciously.

"The ground shook while you were down there," said one of them in an accusatory tone.

"We fought with the dark elves and with the thief we sought to bring to justice," said Esras. We won the battle but did not capture the fugitive or the book he stole."

"Ill luck that," said the elf. His words dripped with doubt. His current attitude made their earlier cold reception seem trusting by contrast.

"What says Freyr to our request for safe passage for our troops?"

"He says no," said the elf.

"Gudbrand, that isn't exactly what he said."

"DL hadn't known anyone was standing behind them. He turned and saw one of the most beautiful women he had ever laid eyes on—with the exception of Ekaterina, of course.

The newcomer didn't glow like the elves that surrounded her, but she still drew his eye more than any of them. Why was she so compelling? More than just physical beauty was involved, though she was beautiful. Her hair wasn't blonde; it was golden. Her skin wasn't fair; it was fine porcelain.

He shook himself. Why was he suddenly thinking in poetic terms? Was he under a spell?

If he weren't careful, he'd be under that woman's spell for sure.

"I meant no offense, my queen," said Gudbrand, bowing low. "My king has not said yes, though."

Queen? Yes, almost invisible in her golden hair, a small crown rested on her head.

"He has not said no, either." She walked closer and studied the group. "Esras, is that you? I have not seen you in centuries."

"It is I, indeed." The druid bowed. "Alas, my purpose is far graver than when last I visited you."

"So I have heard," she said. "Freyr did not wish to give approval for an army to march into our territory without conferring with you personally. He will be here momentarily.

"While we wait, I can meet your friends. I am Gerda, wife of Freyr and queen of Álfheim." She looked at Max expectantly.

"I am Max, sorcerer-in-training, rightful owner of Merlin's grimoire." DL couldn't help noticing that his voice cracked. Apparently, he was at least as rattled by the woman…goddess…whatever as DL was.

"I am DL, the son of a dragon—"

Gerda flinched and stepped away from him.

"But not like the dragons you know," he added quickly. "Eastern dragons are good and peaceful beings."

Gerda squinted at him. "I am relieved to hear it. There is something else about you, though, isn't there?" Looking back at Max, she added, "About both of you."

"Our souls are in the wrong bodies," said DL.

"Strange! I have never heard of such a thing. How did it come to pass?"

Max nervously explained what had happened. Gerda hung on every word and asked many questions. When her curiosity was satisfied, she turned to Ekaterina.

"And who is the mysterious blue woman? I have not seen her like before."

"I am Ekaterina, once princess of Wallachia."

"And why are you enshrouded in some sort of mist?"

"I am very sensitive to sunlight."

Gerda frowned. "I have never heard of such an affliction, except for the dark elves, of course."

"I am not a dark elf, majesty, but I fear it would take too much of your time for me to explain what I am."

Gerda's eyes narrowed as if she was trying to see right through Ekaterina.

"There is more than one kind of magic upon you. Some of it is light, and some of it is dark."

"As is life," said Esras.

"How true," said Gerda, though she sounded unsatisfied. "And you, boy. What is your name?"

"Outcast," he whispered. He was doing his best to hide behind Ekaterina.

"He's very shy," said DL, "and he's been through a lot."

"I can see that," said Gerda. DL braced himself for a whole string of questions about Outcast and Ekaterina. Fortunately, Gerda heard the sound of approaching chariot wheels and turned away from them.

A chariot drawn by large boars was approaching as fast as a race car. The driver was a handsome man wearing a crown that matched Gerda's. He must have been Freyr. Standing at his side was a woman as beautiful as he was handsome.

Freyr came to a stop near them and helped his companion from the chariot. DL found her even more compelling than Gerda. It was almost painful to look away from her.

"That's Freya, Freyr's sister," Esras whispered to him. "It is good she came, for her magic is great. She may even be able to help us to get you and Max back into the right bodies. Be cautious, though. She was once goddess of love, and at times she can be more compelling than she realizes."

"Or perhaps she does realize," said Ekaterina, grabbing DL possessively. DL forced himself to look away from Freya's overwhelming presence.

The elves bowed even lower to Freyr than they had to Gerda. The elf king nodded to them and smiled benevolently. That smile faded when he looked at DL and his friends.

"Esras, what is the meaning of this? You I remember, but I am sure these others have never visited us. They are mortals and have no place here."

"Majesty, we seek both a fugitive, the Amadan Dubh and a priceless book he stole. This one, as the book's true owner, is our best hope of finding it." Esras pointed to Max. "Owing to earlier mishaps, these other two are linked to him. His safety requires their presence."

Freyr looked even less happy with the group than Gerda and made less attempt to hide his feelings. "What of the boy? The one cowering

over there, drenched with dark magic. And why do the others seem so…
unwholesome? Nature is out of balance in them. How can you, a druid,
bring such turmoil into my kingdom?"

Ekaterina sighed. DL wished he could take her somewhere out of
earshot and spare her yet another dissection of whether or not she had the
right to live. For a moment, he imagined picnicking on one of those sunny
hills with her and Outcast while Esras argued with the Norse powers that be.
There was no way for any of them to just leave, though. They were stuck.

Even Esras looked tired of having to explain the same situations
repeatedly, but he did so as diplomatically as he could. He also reminded
Freyr of the request to allow a faerie army into Álfheim.

"An army seems premature as things stand," said Freyr. "You admit
that you don't have any idea where to find this refugee, and I have no
intention of letting an army search the whole kingdom."

"That wouldn't be practical, anyway," said Esras. "My hope was to
find Dubh with magic. The army will not be needed until I find him,
but I wanted the troops to be ready as soon as I discovered where he was.
He is as slippery as Loki, Majesty. He has the support of the dark elves
and extra power from Merlin's book. He could easily create a war
between the light and dark elves—or worse."

"But surely my light elves would be more than a match for the dark
ones without any help from your faeries. And surely I would be more
than a match for this Dubh, particularly if I were supported by Gerda
and Freya."

"I do not mean to cast doubt about your elves or upon you, Majesty.
It is possible for Dubh to hide with the dark elves beneath the ground,
in which case the light ones would be unable to help. He has already
visited their underground lair at least twice, probably much more."

"Majesty," said Gudbrand, "I am skeptical of bringing a foreign army
here as well, but Esras speaks the truth. Whoever this Dubh is, he has
come close to obscuring the sun more than once."

"I have seen this magic from afar," admitted Freyr. "Let us attempt to
find this Dubh first. Once we know where he hides, we can then decide
whether or not a faerie army is needed to assist us. Esras, it will take
Freya and me time to gather what is needed for the ritual. Your party

looks weary. You may wish to take the opportunity to rest. Gerda will see to your needs."

DL had to stifle a chuckle. Never had he heard an invitation that sounded so much like an order.

"Thank you, Majesty, for your help and for your hospitality," said Esras.

Freyr nodded and hurried off. As little as he seemed to like the party or the idea of a large faerie incursion, he did seem to be taking the Dubh threat seriously.

"What's his problem?" muttered Max.

"I mentioned the tense relationship between faeries and elves before," said Esras. "Were the situation reversed, many faerie rulers would respond in exactly the same way."

Gerda continued to eye them with mistrust, but she was not stingy with the hospitality. Once she started giving the light elves orders, it took them only minutes to set up tables for food and tents for rest.

Tired as DL was, he was ready to sleep as soon as Ekaterina's hand was taken care of—until the food arrived. Did the light elves think they were feeding an army?

He must have been as hungry as he was tired. Even the sight of a whole roast pig, which would ordinarily have repulsed him, made his mouth water. If pork hadn't been to his liking, there were also large quantities of beef, mutton, and something Esras told him was goat meat. There was also a stew called skause that looked like a modern beef stew. At first, the only visible vegetables were the peas and carrots, and other bits in the skause, but DL also spotted wild apples and some kind of greens surrounding the pigs. It wasn't clear whether those were intended just for decoration or for eating.

"It's a good thing none of us are vegan," he mumbled.

"Yeah, I never heard of a vegan Viking," said Max.

DL sat next to Ekaterina. "What are we going to do about your hand?"

"Ignore it for a while," said Ekaterina. "I don't know how our hosts would react if I started drinking your blood. Anyway, the injury doesn't cause me pain."

"Last time I saw your hand, it was practically black. How can that not hurt."

"It was tremendously painful while it was happening. Vampire bodies aren't like human ones, though. We stop hurting as soon as no further injury is being inflicted. The injured tissue doesn't rot, either."

"What stimulating dinner conversation!" said Max.

DL smacked him on the back of the head. "I was just making sure she was all right. You got a problem with that?"

"Not at all," said Max, reaching for a large flagon. From the golden color and the honey smell of the liquid inside, DL could tell it was mead.

"Careful, Max. You're not that used to drinking, and mead can be pretty strong."

Max grinned. "Yeah, but your body's pretty used to drinking. And didn't you tell me your body's draconic nature makes it much more resistant to alcohol? My body? Not so much. So, I guess you're the one who needs to be careful how much he drinks."

"Under the circumstances, that's not really funny." DL kept a straight face for about thirty seconds. Then he started laughing so hard he almost fell out of the chair.

"Yeah, I can see how funny it isn't," said Max, laughing himself. Even Ekaterina chuckled a little.

"Why is that funny?" asked Outcast in between gulps of skause. "I don't get it."

"Don't talk with your mouth full," said Ekaterina, patting him on the shoulder.

DL had to smile. He stopped quickly, though. Ekaterina would make a great mother—but could she even have kids? She acted so full of life, so much more than just a reanimated corpse. That's what she was, even though he had a hard time thinking of her that way.

Ekaterina took his right hand in her undamaged left one. "We will get this body switch sorted out soon. Don't worry."

"I know we will," said DL. He didn't want to tell her what he had really been thinking about.

They finished eating, but Freyr and Freya had not yet returned.

"They should be back by now," said Esras, looking around as if he had somehow missed seeing them.

"It's just as well," said DL. "That'll give me time to help Ekaterina heal her hand."

"It'll be better if Max does it, remember? Dragon blood," said Ekaterina, leaning over and kissing him on the cheek. The kiss felt even colder than usual through the mist around her.

"I remember," said DL, but his heart felt colder than her kiss as he watched her go with Max into one of the nearby tents. He was just being silly. He trusted them both. Why did he feel so sad, though?

"It's tough when one is used to being the hero." Esras moved into the chair Max vacated. "When one has to watch helplessly."

"You need a little work on your pep talks," said DL, forcing a smile.

"I'm just saying that anyone would have a hard time adjusting in your position. Hopefully, this won't go on too much longer. As soon as we have time, we'll get this sorted out."

"You're sure about that?"

"Absolutely. It may take a little while, but what is done by magic can always be undone by magic. Anyway, you have nature on your side. Your soul and Max's want to be in their own bodies, and those bodies want them back. In time, the return might even happen on its own. We can hurry it along as soon as we know what's blocking it."

Esras glanced over at Outcast, who had slumped over onto the table and was snoring loudly. "Whoever that is counterfeits a little boy very well."

Despite himself, the druid smiled slightly.

"He's getting to you, isn't he?" asked DL.

Esras thought for a moment. "Whoever…whatever he may be, he has yet to do us harm. I'm still certain he's not what he appears. That doesn't necessarily mean he's hostile. I'm going to keep an eye on him, though."

"I'm sure you will," said DL. He picked up Outcast gently and carried him over to one of the tents. The kid was heavy the way dead weight is, despite his scrawny, even fragile, appearance.

DL put him on the soft ground and lay down beside him. He wanted to be with Ekaterina, but something about watching her feed on

Max gave him the creeps. Besides, he was tired, and taking a quick nap wouldn't hurt.

* * *

DL WASN'T sure how he got there, but he was standing in front of the tent where Ekaterina had gone to feed on Max. His feet moved forward without any encouragement from him, and he found himself inside the tent.

They were underneath some kind of animal skin, but he could tell they were making love. He gasped, and they looked in his direction. Neither one showed surprise or guilt.

"What can I say, man?" asked Max. "Letting her drink my blood was a pretty intimate act, after all."

"It's not as if I'm really cheating," said Ekaterina. "It *is* your body. At least, it was. I suspect after this that Max will want to keep it."

DL jerked awake so abruptly that if he'd been in a bed, he would have fallen out of it. He was breathing too fast, and his heart was pounding.

Outcast was sitting up and staring into his eyes.

"Sometimes there is truth in dreams," he said. That was a pretty weird statement to come from a little kid, but DL didn't have any time to think about it before Max stuck his head into the tent.

"Freya's back and ready to start."

"Uh, I'll be out in a second." DL got up, ran his hand through his hair, and looked at Outcast. "Do you want to come along or stay here?"

"Come along!" The kid grabbed DL's hand and dragged him out of the tent.

Why did DL feel so groggy? Too much mead, probably. Max hadn't been joking about his body not being used to alcohol.

Max...the dream. Yeah, it was just a dream. Nothing to worry about.

DL stepped out into the perpetual sunshine of Álfheim and blinked. Judging from how unworried the light elves looked, Dubh hadn't tried to block the sun again.

Ekaterina came over to give him a hug. Was it just his imagination, or did she seem less passionate than normal?

"It feels as if your hand is healed."

"Yes, Max's blood did the trick."

"Don't you mean my blood?" asked DL. The words came out harsher than he meant them to. Ekaterina looked puzzled.

"Yes, of course, I meant your blood. The situation is confusing, is it not?"

"Not so confusing that I'd expect you to get Max and me mixed up."

"What's gotten into you?" asked Ekaterina. "You aren't still thinking I love you any less because of the body you're in?"

"Freya is nearly ready," said Esras, who had just walked over. "All of us should join the circle around her."

DL, with Outcast once again clinging to his hand, followed the druid. Ekaterina walked next to him and slipped her arm around him. He didn't resist, but the gesture felt wrong to him, as if Ekaterina was just faking interest.

The remains of their feast had been cleared away. In its place was a high wooden platform with a simple chair upon it. Max led them to where Esras was standing. At the druid's side was Freya, though she was dressed very differently.

Over her white gown, she wore a dark blue cloak decorated with stones that caught the light in such a way that they sparkled like stars. The necklace of amber around her neck did the same, as did the stones set in the tip of the rune-covered staff she carried. Her cap, gloves, and shoes all appeared to be some kind of animal skin.

"Greetings, friends!" she said. If she felt the same suspicions Freyr and Gerda did, she was hiding them well. "The hour has come to begin the seidr ritual."

"Seidr?" asked Max.

"Now is not the time for that kind of question," said the druid.

"It is all right. The young sorcerer is naturally curious. In his place, I would ask as well.

"Seidr is the most sacred and powerful kind of Norse magic. It underlies the power of human practitioners and even of the Vanir and Aesir. The Norns themselves, the three who carve and weave destiny itself, make use of it.

"It can be used for anything from changing the weather to changing one's shape, but today we will use it to reveal the unseen. If the Amadan Dubh is anywhere within the Nine Worlds, he will be unable to hide from its power.

"Before we begin, tell me what other questions you have. I sense that finding and defeating this Dubh is not the only way in which I can help."

"My friend and I are in the wrong bodies," said Max. "If it is not too much to ask, can you help us find the way to switch back?"

Freya smiled, brightening the already glowing day. "I would have been surprised if you had not asked. Though I have never seen such an affliction, I will try to find its cure."

"Can you also tell us how to lift the curse from Outcast?" asked Ekaterina.

"There is much tangling of magical forces around that one," said Freya. "I can try, but I cannot promise success. The type of magic used is alien to us."

"We got caught in Dubh's schemes because of his abduction of Adreanna, my...a woman I know. Can you help us find her?" asked Max.

Freya nodded. "If she is within the Nine Worlds, it can be done."

"I hesitate to ask for any more, but there is the matter of my grandmother—"

Freya looked puzzled. "I see no grandmother here."

"She is...a ghost."

Freya frowned. "We have no ghosts here, but I have heard the term. Here the restless dead, draugr and others, walk in physical form."

"She is not physical, but she was with us when we came to Álfheim and has since vanished."

"Did she die a hero's death?"

"She died of old age."

"Then her fate I can reveal without needing seidr. The honorable dead are divided between Folkvang, which I rule, and Valhalla, ruled by Odin. All others go to Helheim."

Max opened his mouth but couldn't get words out.

"I did tell her that was the risk of coming here," said Esras gently.

"But she doesn't belong here," said Max. "There is a way of getting her back, right?"

"If Hel has claimed her, there will be no getting her back," said Freya. "Even Odin himself could not retrieve her."

Max's eyes widened in horror. "There must be something we can do."

"I can check to see if she is truly with Hel, but if she is, then there she must stay."

DL could feel Max's cold despair, and he wanted to shake off the weird ideas that dream had given him and comfort his friend—until Ekaterina walked around him and hugged Max. Seeing them together, touching like that, burned away the memory of Max's icy pangs and left DL only with a raging inferno of resentment.

Ekaterina had lied when she said what body he was in made no difference. Already she was slipping away from him, moving inexorably toward the guy wearing his skin. The guy who would soon have his life.

No! That couldn't be right. He couldn't have misread Ekaterina's feelings so badly.

He barely heard Freya excuse herself to begin the ritual. When he realized she was gone, though, he knew what he had to do.

"Esras, I need to speak with you—alone."

The druid raised an eyebrow. "The ritual is about to begin. This is not the time—"

"This can't wait."

Esras glanced over at the platform. Freya was taking her seat in the chair.

"Well, the beginning of the ritual will take a few minutes, maybe more. I can give you that long. We both need to be in position when Freya begins to explore."

DL led Esras to a position where they wouldn't be overheard by Ekaterina or Max.

"Esras, can you check me to see if I'm under a spell?"

"Perhaps. With all the magic that you've been exposed to recently, I might not be able to tell."

"Please, please try! I feel as if I'm losing my mind."

The druid put his hands on DL's head and closed his eyes. When he opened them, he looked confused.

"The draconic magic—your connection to the Yeouiju—is fluctuating, but that may be normal for your unusual circumstances. I'm not sensing any other indication you're in the grip of a spell. Why would you think that?"

"It's…its, uh, embarrassing. I'm having these weird feelings Ekaterina is cheating on me with Max. I know that's stupid, but I just can't shake it."

"When did you start having these feelings?"

"I had a dream in which I caught them making love, but the feeling lingered after I woke up. If anything, it got worse."

"The kind of dispossession you're experiencing is rare. For all we know, your reaction to it is normal. Maybe anyone in your situation would become jealous of the person possessing his body."

"I can't stand feeling like this, whether it's normal or not."

"I'm reluctant to meddle with your mind when the circumstances are so unusual." Esras leaned forward and stared right into DL's eyes as if trying to read his mind through them. "Can you hold on until we get you back in the right body? I believe that will probably fix the problem."

"I…I'll try," DL mumbled. He felt as if his mind were about to split into parts: the normal, sane DL; and the raving lunatic DL, ready to believe the woman he loved was cheating with his best friend.

"I'm not…I might not be much use in a fight, though." DL had to pry the words out of himself, but he knew it was true. One thing he'd always been good at was fighting, but between Max's scrawny muscles and his own confused mind, he could only be a liability on the battlefield.

Esras nodded sympathetically. "I'm sure the others will understand."

"You can't tell them! They'll think I'm an idiot. They won't understand."

"You should give them a little more credit," said the druid. "From what I've seen, Ekaterina and Max are both sensible people. Anyway, we have to tell them something. It's dangerous not to. What if this mental conflict causes you to freeze up or behave erratically? You could be putting everyone else in danger if they aren't expecting something like that."

DL sighed. "I guess you're right. Let's tell them I'm, uh, having some kind of bad side effect from the body switch. We don't have to give them all the details, do we?"

"No, I think a general explanation will suffice. We'd better get back now. I can feel the mystic energy building."

DL had been so absorbed in the conversation that he hadn't even noticed the elven women circling around the platform and singing, nor the elven men burning herbs nearby.

Freya's eyes were closed, her head tilted toward the sky. Power the color of sunrise swirled around her, vivid even against the surrounding sunlight and the glow of the light elves. DL had never felt or seen so much power from any one person before. Maybe Esras was right about how much help she could be.

Outcast was standing a little farther away from Ekaterina than he usually did, as if he had started fearing her again. DL slipped in between them, and Outcast immediately took his hand.

"What's happening now?" DL whispered.

"Freya is aligning herself with Yggdrasil, the world tree," Esras whispered back. "Once she has done that, she should be able to find anything in any one of the Nine Worlds, for they rest in Yggdrasil's branches."

"I cannot see the Amadan Dubh," said Freya slowly. Her voice reminded DL of the seances he's seen in movies.

"Yet there is a power building beneath our very feet. It can only be his. He is preparing to fulfill his pact with the dark elves."

"So he did return to their caverns," mumbled Esras.

"If left unchecked, he will unbalance Álfheim," said Freya. Her voice, which had sounded detached, began to sound fearful. "The day will become night. The dark elves will rise from the depths and dare to challenge even the rule of the Aesir.

"Should such a thing happen, the Nine Worlds will all be driven from their normal paths. Anything could happen, even the premature coming of Ragnarok."

Freya remained in a trancelike state but stopped speaking. The pause went on so long that the elves began to talk quietly among themselves.

"Ragnawhat?" asked DL.

"The Norse apocalypse," said Esras. "Most of the Aesir and the Vanir will die, as will almost all other living beings. The worlds themselves will largely be destroyed."

"How can Dubh alone do so much damage?" asked Max.

"This plane of existence is balanced precariously," said Esras. "Someone who doesn't care about the consequences of his own actions and who has enough power might easily disrupt that balance."

"Perhaps we will need to focus on rescuing Adreanna, Morfesa, and Maeve and getting out as fast as we can," said Ekaterina. "Is Merlin's grimoire worth getting caught in the destruction of his plane?"

"You don't fully understand," said Esras. "A disaster of this magnitude in any plane that once had close ties to Earth will have repercussions there. How bad they will be I cannot say with certainty. Thousands of deaths are probably the best we can hope for."

Ekaterina nodded. "Then we must stop Dubh."

Freya broke her silence. "It is too late."

Dense clouds swept across the sun, and DL could have sworn he felt rumbling beneath his feet.

AN APOCALYPSE CAN RUIN YOUR WHOLE DAY

"REMOVE THOSE CLOUDS NOW!" yelled Freyr. The elves obeyed sluggishly as the darkness deepened. The cloud cover was thick enough to imitate a solar eclipse.

Max ran to where the elven sorcerers struggled and bathed them in bright sunlight. Esras did the same for the elven women around Freya.

"I'm afraid," said Outcast. DL scooped him up.

"Freya, climb Yggdrasil to Asgard," yelled Freyr. "Ask Odin for aid."

"She's going to climb a tree?" asked Outcast. He looked skeptical. Freya didn't move a muscle.

"She's in a trance," said Ekaterina. "I think Freyr wants her to send her mind to Asgard."

DL looked at Ekaterina. She wasn't looking back. Instead, she was looking over at Max. DL felt his jealousy stir again.

"She's in love with Max," whispered Outcast. "I'm so sorry."

DL looked down at Outcast. The kid's eyes looked different, more knowing than before. The ground shook again, harder this time.

The cloud cover parted momentarily, allowing sunlight to flow for a few seconds, then sealed again.

Freyr walked into Esras's light. Since Ekaterina was drifting in that direction, DL followed, still carrying Outcast.

"No one man could do this, grimoire or no," said Álfheim's king. "Something more is happening."

The druid closed his eyes for a moment as if he was going to join Freya in a trance. When he opened them, he looked alarmed.

"I wouldn't have thought Dubh could do this in so short a time, but he must have taught the best dark elf spellcasters how to reinforce his spell."

"Their magic is powerless above ground."

"What if Dubh were to get the spell going on his own? Could the dark elves get their magic to work above ground if the sunlight was partially masked?"

"Since the sunlight is never clouded this way, I cannot say for certain," said Freyr. "If your guess is right, though, our danger is grave. My light elves could beat back the threat from Dubh and the book—but add the collective power of the dark elves, and the forces of light may fail."

"My lord, if that is the case, surely now is the time to let the faerie army through?"

Freyr nodded slowly. "We have little choice now. Give the signal."

"When I descended into the dark elf tunnels, I left my signal ring with Gudbrand.

"Gudbrand!" yelled Freyr. "Come here at once."

The elf came, but in the growing darkness, he was moving slowly.

"The ring Esras gave you," said Freyr. "Give it back."

The elf raised his right hand. In the gloom, the ring's dull green glow was clearly visible. He slipped it off his finger and started to hand it to Esras. Before he could do so, the ring vanished.

"Treachery!" said Freyr. He stared fixedly at the spot where the ring had been, as if trying to conjure it back.

"In the second before it vanished, I realized the truth," said Esras. "That wasn't the real ring. Gudbrand, what happened to the original?"

"I...I do not know. I felt something odd on my finger for just a moment during one of the earlier periods of darkness. When I looked down, the ring was still there—or so I thought—so I worried no more about it."

"How could you have been so foolish?" asked Freyr.

"Majesty, he is not used to faerie magic," said Esras. "The counterfeit had an energy somewhat like the original. It is not his fault that he failed to detect the substitution.

"All is not lost, however. I will return quickly to my world through the fixed portal and summon the army from there."

The ground shook again, this time so hard that it cracked beneath them.

"Make haste, friend," said Freyr. Esras ran off in the direction of the portal.

Another flash of sunlight broke through, but even briefer than the previous one.

"We are losing the battle to strip the clouds away from the sun," said Freyr. To the nearby elves, he yelled, "Anyone not working to bring back the light, prepare for battle! Sacred animals, come forth—now!"

The elves moved to obey, but so slowly it was painful to watch them. DL noticed how dull their normally glowing skin looked. That glow, like everything else about them, depended on continuous replenishment from the sun.

By contrast, the sacred animals were not hindered by the gathering gloom. Freya's platform was surrounded by cats. Freyr and the group near him were surrounded by large and ferocious boars.

"They are formidable," said Freyr. "They will not be enough, though, if the dark elves attack before faerie aid can reach us."

"What about Odin and the other Aesir?" asked Ekaterina. "Couldn't Freya reach them?"

"She was successful," said Freyr, "but it takes only a moment to send her mind to Asgard. It takes hours for the Aesir army to reach Álfheim from there." He looked up at the sky. "I fear we may not have hours. Ah, friend, what news?"

"Grave news, I fear," said Esras, who had just returned. "The portal has been buried by fallen rock, and some kind of spell is holding the debris in place. There is no way for me to leave or for the faerie army to enter."

Freyr nodded. "My elves could easily have moved the stones, but they are too weak right now."

"The most magical ones—" began Ekaterina.

"Could probably shift the rock," said Freyr. "But they are also all that keeps us from total darkness. I cannot divert them to something else now."

"DL, ask the Yeouiju if it can be of any help."

"Only if I am complete again," said the Yeouiju before he could ask the question. *"Only then can you draw enough power from me to control the weather."*

"There's no way to do that right now," said DL.

"There might be one way," said Ekaterina quietly.

"But it's sustaining your life," said DL. "The only way to make it whole again would be to—that's not what you're thinking, is it?"

Ekaterina hugged him—which, since he was still holding Outcast, became a group hug.

"My darling, I would never want to leave you. But to save your life…the lives of everyone here…is there even a choice?

"It would be easy. I could let go of the mist, walk into the sunlight over there, and—"

"No!" said DL. "Out of the question."

"A last resort," said Esras. "If we're all going to die anyway—"

"There's no guarantee that would even work. Yeouiju, what would happen to you if Ekaterina died?"

The silence that followed was like a condemned man waiting for a last-minute reprieve from the governor. DL was just about to give up when the Yeouiju said, *"I do not know. I might be able to reassemble myself, or the part of me within her might disappear when her existence ended."*

"See! You could end up dying for nothing. In fact, your death might make things worse."

DL wanted to say more, but Dubh and his allies picked that particular moment to escalate their attack. The cloud cover thickened almost to the point of blocking all the light, and the sunlight created by Max and Esras flickered like a candle in the wind. Freya, barely visible as the reflected light of her stones faded, screamed.

"Sister!" Freyr yelled. "What is it?"

"My spirit has been driven back from Yggdrasil," she said so softly that DL could barely hear her. "I can no longer seek help in the other worlds."

DL was nearly knocked off his feet by another earthquake. Could it be that the dark elves were digging their way out of their deep caves? There was little sunlight to stop them. What dim light remained was just enough for DL to see the light elves dropping to the ground, unconscious. Only the ones near enough to Esras or to Max were still standing.

"Expect an attack any minute!" yelled Freyr—a hollow gesture given how few of the light elves were left conscious.

"Brother," said Freya, who had crept through the darkness to join them. "Let us see what we can do if we both turn our entire wills toward breaking that cloud cover. Perhaps—"

Before she could finish, the ground nearby exploded, and dark elves began spreading out in all directions.

DL could barely see anything outside the tiny islands of sunlight against which the darkness was now pressing relentlessly.

"See through me," said the Yeouiju. It managed to give his eyes a pale imitation of the draconic vision he would have possessed in his own body. It was sufficient to let him see the advancing dark elves well enough to attack them—if he hadn't been holding Outcast.

"I'll take him," said Gerda, who had joined them so quietly DL hadn't realized she was there.

"No! I want to stay with you!" DL's shirt was wet with the kid's tears.

"I can protect you better with free arms," said DL, handing him to Freyr's wife despite the kid's continuing protests.

DL turned, grabbed the Spear of Lugh, and did a Max throw in the general direction of the dark elves. As before, the spear streaked at the growing mob of enemies and skewered them with amazing precision. The dark elves looked in his direction and raised their bows. They squinted against the fading sunlight in which DL was standing and fired, but their shots went wide.

DL couldn't do too much more against them. He longed for a bow himself, but what would have been the point? He had never practiced with one.

Ekaterina sprung at the nearest dark elves. She had no weapon, but with strength several times theirs, she had no difficulty overpowering the first few and spreading panic among those a little farther back.

DL longed to help her, to fight at her side as he had before. The

Spear of Lugh was a great, nerd-proof weapon that was essentially fighting on its own, but using it made him feel useless. A trained chimpanzee could have wielded it just as well as he had.

He glanced over at Max, who was still using magic with the remaining light elves to keep the sunlight going. The Sword of Dragon Light was hanging unused from his belt.

DL ran as fast as he could through the dark space between the two patches of sunlight. The moment he was out of the sunlight, arrows started whizzing right past him. One caught his shirt sleeve, just missing flesh. Another embedding itself in the ground right next to him. At least one would surely have drawn blood if Ekaterina hadn't been distracting the nearby elves so effectively. The boars joined her. They charged blind but were fierce enough and heavy enough to make the dark elves take notice. They ran right over some of the front-rank elves, pounding them into the dirt with their hooves. Barely slowed, they sprang forward into the next rank. Only when the dark elven fire was focused on them did they slow.

"What are you doing?" said Max when DL reached his sunlight. "Trying to get yourself killed?"

"Trying to get myself armed. The spear is doing just fine without me, and you're not using the sword. Give it to me."

Max frowned. "Enough dark elves have gotten close to charge us when the sunlight fails. I'll have to use the sword myself. Anyway, you aren't...well suited to use it right now."

"I can't help it if you didn't keep this body in good shape," said DL as anger burned through his blood. "Anyway, I can use the light from the sword to immobilize the dark elves. I don't need to be able to swing it very hard."

Max made no move to hand him the sword. DL realized what was happening. Max wanted to ensure that DL wasn't the hero this time. He wanted all the opportunities to impress Ekaterina for himself!

"No, I meant it's a dragon sword, and right now I'm the one with the dragon body," said Max. "It just makes sense it would work better for me than for you."

DL reached for the sword. In Max's body, he was a lot slower than Max was in his, and Max had no problem knocking his hand away.

"What's wrong with you?" Max asked, looking at DL as if he were a total stranger.

"Give me the sword!" yelled DL.

The light elves around Max subtly repositioned themselves to be ready to come to Max's aid.

Max's eyes widened as he looked at DL.

"What's…something's happening to your part of the Yeouiju. I think maybe it's making you crazy."

"Is it crazy to want to play the role I was meant to play in this battle?"

DL took a step toward Max, and the light elves were all over him. They restrained him with embarrassing ease, though he thrashed like a wild animal caught in a trap.

Maybe the dark elves stepped up their magic. Maybe Max was distracted by DL. Either way, the little patch of sunlight winked out. The light elves holding DL slumped to the ground, and arrows started flying everywhere.

Max had only started to weave protection against the arrow fire when he took a hit in the shoulder. He fell backward and hit the ground hard.

DL felt as if his brain was twisting around in his skull. Part of him wanted to grab the sword and charge at the dark elves. That would have made sense now. There was no one left nearby to wield it. He couldn't make himself move, though.

Something was wrong with him, whether magical or psychological. He felt as if there was more than one mind inside his skull. Were the numerous magical bonds putting too much pressure on him? He felt like cracking glass, ready at any moment to shatter into a thousand pieces.

Max was lying there bleeding, and it was his fault.

DL dropped to make himself less of a target, grabbed the sword, but, instead of charging, just held it up to produce light. Nothing happened.

Work! DL thought to the sword. *Work!* The blade glowed faintly for a second, then flickered out.

"Yeouiju! Can you get the dragon sword to respond to me?"

The dark elves' red eyes were focusing on him like thousands of rifle sites. Redirecting the Spear of Lug wouldn't stop so many in time.

Ekaterina wasn't that close, and Max wasn't in any shape to help.

"*Yeouiju!*"

DL knew it was still there, but he felt alone. He heard the echo of his own thoughts rather than a response.

The sword responded to the supernatural. DL didn't have his draconic body right now, but he still had a draconic soul.

An arrow came close to striking him but bounced off some invisible barrier. Max had gotten further along with the protection spell than DL realized.

Arrows started hitting the barrier as if they were being fired from guns rather than shot from bows. A completed spell wouldn't have withstood that kind of battering for long. This partial barrier wouldn't hold for more than a few seconds.

DL's body was flooded with adrenaline. His mind, equal parts determination and desperation, pumped every once in concentration into activating the sword.

Part of magic was visualizing the outcome. DL pictured the sword's sunlight as hard as he could.

The first arrow pierced the crumbling spell but missed DL by inches.

The blade flared to life, and the nearest dark elves fell back, blinded. For some reason, the nearby light elves didn't revive, but he would have to worry about that later.

Keeping the sword up as best he could, DL looked more closely at the damage. Max had passed out, and there was more blood on the ground than there should have been. The soil was soggy with it.

DL still itched to pursue the dark elves and prove he was a hero, but that couldn't possibly be the right move now. Max was pale and looked as if he might be bleeding out. DL wouldn't have thought a shoulder wound could do that, but the red puddle on the ground kept growing.

Healing. That draconic body should be healing. The arrow was preventing that. DL had to get it out.

Lacking the draconic vision to monitor Max's condition, DL turned to the Yeouiju, praying that this time he'd get an answer.

"I need to see what's happening to Max physically. Can you give me the ability to do that?"

"Perhaps," was all the Yeouiju said. DL's vision flickered, but he didn't gain any new visual insights.

His vision flickered again, but he still wasn't getting any medical insight. Whatever change the Yeouiju was trying to make to his mortal eyes wasn't holding.

DL didn't really know how to take the arrow out without doing more damage. If the body died, he would never be able to return to it, but he wasn't thinking about that. He was only thinking about Max. Even if Max's original body still lived, would he be dead if DL's body died?

Max probably knew more first aid. If they were back in the right bodies, Max could do more to save DL than DL was doing to save him.

DL looked at the light elves again. Any one of them would probably have known the best way to get the arrow out, but they remained unconscious. Perhaps an enterprising dark elf sorcerer had cast a spell on them during the few moments they were in darkness. If so, DL had no way to reverse it.

"Ekaterina! Max is badly wounded. I need your help!" DL got no response. Both the Yeouiju connection nor the blood bond between them might not work over distances with all the magic in the air. DL didn't know exactly where Ekaterina was, but not being able to see her was a bad sign. He would have tried shouting, but the noise of the battle made it unlikely she'd hear him.

He examined the wound again and tugged experimentally on the arrow. It was buried too deeply in the shoulder to come out easily.

DL tried applying direct pressure to stop the bleeding, but working around the arrow made that almost impossible. If anything, the pressure looked as if it might be forcing blood out faster.

He felt a slight breeze and looked up. Ekaterina, shrouded in black mist to protect her from the light of the dragon sword, had answered his call.

"He's bleeding out for some reason," said DL. "He'd heal if I could remove the arrow, but I was afraid to try to do that blind."

"Let's see how well I fare with vampiric senses," she said, kneeling next to Max. "In my day, even a princess would have to be prepared to treat the wounded. This isn't the only time I've taken out an arrow."

Her self-assurance calmed DL a little, but as she worked, he began to feel useless again. This looked like such a simple problem, but he had been powerless to solve it.

Much to his surprise, she ended up tearing the flesh away from the arrow to extract it.

"I wouldn't do that normally," she explained, "but you know how this body heals. It was the quickest way."

As soon as the arrow was out, the wound began healing so fast that DL needed no draconic vision to watch its progress.

His feeling of relief lasted for about twenty seconds. A look at the battlefield sent his mood straight off the cliff.

Only two small groups remained to oppose the dark elves. DL, Ekaterina, and the still unconscious Max were protected by the Sword of Dragon Light, though some of the dark elves started firing blind. Ekaterina moved fast enough to deflect arrows that came too close.

A few yards away, Esras, Freyr, and Freya continued to fight with the aid of the few boars that were left. Freyr had been wounded, and Esras looked nearly exhausted. Freya's staff glowed with magical might, but that glow flickered as more and more pressure was brought to bear on her. She had to maintain the sunlight to keep their position from being overrun by dark elves. To do so, she had to contend with what looked like a much larger force of dark elves than was facing DL and his friends.

The worst part was that Dubh was facing her. His magic, amplified by Merlin's book and by whatever the dark elves contributed, swirled around Freya and the others like a cloud of toxic gas. No, like a sentient cloud of toxic gas, squeezing her defensive spells, probing for weaknesses. Even someone as powerful as Freya would not be able to hold out for long.

Everywhere else was nearly pitch-black, and the dark elves had covered the ground like a swarm of locusts.

"I smell blood...mostly light elf," said Ekaterina. "Their dark kindred must have slaughtered every helpless one they could reach."

Somewhere in the darkness, DL could still hear the disturbing squishing sound Lugh's spear made as it plunged through a body. There was dark elf blood being shed as well. However, there were so many dark elves above the surface now that even the mighty spear was only slowing their conquest down.

"We should do something," said DL. Despite himself, his voice sounded whiney.

"There's not much we can do," said Ekaterina. "We can't very well go into battle with Max slung over one of our shoulders—not to mention the few light elves—and we can't leave them. As soon as they're out of the sunlight, those dark elves will be all over them."

The dark elves stood in rows that stretched as far as DL could see, standing just far enough away from the light not to be overcome by it. They surrounded DL and his friends on every side. Only the light of the dragon sword held them back, and it was only a matter of time before they figured out some way around that.

Max sat up, though his eyes looked unfocused. "What's happening?"

"We're all still alive," said Ekaterina. She didn't turn to look at him. Arrow deflection was taking all her attention.

DL noticed Max staring at the sword and offered it to him. "I picked it up when you got wounded. It was the only way—"

"I know. You don't have to—"

"Yes, I do. Max, you were right. Something is making me act crazy. I'm ashamed I couldn't control it better."

Max patted him on the shoulder. "Magic can make anyone crazy. When we get a chance, we'll figure out how to protect you."

Ekaterina raised an eyebrow. "The shifts in the Yeouiji are not my imagination, then?"

"No," said DL. "I'm not sure that's what's causing the problem, though."

An arrow got past Ekaterina's outstretched arms and almost hit Max.

"Get down!" said Ekaterina. "More of the dark elves are moving into firing range."

Sure enough, the one arrow was followed by dozens. Ekaterina was struck once in the arm, then in the shoulder, before Max managed to get a little protection up.

Ekaterina pulled the arrows out and threw them back with enough force to nick two of the archers. That did not even slow down the attack. In fact, once the dark elves realized the arrows were being stopped by magic, they redoubled their efforts. Max shook from the effort of keeping his spell coherent enough to shield them.

Thunder rumbled in the distance. DL looked around but could see no source.

The thunder sounded much closer. Lightning flashed so brightly that DL blinked.

The dark elves cried out at each flash. They cringed as if the lightning was going to strike them, even though it wasn't that close.

"This might be a moment to go on the offensive, Max," said Ekaterina. "Something is distracting them."

A chariot drawn by goats came into view. It sped rapidly in their direction, cleaving the ranks of dark elves as it went. Riding in the chariot was a tall, muscular man. Power throbbed from his body like an unseen supernatural message. DL knew in his bones that the new arrival was an alpha male—and so did the dark elves, who fell as far back from the chariot as they could get. They didn't flee, but their cries laid their fear naked.

The stranger held a large hammer in his hand, and with it, he struck right and left at the dark elves who hadn't scrambled out of the way fast enough. Each blow sounded like thunder, and lightning crackled outward from it, burning through nearby dark elves.

"That has to be Thor," said Max, breathless.

He didn't look anything like the Thor in movies, so DL wasn't sure how Max could tell, but whoever the guy was, he was wreaking havoc on the dark elf army.

Taking advantage of their distraction, Max shot little balls of sunlight into the nearby rows. Tiny as they were, they must not have taken much effort to generate, but they were great for causing blindness and confusion. DL called back the spear of Lugh and tossed it at the nearby dark elves, who fell to the blood-thirsty weapon by the dozens.

A horn sounded in the distance, and the dark elves began to retreat back into subterranean darkness. Dubh wasn't crazy enough to fight three former gods on his own. He slipped into a portal and vanished faster than Thor's lightning.

With the immediate threat removed, Thor used his mastery of

storms to try to clear the cloud cover. He was sweat soaked and shaking by the time he succeeded.

"What dire magic could have so strong a hold upon the sun itself?" he asked.

"We have guests who may be able to tell you." Freyr came over to greet Thor. "It is so unfamiliar because it comes from the Amadan Dubh, a faerie who intruded upon our peaceful realm."

The realm didn't look that peaceful at the moment. Dark and light elf bodies were everywhere, in some cases piled high enough to look like little hills. The ground was soggy with blood.

"Why would he bring such chaos to us?" asked Thor, looking disgusted. "An honorable battle is one thing, but this is just...slaughter, mindless murder. Wild beasts would have behaved better."

"The dark elves have always wanted to destroy the light ones," said Freya. "They just have not possessed the means—until now."

"Those means must be taken away from them," said Thor. "Alas, that's the kind of task for which we would need preparation. Even I would hesitate to venture down into those narrow tunnels, for in many of them I could not freely swing my hammer. Nor would my mastery of storms be of much use."

"There has been enough death for now, anyway," said Freyr. "The dark elves must face justice, but it is better to take time to bury the dead and mourn them first."

"My king!" yelled Gudbrand, who had somehow survived the fighting. "Gerda and the child she was carrying have been taken."

Freyr turned from mournful to vengeful in just a few seconds. "Who could have done such a thing? Whoever it was, this day may be his last!"

"Now that peace has been restored, I'll use seidr to find her," said Freya.

Her brother was not so easily satisfied. "Thor, could not your father find Gerda even faster? From his high throne, he can see everything that passes in all of the Nine Worlds."

"Aye, Odin can see all," agreed Thor, "but the fastest way to get him a message will be through seidr, anyway. Since Freya must let her spirit free to climb the branches of Yggdrasil, she may as well look for Gerda as she goes."

Freya climbed back onto the platform, though with considerably less ceremony than before. Freyr and Thor stood near her, waiting anxiously for any news.

"This must be Dubh's doing," said DL. "We didn't see him during the early part of the battle. That must be when he managed the kidnapping. He has Outcast—and it's all my fault!"

"Giving him to Gerda was a reasonable move," said Ekaterina. "You couldn't have known this would happen."

"He didn't want to leave me," said DL. "I should have listened to him."

"There's no point second-guessing yourself now," said Esras. "We've lost more people, and our focus should be on getting them back."

Ekaterina raised an eyebrow. "No lecture on how Outcast is not what he seems?"

"I'm still sure that's true," replied the druid. "But nobody deserves to be captured by Dubh.

"The good news—if you can call a kidnapping that—is that the full force of Asgard will be deployed to bring Gerda back, and Outcast is probably with her."

"I guess it's no surprise that Freyr will want to rescue his wife," said Max.

Esras nodded. "She is more than just his wife. She is the woman he's sacrificed his life for."

Ekaterina frowned. "He looks alive to me."

"He is—but he submitted to a fate he could have avoided to be with her. He had a mighty sword, one that would fight on its own much like Lugh's spear does. He gave it up for Gerda's hand in marriage, and as a result, he is destined to be killed by Surt, the fire giant, during Ragnarok."

"Speaking of Ragnarok, did this battle start it prematurely?" asked Max.

"No, I think the dark elves were defeated before the threat to the balance became grave enough—but Dubh is still here," said Esras. "We must capture him and recover the book. As long as he is free and empowered, who knows what he might do."

Freyr walked over to them. "What he has done already is bad enough."

"Has Freya found Gerda?" asked Esras.

Freyr nodded. "Aye, but it will be no easy task to rescue her. Dubh, that vile fiend, has taken her to Helheim."

EVERYTHING'S GOING STRAIGHT
TO HEL

"WHY WOULD HE HAVE DONE THAT?" asked Esras. "She isn't dead, so Hel can't keep her—right?"

"You speak the truth," said Freyr. "Unfortunately, Hel will not just send her back. I must go and retrieve her. Nor is that a simple journey even for the Aesir and the Vanir. Though we know where Helheim is—near one of the roots of Yggdrasil—we cannot find it without an appropriate guide."

"One such is on the way," said Thor as he rejoined them. "Odin himself cannot come just now, but he is sending his horse, Sleipnir, for it knows the way to Hel's gloomy realm."

"That is one problem solved," said Freyr. "Thank you, my friend. Alas, I fear Hel will devise some scheme to keep Gerda. I could not bear that."

"Fear not," replied Thor. "Though my father cannot accompany you, I will go as his representative."

"I will come as well," said Freya. She looked tired but determined. "The more of us who back your request, the harder it will be for Hel to refuse it."

Hooves struck the ground nearby almost as loudly as Thor's earlier thunder. Sleipnir, the massive, eight-legged horse of Odin, had arrived.

"So soon?" asked Freyr.

"My father foresaw your need," said Thor. "Sleipnir started his journey before the battle began."

'May we accompany you?" asked Ekaterina. "We too have people to retrieve from Helheim."

Freya looked at her with a mixture of sadness and alarm. "If you go, Hel will surely try to claim you as her own, for have you not been dead for centuries? And yet…and yet I sense you may have a role to play in this drama, risky as it may be for you."

"I don't like the sound of that," said DL.

"A vision I saw as I used seidr to look for Gerda makes sense now," said Freya. "Brother, these visitors may prove helpful in our efforts to free your wife. But…but only if we can restore these two to the right bodies first. Hel will use their strangeness against us otherwise."

Esras fidgeted a little, clenching his fingers together and twisting them. "While I would like nothing better than to see their situation put right, you have already said that you have never seen such magic before."

"Nor have you if I remember correctly," said Freya. "In any case, you are in my realm now. Magic works somewhat differently here. Druidic magic is not the same as seidr. Drawing power from nature is not the same as drawing power from the runes that both symbolize nature and underly it. It may be we can do something that would solve the problem in a way that would never occur to you."

"It may be that my hammer will prove useful," said Thor. "I know most people see it only as a weapon, but though storms may be destructive, they also bring the rain that gives life to the crops."

"I know the hammer can be used in blessings, but have you ever tried to rearrange souls with it?" asked Esras.

Thor pointed at his chariot with the hammer. "Do you see my goats over there? I have more than once been in desperate circumstances where I needed to eat them. Afterward, I put the bones back into the skin and used Mjolnir to restore their flesh and life."

"That's impressive," said Esras. "This task may be more delicate, though." He had the look of someone needing emergency surgery when a veterinarian was the only doctor near enough to do it.

"Do you have so little faith in us?" asked Freya. "Mjolnir is one of

the most powerful objects in the Nine Worlds. I am the greatest practitioner of seidr next to Odin himself. Freyr is far from being an amateur
at it. If anyone can get souls into the right bodies, we three can."

"I would not wish to force our guests if they are reluctant," said
Freyr. "However, if their presence could help save Gerda…please friends,
at least let us try."

Max glanced at Esras, who still looked unhappy, back at Freyr, who
was practically vibrating with anxiety, and finally over at DL.

"I say we let them try," said DL. "People we care about are in trouble. We could both be more use to them—well, I could, anyway—if we
were in the right bodies."

"Don't agree just because you feel as if you've made mistakes,"
said Max.

"I'm not. I'm agreeing because it's the right thing."

Max nodded. "I feel the same way." Turning to Freya, he said, "We
gratefully accept your offer."

"That is most welcome news," said Freya. "We must begin our preparations at once."

As promising as that sounded, the preparations dragged on for what
seemed like days. Despite Freya's initial confidence, her attempt through
another seidr trance to understand the magic necessary proved unsuc-
cessful. An attempt to move their souls back with magic she already
knew ended with no result.

By this point, Sleipnir was stamping his hooves impatiently. Freyr's
pacing was even louder. Esras had an I-told-you-so expression, though he
said nothing.

"I am a fool!" said Freya suddenly.

"Surely not," said Thor.

"No, I am. The solution has been right in front of me the whole
time, yet I have been blind to it. What happens during a seidr trance?"

"The hugr—soul—leaves the body," said Freyr.

"Then why can I not take Max and DL into a trance with me? Their
souls will leave the bodies they currently inhabit, and I can then steer
them into their proper bodies."

"That sounds promising," said Esras, smiling for the first time
in hours.

Max and DL immediately agreed, but getting them into the right state of mind when neither one had ever practiced seidr was more of a problem than Freya had expected.

Freyr burned the appropriate herbs, but the elven women nearby were too busy with the preparation of far too many bodies to join the chant again. Thor tried to fill in, but the result was more comic than trance-inducing.

Freya eventually sang them into a trance herself. DL found himself staring down at an enormous yew tree that seemed to stretch infinitely in all directions.

"It is Yggdrasil, the world tree," said Freya, who floated nearby.

"It's amazing," said Max. "I know there isn't time now, but I wish we could travel its branches, see the other worlds."

"Perhaps there will be time when everything is set right again. For now, relax as much as you can, and let me guide you back.

Freya took Max first. He closed his eyes, she wrapped her arms around him, and they vanished into a cloud of mist. After a while, DL felt a little tingle and knew that Max was back in his own body. If Freya had succeeded with him, no doubt she could do the same for DL.

Invisible hands that were nothing like Freya's grabbed him, and he fell at incredible speed. The branches of Yggdrasil and the worlds nestled among them flashed by in one big blur.

DL struggled, but he was like a gnat fighting an elephant. His only hope was that Freya would realize what was happening to him in time to save him.

He wasn't sure what would happen if he crashed into the ground he saw rising to meet him. He was only spirit right now—but what if part of that landscape was just spirit, too? Would the end result be like a physical fall from thousands of miles up?

Just when he thought his doom was sealed, his descent slowed, and instead of crashing into the rocky ground, he fell through a crack near one of Yggdrasil's roots.

Once he was below ground, his surroundings blurred again. He might have lost consciousness.

When he awakened, he seemed to be in his body again, but it felt as if his nerves had been wrapped in cobwebs. Nothing felt the way it should. The room he was in only heightened the suspicion that he wasn't in his real body.

Instead of seeing the bright sun of Álfheim, he was looking at the flickering light of torches. He was in a large hall, cold and gloomy. Seated on a crude throne and watching him intently was a woman whose appearance kept shifting so rapidly it was hard to focus on her. Sometimes she was a beautiful blonde who, if not for her pale skin, would have seemed quite at home in a commercial for suntan oil. At other times she was a rotting corpse or a skeleton.

DL had never studied Norse mythology in school—or, if he had, he hadn't been paying attention. He had, however, paid attention to enough of the earlier conversations to realize that he was in the presence of Hel, ruler of the dead.

"Welcome," she said with a voice like the creaking of old, rusty hinges.

LOST

"What do you mean you can't find him?" asked Max. "His soul was just there."

"I know it was," said Freya, "but it isn't now."

"There can be only one answer—Hel has snatched it," said Freyr.

"But he isn't dead!" said Ekaterina. "How could she have managed such a thing?"

"It is true his body lives," agreed Freya. "The circumstances were strange, though. His soul had most recently been in Max's body. I had to cut that connection to get Max back in easily. Though DL's soul still had a tie to his own body, it was weak. Hel must have taken advantage of that to claim him."

"His body's dying," said Esras. The druid put both his hands on DL's empty shell. "I can keep it going for a while, but we must get that soul back as soon as we can."

"We were just about to travel to Hel, anyway," said Thor. "We can reclaim your friend's soul at the same time."

"Then let us be on our way at once," said Freyr. "Our errand grows more urgent by the minute."

"I need to stay here," said Esras. "I have to remain with DL's body, and I fear moving it would be a mistake."

"Perhaps I should stay, too," said Max. "I know a little about keeping a human body from dying. If nothing else, I can lend you my strength if the process drains you too much."

"That is not wise," said Freya. "My vision was clear. Esras can stay here, but you and Ekaterina must both accompany us."

Max looked at DL's barely living body. "My lady, your wisdom is far greater than mine, but visions can sometimes be interpreted in different ways. I know enough magic that I might help save my friend's life if I stayed, but I am not such a mighty sorcerer that I would be much use in Helheim."

Freya might once have been a goddess of love, but there was no hint of love in her eyes now, just steely determination. "There is no one but Odin who can read the signs of fate better than I. Do you question my judgment? If I say you are needed in Helheim, then you are." Her voice was as hard as diamonds.

"Forgive my young companion," said Esras. "He is worried about his best friend, just as Freyr is worried about Gerda. He did not mean to question the truth of your interpretation."

Max couldn't help looking at DL again. He was breathing, but just barely. If the situation were reversed, he would never leave Max, no matter what supernatural being demanded it.

Esras cleared his throat and nodded to Max. The young sorcerer glanced at Freyr. He looked back at Max as if could see right through him and clear down to Helheim, where Gerda was imprisoned. His face was like a calm lake—with a creature like the Loch Ness Monster right beneath the surface, ready to swallow Max in one bite if he didn't do what Freya demanded.

Thor's expression was no more encouraging. He stared at Max impatiently, shifting his hammer from hand to hand and letting random sparks fall from it. There would be no more point in reasoning with him than there would be with an oncoming storm. Freya had spoken. Max's job was to obey.

"Please accept my apology, my lady. Esras has spoken truly. My worry momentarily clouded my judgment."

"I accept your apology," said Freya, the hard-as-diamonds voice replaced by one that was soft as silk. "How could you not be concerned for a fallen comrade? We would feel no differently. Fear not, for you will be back at his side soon."

Max gritted his teeth and nodded. Despite her reassuring tone, Freya offered no comforting vision, no assurance that when they did return, DL would still be alive. However, she did know this plane of existence far better than he did. He said a little prayer that she was right in thinking he could be of some help in bringing back DL and Maeve.

Thor led Sleipnir over. The animal moved gracefully on his eight legs, but his size was intimidating. Max wasn't short, but even so, Sleipnir stood high enough above the ground that the sorcerer only came up to his stomach. How was he going to mount the creature?

Thor laughed and gave Max a boost. Freyr leaped onto the horse's back, landing in front of Max. Freya floated up more gracefully and came to rest just in front of Freyr. Ekaterina jumped as Freyr had and landed behind Max.

Sleipnir *was* big, but Max hadn't thought he was big enough to have room on his back for five people. As Thor seated himself in front of Freya, the horse lengthened to accommodate him.

Max's eyes widened, and Thor laughed again. "Sleipnir is no ordinary horse."

"The eight legs should have been a giveaway," said Max, trying to smile back.

Thor gave Sleipnir a command in Old Norse, and horse trotted off at a speed that should have been jarring for an inexperienced rider like Max but wasn't.

Max tried not to look too shocked when Sleipnir started flying. No, flying wasn't the right word. A magic haze the color of clouds, light gray as Sleipnir's coat, churned around them, obscuring the landscape.

Álfheim faded away, as if they were going through a slow-motion portal. Max felt a little dizzy. Was Sleipnir galloping straight down? That's what the movement felt like, but the horse's magic quickly made it seem as if they were traveling horizontally.

The surface along which Sleipnir ran was rough. It was the bark on the enormous trunk of Yggdrasil, the yew tree that was called the World Tree. In its branches and at its roots rested the Nine Worlds, though from where they were riding, Max could only see the trunk, stretching out in both directions as far as he could see, a wooden superhighway on steroids. Occasionally, branches bigger than skyscrapers loomed before them, but Sleipnir gracefully veered around them.

There was light all around but no obvious source. Was it coming from Yggdrasil? Though Max saw no light flowing from the bark, he did feel power radiating from the tree. The sensation was gentle, like sun warming his skin, and constant. The tree provided more than just a physical connection among the Norse worlds. It empowered and organized their magic as well. If the myths were accurate, the Norns carved the fate of the worlds into the same bark on which they rode.

Max had picked up a few details about Yggdrasil from studying Norse mythology in school. He had learned something about the magical properties of yew trees from Maeve. Because the new trunks could sprout from old branches that touched the ground, the tree was associated with life and with resurrection. However, because its needles were toxic, it was also associated with death.

The old stories did not prepare Max for the way being so close to the tree made him feel. If he touched it with his mind, he could sense the whole life cycle vibrating deep within the tree's core, pulsing in its sap, surging out into its branches.

If DL had been here, he would have told Max not to geek out over the experience.

Thinking of DL while his mind was still touching the tree caused a momentary shudder in the tree's flow as if it feared for him as much as Max did.

"*He'll be all right,*" Max thought to the tree. The shudder stopped instantly. Too bad Max's own fears could not be so immediately quieted.

The lower they got on the trunk, the mistier the air got.

"We are nearing the roots," said Thor. "It won't be long now."

The air darkened until it was night black, but without a moon or stars. Freyr and Freya conjured a little light, by which Max could see one of Yggdrasil's massive roots as Sleipnir rode down it and into the ground the root had split.

"Is this Helheim?" asked Max.

"Not yet," said Freyr. "We are close but not quite there."

Light, still without an obvious source, fluctuated from a completely unnoticeable reduction in the blackness to a minimal gray. Beyond the path they traveled, Max saw vague hints of enormous trees, of dark forests no one could ever explore because the trees grew so close together and were so tangled.

Max heard the sound of metal clanging before he saw what looked like a wide river, except that instead of flowing water, it was filled with gradually moving swords.

"A way to bar intruders," explained Thor. "There is magic here that prevents even Sleipnir from jumping over, and no one could survive trying to swim across. The only way forward is that bridge.

Max's eyes had been so drawn to the dull gleam of the swords that he hadn't even noticed the bridge—odd, considering how much its golden glow stood out against the surrounding darkness.

The bridge was wide, but standing in the middle and blocking the way across was a female giantess who looked at them with undisguised contempt.

"Go back," she said in a voice as loud as the battle cry of many men. "You have no business here."

Thor was the one sitting nearest the front and holding the horse's reins, but it was Freyr who spoke for the party. "Modgud, you speak too hastily. We come for an audience with Hel, for she has within her grasp some who are not dead and others who are dead but who came from far beyond this realm."

"Such petty disputes are none of my concern," said Modgud. Eying Thor's hammer, the giantess grudgingly added, "You may pass, but see to it that you keep the peace. Any attempt at violence against Hel or her servants will do you more harm than it will them."

"We know how the place works," said Thor impatiently.

"Yet we are thankful for the reminder," added Freyr, bowing slightly to the giantess. Scowling, she stepped aside just enough for Sleipnir and his riders to get past.

"I see one of you belongs after all," said Modgud as Ekaterina rode past. The vampire gave no hint that she even heard the remark, but Max shuddered. What if Hel saw Ekaterina as her property? Freya had said Ekaterina was vital to the success of the quest. Now that he thought about, though, the former Norse goddess had never said Ekaterina would be safe in Helheim.

Not far from the bridge, they came to a wall so high Max couldn't see the top in the moonless-night darkness. There was a massive gate, but it was completely shut. Thor rapped on it gently with his hammer, but no one answered.

"Aside from Hel herself, no one knows the way to open that gate. It seems to open on its own when someone who is dead arrives, but there is no way for anyone living to enter," said Freya.

"Sleipnir has jumped this very wall in the past, but he seems reluctant now," said Thor. "Perhaps Hel increased the defenses at some point. I may have to smash through the gate."

"I'm sure you could, but that's hardly keeping the peace," Freyr pointed out. "Even though you are Odin's son and come as his spokesman, Hel rules here, remember? She is bound by laws, but she could easily use such an attack as an excuse not to see us or to refuse our requests if she does."

"I know, I know," said Thor, staring up at the wall. "How are we to get in, then?"

"Perhaps I can help," said Ekaterina, dismounting.

The vampire walked over to the gate, which creakily swung open to admit her. Standing so that the gate could not close behind her, she gestured for Thor to lead Sleipnir through.

The horse pulled against the reins and whinnied in protest.

"Something must be—" began the Aesir.

A gigantic hound, face and neck covered with blood, raced forward. Ignoring Ekaterina, it turned its attention to Sleipnir and its remaining riders.

A pack of wolves followed it out of the gate, snarling and baring their sharp teeth.

"There's no keeping the peace now," said Thor.

NO PLACE LIKE HOME

"What...what am I doing here?" asked DL.

Hel gave him a skeletal smile. "You're dead. This is the place where souls come after death."

"I'm not dead. My body is still alive."

"A druid is keeping it alive. It should be dead. That is what matters to me."

DL tried to awaken his dragon, but he got no response. It was as if the dragon wasn't just asleep—it was gone, leaving an aching void where it had once been. This body looked like his own, but it was obviously not an exact copy.

"*Yeouiju?*" Nothing. It often didn't answer immediately, but this was like the difference between not having someone pick up the phone and getting the "This number is no longer in service," message.

Hel laughed. The sound reminded him of breaking glass. "Did you expect that your body here would perform the way your mortal body did? How foolish!"

Draconic or not, DL wanted to smash his fist into that everchanging face. That really would have been foolish, though. This...creature had once been considered a goddess, and this was her realm. He probably couldn't have won a physical fight with her, even at full-strength.

"You've made a deal with the Amadan Dubh, haven't you?"

"Ah, you're not entirely stupid. I did have a visit from this Amadan Dubh. He made me a most persuasive offer."

"He'll betray you. His only interests are his own."

This time Hel's laugh sounded like metal scraping against metal. "Of course, his interests are his own! So are mine. I'm not taking him as a husband. I'm using him to my own advantage."

"What could he possibly have that you would need?" asked DL, looking around. "You are the mistress of the land of the dead. He is a friendless fugitive."

"Not quite friendless, from what I hear of the dark elves. You are most presumptuous to question my wisdom, mortal. Do not forget that you are my subject now and owe me your obedience."

Taking a gamble, DL went down on one knee. He'd seen enough of royal customs among the faeries to have some idea what he was doing. "Majesty, I mean no disrespect. I have witnessed some of Dubh's earlier actions, that is all. I feared you might not be aware of how he disrupted another plane of existence."

"I have no need to explain myself to you." She sat down on her throne as if to underscore her position. "However, I find you more amusing than most of the dead who pass through here, so I will tell you why I do not care how much he has disrupted. Seeing your face when you know the truth may be worth a laugh.

"I am in the unique position of having absolutely nothing to lose. As my fate is woven now, I will be destroyed at Ragnarok, as will all of my family and the army I have built. But the Norns accounted only for forces that dwelled on this plane of existence. They never foresaw the intervention of someone like Dubh. It may be that he can change my fate.

"Suppose Ragnarok could be begun before its appointed time. That might catch even Odin off-guard. The current prophecy is that the two opposing forces will largely destroy each other, leaving a small number of Aesir to rebuild. What if the outcome could be changed? What if my father Loki and his allies could defeat the Aesir and their allies?"

"How can one faerie have that much power?" DL asked.

"As I said, I have nothing to lose by letting Dubh make the attempt."

"What does he get out of it? You know he wants something."

"Of course he does—his own world. At some point, it occurred to him that, under the right conditions, he could build it here rather than seeking out some far-distant plane. If the current order perishes, he will be able to achieve his dream."

"He tried great schemes before and failed at them."

Hel sighed. "I see you will not be as interesting as I hoped." A side door in the hall creaked open. "Go and find your home among the other dead."

There was no point in arguing, so DL rose and walked out the door, which slammed shut loudly behind him.

He found himself in a place that looked like an old Norse village. The houses were little more than primitive huts with thatched roofs and turf walls. Occasionally, the turf was reinforced by wood supports, but the buildings still looked more like hills than houses. Sometimes the walls even had grass sprouting from them.

A door creaked open, and a woman slowly walked through it. She must have been old when she died, for her face was wrinkled, and her hair was white. She wore an ankle-length linen gown with a strapped wool dress over the top. The straps were held in place by large, ornately patterned brooches. Like the hut from which she came, she looked as if she had popped out of a museum display.

DL hesitated. Should he say something to her? He could use some advice about how to navigate this world, but he didn't know how she'd respond.

She turned and walked in his direction, but she looked right through him. As she got closer, he took a good look at her. Was she blind? Her eyes appeared perfectly normal, but if she saw him, she gave no sign, not even the slightest change in her expression. He had to step out of the way to keep her from walking straight into him.

He turned and watched her shuffle slowly down the dirt path. The more he watched her, the fuzzier she became, as if his eyes were unfocusing. The huts around him also became less distinct. He blinked a couple of times, and they snapped into sharper focus, then faded as if covered by mist.

There was nothing to be gained by just standing there, so he started walking. The mist surrounded him. Even the path beneath his feet was no longer visible.

The path felt harder. He looked down. He was walking on cobblestones instead of dirt. The mist thinned, and he found himself in a town whose Victorian architecture reminded him of the Eau Claire house. There were several people on the street. The men all wore expensive looking suits, overcoats, and top hats. The women carried parasols and wore dresses heavy with brocade that looked more suitable for a ball than a quick stroll. They greeted each other but paid no more attention to him than the old woman had.

DL looked down at himself to make sure he wasn't invisible. An Asian in twenty-first-century clothing should have stuck out like a neon sign in what appeared to be a Norwegian nineteenth-century town. Yet no one even glanced his way.

He touched the side of one of the buildings. It felt solid—but also strange. A slight vibration ran through it, as if it were constantly changing.

He squinted. Making a real examination of the place was hard without his draconic senses. He hadn't been wrong, though, the buildings were changing. He looked away from the building he'd touched—a men's clothing store, judging from the display. He watched the people on the streets for a short time, and when he looked back, there was still a building next to him—but now it was wider, several stories taller, and had a lobby just beyond the front door that looked like a hotel's.

He looked back at the street. The buildings were still Victorian, but they were completely different buildings than the ones he had seen originally. The people he had seen were also gone, replaced by others.

He started walking again. The farther he walked, the less the place seemed like the living world. Not only did it mutate from time to time, but he became more and more aware of a pervasive grayness. It didn't obscure the colors underneath it, but it dulled them, making them look like colors in an old, faded photograph.

He walked his way into another Viking era village. He was still invisible to other passersby. As with the Victorian town, if he stayed in the same place long enough, it changed, sometimes dramatically, as people entered the area and left it.

What caused the changes? Figuring that out might be the first step to finding a way to escape from the land of the dead.

He followed one of the villagers, a tall, broad-shouldered man whose hands were callused from farm work. DL watched him inspect the cattle which were grazing on a nearby hillside. He watched him feed hay to the cows in the barn and milk them.

As long as he shadowed the farmer, there wasn't even a slight twitch in reality. The barn was still the barn. The grazing land around it didn't shift a single blade of grass. The village in the distance remained the same village.

Bored out of his mind, DL walked out of the barn—and straight into a fog bank. He emerged next to a Viking hall only a little less magnificent than Hel's own. DL took a quick glance and confirmed that a chieftain and his warriors were gathering around the fire pit, feasting on roast boar.

The dead saw the homes and towns where they had lived. That much made sense.

Why could he see them and their times when they couldn't see him —or, as far as he could tell, anyone they hadn't known in life? The Victorians and the Vikings didn't mingle.

He walked again, but he found no answers. However, the harder he looked at his surroundings, the less coherent they became. Instead of seeing one consistent landscape, he saw a patchwork quilt of different eras. To his left was a dirt road bordered by turf huts. To his right was a concrete street bordered by glass and steel office buildings.

Perhaps Hel's kingdom didn't know what to make of him. If he ever wanted out, though, he needed to figure out what to make of it.

He needed Maeve. She was here, somewhere.

He'd come in with an exploring mindset, and the place had let him explore. The exploration led to nothing but dead ends, though. Getting out required a different mindset.

DL walked more quickly and purposefully, his mind focused on one goal. The scenery shifted around him in a way that reminded him too much of the chaotic world in which he had first met Dubh. That didn't deter him.

He spotted it—the second story of the Eau Claire house, visible above some much lower huts that were vibrating in and out of focus with sickening rapidity. He ran to reach his house in case it, too, faded away.

He got past the huts and was on the right street in Eau Claire, grayer than normal but still a welcome sight.

The house was right in front of him. He bounded up the steps and through the open front door.

Maeve was standing in the entry hall, very solid and looking as old as she must have been when she died. "Well, it's about time you got here!"

He surprised her—and himself—by hugging her. "I've been wandering for hours out there. Days, maybe."

"It took you that long to realize getting here was as simple as thinking of home?" Maeve looked at him critically, but she smiled more broadly than he'd ever seen her smile.

"Hey, it took Dorothy the whole *Wizard of Oz* movie to figure out how to put on those ruby slippers, click her heels together and say, 'There's no place like home.' Besides, there's no Glinda out there to offer pointers."

Maeve shook her head. "Always with the movie trivia. You're not wrong, though. Hel's usual guests are thinking of home when they first arrive here. If you're in a different state of mind, you end up lost. I didn't find this place immediately myself."

"Knowing you, I bet the moment you found it, you started working on a way out of here."

"I wish it were that simple. This place is well-designed to keep the dead from wandering off. If there is an exit, I've yet to find it. The one blessing is that, in giving me physical form, Hel enabled me to use my magic again."

"But you can't just open a portal, or you wouldn't still be here."

"Oh, I can. The Norse don't know enough about portals to specifically block one, but I can only travel within the Nine Worlds, and as soon as I step through, this body disintegrates, and Hel grabs me again.

"What really worries me is that I think I may have accidentally inspired a new interest in portals. Hel didn't ask me for details, though. She just warned me not to try again. I think she plans to get the details from Dubh."

"That doesn't seem like our worst problem," said DL. "Dubh plans to do far worse for her."

"Hel may rule this place, but keep it in mind Odin imprisoned her here. She can't get out until Ragnarok—but, as I've already said, Helheim doesn't block travel out by portal. Hel could theoretically escape from here any time she wants."

"Damn! She told me Dubh is going to help her start Ragnarok early and rig it so the bad guys win."

"It does make getting out of here our first priority," said Maeve. "We need to warn the others and get the attention of someone in Asgard before this scheme goes too far."

"But you just said you couldn't successfully portal out."

"I can't, and in that body, you can't either. However, your special nature gives us access to that Yeouiju connection of yours. We can get a message out that way. It's another kind of power Hel knows nothing about. Even Dubh doesn't."

DL frowned. "I already tried. This body doesn't have any connection with the Yeouiju or any inner dragon to wake up."

Maeve put a hand on each of DL's temples and closed her eyes. After about ten minutes, she opened them again.

"This body isn't a perfect copy, but it may be better than Hel realizes. The dragon is dormant, as it was before you met Ekaterina, but it is there. Perhaps we could awaken it. Are you game?"

DL grinned. "Well, I'm not sure if I am game, but I certainly have game, so let's give it a try."

Someone pounded on the front door so hard DL expected a fist to come crashing through it at any moment.

"We may be too late," said Maeve.

"The house is protected, though—right?"

"It lacks all the magical protections I built into the real house over the years. I haven't had time to do anything with this one.

"If that's some emissary of Hel out there, there's nothing I can do to prevent our capture."

HEL'S HOSTAGES

THOR JUMPED down from Sleipnir to confront the gigantic beast. "Garm, stay back! We come on orders from Odin himself."

The monster hound, unimpressed, tried to chomp Thor's head off. Only the Aesir's greater speed saved him from decapitation.

"If you kill Garm, Hel is sure to deny our request!" yelled Freyr. He dismounted, but it wasn't clear how much help he could be to Thor.

Freya also dismounted, and the runes on her staff glowed. Garm looked in her direction, then back at Thor. He seemed resistant to whatever magic she was using against him.

At least Garm didn't get reinforcements. Ekaterina caught the wolves by surprise. Moving faster and striking harder than the dead they were used to seeing, she kept them from following the hound out to attack the others, but she wasn't able to force them to retreat. If they recovered from their shock fast enough to gang up on her, she was going to be in trouble.

Thor struck the ground with his hammer. Lightning flashed, thunder roared, and Garm shuddered, but only for a moment. Then he sprang at Thor, who dodged again. Garm's fangs only barely missed Thor's arm.

Switching tactics, the storm lord ran as fast as the wind. Garm bounded after him. Thor managed to say ahead, but he couldn't widen the gap between them. An occasional spark from the hammer diverted Garm's attention, but only for a moment.

Max dismounted awkwardly, but he didn't throw himself into the battle immediately. Thor was in more trouble, and the Sword of Dragon Light was powerful enough to slow the beast down. However, attacking the fast-moving hound with enough precision to wound it without killing it was far beyond Max's skill level. Garm could end up lying dead in a pool of his own blood. Hel could declare all-out war. No, helping Ekaterina fight off the wolves was less risky.

Max headed toward the vampire and drew the sword. Nothing happened. He was no longer in DL's body, and the blood bond between them wasn't enough by itself to trigger the weapon. He managed to toss it close enough to Ekaterina for her to pick it up. It flashed sunlight the moment she touched it, and the wolves backed away, eying her suspiciously.

"Let's try not to kill them," said Ekaterina. "They've been magically enhanced, but they're still basically ordinary wolves. Their reactions look more instinctive than evil."

That sounded reasonable, but the wolves didn't take long to become less afraid of the light. Not only that, but more kept arriving.

Ekaterina handed the sword back to Max. Now that she had gotten it working, its glow remained, even in his hand.

She knocked the first wolf back with one blow, but that did not deter his fellows from throwing themselves at her and at Max. He tried to follow her suggestion and aim only to wound, but the blade was so sharp that it sliced through the wolves like butter, leaving them dead and him blood-spattered and shaking.

After a short time, the wolves pulled back to just inside the gate. Their eyes followed every move Max and Ekaterina made, and they kept their teeth bared, ready for the first opportunity to attack.

"I'm sorry," said Max. "I tried to keep from killing them. I'm just... just not very good at this."

Ekaterina moved close enough to give him a cold hug. "You did better than a lot of people would have. When that many beasts are moving in for the kill, some of them will die. I had to kill a few myself."

Max looked down at his aching sword arm. "I'd have done better in

DL's body. I just fought for a few minutes, and already I can barely hold the blade up."

Ekaterina rolled her eyes. "Men! Always fretting over their physical limitations, as if their bodies are all that they are."

Max smiled. "That's easy for you to say. You're strong—and beautiful."

"And basically dead. Anyway, strength isn't just how hard or how long you can swing a sword. You had the strength to throw yourself into battle. You might have been injured or killed, but you did it. That's strength, too."

One of the wolves snarled. They kept their distance, though.

Max glanced back to see how the rest of their party were faring. Freya stood alone, eyes closed, gathering power. It looked to Max like a spell to put Garm to sleep. Thor and Freyr were so far away they were barely visible in the shadows, though the occasional lightning flash lit them up. Garm kept pace with Thor as the storm lord led him farther and farther away from Hel's gate. Freyr followed some distance behind. If the Aesir were trying to wear the beast down, they weren't having much luck.

"Who dares do violence to the guardians of my realm?"

The voice was as cold as an arctic wind. Max spun around and saw a woman who could only be Hel. She looked both living and dead, her form shifting from a beautiful blonde to a decaying corpse with such rapidity that it was hard to look at her.

Ekaterina bowed, so Max awkwardly followed suit.

"Pardon us, but the wolves attacked despite the fact that we are your guests."

Hel started to raise an eyebrow. She never completed the movement because her eyebrows flickered away in the middle of it.

"By what right do you claim to be my guests?"

"Your guardian at the bridge admitted us."

"You are not my guests until I open my gate for you. You should have waited."

"Great ruler of the dead, the gate is open. As there was no gate-keeper, we took that as an invitation."

Hel looked at Ekaterina more closely. "The gate opened for you. You are no guest, but a subject. Get yourself inside, for you are dead. The wolves will no longer block your path."

"She is a visitor from outside the Nine Worlds," said Freya, who had walked up behind them. "As such, she is not your subject."

Hel scowled—an especially ghastly expression in her corpse phase. "She is dead, and she is at my gate. How she got here or where she came from is of no consequence."

"If she is to be treated as our dead are treated, then as a warrior, I may claim her for Folkvang, and I do so now." Freya had grown taller during the conversation, and her eyes had a savage gleam in them.

"Yet I sense she did not die in battle," said Hel. "Warrior or not, if her death was not honorable, she is still mine."

"We can discuss your claims in a civilized way if you will call off your watchdog so that Thor and Freyr may join us."

Hel gave an ear-splitting whistle, and Garm trotted back. The ground shook from the impact of his running paws. Thor and Freyr followed in a surprisingly short time.

"Ruler of the dead, I have come on behalf of Odin to arrange the release of those who are being held in your domain unlawfully," said Thor.

"I will respect the law if you will," said Hel. "State your *request*."

"The first request is for Gerda, my wife," said Freyr.

"She is indeed not dead. She will be returned to you."

"The second request is for the boy known as Outcast," said Thor.

Hel laughed in a way that sounded like metal grating on metal. "Whatever Outcast may be, he is no boy. In any case, you have no more claim on him than you do on my wolves. I reject that request."

"But he's alive!" Max said. Hel looked at him as if he were a fly that had just landed in her stew.

"Silence, mortal! You have no right to speak here, nor even to be here."

"The mortal is...unusual," said Freya. "He will hold his tongue from now on." She looked at Max to make sure he understood. "However, we require his presence. In any case, he makes a good point. Never since you became ruler of the dead have you kept one who is alive in your domain."

"That may be," said Hel. "However, what I said before is also true—you have no claim on him. Let those who do come forth and make the request."

"He was under our protection when he was abducted, and therefore we do have a claim on him," said Freyr.

"How are you sure he is alive?" asked Hel. "Do you truly know what he is? Present me proof that he is a living human being, and I will return him to you at once."

"I care not whether he is a human, an ash tree, or a boar," said Freyr. "He was under our protection."

"But if he is not truly alive, then he could be considered mine, regardless of whether he was receiving your hospitality or not."

"I am weary of this legalistic bickering," said Thor. Sparks crackled from his hammer. "Bring forth the boy, or face the consequences!"

"You dare threaten me here, in my domain?" asked Hel. Her eyes gleamed like ice crystals. "Do you really think you could defeat me here? Even if you could, I am destined to play a role in Ragnarok. Kill me now, and you risk the fabric of reality itself."

"Let there be no talk of killing," said Freya, putting a hand on Thor's shoulder. "There will be further discussion of the boy's status, but we have other requests to make as well."

"Make them then, but be quick about it." Hel practically snarled the words. "I have other matters to attend to…important matters."

As the ruler of the dead spoke, the remnants of the wolves shuddered and began to slowly reassemble themselves. As if that were not unnerving enough, warriors began to gather behind Hel. The grayish color of their skin suggested that they had been recruited from among her dead subjects. However, they were nothing like Hollywood zombies. They looked alert, and they moved as fast as living men.

"The third request is for the one known as DL," said Freya, ignoring the horror movie buildup all around them.

"He is dead," said Hel. "You have no possible claim there."

"He was no more dead than someone in a seidr trance. His soul was out of his body. That much I will grant. However, his body lived when he was taken. With any luck, it lives still."

"At that moment, he was unconnected to it. I was within my rights to claim him."

"He is a warrior, and if he were dead, Odin would claim him for Valhalla," said Thor.

Hel sighed, a sound like air escaping from a corpse. "Yet he did not die honorably in battle. You know as well as I that Odin and Freya may claim only those who have so died. Even an Aesir would be mine if he died in some other way. Have you forgotten your brother, Balder, who even now remains my subject? Though almost every living creature begged for his release, he is still mine."

Thor cursed her and raised his hammer, but Freyr placed his hand gently upon it.

"Can you not see she is trying to goad you? If you strike in anger, she will use it to her advantage."

Thor slowly lowered the hammer. Freyr turned his attention back to Hel. "In Balder's case, there was no question he was dead. In DL's case, there is."

"Will you at least agree he is mine if his body dies?" asked Hel.

"Not if you delay us on purpose to ensure the body's death," said Freyr. "Give him to us at once, and his body will not die."

Hel gave him a blood-chilling smile. "What makes you think the body is not already dead?"

Max's heart sunk. He wasn't sure how long Esras could keep the body alive with no soul. He wasn't even sure how much time had passed since they had left. All he knew was that Esras alone couldn't sustain DL's life forever.

"Deal with us honestly, and we will do the same with you," said Freyr. "If you deliberately withhold a living person from us, you risk tearing destiny as much as we would if we killed you before your time."

"Are we at last at the end of your requests?" asked Hel.

"We are yet ready to concede the justice of your decision on those you have denied," said Freyr. "Nonetheless, that you may have all of them to consider, I will tell you the other three. The woman Morfesa, druid of Falias, and the woman Adreanna, whom I believe an ally of yours brought here, are both alive. The third, Maeve Murphy, belongs in another realm beyond the Nine Worlds."

"The live ones I will concede to you—though I must check. I do not recall seeing either one of them. As for Maeve, I care not whether she came from another world or not. If she did not wish to be claimed, she should not have come here."

Max longed to argue on his grandmother's behalf, but he would just make Hel angrier if he did.

"The keepers of the dead in the world from which she comes have a prior claim," Freyr pointed out.

"Then they should have kept her instead of allowing her to roam free. Let them make the claim themselves if they so wish."

"We dispute your rejection of our requests," said Freyr.

"You may dispute them until Ragnarok—and beyond for all I care. I have made my decision. It is firm as the roots of Yggdrasil themselves."

Thor raised his hammer. Following his lead, Ekaterina crouched as if to spring, and Max raised the Sword of Dragon Light. Hel might have flinched, but it was such a slight movement Max could not be sure.

"Do you really choose battle?" asked Hel. Her wolves were fully restored and snarled in unison. Garm growled loudly enough to make the ground tremble beneath their feet. Her dead army now looked as if it numbered in the thousands.

"Though I have offered all I am required to, yet I will give you a chance to reverse those decisions you find so displeasing. If Odin will come to me in person and plead for those whose release you wanted, I will release them."

"My father is not one to be ordered about by the likes of you," said Thor. His hammer sparked again, this time so violently that Max's hair stood on end.

"Is that really too much to ask? Surely, if you speak on Odin's behalf, and all he has to do to gain you everything you seek for him is to come and make the request in person, why would he not do that?"

"Perhaps by seidr trance—" began Freya.

"No, in person. In the flesh, so to speak. Only then will I do as you ask."

"Allow us to confer for a moment," said Freyr, gesturing for Thor, Freya, Ekaterina, and Max to follow him. Hel did not object, though she did begin tapping her foot in a heartbeat rhythm.

When they were far enough away to be out of earshot, Freyr waved his arms, and Max could feel the magic rising up around them.

"That should keep her from eavesdropping," said Freyr.

"Probably not," said Freya. "Still, what must be said must be said."

"Can we not just kill her?" asked Thor. "We could be on Sleipnir and away before her army could surround us."

"And how would we then retrieve the prisoners?" asked Freya. "We would need the forces of Asgard at our back to fight our way into the dwelling place of the dead—and it is vast. We could search for months and never find even one of them. No, we need her alive."

"Why not just do as she asks?" said Ekaterina.

"Because what she asks is insulting," said Thor.

"Because it is too little," said Freyr. "She set the condition for Balder's release as universal mourning for him, and when we could not convince one giantess to join that mourning, she refused to release him. Now she has five prisoners to bargain with, including one indisputably dead, and all she asks is a personal visit from Odin. I like it not. She would not ask if she had not seen some way to profit greatly at our expense."

"What choice do we have?" asked Max. "I know my grandmother shouldn't have come in the first place, but she and DL came to help me save Morfesa and Adreanna, two of Dubh's innocent victims. They deserve better than that. As for Outcast, he's just a little boy."

"Maybe not," said Freyr. "In any case, it is presumptuous for a mortal to offer advice to us. However, your motive is noble, even if your manners perhaps leave something to be desired."

"She did not specify that Odin come alone," said Freya. "The only way for her to profit that I could see would be to kill him or capture him. If he comes at the head of the army of Valhalla, she will not be able to do either, and we might have enough force then to compel her to free the prisoners. Even if she plans some kind of treachery, I would wager on the victory of our forces against hers."

"You're forgetting how long it takes to transport armies here," said Thor. "We could send Sleipnir back to Asgard to fetch Odin and some few others, but even Sleipnir can't carry an army."

"What choice do we have?" asked Freyr. "I think it unwise at best to bring Odin here without an army to match the one Hel has."

"But if it takes too long, DL's body will die," said Max.

Freyr didn't reprimand him for speaking again. Instead, the Vanir looked away. No one else was meeting Max's eyes, either.

He should have realized sooner. The Aesir and Vanir would do what it took to save their own. They might extend themselves also to save someone like Morfesa to avoid further conflict with the faeries. But someone like DL? How much did they really care about him?

Thor patted him on the back. "If it comes to it, we will give him a hero's funeral."

UNEXPECTED GUEST

"WHAT ARE WE GOING TO DO?" asked DL.

"Answer the door," said Maeve. "That'd be better than having whoever it is break it down. I've thrown up what little magical defense I can manage at short notice."

The druid walked toward the front door. DL followed, though he wasn't sure how well he could protect her without his inner dragon.

"I'm coming!" she yelled. The knocking had caused thin cracks that ran almost the full length of the door.

When she opened it, they both gasped. DL had been expecting a giant of some kind, or perhaps some other very strong supernatural creature. The stranger on the porch was no giant, though he was a slenderer, slightly taller version of Thor. He had the grayish tinge of everything and everyone in this place, but he had a vibe that defied the shadows. No, more than that—he was actually glowing. His light was not as bright as the elves DL had seen earlier, but it was the brightest thing he'd seen in Helheim.

"I'd have come sooner if I'd known it was you—my lord Balder, is it not?" asked Maeve.

The stranger nodded. "I am indeed Balder, but I know you are not from this plane. How is it that you recognize me?"

"Even in all this grayness, you find ways to shine. Oh, where are my manners? Please come in, my lord, and be welcome in my home."

Balder nodded, stepped inside, and looked at DL, who managed an awkward bow.

"I am called DL, my lord." Balder nodded again. Evidently, hand-shaking was not a custom among the Norse.

Maeve ushered them down the hall, got them comfortably seated in reasonable replicas of plush chairs, and offered them refreshments.

"Do the dead eat?" asked DL.

"We can," said Balder, "though I doubt we need to. However, I came not to break bread with you, but to know who you are. The other eight worlds have long been separated from the original Midgard. What rests on that branch of Yggdrasil now is but a pale reflection of what Midgard once was. Few mortals reside there, and so the number of dead who have come here recently has been small.

"I felt you both when you arrived. Neither of you was an ordinary mortal in life, yet you are not Aesir, Vanir, alfar, duergar, or any other race that inhabits the Nine Worlds."

"In life, I was a druid and have a fair amount of magic, if I do say so myself. Also, I have some faerie blood, for I am descended from Maeve, queen of Connacht."

"Ah," said Balder, "it has been long since I have seen a faerie, but yes, that is what you remind me of. And what of you, young man? You are nothing like a faerie, nor like anything I have ever encountered before."

"I am an imugi, a kind of young dragon," said DL.

Balder looked at him suspiciously. "You are no dragon. I've seen many in my time."

"I am a Korean dragon, different from those you would have known, my lord. My...people, I guess you could say, are not destructive in the way the dragons you have known are. They can also assume human form at will."

"How did you come to be here?" asked Balder. "You are far from home."

"We traveled here as part of a group seeking a faerie fugitive," said Maeve. "Let us just say things did not go quite as planned."

"I'll say," said DL. "And I'm not even dead."

Balder sat forward in the chair, and his entire body tensed. "What? How can this be?"

DL explained as well as he could what had happened to him. Balder became progressively more outraged.

"This is unbelievable. I am no friend of Hel, but even I would not have accused her of violating the basic laws of this place in such a fundamental way."

Balder looked as if he was about to jump up and race to Hel's great hall to demand DL's release. Instead, he slumped back in the chair and reminded DL of a deflating balloon.

"What's wrong?" asked Maeve.

"I long to right this wrong, but I have no power to do so. Hel cannot compel me to follow her orders, but my former might is so blunted here that I cannot force her hand, either.

"Once, I was a mighty warrior among the Aesir, strong not only in arm but in magic. The body I have here in Helheim is more like the one mortals receive. It looks like mine, but it is no longer as strong as mine. Nor do I have the powers I once did. Only my invulnerability to most kinds of harm remains. I suppose I still have that because it is the result of the oaths my mother Frigg had almost everything in the Nine Worlds swear. They all took an oath not to harm me, and ironically those oaths still bind them, even though I am dead."

"I don't understand," said DL. "If nothing can harm you, how did you die in the first place?"

"I said 'almost everything.' Frigg forgot to request an oath from the mistletoe. Later, she remembered, but she figured that tiny plant was harmless. Alas, vile Loki learned of my one weakness, fashioned a mistletoe spear, and tricked poor, blind Hodr into throwing it at me.

"Unfortunately, Hel knows my one weakness, too, so even if I could launch a strong enough attack to be a threat to her, that same small plant is all she would need to bring me down. If I went to her to plead your case, she would just laugh at me."

"There may be a way for you to help DL if you are willing," said Maeve.

Balder looked much less deflated. "I will do whatever I can."

"This may not work, but we risk little by trying. As far as I can tell, my magic is as strong as ever. DL's draconic powers are inactive, but it would only take a slight nudge to bring them back. I imagine they will also work as normal."

"But are you strong enough to challenge Hel in her own realm?" asked Balder. "Even a living Aesir would find that difficult. Several living Aesir might not be able to do it. Though some of us are stronger than she, none of us is her equal here, in this realm that is both her prison and her kingdom."

"You still have the power you always had, correct?" asked Maeve. "Blunted, you said—but not gone?"

"I can feel it within me, but I cannot use it as well as I used to. Can you free me of whatever constraint binds me?"

"I fear not," said Maeve. "Changing the nature of the body you have here or the basic rules of this realm could take years to figure out —if it could be done at all. However, Celtic magic provides a way for you to share your strength with us. You may not be able to wield your power—but DL and I can. All I need is your consent and some time to prepare."

Balder's eyes narrowed. "I am familiar with this power-sharing, for seidr can accomplish something similar. However, to lend you my power is to place a great trust in people I have known for only minutes."

"The sharing depends on your continued consent," said Maeve. "If we do something of which you don't approve, withdraw your permission, and we lose your power. You risk nothing."

Balder took a little coaxing. DL marveled at how the often-grating Maeve could handle him so diplomatically. Her efforts were aided by his distrust of Hel. In a few minutes, he was convinced to let the druid try.

As Maeve worked to create the necessary psychic links among them, she laid out her strategy.

"When we start drawing on your power, Hel could feel the surge. I've done what I can in a short time to mask what we are doing, but speed will be essential. Balder, you will still be able to move, but you could be slowed down. Once I've awakened DL's inner dragon, he can carry you."

Balder looked as if he'd just been asked to wear a dress. "It seems unmanly for a warrior to be carried."

"We'll only do that if necessary," said Maeve. She gave DL a look indicating she was sure it would be necessary.

"As soon as we can move, we'll head for Hel's hall with Balder's guidance. Once there, we'll try to confront her before she can summon help. Even with Balder's strength, our only real hope is to catch her by surprise."

"That may prove difficult, for she has eyes everywhere," said Balder. "However, I cannot fault your strategy. Only if we can reach her fast enough will we have a chance."

Maeve reached out to Balder through the new links and began to gently direct his energy back toward herself. DL felt a sudden surge, as if his heart was pumping liquid sunshine rather than blood. His inner dragon awakened with a roar that shook the house.

He glanced over at Balder, who looked groggy, but not so much he had missed the change. "You are indeed formidable," he whispered.

"Maybe you won't need to carry him after all," said Maeve, swirling a portal into being with a wave of her hand. Its energy looked more golden than its usual silvery glow. "With Balder's knowledge of the place, we can just step through into her throne room. Let's be quick about it."

DL had to support Balder, but the Aesir made it to the portal under his own power. One quick flash, and they stood in Hel's great hall—her empty great hall.

"This is bad," said Maeve. "We need to find her now."

The druid closed her eyes. *"She's just behind the gate. Max, Ekaterina, and some of the Aesir are confronting her."*

"Let's portal out there now!" thought DL.

"Give me a second! She has an army of the dead with her. I'll have to make this very precise."

Another portal flared open, and DL led Balder through it—and right behind what looked like a thousand rows of dead warriors. Hel was nowhere in sight. Even worse, the portal collapsed, separating them from Maeve.

"The geography of this world is everchanging," thought Balder. *"The dead often see not the reality of it, but an exact replica of their home. Sometimes their perceptions affect where different places are in relation to each other."*

"You could have mentioned that earlier," thought DL. He wasn't really annoyed with Balder. He was angry with himself. He'd seen enough of the land of the dead. He should have known something like this could happen.

Swords flashed in the gray light. Arrows whizzed past.

Thanking God for his combat experience, DL grabbed a sword from the nearest dead warrior and attacked them furiously. They weren't as slow as Hollywood zombies. They moved at regular human speed. Fortunately, DL's speed was considerably greater. That and his greater strength compensated for his lack of armor.

Hacking through the ranks of gray fighters was psychologically tough, though. They didn't fall from wounds that would have been painful enough to drop a living man. He sometimes had to chop them to pieces to get them to stop attacking. He had to keep reminding himself that these men had all been dead for centuries. Their severed limbs still looked enough like human flesh to make him queasy, though.

The dead began to compensate for his speed by rushing him from several directions at once. To counter them, he had to turn fast enough to slash in a complete circle. That meant a lot more spinning around than he was used to in combat, so much so that he started to feel dizzy and unbalanced. Even his inner dragon was disoriented after a few minutes.

DL was enormously relieved when Maeve finally got another portal open in the area and managed to step through it before it collapsed. She hit the ground running, joining the battle with fire magic. The dead didn't cringe away from the flames. They didn't even twitch or slow their attacks when they started burning. The fire consumed them, but with maddening slowness.

DL dodged one whose arms were reaching out to catch him in a flaming bear hug. He stumbled, and another burning adversary grabbed his shoulder with fiery fingers. He broke away, taking three of the fingers with him.

Maeve switched tactics after that. Fueled by Balder's Aesir power, she whipped up enough storm wind to blow the dead backward. Though they could still struggle their way forward, it was harder for them to gang up on DL.

Even taking them a few at a time was tough. DL quickly lost count of how many he had felled. He couldn't move very far forward before the next wave hit him, and a mixture of bodies and severed limbs piled up all around him. He had to keep shoving bodies out of the way to strike at the next group. He glanced at the advancing mob. No matter how many of the dead he took out, the approaching ranks never seemed to diminish.

He noticed small movements out of the corner of his eye. He took a quick look around as soon as he had a few seconds. The shredded flesh of the fallen was pulling back together. A severed arm was crawling toward its body.

Dropping the oncoming opponents as fast as he could was not enough. He had to fall back every so often to hack at the already vanquished.

Maeve switched tactics again, alternating between blasting the active dead with wind and using fire to give the shredded ones a Viking funeral. That worked to some extent. The ashes did struggle their way back to flesh eventually, but the process was much slower than the pieces reknitting themselves back into a body. However, the smell of burning flesh sickened DL, and he began to feel as if he were fighting in an oven.

He kept looking forward, but the number of the dead surging forward never seemed to diminish, and he could never get a clear view of what lay beyond them. His arm ached, but he kept hacking away at each opponent as fast as he could. There was no choice.

"We're losing," thought Mave.

"Tell me something I don't know. Have a better idea?"

"Yes, but it's risky. Max and Ekaterina are nearby, together with some Aesir, but I don't think they'll try to fight Hel or her army. We can't reach them—but a dragon could probably do it."

"I don't have enough Yeouiju power—"

"I know that. I think Balder's power would provide enough raw energy. The risk is it's a very different kind of energy. It worked to trigger your inner dragon, but I'm not sure whether it will work as well with a complete transformation."

DL looked at the seemingly endless rows of enemies surging in his direction like a tidal wave from a gray sea. *"Try it. What have we got to lose?"*

"You could be hurt or killed."

"I'm being treated like I'm dead, anyway. I'm willing to risk the real thing for a decent shot at getting out of here."

DL spent another minute or two chopping off limbs and heads. As he felt more power humming through his muscles, he jumped back to give himself room if the transformation worked.

He almost immediately regretted agreeing to Maeve's idea. The one time he had become a dragon before, the process was quick and natural. This time it was slower—and much more painful. His body felt as if it was resisting the change and being beaten into it by magic that felt dark inside him.

He became bigger, so much so that even the dead warriors paused for a moment, uncertain how to proceed. They might have been less reluctant to attack if DL hadn't been so successful at choking back his screams.

His flesh and bones writhed within his skin. His blood boiled. Dark scales the color of burned skin sprouted all over him.

Maeve was yelling to him, but he heard her thoughts as far-away shouts. He could not make out the words. She was no longer real. Only the pain was real. His own thoughts were burned away by it.

He had teeth like scimitars, claws like great swords, and wings with a span greater than a small town.

As the pain subsided, he looked through a blood-red haze at the ranks of the dead army whose warriors stared at him, their mouths hanging open. They were puny, insignificant. A few puffs of his fiery breath would burn them all away.

His battle roar shook the walls of Hel's hall, and he prepared to unleash massive destruction, just as he had been born to do.

REUNION

"THERE'S a way to save DL and get Odin and his army here fast." Max spoke as quickly as he could, hoping no one would interrupt. "Send Thor, Freya, and me back to Álfheim on Sleipnir. Esras knows how to open portals from one place to another. If Freya takes over the task of keeping DL's body alive, Esras can use Thor's memories of Asgard to open a portal to it, then use any of our memories to portal Odin, his warriors, whoever you want back here. That couldn't all be done instantly, of course, but the portal part would take minutes or hours, not days."

"If it is truly as you say, then it may be worth attempting," said Thor. "DL has fought by your side, Freyr. That is no small thing."

"I hear the sounds of combat," said Ekaterina. "They are faint. I think someone is fighting near the back of Hel's army."

Max was tempted to make a joke about speaking of the devil when he saw Hel striding in their direction with anger in her eyes.

"How dare you try to mount an attack in my own territory?" Instead of switching between living woman and corpse evenly, she was staying a corpse for longer periods of time.

"We were discussing bringing an escort to protect Odin, not an invading army," said Freyr.

Hel glared at him, a living incarnation of the expression about looks killing. "I'm not talking about what you may do but what you have done. Even now someone is attacking my army in the rear."

"How could we have gotten troops in there?" asked Thor. "Would they not have had to pass the same army they now attack?"

"Yet someone is attacking," said Ekaterina. "I hear them even more clearly now."

"Whoever it is, we didn't bring them," said Freya.

"I do not believe you," said Hel. "In any case, I will keep all those you asked about, even the ones I earlier agreed to free, until you cease these aggressions against me."

"I will have Gerda freed," said Freyr. "She is alive, and you have agreed already."

Max wondered if Hel had made a serious mistake. When she had been standing behind her own gate, the Aesir had no way to reach her. Now that she had stepped outside the protection of her own walls, she was more vulnerable—and Freyr was blocking her path back. Thor quickly joined him. Freya closed her eyes, probably headed into another seidr trance.

"You will not attack me," said Hel. "You cannot risk the disruption of the natural order if you should kill me. It could be worse than Ragnarok."

"Nonetheless, you shall not keep my wife," said Freyr, drawing his sword. Thor let tiny bolts of lightning shoot from his hammer.

"Fools!" shouted Hel. "This is not Asgard—as you will soon see. Attack!"

In response to her command, a large mass of dead warriors surged through the gate. Freyr tried to grab Hel to use as a shield, but she vanished into the ground with such speed that he clutched at empty air.

Thor's war cry was loud enough to deafen Max for a moment, but Hel's warriors showed no sign that they had even heard it. The booming thunder and flashing lightning when he hit the ground with Mjolnir got their attention—but they kept coming. Throwing himself at the front line, the storm lord swung his hammer so fast that he took down several of the dead before any of them could react. The lightning crackling from each hammer strike took down several more.

Freyr swung his sword as if he had been born with a blade in his hand. His aim was always true, and his movements were as graceful as a dancer's. The dead might have been warriors in life, but their movements looked clumsy compared to Freyr's.

Unfortunately, his sword could only take down one opponent at a time. The dead surged forward rapidly enough to force Freyr to face ten, all slashing at him with spears and swords. His movements became more erratic as they tried to parry all those strokes at the same time.

Ekaterina came to his aid. Despite being barehanded, she was strong enough to rip off arms and punch right through chests. To Max's amazement, those kinds of injuries didn't stop the dead, but at least they slowed them down.

Standing a little farther back, Max tried to cast a spell to slow the dead down. He stretched the magic out further and further in an attempt to encompass as many of the dead as possible. Stretching became tearing. Tearing became shredding. The spell ended up as powerless, disjointed fragments—as useless as Max was.

He raised the Sword of Dragon Light. He couldn't get it to flare. Ekaterina was pinned down by the dead now, too preoccupied to help.

Thor's attack slowed the advance of the dead army, but its numbers were so great that some slid around him and charged the others. Freyr and Ekaterina stopped a lot of those, but they couldn't get them all. A few of the warriors headed toward Max.

"Going after the weakest link, huh?" he muttered. The sword already felt heavy in his hand.

One of his opponents had only half of a body—the other half had been pulped by Thor's hammer. Another had lost his sword arm to Ekaterina but had shifted the sword to his remaining hand. Two more got through and moved at a run in his direction.

Standing back to cast spells had looked like a good idea—but it only worked with a front line that kept attackers off him. Dodging the dead as best he could, Max ran until he stood right behind Freyr and Ekaterina, then turned to face his pursuers. At least now, they couldn't surround him.

The unwounded dead both lunged at him at the same time. Instead of knocking the sword out of his hand, they struck an invisible barrier and fell to the ground, confused.

Max looked back at Freya. She had once been a goddess of love and fertility, but that didn't limit her use of magic outside those fields. She had surrounded herself, Freyr, Ekaterina, and Max with a shield whose power increased so fast that even the dead became aware of it. They cringed away from the throbbing power. Their eyes darted back and forth, looking for weaknesses.

Max doubted they would find any. He focused enough to see the magic pulsing around them. Even though she had to craft the spell quickly and extend it over a wide area to encompass all four of them, the shield was flawless.

The dead might not be able to see what Max could see, but their experimental poking and prodding of the barrier found no niche to slip through, no crack to pry open.

"They aren't going to give up unless Hel orders them to," yelled Freya. "We would do well to work out a better strategy."

Thor scowled at the dead. The wounded ones close enough to see were healing at an alarming rate. "What trickery is this?"

"You cannot kill the dead," said Freyr. "You've seen how the warriors of Valhalla heal. This is no different."

The dead spread themselves out, surrounding the group. Abandoning poking, they started hacking at the shield with their weapons.

Freya moved toward the others, contracting the shield as she did so.

"That will conserve power and give them a smaller surface to hit. None of their weapons have any particular magic I can sense, but even this physical pounding will wear me down eventually. We must find a way to beat them."

Her words were underscored by the incessant clanging of swords against Freya's shield.

"We should trade swords," said Max, holding out the Sword of Dragon Light for Freyr. "You could make much better use of this one than I can."

Freyr nodded and made the exchange. "It is a truly noble man who puts the welfare of his army above his own glory." The Sword of Dragon Light flared in his hand.

"I wasn't headed for glory, anyway," said Max. "I can barely lift the thing."

"You would be more use with a spell than with a sword," said Freya. "Start smaller, though. Don't try to cast a spell that covers all the dead."

Max felt his cheeks redden. He hadn't realized Freya was watching his casting efforts.

"How do we defeat an army whose warriors can heal before we can bring all of them down?" asked Thor. "Will we not be at this forever?"

"We can't defeat them," said Freyr. "What we need to do is find a way around them—open a gap big enough to run through. I don't know how we can do that if we have to stay behind a communal shield, though."

Tiny cracks formed in the barrier. Freya sealed them with a wave of her hand, but she looked pained as if all the pounding was giving her a migraine.

"I can protect you individually," she said. "I can give you more freedom to attack. That will drain me faster, though. You'll need to break through their lines soon. Make a gap through to the gate, and I can ward it long enough for us to get through without interference."

"Do it," said Thor, clenching his hammer.

Freya raised her glowing staff, and the shield shifted, becoming four smaller shields.

Max had only a second to admire how smoothly she worked her magic before the dead figured out the barrier no longer held them back. They hurled themselves at all four group members.

The first wave floundered against the personal shields. Thor crushed half of them with a few well-aimed hammer blows, and the sky was bright with his lightning. Freyr charged forward, bathing the dead in the sunny glow of the sword. They cringed away from it, but not fast enough to avoid having limbs lopped off by his blindingly fast strokes. Ekaterina grabbed up one of the fallen who had lost both arms and used him as a gigantic club, knocking aside his comrades with her powerful swings.

"Will the shields protect against fire?" Max asked Freya.

"Absolutely," she replied. She smiled as if she knew what Max had in mind.

Keeping in mind Freya's advice to start smaller, Max shot sparks at the warriors. The sparks clung to the dead, who ignored them—until Max fed more power into the spell, igniting the dead. A little more power, and the flames became an inferno.

Instead of trying to cover all the dead at once, Max let the fire spread in an almost natural way. Each blaze shot sparks at the nearby dead, who in turn burst into flames. He used magic to guide the spread of the conflagration but let nature do as much of the heavy lifting as possible.

Despite the fire, the dead kept pressing forward, but the more they crowded, the faster the flames spread.

Freya put her hand on his shoulder. "Well-done! Your magic is more sophisticated that I at first thought."

The dead continued to flow forward, a flood of flesh trying to extinguish the flames. Thor, Freyr, and Ekaterina pushed back. They made far less progress than Max expected, though.

"Do more dead keep coming? I can't see where their lines end."

Freyr squinted at the mob. "It could be. We are not making as much headway as I would have expected."

The gate wasn't that much farther away than a couple of city blocks, but they had only moved inches closer to it.

Ekaterina staggered as if someone had hit her from behind.

"Max!" she cried. "I can't feel DL anymore!"

The dead took advantage of her distraction to jump on her, burning and unburning alike. She would have gone up in flames herself if not for Freya's shield. She pushed her way out of the pile with a little help from Freyr. His well-placed slices disabled the dead nearest the top of the pile.

Max reached out for DL. Ever since DL had healed Max with his blood, Max had felt DL's presence. Their body swap and the Yeouiju's efforts, erratic though they were, had heightened that tie. Now he felt only emptiness where his connection with DL should have been. It was as if his friend had been erased from existence.

Max tried and failed to send his mind out in search of DL. He didn't know how to achieve a seidr trance, and the druid method of separating mind from body didn't seem to work with a battle raging all around him.

Thor's eardrum-shattering war cries weren't helping, either, but at least his combination of hammer strikes and lightning bolts did enough damage to the dead to compensate for Ekaterina's preoccupation.

"Yeouiju, what has happened to your master?" thought Max. Even though he was in his own body, he could still feel the Yeouiju's subtle presence deep inside. It didn't answer, though. Maybe it was as baffled as he was.

Max started to cast a locator spell, but his concentration was shattered by a roar far louder than Thor's war cry. The sound burst deafened him and caused the dead to turn toward something Max couldn't see.

Freya, pale and wide-eyed, stared at the sky. "A dragon!"

"DL?" Max asked Ekaterina.

"The one time he became a full dragon, his roar was nothing like that," she said, squinting in the direction from which the roar had come. "Anyway, with the Yeouiju split among us as it is, he has no way to— God preserve us!"

An enormous dragon far blacker than the gloom that surrounded him cast its gargantuan shadow over the dead army. Its eyes flashed red as it poured its flaming breath on the warriors, wiping out rows of them with a single scorching puff. Max's fire magic looked like a candle flame in comparison.

Thor poised himself to strike the creature with lightning, but Freyr put a hand on his shoulder. "The dragon is doing our work for us, or so it seems."

"Aye, that it is—but for how long? When it finishes with the dead, will it not turn on us?" Thor's hammer sparked as he spoke. "It has weakened the army of the dead enough for us to beat it. Now is the time to kill it."

"If we can," said Freya. "This looks like an unusually strong dragon." She closed her eyes again. Her calm expression suggested she was back in a seidr trance, perhaps to study the dragon.

"This is not my master," thought the Yeouiju. It had not spoken in hours. Why was it speaking now just to state the obvious?

"And yet it is."

"What do you mean?" asked Max. He could tell from Ekaterina's expression that she was hearing the Yeouiju as well—and was just as puzzled as Max was.

"It…it was him. It is no longer. He has been changed."

"How could this have happened?"

"I know not. I only know there is still a little of him left, but very little. What is left is like a snowflake in an inferno. It will not last."

"How do we change him back?" Max was already frantic, and the fact that the Yeouiju was silent again didn't help.

The dragon flew closer as it exterminated the dead warriors. "It can't be!" said Ekaterina. "This is a Western dragon, absolutely nothing like DL in dragon form."

Thor raised his hammer. Before he could throw it or use it to strike the dragon with lightning, Max grabbed at his arm.

"Mortal, how dare you try to stay my hand? Learn your place—or I will teach you what it is!"

Faeries were a little easier to deal with than the Aesir, but Max kept that thought to himself. He fell to his knees before the angry former god, mostly because he couldn't think of any other way to salvage the situation.

"I'm sorry. I meant no offense, but the dragon may not be what it seems. The Yeouiju within us has told Ekaterina and me that that beast is really our friend and your guest, DL. Please don't kill him!"

"How can such a thing be?" asked Freyr. "He told us he was a dragon, but of a different kind."

"Fafnir the duergar became a dragon from greed," said Thor, looking suspiciously at Max. "Never have I heard of someone becoming a dragon who wasn't evil. Perhaps we have been deceived."

"No, my lord," said Ekaterina, doing her best to squeeze in between Thor and Max. "We have always been truthful with you. Our friend has been transformed, but not through any fault of his own. Some vile magic in this dark place must be responsible."

"I doubt that," said Freyr. "If Hel could transform people into dragons, she would long since have created a dragon army and conquered the Nine Worlds."

"Let us not be too hasty. I cannot tell whether this dragon is the one called DL or not, but I know this much—there is something of Balder within him," said Freya.

"You err," said Thor angrily. "Balder had nothing but good within him. He was the best of us. Could he have created a dragon? Never!"

"Nonetheless, he is connected to this dragon in some way," said Freya. "I can see that much as clearly as I can see you."

The dragon roared again. This time he was so much nearer Max thought his eardrums would split. The dead archers were shooting arrows at it but with little effect. Much of Hel's army had already been reduced to ashes, though from what Max had seen, they would eventually return to their human forms.

"Pardon me if I'm speaking out of turn, but Hel's forces are all focused on the dragon now. Her gate's open. Isn't this a good time to free the hostages?"

"You always speak out of turn," grumbled Thor. "You may be right, though. What think you, Freyr?"

"There will doubtless be traps," said Freyr. "However, it's not likely Hel would have anticipated a dragon attack. We may be able to slip in while she is fretting over the beast."

"There may never be a better chance," said Freya. "And whoever the dragon may be, getting out of its path would be prudent."

Max looked in the dragon's direction again. It was still focused on destroying the dead warriors, but it would be done with them in five minutes at most. Even if it was DL, how would it react to them?

Based on the Yeouiju's snowflake analogy, what Max really wanted was to try to rescue DL and then go after the hostages, but he didn't have the first idea how to save him. Morfesa and his grandmother might be able to figure out what needed to be done.

Of course, nobody in this group except Ekaterina was likely to care what he thought. Thor at least had made that very clear.

"Follow me, then," said the Aesir, pointing toward the unguarded gate with his hammer. He, Freyr and Freya moved in that direction so fast that Max would not have been able to follow if Ekaterina hadn't scooped him up off the ground and practically thrown him after them. Once he was on his feet, he was able to conjure up enough speed to keep up.

Max could have sworn the dragon glanced in their direction as they ran through the gate. What was in those furnace-red eyes? Recognition? An appeal for help? Or just curiosity about how well they would burn? There was no way to know.

TRESPASSING

HEL'S DOMAIN was just as gloomy as it had appeared from outside. They ran down gray streets, some of them cobblestone, many little more than dirt roads. On either side were gray buildings from many different time periods. They looked as if they had been jumbled together at random from the memories of the dead.

Max would have become hopelessly lost among those twisting streets and mismatched buildings, but the former gods moved with the confidence of people navigating the place where they grew up.

"How do you know where you're going?" Max asked Freya.

Freya laughed. "This place greets the dead with images from their lives. They are drawn to those images and end up dwelling in permanent illusions of their old homes. The living get no such greeting. Instead, we are surrounded by bits and pieces of the memories of the dead.

"Luckily, there is a way through the tangled pathways of Helheim. We keep in mind the place we seek, Hel's hall. Thor, Freyr and I know what it looks like, and as long as we cling to that image, our feet will sooner or later lead us to it."

"Unless Hel tries to block us," said Freyr. "Then we might wander for years without finding what we seek."

"*I* could still find my way, though it would take longer," said Freya. "But let us hope the dragon keeps Hel busy for a while longer."

"Look!" said Thor, pointing his hammer at another gate. It and the walls extending from it in either direction looked wooden, just like the walls around Viking circular forts, but the wood was filled with magic. It wouldn't be easy to break through.

"Ekaterina, we will need your help again," said Freya. "The dead come here when they first arrive, so the gates must open for them. Perhaps they will open for you, just as the main gate did."

"I'm happy to try," said Ekaterina, stepping forward. As soon as she touched the gate, it swung open.

"Be wary," said Freya. "Hel probably has at least some warriors garrisoned here, and her own magic will be at its strongest within these walls."

They all moved cautiously as they entered, even Thor. Aside from the prevailing grayness, the interior layout was much like the Norse ring forts Max had studied. There were at least four square enclosures, with each "wall" being a longhouse. Like the historical longhouses, these had no windows, though Max couldn't help feeling watched, anyway. Some kind of supernatural surveillance was likely. He expected several dead warriors to charge out of every longhouse door they passed, but they met no sign of opposition.

Near what could have been the center of the compound stood a much larger and less historically accurate structure. It was still nominally wooden, but it was even more magically charged than any of the surrounding buildings. It had to be Hel's hall.

"Is this where Hel is keeping the hostages?" asked Max.

"It is the best-protected spot," said Freyr. "That doesn't mean they are all here, however. Hel could have scattered them throughout her realm."

"There is only one way to know," said Thor, shoving the door open and striding in as if he owned the place. The others followed more slowly. Freya, in particular, studied each step in front of her as if looking for traps.

The inside of the building was one large hall lit unevenly by flickering torches. In the middle was a fire pit, but the flames rising from it put out no heat and very much less light than they would have if they had been actual fire. To either side of it were long wooden tables. At the far end was a large throne that looked out of place. A Viking leader would have dined with his men, not separated from them. Maybe the tables were just for show. Max couldn't imagine Hel presiding over a feast.

"There's no one here," said Thor, looking from side to side. "At the very least, I would have expected Hel to be here."

"It is likely she seeks a way to defeat the dragon," said Freyr. "That could work to our advantage. It is better not to face her in the place where she is the strongest."

"Except that she alone knows where her captives are," said Thor. He looked as if he wanted to take his hammer and smash the whole place to splinters.

Freya put her hand on Thor's shoulder. "She may have concealed them, but even she cannot have hidden them so completely that I cannot find them if I have enough time."

"I suppose you'll want to go into a trance again," said Thor in a tone that suggested he didn't think much of trances. From what Max had seen, solving problems with hammer strokes and lightning was much more his style.

"Yes," said Freya, giving him her sweetest smile. "Will you stand guard while I send my mind out to search for the hostages?" Thor nodded. "Perhaps the rest of you could search for a hostage with whom you have a connection."

"I will reach out for Gerda," said Freyr.

"I cannot reach DL…as things stand now," said Ekaterina. Her face was tight with frustration. "Perhaps I can track Outcast's scent."

"I'm not feeling DL, either," said Max. "Maybe I can reach Maeve."

Freya nodded to each of them and closed her eyes. In seconds, her face became expressionless. Freyr sat down next to her and initiated his own trance. Ekaterina walked around the room frowning and sniffing. Thor paced back and forth, tension sparking like electricity from his hammer.

Max sat down and reached out with his own mind. Even though he kept Maeve's image in his mind, he couldn't break through the dense psychic fog around him. The atmosphere was so thick with the thoughts of the dead that connecting with an individual spirit was like trying to find a drop of blood in a vat of blood-colored paint. He could probably reach her eventually, but who knew how long they had? Hel might return at any moment.

It was Ekaterina who scored first. "Outcast is nearby!"

Freya opened her eyes. "I see no sign of anyone nearby."

Ekaterina smiled. "In your trance, you could see more than I could ever hope to—but Hel is familiar with seidr. She'd have tried to counter that. She has no experience with vampires and has no idea I could sniff out the hostages if they were close enough."

"He is the cursed one," said Freyr. "Perhaps Hel deliberately made him easier to find."

"If he were intended as a trap, why not just leave him with us in the first place? We have little to lose by finding him now," said Freya.

"Unless 'near' means in this hall, I fear we may not find him at all," said Thor, pointing to the door—no, to the spot where it had been. All they could see now was an unbroken wall.

"Hel may be focused on the dragon, but she knows we're here," said Freyr.

Freya verified that the vanishing door wasn't just an illusion, after which Thor spent a while bashing away at the wall with his hammer. He didn't do much damage, and, much like the dead warriors, the wall repaired itself. He tried pounding harder and more rapidly. The whole structure shook, but the more damage he did, the faster each splinter flew back into place.

"Perhaps lightning—" began Thor.

"Will bounce back and strike us," said Freya, putting a hand on his hammer. "Let me study the magic in the walls before we try anything else."

Max's ability to analyze magic was far less well-trained than Freya's, but it looked to him as if it would be hard to overcome the magic radiating through the wood. It twined through every speck, as much a part of the wood as the grain was. It held onto each splinter with unshakable determination.

The rescuers were now in need of rescue.

SPLIT DRAGONALITY

DL HAD BURNED through the ranks of dead warriors. That should have been more satisfying than it was, but his draconic eyes told him the warriors were not really gone. He flew back and forth, relentlessly burning everything that moved until the soil became like volcanic glass. Even then, the ashes twitched as they began to reform themselves back into bodies.

There had been some reason to annihilate the dead, but he couldn't remember what it was. He couldn't remember much of anything, but he didn't care. The world seemed full of things to burn. That was good. There was no need to keep burning this one recalcitrant group.

There must be other things to do as well. DL felt the instinctive urge to look for treasure. He didn't think he had a trove of any kind yet. Now might be the time to search out shiny things and to begin accumulating them.

"DL!"

He heard the frantic tone of the voice in his mind, but to him, it was like a whisper—and unimportant. Whoever was calling out to him was too weak to be a credible enemy or a useful ally.

"DL, look down!"

Irritated, DL glanced downward. Just as he thought, weaklings! An old woman and a younger man who could barely stand. Still, there was something shiny about the man. Gold armor, perhaps?

DL flew downward and landed near them. He must have come to rest harder than he thought, because the old woman was knocked over. She was one of the dead, though, so no harm done—not that he would have cared.

"Why have you summoned me?" he asked. His roar must have been painfully loud to human ears, but he didn't care. He had only just landed, yet he was already impatient to be on his way. The man had no gold, just a golden glow. There was nothing here to add to his hoard.

"To...to apologize," said the old woman, who had managed to pull herself back to her feet. DL had to admit she was brave for a dead mortal.

"What could you possibly have done that could have harmed me in any way?"

"Allow me to show you." With a wave of her arm, she conjured up strange images in the air next to her. Not completely strange, though. There was something familiar about them. One man, in particular, he was sure he had seen before.

He had seen him in a mirror.

"What is this sorcery?" he said. "Why do you seek to put strange thoughts in my head?"

The old woman looked alarmed but stood her ground. "Please allow me to explain. If you are still dissatisfied when I finish, I will not resist if you wish to burn me to ashes."

DL laughed, and the sound was like thunder. "Resist? What could you do to resist me? Your petty magics would not protect you."

The old woman bowed. "You are right, of course. But what I have to say could do you much good."

"That is almost as funny as the idea that you could resist me."

"Yet I know things that you do not. Where is your lair, dragon? Where is your hoard?"

"I have not yet made one," said DL slowly.

"How can this be?" asked the old woman. "You are no hatchling, are you? By your size, I would take you for a full-grown dragon—but what full-grown dragon has no dwelling, has no treasure put aside?"

DL did not know how to answer that. He could remember nothing of life before he rose up to smite the dead army. A dragon of his age should have at least a cave somewhere, as well as a fair-sized hoard. He had neither, or, if he did, he had no idea where to find them.

"What do you know of me?" he asked. "Will you tell me where my hoard is? That is the only thing you could say that would be of value to me."

"Treasure is not always gold," she said. With another wave of her hand, she showed him an image of a pale, dark-haired mortal woman. No, not quite mortal. Stronger than mortal. How did he know that, though? And why did something stir in his heart at the sight of her?

"Who is this woman? And of what use would a woman be to a dragon?"

"You were not always the kind of dragon you are now, and you have lived most of your life as a man."

DL laughed again. "Men cannot be dragons, and dragons cannot be men."

"I have known of at least one man who became a dragon," mumbled the shining man. "Well, duergar rather than man, but the idea is the same. His name was Fafnir."

"That name means nothing to me," said DL. "I should burn you both to ashes and go about my business."

"Ah, but what exactly is your business?" asked the old woman. "You have neither home nor hoard, and I would wager no idea of where you are."

"This…this must be the land of the dead."

She nodded. "Yes, but where is the way out? What lies beyond it? You have no idea, do you?"

DL should have incinerated her at this point. He knew he should—but he still remembered nothing. If there was treasure to be found, he had no idea where it was. A little conversation with this annoying mortal might prove worthwhile.

"What can you tell me of this place and its doorways?" he asked.

"To understand my answer, you need to know what I know about you. Will you listen?"

DL nodded reluctantly. He would probably regret this, but he did at the very least need to discover how to get out of here.

The old woman conjured up more images of the man he recognized and that man's friends, whom he also began to recognize. His thoughts became increasingly uncomfortable, as if they could no longer fit in his head, but he endured them in the hope of learning something more useful.

"I don't know why your transformation went so…had such an unexpected result," said the old woman when she finally finished showing him images.

"It was my fault," said the shining man. "I fear that you drew not only power from me, but some of my perspective as well. I have never met a good dragon, such as you describe DL as being. My experiences must have poisoned the spell somehow, creating the kind of dragon I knew rather than the one he should be."

"This is all nonsense as far as I can tell," said DL. "You did, however, give me one useful idea. Dragons accumulate treasure, but they often add at least one maiden to that treasure. You have shown me one that would be worthy of my attention. I will seek her out."

The old woman looked dumbfounded. "But this woman cares for you—the real you. She will not accept you as a dragon."

DL's laugh once more shook the ground. "She does not need to 'accept' me. What maiden ever did accept a dragon? Nonetheless, I will have her. For giving me the idea, I will spare your lives—but do not trouble me again!"

He took off so fast that the rush of air knocked the woman to the ground. Despite his warning, he heard her in his mind almost at once.

"I don't know whether this transformation will last. I channeled power from Balder to you, but you are no longer joined to him or me. If you become yourself again in a dangerous situation, you could die."

He couldn't understand why the woman would care whether he died or not. She was just being foolish, anyway. He was who he was—who he would always be.

He would not reply. The only answer she would get would be his thunderous laugh as he glided away in search of his maiden.

HOSTAGE SCAVENGER HUNT

"Try the Sword of Dragon Light," suggested Ekaterina. "This place is unused to real sunlight, and the magic is of a different type than what Hel would recognize.

"We have little to lose by trying," said Freyr. He swung the blade at the space on the wall where the door had been. It struck with a sunny flash and dug into the wood. A few more strikes caused the door to reappear.

"Well done!" said Thor. "It is a shame we cannot obtain more such weapons. We might catch our enemies by surprise at Ragnarok."

"And perhaps unravel the universe in the process," said Freya. "At any rate, we have a way out again. Ekaterina, lead us to Outcast, and then we will see what we can do about the rest."

After a few sniffs, Ekaterina led them to one of the longhouses that surrounded Hel's hall. It was as empty of guards as the hall had been, and for a moment Max feared she was wrong. Then he saw the flickering of odd magic from the far the side of the room. They had found Outcast after all.

The boy didn't look as if he'd been harmed physically, but his hands were bound, and he was sleeping so soundly that they couldn't wake him up.

"Can we break this spell?" asked Ekaterina.

"The binding on his hands seems to be the source," said Freya. "From what I can tell, though, cutting it might be dangerous."

"The boy would be of no use in battle, anyway," Thor pointed out. "Leave him be for the moment."

"We should not just leave him here," said Ekaterina. "I'll carry him."

"Why would Hel have put him to sleep?" asked Max.

"Perhaps she feared his curse," suggested Freyr. "We might do well to follow her example. We've had nothing but ill luck since he came among us."

"Because of the Amadan Dubh, not because of this boy," said Ekaterina. "The curse does affect him, but we've seen no sign that it affects those around him."

Freyr looked as if he wanted to object but thought better of it. Max was a little stung by the fact that he got shot down every time he made a suggestion, but Ekaterina never did. One social rule, apparently, was as true in the Nine Worlds as it was on Earth—the hot girl always gets what she wants. No, that wasn't being fair to Ekaterina. Given how much the Norse valued success in battle, Freyr was just as likely to be swayed by her combat ability as by her looks. Max hadn't been able to contribute nearly as much. If he could just get his hands on Merlin's book, Freyr and the others would have a better idea of how much he could contribute.

"Can you tell where the others are?" asked Freyr.

"They were here once I think, but I don't smell anything recent," said Ekaterina.

"They could be anywhere," said Freya. "The realm of the dead is vast. It hasn't received many new souls since…since we were separated from the real Midgard, but it holds a huge number from earlier times, each one seeing the world in which he used to live. As they move about, the geography shifts to accommodate them. Visitors like us see only bits and pieces of that complex reality, so it's difficult for us to even measure its size."

"Is there a way for us to focus on one of the dead and see this place as she sees it?" asked Max.

Freya frowned. "I have never tried such a thing. What would be the point?"

"Most of the hostages are still alive, but my grandmother is dead. If we could see what she sees in this place, we could find her. She may know where the others are."

"That may be a good plan—if we can figure out how to do it," said Freya.

"Would it not make sense to take advantage of Max's hereditary connection to her?" asked Ekaterina. "Surely it would be easier to link him to her than to try with any of the rest of us."

"That idea too has merit," said Freya. "If I could take him with me into a seidr trance, the combination of his bond with his grandmother and my magical skill might just make such a connection possible."

"I'm willing to do whatever I need to," said Max.

"Then let us make the attempt quickly," said Thor. "The longer we delay, the greater the possibility that Hel will stop being distracted by the dragon and realize that we have invaded her hall."

As if the dragon had heard what Thor said, a roar like a thunderclap sounded overhead, and enormous wings flapped hard enough to raise a storm.

"If he gets close enough, perhaps we can reason with him," said Ekaterina. "If he truly is DL, we might reach the part of him that remembers his old self."

Thor stared at her wide-eyed. "Are you mad? Whoever he might have been, he is a dragon of the Nine Worlds now. There will be no reasoning with him." His hammer sparked bluish electricity as he raised it and moved toward the door.

"We don't know that," said Max. Visions of Thor's hammer crushing DL's draconic skull flashed through his mind. "If we can communicate, he could be a valuable ally, right?"

"If any part of him remembers who he was, then yes," said Freyr. "A friendly dragon could be invaluable—but such a thing has never existed in the Nine Worlds."

The dragon must have been circling. The flapping of its wings was a constant drumbeat in the distance.

"We will not know unless we can get close enough to examine him," said Freya. "I might be able to tell if something of the original person still remains. Perhaps I can even find a way to change him back—which is, I suspect, what you really want, is it not?"

"Yes." Max and Ekaterina spoke almost in unison.

"But surely approaching the dragon is folly," said Thor. "Humans are not the only ones who can die, remember. Aesir can die. Vanir can die. Then we would truly be at Hel's mercy. The risk is too great."

The flapping sounded louder, closer, like an approaching tornado.

"If there is even a single particle of the original DL in him, he will not hurt me," said Ekaterina. "I would bet my...existence on it."

"I don't think he'd hurt me, either," said Max. "Both of us have some aspect of the Yeouiju within us, too. We have the best chance of reaching him."

"We cannot allow you to risk yourselves in that way," said Freyr. "Max, you are the only one among us with a link to your grandmother. Ekaterina, you are the only one among us able to sniff out the hostages. If we lose you, we lose our chance of rescuing them."

Max could hardly blame Freyr for making the rescue of his wife his first priority. That didn't mean he was willing to sacrifice DL, but he wasn't sure how to defy his hosts. He had no way of stopping Thor from striking DL out of the sky with lightning if the Aesir deciding that was the best plan.

"My lords, I am grateful for the help you have given us, but I am not of your world and do not consider myself bound by its rules," said Ekaterina. "I will risk what I must to save the man I love." She turned and was out the door before their hosts could protest.

Open defiance by mortals—or beings who had once been mortal—wasn't something the former gods would have encountered that often. They froze, eyes wide and mouths hanging open. Max took advantage of their distraction to slip out the door and follow Ekaterina.

He had barely gotten out the door when Thor charged out. He was only a few footsteps behind Max. The storm lord stopped so abruptly to look up at the dragon, though, that Freyr and Freya ran into him on the way out.

Max moved away from them as fast as possible, but the dragon's flapping wings produced high winds that pushed him back. The beast hovered above them, squinting down at them, its shadow turning the grayish Helheim day into night.

What had drawn it here? Could it have been looking for them?

"Yeouiju! Can you try to connect with DL?" asked Max frantically.

"I never stopped trying," it replied. *"I have failed. Perhaps if I were closer—"*

"DL!" yelled Ekaterina. "DL, let us help you!"

The dragon circled even closer. Max had a hard time standing against the wind.

Thor had Mjolnir ready, and Freyr held the Sword of Dragon Light. Neither of them looked as if helping the dragon was the first thing on their mind.

It was impossible to tell whether the dragon heard Ekaterina or how clearly it could see the weapons brandished by the ex-gods. Maybe its descent was caused by both—or neither.

Thor raised his hammer for a potentially fatal throw. Ekaterina, thinking faster than Max, tried to tackle the lord of thunder. His strength was greater than hers, but she was far enough above the human norm to keep him from throwing before the dragon landed with a building-rocking thud.

Thor tossed Ekaterina aside and tried again, but this time Freya interfered.

"The beast is not attacking. Let us see what it wants." Thor looked angry with her, even angrier with Ekaterina, and just generally outraged at not being able to kill the dragon—but he stayed his hand.

"Lord Dragon, what is it you wish of us?" asked Freya.

"I wish the maiden in black," rumbled the dragon, raising a claw to indicate Ekaterina. "Give her to me, and I will let you depart in peace."

"Let us?" Thor's hammer sparked, but this time it was Freyr who restrained him.

"The beast is too close," Freyr whispered. "It might breathe fire upon us before you could strike it."

Ekaterina stepped forward. "I will go with you willingly, DL."

The dragon's forehead wrinkled beneath the scales as if it didn't understand her. "Di-El?" it asked. "My name is Di-El?"

"Yes, it is. There is much else about you that I could reveal if you give me a chance."

Ekaterina was smiling, but was she jumping the gun a little? Max couldn't interpret the dragon's expression, but he didn't see any sign of recognition in those giant red eyes. If the dragon wanted Ekaterina, it was not because the DL part of it remembered her. As far as he could tell, it might be just as likely that it wanted to eat her.

The dragon's enormous black claw reached toward Ekaterina. Max wanted to scream, but Ekaterina didn't even flinch.

"Before we go, let me suggest that you take Max as well."

Ekaterina spoke in a surprisingly casual tone. Max froze when the dragon's eyes stared into his. There was still no trace of recognition.

"I have no need of him." The dragon snorted and shifted his attention back to Ekaterina. Either it really wasn't interested in eating human flesh, or Max looked too scrawny to be worth it.

"There is a power source that could make you even stronger than you are," said the vampire. One of the reasons you don't remember anything is that the power source is now scattered. Part of it may still be within you. The other two parts are within me and within Max. Only if the three of us are together is there any hope that you can access that power."

The dragon snorted and looked back at Max. "By the look of him, he has a little magic, but I see no great power source, no more than I do in you."

"You wouldn't be able to see it, for it is faint. When the power is reunited, then you will see it easily."

Max became uncomfortably aware that Thor and Freyr were moving slowly in opposite directions, one toward the dragon's left and the other toward its right. Could they be planning to attack it from both sides? No good would come of that, but if Max tried to warn them off, the dragon would realize what they were up to and might attack.

Freya must also have spotted Thor and Freyr moving into an attack position. Looking unhappy, she moved closer to the dragon. Both Freyr and Thor tried to wave her back, but she kept going until she was standing right next to Ekaterina.

The dragon's eyes narrowed. "And what of you? Do you wish to be taken as well?"

"Lord Dragon, I wish only to bestow a parting gift upon my friend if you will be kind enough to allow it."

"What gift?"

"One that will help reunite your power source." From amongst her seidr paraphernalia, she pulled a gold necklace set with highly polished amber. Max was surprised he hadn't noticed it before.

Freya glanced at the dragon, who eyed her suspiciously but said nothing. She put the necklace around Ekaterina's neck and fastened the clasp. As she did so, she leaned close enough to the vampire to whisper to her. Max saw what was happening in time to magically amplify his hearing.

"This is Brisingamen," Freya whispered. "It's a symbol of my power. It can help you if you unlock it. Love is the key."

The dragon was looking at them so intently that it must have been able to hear even the whisper, but if so, it said nothing. Freya's words were cryptic enough not to seem like a threat to it.

Freyr looked worried, and Thor looked appalled, but neither of them made a move. Freya was still standing right in the line of dragon fire.

The dragon reached out an eager claw for Ekaterina. Very slowly, it extended the other one for Max. Freya stepped back slightly but kept herself close enough to keep Freyr and Thor from getting any aggressive ideas.

Max froze again. One casual squeeze of that claw would crush him.

On the other hand, was he really willing to let Ekaterina go off with this dragon alone? Was he willing to give up any hope of getting back the original DL?

Trying not to shake, he walked as quickly as he could toward the waiting claw. Moving more slowly would give him more time for second thoughts.

As soon as he stood in its palm, the claw closed.

In the distance, someone screamed. It sounded like Outcast, but the claw held him too tightly for him to look and see.

The dragon roared loudly enough to shake the ground, then took off. Thor cursed, but, though the hammer shook and sparked in his hand, he didn't throw it.

That looked as if it could be the last luck Max would have for a long, long time.

WINGS OF LOVE

THE DRAGON ROSE into the air so fast that Max's ears popped from the altitude change. Looking down at the motion-blurred scenery made him dizzy. He managed to turn his head enough to stare at the side of the dragon's head. It looked so unlike the dragon DL had changed into months ago that Max had a hard time keeping his doubt from getting out of control.

As the dragon accelerated, the air was torn out of Max's lungs, and he struggled for breath. Would the beast kill them by accident? No, Ekaterina didn't need air to survive. It would just kill Max. If that happened, he doubted the dragon would even care.

The dragon slowed, and breathing became easier. Was it trying to accommodate Max? Either way, the cold wind still knifed him clear to the bone. Warming himself up with magic was tricky while he was in constant motion. A combination of a spell to warm the air and one to pull the warm air after him was better than nothing.

The trip lasted hours. Max could sense when they left Helheim, but he had no idea where they were going, nor any inclination to ask the dragon.

Ekaterina, more comfortable with the beast, was not as hesitant. "Lord Dragon, where are you taking us?"

"I seek a place for my lair," he rumbled. "An uninhabited place would be best until I come into my full power—which, with your help, will be soon."

Was that confidence in the dragon's tone or a threat? If he and Ekaterina couldn't deliver the power she had promised, Max had no doubt the dragon would burn them to a crisp.

Max was no expert on the Nine Worlds, but Maeve had mentioned them to him in passing when she introduced him to the study of runes. He learned enough to know that none of them were uninhabited, though any of them could have isolated areas the dragon might find usable. However, the vast areas the dragon would have to search might leave Max close to starvation by the time it found just the right spot.

Nor would Max's problems be over when the dragon found its spot. If it wanted to make its lair in Niflheim, Max could freeze. If in Muspelheim, Max and Ekaterina might both roast. There were also the frost and fire giants to consider, as well as the regular giants if the dragon picked Jotunheim. There were many other undesirable alternatives—too many for Max to keep track of in his dizzy and frightened brain.

The dragon slowed to a leisurely glide. Max giggled with relief at the sight of dark mountains below them. The mountains looked shadowy, even sinister—but they were a place to land.

By the look of the place, it could be somewhere in Nidavellir, the gloomy home of the duergar, the dwarf craftsmen who fashioned weapons like Thor's hammer and Odin's spear. They weren't universally good in the Norse stories, but they weren't invariably evil, either. Like the dark elves, they lived underground, and they had a reputation for greed, but unlike the dark elves, they weren't in a state of constant war with the forces of light.

The dragon glided into an enormous cave high up on one of the mountains and probably well away from any duergar colony. That made any unwanted encounters unlikely.

Of course, it also made escape unlikely. But Max's only exit from certain death was to revive the real DL. That much was clear to him the moment he stepped into the dragon's claw.

The dragon sniffed around. "The cave is empty," he said, letting go of

Max and Ekaterina in what—based on its previous behavior—was a reasonably gentle way.

"I shall return with food," it rumbled. It flew off in a gale-force blast.

Max conjured up a little light and looked around suspiciously. The cave was deeper than he thought, and he didn't try to walk all the way to the end of it. He did go far enough to satisfy himself that the dragon was right—there were no obvious critter roommates to worry about.

Ekaterina chuckled. "The presence of a dragon would scare away any small creatures—or big ones, for that matter. It has to be at the top of the animal food chain."

"Speaking of food, the dragon at least remembered we have to eat. That's a good sign, right?"

"You can't make yourself think of him as DL, can you?"

Max sighed. "I hope DL's in there just as much as you do. What we're dealing with right now is not DL, though. He doesn't remember us —or himself—at all. He doesn't act anything like he used to, even the one time he became an Eastern dragon."

"Yet he doesn't really behave like a Western one, either. I'm no expert, but remember my grandfather and father were both part of the Ordo Draconum, and tales about dragons were popular at the time, even though nobody really believed in dragons anymore.

"Western dragons are evil. One would be more likely to fight with Hel's dead army than against it as he apparently did. Also, he didn't attack our hosts like some mindless killing machine. He asked for me relatively politely—for a dragon, anyway."

"There are a lot of stories about dragons holding beautiful women prisoner, though. That seems right in character."

"I thought about that. Do you remember any Norse myths like that, though? I can't think of a single one."

Max had studied Norse mythology in freshman year of high school, and he had to admit he couldn't remember a single princess and dragon kind of story.

"Wait a minute," he said, his eyes widening. "I remember DL talking once about a fairy tale he'd heard when he was young about a dragon holding a princess captive."

Ekaterina smiled. "Do you see? DL has to be in there. If this dragon were behaving as dictated by the instincts of his Norse kin, he would be interested in eating me or killing me, not keeping me as some kind of prize. That behavior comes from DL remembering that story."

Max didn't want to say what he was thinking, which was that Ekaterina was grasping at straws. Instead, he asked her about the necklace.

"I sense it has magic," she replied. "Vampires can do that, but we can't usually tell what kind of magic. Do you have any ideas?"

"I wish I'd had more practice. I can see some magic, but I can't really tell what it does, either. I remember from reading Norse myths that Freya was a goddess of love and fertility."

Ekaterina sighed. "Well, if this is fertility magic, it's not going to do me any good, but she did mention love was the key. However, I've been feeling love for DL the whole time, and the necklace has done nothing."

"Norse myths aren't going to be much help there," said Max. "Brisingamen pops up in one or two of them, and it's clearly very valuable, but what it does is never described. Wait, Freya said it was fashioned by the duergar, and I think we're in Nidavellir right now. We might be able to find out what it does from them."

"If we weren't high up in the mountains. They're underground, are they not?"

"Yes, but *underground* could mean right beneath our feet. It doesn't have to mean below sea level." Max closed his eyes and let his mind wander downward. If there were duergar nearby, they were using concealment to avoid detection—and that seemed unlikely in their own realm.

"No one close as far as I can tell." Max looked nervously in the direction of the cave entrance. "Shouldn't the dragon be back by now?"

"I didn't see many signs of animal life outside," said Ekaterina. "He might have had to fly some distance to find something we could eat. He might have had to eat, too. Dragons are big, so it stands to reason they'd have to consume a great quantity of food."

"Speaking of food, I haven't seen you drink blood in hours, or…well, however long we've been in the Nine Worlds, actually, except that one time you used DL's blood to heal when I was still in his body. I know DL might not be happy with the idea, but you can have a bit of mine if you need it."

Ekaterina frowned. "You know, I don't feel the thirst at all. I think the Yeouiju has been feeding me on its energy—just as it would be feeding DL's dragon powers if it were whole again."

"Is that a good thing or a bad thing?" asked Max. "I know that isn't what it's designed for."

"I feel fine, and it isn't complaining. Actually, it's silent at the moment, but it seems fine, too. Its power level is remaining constant, anyway.

"Oh, it just occurred to me how to use Brisingamen's magic. My love for DL isn't working by itself. If we could awaken DL's love for me, I think the combination might bring the necklace to life. Freya did say love was the key. Might we be able to restore DL with it?"

That seemed like a reach to Max, but rather than say that, he decided to switch to a safer topic. "How do we go about doing that?"

"The Yeouiju is the best way. I'm certain of it. It wasn't able to reach him before, but perhaps you can use your magic to amplify its power somehow. I'm sure the part of it that is within him must still be there."

Max wasn't at all sure that was true, but there was no harm in trying. *"Yeouiju, can you reach the part of you that is within DL?"*

"I still feel nothing, Not My Master."

"Can you work together with the part of you in Ekaterina to try harder? Use my magic to boost your signal, maybe?"

"Perhaps, but it will take time."

Max felt a faint tingling as the Yeouiju did what it could to collaborate with the part of it inside Ekaterina.

"Any luck?" he asked.

"I do not know what luck is. I do know that it is best for me to work uninterrupted."

"I guess that's its way of telling me not to ask for status reports," said Max.

Ekaterina nodded. "It will tell us when there is something to tell. Perhaps exploring the cave will occupy us until it reports."

Max shrugged and followed her lead. They walked deeper into the cave than he had during his vermin check. The place wasn't exactly a spelunker's dream. Though high-ceilinged and deep, it was remarkably featureless.

"I think this cave is manmade—or duergar made. The walls look too smooth to be natural," said Max.

"In that case, why did they make it? There is no sign of—"

"*I can feel my master, though just barely. My master is getting closer.*"

"*Can you join with the part of you that is within him?*" asked Max.

"*I think so.*"

"*I'll signal you when I want you to try.*"

Enormous wings flapped, and a thud shook the cave. Max and Ekaterina rushed back to where the dragon had left them. As soon as they appeared, it dropped a couple of mountain goat carcasses in front of them, then used a light burst of its breath to cook them whole. The sight was enough to make veganism look much more attractive.

"You are a sorcerer?" asked the dragon, noticing the light floating near Max.

"I am, though not a very experienced one. Would you like to see a trick?"

The dragon snorted but did not say no.

"*Now, Yeouiju!*"

The tingling in Max's head escalated to an all-consuming psychic throbbing as the part of the Yeouiju within him bonded as closely as it could with the part in Ekaterina. The throbbing became an incessant, frantic drum beat as the Yeouiju reached toward the dragon subtly but rapidly. The creature blinked, then looked accusingly at Max.

"What are you doing?" it roared.

"Getting your power source back together, just as Ekaterina promised. Be patient for a few minutes."

Max had no idea whether the process would take a few minutes, a few hours—or fail completely. He wasn't going to let the dragon pick up that vibe, though.

The Yeouiju probed deeper and deeper into the dragon's mind. Max got flashes of its savage thoughts, but the connection didn't feel complete. The drumbeat became a jackhammer. The dragon's thoughts burned in Max's mind the way its breath would have burned his body.

The Yeouiju connection to its dragon should have been smooth and natural. This attempt was forced, twisted, the ultimate jamming of a square peg into a round hole.

"Stop!" Max tried to scream but only managed a whisper, and the Yeouiju ignored him. He was picking up some of its thoughts. Having come this close to reconnecting with its master, it wouldn't stop.

It didn't understand the limitations of nondraconic flesh and blood. Max tried to make it understand, but it responded with blank incomprehension.

He shuddered toward unconsciousness, knowing he might never wake up.

The sensation of brain-crushing overload faded as rapidly as it had struck. The Brisingamen began to shine, soft gold at first, then brighter gold, then blindingly brilliant white. Ekaterina, looking more like a goddess than a vampire, reached out to the dragon.

"DL! DL, come back to me!" She took one step toward him, then another.

The dragon roared in pain. It fell to the cave floor and writhed, sending shock waves through the stone that escalated to a small earthquake. The ground shook, and dust fell from the cave roof. Ekaterina and Max fell, but the Yeouiju kept pushing farther and farther into the dragon's brain, insinuating itself into every nook and cranny of gray matter.

Ekaterina managed to stand despite the tremors and reached out to the dragon again. The Brisingamen was like a miniature sun by now, though Max wasn't completely blinded by it.

Dust hit him in the face, and he blinked repeatedly. Looking up, he could see cracks forming in the ceiling. Most were hairline, but a few already looked like giant fissures. A chunk of rock hit the ground next to his foot.

Another shockwave through him against the wall. Crunching sounds loud as gunshots filled the air as more fragments broke loose right above him.

DREAMING THE IMPOSSIBLE DREAM

"WE NEED TO STOP!" yelled Max. The floor was shaking too much for him to stand up. He had to keep rolling back and forth to avoid getting hit by increasingly large rock fragments.

"We almost have him! I can feel it!" Ekaterina yelled back.

Max could feel something, too, but it might have been feedback from Ekaterina's wishful thinking. The dragon continued to writhe on the floor. There was no sign of any returning consciousness that it had once been DL. It could obviously feel the Yeouiju's questing tentacles twitching through it—and it must not have liked that sensation. That was all Max could be sure of.

The dragon jumped to its feet with an echoing crash, and roared, "I am not Di-El! I am not!"

The Yeouiju was getting to him, but the new dragon persona was giving it one hell of a fight.

The dragon fell over again, and this time Max was sure the ceiling was going to collapse. The falling rocks kept getting bigger, and the ceiling was webbed with cracks and fissures.

A distant crash echoed through the cave, and a cloud of dust blew from the direction the entrance used to be. Max reached into the surrounding rock with his mind. Could he hold it together well enough to prevent complete collapse? The cracks already extended far into the mountain. He could feel them widen and deepen with each tremor of the dragon.

Ekaterina moved closer to the convulsive beast one slow step at a time. Watching her get so close was like watching someone fall off a cliff. She was only feet away from a monster that could crush her in a single twitch.

"Stay back!" yelled Max.

"I…can't," Ekaterina's voice shook almost as much as her body. She took another step.

A flailing dragon leg swept over her. Had it been a couple feet lower, it would have taken off her head.

The dragon convulsed again. Somehow, Ekaterina stayed on her feet. She glared at the ground as if willing it to be still.

The dragon's movements became less spasmodic and more like a continuous, heavy vibration. The rapidly disintegrating cave throbbed in unison with the dragon's distress as if it were an extension of the beast's massive heart.

Max's magic gripped a small part of the cave roof from where he was to where Ekaterina was. It was more splinters than stones—and tons of unstable rock were above it. He gritted his teeth, determined to hold it together as long as he could.

Ekaterina took another labored step and stretched as far as she could. Her fingertips barely touched the dragon. The moment her skin touched his scale, the beast stilled so completely that it looked frozen in time. The light from Brisingamen expanded until the two of them were completely surrounded by it.

The ensuing explosion of brilliance forced Max to close his eyes. Even through his eyelids, the brightness was painful.

The light faded, and he opened his eyes. The dragon remained calm —though it also remained a dragon. No, not quite. It looked in Max's direction, and the recognition shone in its—his—eyes. DL was back—at least in spirit.

Ekaterina was holding one of DL's claws and sobbing with relief. DL looked away from Max and back to her. He blinked several times as if he wasn't sure what was happening. He leaned down awkwardly to kiss her, and his eyes widened in shock.

"I'm…I'm still a dragon!" He didn't sound happy about it.

"One thing at a time," said Ekaterina in her most soothing voice. "With the help of the Yeouiju and Freya's magic, we have brought back your mind. Given time, I'm sure we can restore your body as well."

DL looked down at his body. "I'm a monster! How can you even look at me?"

"And I'm a vampire. How can you even look at me?"

"That's different," said DL. "You're beautiful."

"And do you love me only for my beauty?"

"Of course not!" He was beginning to sound defensive.

"Then why would you think I love you only for your looks? I love *you*, DL, not just the particular physical form you happen to inhabit."

Max wanted to join the reunion, but he paused long enough to check the condition of the ceiling. It had lost so much of its stone that it was like geological Swiss cheese. It wouldn't collapse immediately—unless DL sneezed—but he couldn't afford to let go of it. He longed to make it whole again, but he lacked the magic to do that. The best he could do was set in motion a slow-moving spell that would fuse the stone together, eliminating the most threatening cracks. To give that spell time to work, he made the magic holding the stone in place self-sustaining—at least, that's what he hoped he'd done. He was dangerously close to exhaustion, so he had less power to spare for the spells than he would have liked.

Max got to his feet and hobbled over to DL, who was still fretting over his transformation.

"You look a little fiercer than you did as an Asian dragon, and your scales are black instead of green, but otherwise you look pretty much the same. You weren't horrified by your appearance then."

"That's because I knew I could change back. Now I try, and nothing happens."

"That's just temporary," said Ekaterina. Her optimism sounded a little forced to Max, but it was still better than the pessimism he was keeping tightly bottled up inside.

"Who is it that intrudes in our domain?" asked a loud, harsh voice behind them. Max turned to see that a large party of duergar had sneaked up on them while they were preoccupied with DL.

Though they were somewhat shorter than Max, what they lacked in height, they made up for in muscle mass. Not that he could see their muscles very clearly. Most of them were heavily armored, and all of them carried impressively sharp battleaxes or long swords that sparkled in the glow from Max's light.

The one who had challenged them stood proudly in the front row. Both his armor and his crown were golden, as was his ax. Gold wouldn't normally be a practical material for weapons, but these glistened with the magic that had been forged into them.

"A dragon!" one of the duergars yelled. All of their eyes focused on DL, and they all raised their shields.

"Yes, he is a dragon," said Max, "but he is unlike any you have ever seen. He means you no harm."

The duergar king snorted. "No harm? He shook this whole mountain. Very nearly brought it down on our heads."

"That was an accident," said DL. Like all of his words while he was in dragon form, it was a roar, and the duergar raised their axes. The weapons were tiny compared to their intended target—but each one had been forged with magic, and there were a lot of them.

"He is a good dragon," Max protested. Despite how tense they were, the duergar warriors laughed at that.

"There is no such thing," said the king. "All dragons are evil—but at least most of them stay and their lairs and do not trouble us. That this one invades our territory is an ill sign indeed."

"I can prove our words are true," said Ekaterina. "I carry a token from Freya herself." She held up Brisingamen, which glowed as if she had commanded it to.

The king squinted at it. "That must be a copy of some kind. Freya would never part with Brisingamen—unless perhaps the dragon took it by force."

"She gave it freely," Ekaterina insisted. "I can prove my words in trial by combat."

"You challenge me to a holmang?" The king looked her over incredulously. "You are a woman—and unarmed at that. How could you hope to prevail?" He squinted at her. "There are at least two types of magic about you, but I recognize neither. Is this some kind of trick?"

"The magic keeps me alive," said Ekaterina.

"It does more than that," said the king.

"What if it does? Surely it could never do enough to make an unarmed woman a match for a duergar king? Unless, of course, the reputation of the duergars has been much exaggerated. I wonder—is that the reason why you hide underground?"

The king waved his battle ax at her. "Were you a man, you would lose your head for that!"

"Though I am a woman, you may have it—if you can take it. As for me, I will be content to call myself the victor if you yield to me or are rendered unconscious. Agreed?"

"What are you doing?" Max asked.

"Trust me," replied Ekaterina.

"I agree—provided neither the dragon nor the sorcerer interferes. They must also agree that they are mine to do with as I please if you lose."

Max's heart pounded like a drum. It wasn't that he didn't trust Ekaterina, but the duergar king was bound to be a formidable fighter, and his armor and ax were both enchanted.

If a dragon could look unhappy, DL did. Nonetheless, he roared his agreement. Max had little choice at that point. He agreed as well—though he dreaded the outcome.

"You and your men must likewise agree to respect the outcome," said the vampire. "If I win, my friends and I will be allowed to depart in peace."

"Done," said the king. The duergar warriors roared their agreement.

"Ready?" said the king. Ekaterina nodded.

The king's battle cry wasn't as loud as DL's roar, but it was strong enough to echo frighteningly in the confined space. He charged, readying his ax to strike. Ekaterina stood still until the last second, then dodged his first stroke, his second, his third. The king roared and swung with all his might, but still the vampire dodged him.

Elves, like faeries, could move faster than the human norm. Max suspected the duergar could as well. The problem was that they had come heavily armored. That was bound to slow the king down.

The warriors grumbled and shifted uneasily from one foot to the other. Their faces betrayed little emotion, but they frowned slightly every time one of the king's blows missed its mark.

"The woman is more of a fighter than she appears," muttered one of them to the warrior standing next to him. He raised his ax as he spoke, making him look more like a combatant than a spectator.

"It is as it is," said the other, placing a restraining hand on his ax handle. "We are sworn to respect the outcome—whatever it may be."

Ekaterina slipped around the king as he lunged at her, leaving him off-balance. She tripped him, and he fell with a resounding crash. The duergars mumbled unhappily, but they fell silent when, instead of taking advantage of the king's vulnerability, she stepped back and allowed him to struggle to his feet.

The king struck with more calculation, but it did him little good. His stance prevented Ekaterina from tripping him, but she still slipped around him, this time striking him in the side with her fists hard enough to jolt him despite his armor. The armor itself wasn't dented, but the king's pained expression suggested the skin beneath the armor was badly bruised.

Ekaterina's fists were bruised as well, and the left looked as if at least some finger bones were broken, but they healed fast enough to make the duergars close enough to see the fight gasp. Had the Yeouiju found a way to boost Ekaterina's regeneration?

The ax whooshed through the air as the king gave his hardest swing yet. Max's heart skipped a beat. Ekaterina wasn't moving!

The vampire threw herself out of the way at the last second—too late for the king to adjust. His ax blade hit the cave floor with a crack as loud as a gunshot and drove deep into the stone. He pulled with all his might, but ax shifted only slightly.

The king let go of the ax handle and turned toward Ekaterina.

"I yield." He yelled loudly enough to be heard by all of his warriors.

"Majesty, you are not beaten!" protested the one who had raised his ax.

"Aye, but I am enough of a strategist to know when defeat is inevitable," said the king. "Also, I am wise enough to perceive the truth of her words. No ordinary dragon would agree to leave his fate to a holmang. He would have attacked us instead. These strangers speak the truth!

"I am Sindr, king of the duergar, and you are welcome here in my kingdom."

"I am Ekaterina, princess of the Wallachians. This is Max...sorcerer of Eau Claire, and this is DL, dragon of the East."

"I would invite you to my hall, but there are many narrow passageways between here and there through which a dragon could not hope to pass. Is there perhaps something I could offer you by way of hospitality before you go?"

"Majesty, information is what we need most," said Max.

The king frowned. "Information is a bit more...expensive than what I had in mind." Apparently, the duergar reputation for greed was not exaggerated.

"King Sindr, we are on a very complicated quest," roared DL. "We seek a fugitive, a magic book, and hostages that may or may not be in Helheim. We have a serious need for information on any or all of those subjects. How much gold would you require?"

Sindr's eyes widened. "That is a great deal of information indeed. I fear it would take my weight in gold."

"Done!" said DL as if the king had asked for a pile of rocks.

"Do you know what you're doing?" asked Max.

"Apparently, Western dragons can smell gold—from miles away if need be" replied DL. *"I can give him what he wants, and then some!"*

"Uh, I seem to have accidentally sealed the cave mouth earlier," said DL. "It will take me time to remove the fallen rock. Perhaps my friends can explain what we need while I work."

"Of course," said Sindr. "By the time you return with the gold, I will be ready with such answers as I have."

That didn't exactly sound like a money-back guarantee if the king had no answers, but DL plodded away as if everything was fine. It wasn't likely the duergars would try to cheat a dragon—or so Max hoped.

With DL gone, Sindr could theoretically have invited Max and Ekaterina into his hall—but he didn't. Instead, he called for food, drink, a table and chairs to be brought from somewhere. They appeared so fast that Max was suspicious magic was somehow involved, but he didn't see any obvious sign of it.

Despite being served by a king, the meal was far from the best Max had ever had. Even though he was hungry, he could only get so excited about boiled mountain goat and dried fruits. From what he had seen, not much vegetation grew in the immediate area, so the duergars had to import fruit and vegetables from somewhere else. The same must have been true of the mead, which Max sipped very carefully. This time he wasn't in DL's alcohol-resistant body, and he needed to keep his mind sharp.

The meal was even more awkward for Ekaterina, who nibbled a little to avoid appearing impolite. She even pretended to enjoy it, though she had once told Max she couldn't really taste anything except blood, and nothing else provided any nourishment for her.

Sindr and a few others, probably his advisers, sat with them while Max explained their desperate situation. The king tried to maintain a poker face but became more and more agitated as the story progressed.

"This Amadan Dubh is dangerous indeed," said Sindr at one point. "We have long accepted the inevitability of Ragnarok, but Nidavellir is not destined to be destroyed, and those worlds that are, such as Midgard and Asgard, will be restored once the war ends. Who knows what will happen if Dubh interferes too much? Perhaps all nine of the worlds will be destroyed. Perhaps none of them will be restored. There is no way to tell."

"From what I have seen, Dubh wants what he wants and doesn't care what he has to do to anyone else to get it," said Max. "He has Hel convinced that the outcome of Ragnarok can be changed, and she seems determined to provoke its early start, with or without his help. Before that, he aided the dark alfar to start a war with the light alfar that resulted in many deaths on both sides."

Sindr frowned. "Those Dökkálfar are not to be trusted. It doesn't surprise me they would align themselves with someone like Dubh.

"Centuries ago, they tried to invade our land. We might have accepted them as settlers in—and below—the flatlands, but they wanted to rule all of Nidavellir. They even tried to rename it Svartálfaheim. As for us, we would have been their slaves—or worse. Only our superior digging ability enabled us to triumph underground, and the Dökkálfar, who could not live above ground because of the daylight, were forced to flee."

The table and dishes vibrated with DL's steps. "Majesty, I have your gold. You may inspect it whenever you have the time."

"There is always time for gold," said Sindr, winking at his guests. "Let us all go and see what our dragon friend has brought us."

The duergars moved quickly toward their reward with Max and Ekaterina following behind them.

The duergars could see in the dark, as could Ekaterina, but Max kept his light with him. He was glad he had done that, instead of giving himself dark vision, because the gold looked even more spectacular in the glow.

"I hope I did not bring too much," said DL, winking at Max and Ekaterina. "You asked for your weight in gold, but I wasn't sure how much you weighed."

After clearing the fallen rock from the cave entrance, DL had dug up enough gold to reseal the opening twice over. It was lying in large chunks along both cave walls. Even the duergar were awestruck by the display.

"I have seen much gold in my time," said Sindr. "Never have I seen so much assembled so quickly. You can have all I know that might conceivably aid you in your quest—and more."

"We appreciate any help you can provide," said Max. "You've heard our story. What can you tell us that might be helpful?"

"Let us begin with the most important," said Sindr. "If this Dubh really means to honor his agreement with Hel and provoke Ragnarok early, there is one place he must visit—the very spot where the trickster Loki is imprisoned.

"The great wolf, Fenrir, and the Midgard Serpent are both children of Loki and will see his liberation as a signal to attack Asgard. So will the frost and fire giants. Loki himself will lead Hel's army of the dead, for she too is his child. I can see no other way for Dubh to succeed with his plan."

"How could Dubh get into this prison?" asked Ekaterina. "Surely, it is guarded, is it not?"

"It is warded by powerful spells, as are the chains with which Loki is bound," said Sindr. "Both will fail at the moment Ragnarok is destined to begin—or so the prophecy says. If this Dubh, armed with Merlin's book, is as powerful as you say, he might be able to break those protections earlier. Those charms are supposed to be immune to manipulation by seidr, but they may not be as durable against magic from a completely different plane.

"Of course, I know not how different his magic truly is, but if I were you, I would not take the chance. At any rate, that prison is where you will find him sooner or later—and surely, the book will be with him. Strike well, and in one stroke you can achieve two of your objectives at once."

"That's great information," said Max. "What about the hostages?"

"Alas, there is no reason Dubh would bring them with him," said Sindr. "They are likely still in Hel's domain somewhere."

"The place is vast," said Ekaterina. "Can you offer advice on finding them?"

"No magic is likely to help if Hel is determined to keep them secret, but remember your approach in sniffing out the one you call Outcast? Your dragon was not then in his right mind, to judge by your story, but his sense of smell should be equally acute—and over a much wider area."

"That makes sense," said DL, sniffing as if he could smell them even from another world. "May I ask one more thing?"

"Of course," replied Sindr, the nearby gold glittering in his eyes.

"Perhaps my friends have told you that this is not my natural form. Do you know a way to return me to my original state?"

"I cannot be sure, for such a thing has never been attempted in all of the Nine Worlds. There have been a few men who became dragons, usually as a result of greed, but no one has ever tried to turn a dragon into a man."

"Freya's magic helped restore your mind," said Ekaterina. "Perhaps she can help."

"If there were a way to get the dragon king your friends told me of here, he and Freya together might be able to provide the answer you seek," said Sindr. "You have both Eastern and Norse magic within you, so it stands to reason that you need practitioners of both to set you right."

"Eastern, Norse, and Celtic," said DL. "Maeve tried to empower me using Balder's strength."

"My grandmother is responsible for this mess?" asked Max. He felt a twinge of guilt, even though he knew that wasn't logical.

"She warned me it could be dangerous," said DL. "I'm the one who took the risk."

"Balder's strength?" asked Sindr. "How is such a thing possible? And why would it miscarry in such a way? We duergar have our reasons to dislike some of the Aesir, but even we have not a single word to say against Balder. He was the best of the Aesir by far—and will be again after Ragnarok, when he is freed at last from death."

"Balder is as good as you say," replied DL. "He just couldn't visualize such a thing as a good dragon. Without meaning to, he transformed me into the one kind of dragon he was familiar with—evil.

"As for the other part, Celtic magic provides a way to share strength. Maeve should have been in control, but I guess Balder's strength was too great for her to channel as well as she thought she could."

"We have no way to get the dragon king here, but perhaps Freya, Maeve, and Balder could work out the problem," said Ekaterina. "They are probably still relatively close together in Helheim, and DL could fly us there quickly."

"No," said Sindr with surprising vehemence. "You must stop the Amadan Dubh first. Even now, he may be nibbling away at the defenses of Loki's prison. If he succeeds in releasing the trickster and starting Ragnarok early, who knows what may happen? Such a blatant break in our destiny may destroy the Nine Worlds—and all of you with them.

"DL can fly you to Helheim must faster than you could reach it in any other way, but rescuing the hostages would still take hours at best, days at worst. That is more than enough time for Dubh to work his evil."

"Even if the outcome isn't that cataclysmic, Sindr is right," said DL. "Dubh needs to be our first priority. I'm not happy being like this any longer than I have it be, but I'll live."

"Well said!" replied the king, looking intently at Max and Ekaterina in a way that suggested the subject was no longer open for debate.

"Where can we find Loki's prison?" asked Max.

"It was placed in Midgard while the Aesir could still reach it."

"You mean it is somewhere on Earth?" asked Ekaterina.

"No, when the Aesir and the rest of us lost the ability to travel to Midgard, a sort of copy of it appeared to keep the Nine Worlds in balance. Locations like Loki's prison remained with the copy rather than the real Midgard. Seek the highest mountain you can find. At the top of it is a large hall with four doors, built so that Loki could see his enemies coming from any direction. That didn't help him, however, and he was captured. The Aesir took him to a cave somewhere in the mountain beneath his four-doored hall. There he is chained, and a serpent drips venom on his face. His wife, Sigyn, puts a bowl in between him and the serpent to catch the venom, but he still gets a few drops every time she has to empty the bowl."

"It is the cave that is warded against magic, right?" asked Max.

"Yes, I'm sure none but the Aesir can enter. However, we know the spell is flawed. All Dubh has to do is get it to fail earlier than it was destined to."

"Then we should head for Midgard as soon as possible," said DL. "If there is only one spell, I have a hard time believing it will hold off Dubh for long."

"Before you depart, I have some equipment that may help. Lady Ekaterina, formidable as you are, I cannot help but think you would be even more formidable with a proper weapon." He gestured, and two of his men stepped forward with a sword and scabbard. "This sword cuts far better than any mortal blade. Had we the time, I could craft one designed specifically for defeating the Amadan Dubh, but I fear what we have at hand will have to do. It has been crafted from cold-forged steel and marked with runes that will make it especially deadly to one of faerie blood, as well as disruptive to faerie magic."

"That's an excellent gift, Majesty," said Max. "Unfortunately, I have some faerie blood. Will it disrupt my magic as well?"

"Only if she wields it against you," said Sindr. "It respects the intent of its wielder."

"How could you have crafted such a thing so quickly?" asked Ekaterina.

Sindr chuckled. "I would like to claim I could just snap my fingers and produce such a weapon, but in truth, we have had it a long time. We crafted a few such weapons during the war between the alfar and the fey in Elphame, but the war ended before they could be used."

"I will endeavor to be worthy of such a blade," said Ekaterina as she bowed to the king.

"I have no doubt of that," said Sindr. "We have not forgotten you, either, Max. I'm afraid you too must settle for what we have on hand, but I do not think you will be disappointed."

Sindr gestured, and one of his men stepped forward with a highly polished wood staff that looked just like the one Freya used for seidr. Runes were carved deeply into it, and it was capped by a bronze ball inlaid with jewels. Though the craftsmanship was excellent, what really drew Max's eye was the amount of magic pulsing in the wood. The staff might not be as strongly enchanted as Merlin's grimoire—but it was close.

"No sorcerer should be without a staff," said Sindr. "I could not help noticing you lack one." The king took the staff and held it out for Max.

The nearer it got, the more Max could feel its power. It was immeasurably old—and immeasurably tempting. Part of him longed to hold that power, to wield it against Dubh. Another part of him wished Sindr had never offered it to him. There was no remotely polite way to decline it, but would it just bring more trouble? Merlin had trusted him with his book, and that had turned out catastrophically.

"It looks as magnificent as all your other craftsmanship, Majesty, but, to be honest, I haven't really learned the use of a staff yet."

Sindr raised an eyebrow. "I hadn't realized you were that young in the craft, but I am doubly honored to be able to present you with your first staff. As for learning its use, fear not. Though experience will make you more adept, yet, like your book of Merlin, the staff has power of its own. The wood is yew from Yggdrasil itself, and the runes were inscribed on it by Freya herself. She likes to have a spare available, and this one was crafted for her use."

"Is…is she going to be upset that you're giving it to me?" asked Max, sounding more worried than he intended to.

"She gave Ekaterina Brisingamen, her most prized possession. Surely, she would not begrudge you a staff, especially not if you succeed in thwarting Dubh. If you fail…well, she will have bigger things to worry about then. If she asks, just tell it was a gift from me.

"Staffs, in general, are used to concentrate and amplify power. Visualize your spell running through the staff, and it will emerge stronger than you could cast it on your own. This particular one, imbued as it is with the life force of Yggdrasil, can also renew your strength if it should wane before your task is done. Take note of the gems set into the bronze at the top. This amber is from the tears of Freya herself, just as the ones on Brisingamen are. It provides balance and harmony, and it can draw on the warmth of the sun if need be. This emerald reinforces order and stability. It could be useful in strengthening the spell over Loki's prison if it is still intact. This jade is for cleansing, and it will make you more resistant to disease. This malachite will ward off physical harm. This moonstone enhances your mind's ability to reach out, both through the seidr trance and in other ways. This diamond amplifies the effects of all the other stones."

"And the runes?" asked Max, getting more wide-eyed by the minute.

"They strengthen runic magic. Just concentrate on the rune or runes related to the magic you are attempting, and the runes on the staff will respond."

"I'm afraid I know little of runic magic," said Max. "Having a staff like this is certainly an incentive to learn, though."

"The staff sounds powerful, as does Freya. I'm surprised she didn't use her own staff to overcome Hel," said Ekaterina.

"In Helheim, Hel will always have the upper hand," said Sindr. "Even so, I think Freya might be nearly her equal with the staff. She is wise, though, and knows defeating Hel might create an imbalance in the Nine Worlds. Certainly, destroying her would do so. If Freya launched an all-out attack against the ruler of the dead, it would be only as a last resort.

"My friends, I wish we could spend a longer time together, but I have detained you as long as I dare."

Sindr pushed the staff in Max's direction. This time the young sorcerer took it from him and bowed. Despite his misgivings, it felt right in his hand.

"I cannot thank you enough, Majesty. I will do everything I can to prove worthy of such a gift."

"I am sure you will. Farewell, my friends."

"Wait, Majesty. I don't know how to find Midgard," said DL.

"I had forgotten for a moment how new you are to the Nine Worlds. How did you find Nidavellir?"

"I wasn't looking for it. I just knew I didn't want to be in Helheim. I searched until I found mountains that had a suitable cave for a lair. The smell of gold helped seal the deal."

Sindr chuckled. "You may have to use your nose again. The geography of the Nine Worlds is difficult to explain. It's not quite as fluid as the inner workings of Helheim, but the ways in which the worlds connect and even how they are located in Yggdrasil's branches would defy any normal map.

"Roughly speaking, Helheim is the lowest point in this plane of existence, and Asgard is the highest. On that everyone agrees. Most people agree that Midgard is somewhere above Nidavellir. If you fly in the same direction you did when you traveled up from Helheim, and if you sniff for your own kind, you will eventually smell another dragon. If the area looks like an icy wasteland, move on, for you are smelling Nidhogg, who dwells in dismal Nifleheim, close to Helheim. If, on the other hand, the area looks more like your own Earth, you are smelling the Midgard Serpent. Avoid making contact with it, for it will be as hostile as Nidhogg. Find the highest mountain, and search from there to find the cave that is Loki's prison."

DL looked skeptical.

"Max, is it just me, or does that seem like searching for a needle in a haystack, even with draconic senses?"

"It won't necessarily be easy, but Sindr has as much reason as we do to want Dubh stopped—more, really. Why would he hold back information?"

"Thank you, Majesty," roared DL.

Max, Ekaterina, and DL said their good-byes and prepared to leave as rapidly as they could. That should have been easy, but now that DL was himself again, he didn't particularly want to carry Max and Ekaterina in his claws.

"There's really no choice," said Max. "If you're flying fast—and you need to be—how will we be able to stay on your back. At least if you hold us, there's no way we'll fall."

"No, you won't fall—but what if something surprises me and causes me to reflexively crush you?"

"When you were just a dragon, you managed to avoid that," said Ekaterina. "I'm sure you can as yourself."

"What if I have to fight? I couldn't use my front claws."

"Who are you going to be fighting?" said Max. "Just stay away from Nidhogg or the Midgard Serpent. No other creature is going to want to take you on."

"There could be other dragons, though, and—"

"Stop worrying so much," said Max. "Yeah, there are dangers. Anything we do at this point is dangerous. Standing around fretting over the future is dangerous. Let's just get on with it."

DL sighed and laid his claws on the cave floor so that Max and Ekaterina could climb in. To make him feel better, they made sure their arms were free. Max gripped his staff and Ekaterina her sword in case of possible attack.

He closed his claws gently around them and took off. His lizard face wasn't easy to read, but to Max, he still looked apprehensive—or was his perception colored by traces of emotion leaking through the Yeouiju connection? Either way, Max hoped it was natural anxiety and not some deep draconic instinct that told DL trouble was on the way.

LOKI'S PRISON

DL HAD NEVER BEEN so conscious of how fragile a human body was. Just a little too much pressure, and even Ekaterina would be a bloody pulp.

Crazy as it sounded, he didn't like having this much power. Sure, he could find Dubh days sooner than he could have as a man. For that matter, Dubh would find him a lot harder to beat in this form.

Aside from the fear of crushing his friends, DL wasn't liking how much saving the world—well, in this case, nine worlds—rested on him. He would much rather have had the kind of allies he had when he took on the Collector. Merlin, the original Lady of the Lake, all four druids of Tír na nÓg—those folks knew what they were doing.

It wasn't that Max didn't. He knew a lot more than DL. However, he had been studying magic for only about a year, not centuries, like the Amadan Dubh.

Yeah, Max had a great new staff—which, by his own admission, he didn't know how to use. Maeve had given him a little background in Norse runes, none at all in seidr. Freya, the expected user of the staff, knew both backwards and forwards.

Nope, as great a person as Max was, he didn't seem likely to save the day. Ekaterina, armed with an anti-faerie sword, might stop Dubh—if she could get within swinging distance of him. Dubh could fly, though, and she couldn't.

The Aesir could lend a lot of firepower, but they were still probably in Helheim hunting for Freyr's wife and the others, and even if they were riding Sleipnir full-speed, they wouldn't necessarily know to head for Loki's prison. DL only knew about Dubh's intentions because of a conversation with Hel he'd had no way to share with the Aesir.

Cool as it had been to be in some ways superhuman from his Eastern draconic heritage, maybe DL wasn't really the superhero type. He longed to be a sidekick in somebody else's story, rather than the hero of his own.

"You guys all right down there?" he asked.

"I'm fine," Ekaterina yelled back.

"Warmer now that I have the staff harnessing sun power for me," yelled Max.

At least they sounded all right. Their voices would have been lost in the wind without DL's draconic hearing, so that was one thing to be thankful for. Of course, if he weren't a dragon, they wouldn't be flying so fast he couldn't hear them.

He had no idea how long they'd been flying. It probably wasn't days, or his passengers would have complained, but it could easily have been hours. He came close to a world of ice and veered away from it, just as Sindr had advised. Much later, he spotted a world that looked a little like Earth viewed from space—if one looked at it from the right angle. These Norse worlds were all disks, and this one did indeed have a giant serpent coiled all the way around it—the Midgard serpent for sure! DL would have known it even without that draconic scent.

Gliding in as quietly as he could so as not to draw the serpent's attention, DL had little trouble finding the high mountain with the four-doored house. There was no sign of Loki's prison, though. Fog so thick he couldn't see anything through it clung to the mountain from just below the summit all the way to the base.

"It's a spell from Merlin's book," said Max. "The fog isn't just hard to see through. It's hard to send my mind through as well. Can you pick up a faerie scent?"

"Yeah, there's one somewhere in there," said DL. "It's hard for me to tell where, though. Maybe I can improve the visibility a little." He flapped his wings hard enough to whip up a gale. The fog continued to cling through the first few flaps, but eventually, quite a bit of it was torn away from the rock.

"Got him!" said Max. "He's at a cave mouth about halfway down."

DL dived toward it, hoping to catch Dubh by surprise.

Just as Sindr had predicted, Dubh was trying to work some magic on the cave entrance. He had managed to not be distracted by the wind, but the flapping of a dragon's wings coming so close was much harder to ignore. The faerie looked up. His eyes widened, all color faded from his face, and his mouth opened as if to scream, though he didn't make a sound.

DL knew the smartest strategy would be to incinerate the faerie with a burst of dragon fire before he had time to weave some magical protection around himself. He still wasn't used to killing, though. So far, he'd only taken lives in kill-or-be-killed situations—and those had mostly been vampires. Did they even count?

The moment's hesitation gave Dubh a chance to fly away at an improbably high speed.

"He's super-speeded himself somehow using Merlin's book!" Max yelled. "Don't let him get away!"

Faeries were natural fliers, but from what little DL had seen in the past, Max was right—this was one hyper-fast faerie! DL flapped with all his might, but Dubh was getting farther and farther away. His body blurred. Snow slid from mountain tops as he screeched by them.

"Max, slow him down!"

"I'm not used to spell-casting at high speeds! There's no way to— wait, that isn't him!"

"You sure? It looks like him." DL stayed at maximum speed just in case.

"We're chasing an illusion. I'd have realized sooner if it hadn't been moving so fast. That means—"

"I know—the real Dubh is still back at the cave."

DL turned at vertigo-inducing speeds, then headed back fast enough to break the sound barrier on Earth. Despite his efforts, it still took a few minutes to return.

There was no sign of Dubh at the cave mouth.

"He's got to be inside! Let us down!" Max had become a lot more confident about giving orders, but DL had little time to be proud of him. He had no problem leaving them on the ledge. The problem was that the cave entrance was too small for him to fit through.

"It's going to take time to get me in there without bringing down the whole mountain," said DL.

"Time we don't have," said Max. Already free of DL's claws, Max and Ekaterina headed for the cave mouth. DL didn't want them going in alone, but there was no way he could stop them from entering without hurting them.

When they reached the entrance, they hit an invisible barrier and bounced back, much to DL's relief.

"He hasn't broken the spell yet," said Ekaterina.

"No, I think he has," said Max. "The barrier feels Celtic, not Norse. After he broke the original spell, he must have put up one of his own to keep anyone from interfering."

"How long have we got?" asked DL.

"I don't know. Depends on how long Dubh's been here. He has to find a way to break Loki's chains. He could have been at it for hours, though. We have to assume he's close to done. I better try to get that barrier down now."

Max raised his new staff and chanted for all he was worth. The gems glowed brightly, and magic crackled from the tip. It snapped and sizzled across the barrier, raising multicolored sparks. Dubh's spell didn't budge an inch.

"Reinforced by the power from Merlin's book!" said Max, disgusted.

"You've got the power of Freya's staff," said Ekaterina. "Shouldn't that be at least as strong?"

"If I knew how to use it better. There hasn't exactly been time to practice. If I could figure out how the spell was constructed, I could counter it more easily, but there's no time to study it, either. I could try brute force."

Max's brow furrowed in concentration. A ray of amber-colored power poured from the staff and struck the barrier. Its brightness escalated rapidly from lightbulb to spotlight to solar flare. The barrier sagged but didn't break.

Max was shaking. The staff glowed vibrant brown as the wood of Yggdrasil lent him energy. The ray brightened again, and the barrier began to shake as if it was about to shatter—until Ekaterina screamed and fell backward, covering her face.

Max stopped casting and ran to her.

"What happened?" said DL, trying to see through Max.

"I was using solar energy, and I must have amped up the power high enough that the Yeoiju couldn't shield her." Max sounded guilty and didn't look DL in the eye.

"Is she all right?" DL didn't know what he'd do with himself if something happened to her.

"I'm all right," said the vampire weakly. "I think I would have been blinded temporarily, but I covered my eyes in time."

DL maneuvered himself into a position from which he could see her. Her hands were red like a bad sunburn. Her face looked much the same. Despite himself, he gasped.

"It's nothing," said Ekaterina, walking over and patting him on the snout. "See, it's healing already."

"I'm so sorry," said Max.

"Don't be," she replied. "You couldn't have known what would happen. I didn't, either."

"We can't try that again, though," said DL quickly. "You might be hurt worse the next time."

"Can you think of a different way in?" asked Ekaterina. "How about a different kind of brute force?"

"I could theoretically use another natural force, like lightning, but the staff isn't specifically attuned to that, at least as far as I can tell. I might not be able to generate enough energy that way."

"Maybe I could knock down the barrier with my fiery breath," suggested DL.

"You could, but you might superheat the rock that way. Ekaterina and I couldn't enter then without burning up—which would sort of defeat the purpose."

"I'm a fool!" said Ekaterina. "Sindr told me this sword disrupts faerie magic, did he not? We should at least give it a try."

"Be careful," said Max. "We don't know how it disrupts a spell. The last thing we need is an explosion."

"I have a very soft touch," said Ekaterina, winking at DL. She drew the blade and ran it gently along the entrance. The runes on the sword glowed red, and the barrier tore with a crackling sound. A few more strokes, and the faerie magic was completely destroyed.

"Now, we just have to figure out how I'm going to be able to get in there and help you," said DL.

"Short of digging a much larger hole in the rock, I don't see how you can," said Max. "Those dragon claws could probably do it fast, but there's no way they could do it quietly. Dubh would be able to open a portal and flee long before you could break through. Don't worry, though—Ekaterina and I can handle him. The gear Sindr gave us should cancel out the advantage Merlin's book gives him."

"If you get into trouble—"

"You can still hear my thoughts, right?"

"Yes, but—"

"How's this?" Max waved the staff a few times, chanted in Irish Gaelic, and DL's whole perspective shifted. He was looking at his own horrendous dragon face—through Max's eyes.

"How'd you do that?"

"We already knew that more than just thoughts can flow through those channels. With a little help from the Yeouiju, I've worked it out so that you can see and hear what's going on from my perspective. That way you'll know everything is OK."

"Great," thought DL. He wasn't satisfied, but what choice did he have? Max was right about Dubh being able to escape if he had too much warning, and there wasn't any quiet way to get DL into the cave.

Through Max's eyes, he watched as Max and Ekaterina crept quietly down a surprisingly long cave. Every step carried them deeper into the mountain.

DL felt something stir inside him. It was more than just concern for his friends. A warning from some draconic instinct? No, it wasn't that.

Something was looking out at him from the depths of his own mind.

Ekaterina hadn't completely banished the evil dragon persona that came with his current body. It had just been asleep, or stunned, or even comatose. Now it was squirming inside of him, longing to be in control.

Max and Ekaterina might need him. Even if they defeated Dubh with no problem, he was their only way out of Midgard.

Ekaterina could probably stabilize him, but he'd have to call her back out of the mountain. The tunnel she and Max were in was widening, meaning they must be close to Loki's prison. It was too late for her to help him. He'd have to hold on somehow until she got back.

How had she saved him? Through love. He tried to visualize that love, to remember their best times together, to feel her in his arms even though she was separated from him by tons of rock.

The beast within wouldn't be denied so easily. It surged forward like a tidal wave of flaming blood, seeking to drown and burn his mind, to destroy it and leave only itself within that great, scaly body.

His mind filled with an image of what the dragon wanted—to fly through the darkness between worlds, to travel so far away that DL's friends could never find him. He would *be* the dragon, be it forever.

DL couldn't let that image swallow him. He called on the Yeouiju, but it did not respond.

He was used to being alone, but not like this. In the past, he had been alone by choice—or so he told himself, anyway. Now he was trapped in an alien body with an alien mind seeking to bend him to its will.

"You are weak," the voice of the dragon whispered to him. *"You are tired. Lose yourself in me, and you can rest forever."*

He did feel weak. The weight of the world—or even all nine—was pressing down upon him, crushing him.

The dragon would get what it wanted. He knew that now with a sick realization that he couldn't deny.

"Ekaterina!" he screamed into the red madness that was engulfing him.

She didn't answer, either.

ROLE REVERSAL

EKATERINA WAS sure they were close to Loki now. She was pretty sure she could smell Aesir and faerie just up ahead—Loki and Dubh.

That thought was torn from her as her bond with DL writhed and burned in her head. Next to her, Max staggered.

"Something's wrong with DL!" she whispered, afraid Dubh might realize they were there. Max had cloaked them in some kind of stealth magic, but if Dubh was keeping a magical eye on the entryway, that might not fool him.

"Yeah, I think the dragon's taking over again."

"I've got to go back to him!"

Max looked down the passageway. "Let's see if we can help from here first. We don't have much time."

Max did what he could to amplify the links among them. Ekaterina tried to reach through those links, but she caught only distorted fragments of DL's thoughts. He gave no sign that he heard her.

"This isn't working!" she said, turning to head back down the passageway.

"Let me try something else," said Max. "We're close enough. Moving back to the surface won't help that much."

Ekaterina, unconvinced, started running back the way they had come. Before she could get more than a few steps, a tremor struck the mountain, knocking Max and her to the rocky floor. They moved to get up, and a second one hit. Ekaterina's head thudded against the ground with enough force to make her glad she was a vampire. The pain hit her like a spike through the brain, but it faded almost immediately instead of driving her straight into unconsciousness.

She and Max braced themselves against the wall, which was still trembling from the last tremor. A distant crash sounded, massive enough to shake the floor a third time.

"Cave-in," said Max.

Max kept talking, but Ekaterina stopped paying attention. She was feeling DL again—not his thoughts, but his physical sensations. They were as dragon-sized as his body, towering over her senses like a mountain range so tall it blotted out the sun.

"Ekaterina, what's wrong?" She was on the floor, and Max was shouting at her. She tried to force a reassuring expression onto her face, but the most she could manage was a nervous tick.

"DL is fighting so hard he's in convulsions," she whispered. "He's striking the side of the mountain. I can feel it as if it were my own body hitting solid rock."

A fourth tremor struck, covering them in dust and rock fragments.

"We're far enough in that this part of the cave won't collapse immediately," said Max. "I can feel the stresses in the rocks, though. He's striking with greater force than he did in Nidavellir. If he keeps hitting the mountain, we'll be buried alive. Even now, the cave mouth is sealed. We need to do something from here to help DL regain control, or we're all lost."

"When DL nearly brought down a mountain before, you stabilized the area around us. You have Freya's staff now. Could that not help?"

Ekaterina would never admit this to Max, but she wished they had Freya to go along with the staff.

Max rolled the staff in his hands as if he hadn't seen it before. "I can try." The mountain shook again. "I'd better try."

He threw himself into the task like a man possessed. The emerald power of the staff flowed into the rock all around them. The cave made crunching sounds as the magic pulled it together.

Max wiped sweat from his forehead. "I've stabilized the cave as much as I can, but if the whole mountain comes down, even the staff won't give me enough power to hold this place together."

Ekaterina couldn't see into the stone the Max could, but a quick glance at the surface told her the rock was laced together with magic. The power shielded them from the vibration enough that the next tremor didn't come close to knocking her over. However, the emerald radiance among the rocks dimmed. Max reinforced the magic, and the glow brightened.

Max's eyes narrowed as he examined the cave walls. "This is makeshift at best, even with the boost the staff provides. Another hit or two, and I won't have large masses of rock to work with—the whole thing will be pebbles. Pebbles against an earthquake."

"We brought DL back before. Could we not do it again?"

Max nodded slowly.

"The cave may hold together long enough to enable us to help DL," said Max. "We'll have to be quick about it, though—and DL isn't as close this time. Can you connect well enough to find his real personality?"

"I'll have to." She closed her eyes and reached out for DL's mind. Only the overwhelming physical sensations were there. Finding DL in that swirling cloud of static was like digging through a mountain with a fingernail.

"Yeouiju, help us reach DL," Max thought. The part of the Yeouiju within her reached out for the part in Max and found it much faster than before. Ekaterina blocked out the distracting bits of thought pouring into her from the heightened bond and stretched her mind desperately toward DL. Still nothing.

Max raised the staff, and the diamond at the tip sparkled. The air around them filled with glittering power, sharpening until it created the illusion that they were standing within an enormous diamond. Ekaterina could feel Max's power building as the diamond amplified it.

Ekaterina caught a hint of the dragon's thoughts, flashing through her mind like its fiery breath. One moment the fire burned her. Then it faded, leaving desperate darkness more complete than the depths of the ocean. Fire and darkness, anger and despair, flashed back and forth until a scream welled up inside of her. It was the cry of the dragon, and she had to clamp her jaws shut to keep it from ripping out of her own mouth.

"Max, I can't feel DL!"

"He's still there somewhere—he has to be. Maybe we aren't close enough."

She felt Max push through the Yeouiju bond, linking them even more closely. His reassuring presence glowed in her mind like diamonds touched by sunlight. It wasn't as strong as the dragon's gargantuan presence, but as Max shared his enhanced power with her, the dragon's agonizing struggles receded.

Her own thoughts became clearer, more focused. The dragon's mental roar was not as far into her head. It sounded distant, like a shouted argument in a neighbor's house. She still couldn't hear DL, not even as a faraway whisper.

"We're close—I can feel it. Reach out to DL as hard as you can!"

The dragon struck the mountain again, and the mountain screamed in the sound of stone scraping against stone. The emerald light of the spell holding the rock together dimmed, and splintered pieces of stone sprinkled down around them like hard, jagged rain.

"Stay focused!" Instead of reinforcing the magic that kept the cave from collapsing, Max poured even more power into Ekaterina. The staff burned with crystalline intensity. Brisingamen flared with answering power and felt hot against her skin.

Sweat poured from the young sorcerer's brow, and the magic shook him harder than the dragon tremors had.

"Are you all right?"

"Focus on DL!" His thought was a scream almost as violent as the dragon's cry. It was the sound of someone about to break under the weight of the magic he had summoned. She looked into his eyes. Fragmented as much as the roof above him, he was held together only by sheer willpower.

"Yeouiju, Max has given me power, but I don't know how to use it. Can you help?"

"Visualize. Visualize your love reaching DL," thought Max. *"I'll guide you as much as I can."*

Judging from how hollow his thoughts sounded, Ekaterina wasn't sure he'd be able to help. The Yeouiju didn't respond, but she felt it trying to bond her and Max even closer together.

Ekaterina didn't have a sorcerer's ability to focus her thoughts, much less visualize them in vivid detail enough to transmute them into reality. Her desperation was all she had to work with. She sent her love flowing toward DL like a mighty river, ready to put out the tormenting fires inside of him. Someone—or something—gently guided the flow. The chaos all around her made it impossible to tell whether it was Max or the Yeouiju.

She connected with DL's mind so abruptly that the feeling was like going from night to day in the fraction of a second. No, it was more like going from night to…not night. She could feel how miserable DL was. Being inside his head wasn't like day, but there was still a tiny flicker of hope inside him. He hadn't given up yet.

DL sensed them now, knew what they were trying to do, but he had been inside the dragon so long that he was having trouble separating himself from its persona. Ekaterina kept pushing, not just with her love, but with her entire mind. Taking Max's advice, she visualized herself in his dragon body, fighting by his side against the evil dragon mind that had no right to exist.

The image of DL in her mind was faint, translucent as a ghost. Or was that really DL, so insubstantial because that was all that remained of him? She felt as close to the edge of exhaustion as Max had looked earlier, but she pushed even harder, willing DL to become substantial, to be fully himself again.

DL became more solid, but the dragon attacked before he was fully restored. She could feel its thoughts biting into her like sharp fangs, burning her like dark fire, but she ignored the pain. Rather than succumb, she pushed harder and harder.

Heartened by her struggle, DL pushed harder himself. He was solid now, and he raised a sword that looked like Excalibur and flashed as brightly as the dragon's fire.

The beast pulled back, its eyes full of fear. DL pushed forward, the light from the sword matching that of Brisingamen as it flared on Ekaterina's breast. The light coalesced into a sword in her own hand. Together, they struck at the dragon, cutting through its armorlike scales, switching to a defensive stance to parry its fire, which struck their crossed swords and was deflected back at the bleeding beast.

They were winning—she was sure of it.

She was so intertwined with DL's thoughts by now that she only barely heard a new sound through her physical ears. It was music... almost. It was more like a collection of discordant notes.

It was—Dubh!

Of course, he would have felt DL hitting the mountain. He would have sensed the enormous accumulation of power nearby. How could he not have? And how could Max and she not have anticipated that he would try to interfere?

Max tried to divert enough energy to defend against whatever Dubh was doing, but Ekaterina could feel the massive power created by the union of Brisingamen, staff, and Yeouiju ebb as Dubh's manic tune assaulted them.

DL slipped away from her like sand through her fingers—and the battle was not yet won. The dragon roared triumphantly, grabbed DL in its swordlike claws and tossed him into its gaping mouth. Ekaterina tried to strike it again, but it too was slipping away from her. She ran toward it, but the distance between them kept increasing, and her speed kept diminishing. It was her worst nightmare made real.

"Yeouiju! Help me stay in DL's body. It's the only chance he has...the only chance any of us have."

"I will try," said the Yeouiju.

The cursed music was becoming more obtrusive by the second, like growing static from a bad phone connection. Max's magic still surrounded her, but Dubh's music was warping it, making it pulse in rhythm with his anti-melody.

She tried visualizing her river of love, but she got an alligator-filled swamp instead. She tried switching metaphors and imagined her love as fire that would burn away the distance between her and DL. Instead, the fire turned on her. It was a flaming sea that blocked her from moving even one step toward DL.

The sword. Sindr had given her a sword that could disrupt faerie magic. Without dropping completely back into her body, she managed to move her arm. She felt the hilt of the sword. She drew it, and Dubh screamed in frustration as the blade's protective charms ripped an Ekaterina-sized hole in his magic. The music stilled.

She was free, but she couldn't undo the magic Dubh had done around her. The only way to do that would be to fully reenter her body and attack Dubh—if he was within sword's reach.

How much energy could Max and the Yeouiju possibly have left? The pathway to DL was twisted and blocked by fire—but still there. Going after Dubh now might mean losing her only chance to save DL.

Abandoning visualization, she took every ounce of willpower she had left and reached for DL. Her love wasn't a river or a fire. It was the pure light of Brisingamen. Dubh had twisted Max's magic, but he couldn't twist her love. It banished the traitorous fire, and she flew forward with the speed of thought.

No crazy faerie was going to beat her. Dubh might be the bringer of madness and oblivion, but this time he would be the one consigned to oblivion—if it was the last thing she did.

She was back in DL's mind—but the dragon was still there, eying her like she was his next snack. Blood still dripped from his wounded legs, though. The magic that supported her might be weaker—but so was the dragon.

Brisingamen's glow engulfed her, and she expanded. She was a giant, the equal of any dragon. No, its superior. She towered over it as if it were a mouse.

It squeaked—but the squeak morphed into a roar as it expanded to match her. She grabbed its jaws, forced them open, and reconnected with DL. Energized by the power of her love, he sprang out of dragon's mouth. The beast broke away from Ekaterina and flew away as fast as it could manage.

She felt DL in her arms, but only for a moment. She heard the distant sound of Dubh's discordant notes again. He already knew his magic couldn't touch her. What could he possibly hope to gain?

She felt what was left of Max's magic twisting again, pulling DL away from her. She clung to DL so hard she would have crushed him if they'd been physical. She let the power of Brisingamen flare around both of them. Despite that, DL slipped away once more. Ekaterina reached after him, even got the light of Brisingamen to reach after him, but it was too late.

That little faerie rat couldn't get at her with his magic—so he used it on DL instead. She would wring his little neck as soon as she returned to her body.

The magic around her continued to warp. It no longer sparkled like diamonds. It had the cold gleam of obsidian instead.

The pathway back was gone, erased by the magic sludge all around her.

She heard the flap of enormous wings. Without DL nearby, she was no longer a giant—and the dragon was coming back for a rematch.

NOWHERE TO GO BUT UP

DL WAS in Ekaterina's arms one second—and all alone in the dark the next.

He recognized the feeling from the seidr trance. He was out of his body. Or was he? He felt flesh around him again, but it was different—wrong. It was colder than it should have been. At least it didn't feel scaly or reptilian.

The rock he was sitting on was cold, too. Cold and hard.

He could hear music nearby—Dubh's music.

His eyes. He was in the dark because they were closed. They came open slowly as if he had forgotten how to open them.

Dubh was smiling and playing his panpipes maniacally. His eyes glittered with their usual madness. Merlin's book floated at his side, pulsing magic in rhythm to the faerie's music, waiting for his next command.

Max was fighting Dubh. Judging by how tired Max looked, the battle had been going on for a while. His face was an emotionless mask so pale it looked as if it had been carved from ivory. It shined with sweat. His eyelids drooped over his eyes as if he were having difficulty keeping them open. His hands shook so much it was hard for him to hold Freya's staff.

Emerald light poured from the staff, but as it flowed toward Dubh, it mutated into a sickly, grayish green that DL could hardly bear to look at.

He needed to join the battle, but his legs refused to lift him off the ground. He looked back at Max. Bloodless as Max's face looked, his heart was still beating, and blood was still pumping through his arteries and veins. DL could feel it. His draconic senses enabled him to tell a lot about someone's physical condition, but they had never been so focused on the circulatory system before. He could even see the pulse in Max's carotid artery.

Where was Ekaterina? Groggy as he was, it took him only a couple of seconds to realize the truth.

He didn't see Ekaterina because he was in her body.

Even worse—if such a thing were possible—she must be in the dragon's body, fighting all alone against its raving, animal desire to become a force of destruction.

With all his heart, he longed to find a way back to her, but first things first. She might not have a body to come back to if Dubh won.

Max's knees almost buckled. Dubh laughed and grabbed Merlin's book. One spell from that, and Max would be finished.

DL struggled to his feet, still having a hard time thinking. His right foot clanged against something. Looking down, he saw a sword.

Not just any sword. There were runes. What did they mean? He knew he should remember, but his mind, still throbbing from the battle, was working sluggishly.

Dubh was chanting, and the air had become so thick with magic DL could hardly breathe. No, that was a phantom feeling. This body didn't need to breathe.

DL bent far enough to pick up the sword. The moment he touched it, his head became clearer, and the body, new as being inside it was, felt more responsive.

That's what the runes were for—the sword was anti-faerie!

The magic swirling and flaring around Dubh suggested he was near the end of his spell. Max's magic looked too discolored and twisted to stop him. Unsteady on his feet but feeling more confident in his arms, DL hurled the sword at Dubh. It spun as it flew through the air, cutting through the mystic energy around the faerie. It didn't disrupt the magic closest to him—Merlin's spells weren't faerie magic—but the spell wasn't shielding Dubh. He had to dodge to avoid being skewered.

He slipped, and the book flew out of his hands. He clawed for it, slipped again, and hit the floor with a thud. The book fell a few feet from him. The complex spell he had been weaving unraveled into tiny threads, which dissolved in seconds.

"Max, the book!" DL was still not moving very fast, and the young sorcerer was struggling with the residual effects of Dubh's magic. He was barely able to stay on his feet. Dubh retrieved the book. He grabbed Ekaterina's sword, too, but its cold steel burned him, and he dropped it. Even so, he had the upper hand.

DL tried to charge Dubh at full vampire speed, but his legs felt rubbery, and he could barely manage a hobble. That gave Dubh plenty of time to hit DL with enough force to pin him against the wall.

That kind of collision with the wall would have knocked a human unconscious at the very least, but the vampiric body could take that kind of punishment better. It also had the strength to allow DL to break free —if only Max would be a more effective distraction for Dubh.

Dubh was no longer warping Max's magic, but the glow from his staff was as small as a firefly's. His face was slack, expressionless. His eyes were almost lifeless. DL would have thought he was dying If not for the sorcerer's steady heartbeat.

"Yeouiju, can you help?"

"Master! Your mind and the biggest part of me are in the same body for the first time. Perhaps I can do something. What should I do?"

"Split up the way you are, I know you can't give me control over the weather, but how about a single bolt of lightning for the faerie over there?"

"Master, we are indoors."

"I know that. Can't you do something with the static electricity in the air?"

"The conditions are not good, but I will do what I can."

While he was waiting, DL pushed with all his might against the magic holding him in place. He knew he couldn't break free right away, but at least he could force Dubh to expend more energy to hold him. Dubh had cast the spell much too quickly to have made it self-sustaining.

The spell felt like thick steel pressing against him. He could break it —but not fast.

Dubh looked more wide-eyed and frantic than usual, but his slow and shaky movements suggested that the battle with Max had taken a toll. He was still on his feet, though, and looked less exhausted than Max did. DL kept pushing against the restraining magic, but it bent only slightly.

The faerie focused his attention on the drained and shaky Max. DL shuddered as the lunatic looked down at Merlin's book.

Dubh, frowning, looked up at Max, back to the book, back to Max again. The faerie smirked. "I don't even need this to finish you off." With his free hand, he made grasping gestures that sent magic swirling in the young sorcerer's direction. A sucking sound echoed in the cave as Dubh pulled the air away from Max.

The faerie's spell didn't feel that powerful. Max should have been able to counter it, but his feeble staff-waving didn't make a dent in it. His breathing already sounded more labored.

A jolt of electricity shot at Dubh, but he dodged it.

"Yeouiju, do you have enough power to break the spell holding me against the wall?"

"The lightning attack has nearly exhausted my power for the moment."

"Max is about to run out of air. Can you channel what power you have to generate enough air to keep him alive?"

"I have never done something like that."

"At full power, you could cause a great wind, couldn't you? This is a much smaller thing."

Max was breathing in short, ragged gasps. The firefly glow of his staff dwindled to a single spark. A faint brown glow spread around him. DL could tell just enough from the bond between them to feel Yggdrasil's wood transferring energy into him—too slowly.

"I'm sorry, master. I cannot. There is too much other magic in the air."

Max fell to his knees. The brown glow flickered. DL had one more idea and perhaps only seconds to implement it.

"Ekaterina!" No answer.

"Yeouiju, can you connect me to Ekaterina?"

"The one who is usually in this body? She's in the beast that calls itself a dragon now. It is hard—"

"JUST DO IT!" DL felt guilty for pressing the poor Yeouiju so hard when it was clearly exhausted, but Max was dying right before his eyes.

"Ekaterina!"

"DL?" The voice was faint as a whisper.

"If you can still control the dragon body, hit the mountain as hard as you can with it and as often as you can. Don't stop until I tell you."

"The cave will collapse on you and Max if I do that."

DL looked up at the ceiling, more crack than rock. Max's stabilizing magic still held it together, but its glow was weak, and it flickered as if it was running out of power.

"Hit gently then, and just a few times. We have no choice."

The connection broke violently enough to make his head throb.

Yggdrasil's brown power flared, and Max almost succeeded in standing up. He came agonizingly close, but he grasped at his throat and sank back to the floor. His chest was heaving frantically.

The mountain shook, and DL felt a psychic pain in his ribs.

Dubh stayed focused on Max, creeping closer like a predator moving in for the kill.

The mountain shook again, and the air smelled like dust. The wall behind him lost pieces of rock, and that, combined with another vampiric push, broke him free.

Max wasn't moving. DL could hear his heart beating, but that beat was weaker, more erratic.

DL's legs no longer felt rubbery, and he shot in Dubh's direction with full vampiric speed. He managed to keep his footing at the third shake. Dubh nearly lost focus on his spell. He saw DL racing in his direction, and his eyes widened in panic.

The faerie raised his hand to stop DL's charge, but the need to multi-task hindered him, and DL dodged the spell. Dubh tried again, but DL fooled him by changing direction and heading for the sword. Dubh's spell hit the wall behind where DL had been standing. DL grabbed the sword. Another spell intended to immobilize him shot right past, missing by inches. Dubh tried again but missed again, his aim spoiled by a mountain shake.

DL lunged at Dubh, sword extended, and the faerie had no choice but to dodge him. To have even a shot at that, Dubh had to move at full speed—which meant he had to let go of the spell that was pulling the air away from Max. DL prayed it wasn't too late.

A large chunk of rock crashed less than a foot from DL. He couldn't take his eyes off Dubh long enough to check the ceiling, but he could hear the stone shifting. Max's spell would not hold much longer.

Dubh opened Merlin's book. Power crackled in the air around him, but no matter how much power he had, he needed to concentrate to aim it, and DL was good enough with a sword to make that difficult. The fact that the sword was cold steel didn't hurt, either.

Unfortunately, Dubh did manage enough concentration to hit DL with raw power hard enough to knock him backward. That gave the faerie just enough time to pin DL to the wall again. The magic felt different—less steely and more serpentine, as if a giant snake were holding him in place.

DL still had the sword and just enough arm movement to slash at the magic. The sword bounced off harmlessly.

Dubh laughed at him. "That sword would work on me or even on my magic, but this time I'm using a spell from Merlin's Grimoire rather than a faerie one. Cold steel has no effect on it." The spell squeezed DL tighter in its snakelike coils, suppressing any further arm movement.

"Now that you are properly restrained, allow me to demonstrate a little of my faerie power—in this case, one that is unique to me. My touch can bestow paralysis or madness. Which shall it be in your case?"

"Your touch doesn't do much to a vampire, remember?"

"Ah, yes, but that was before I had Merlin's book to amplify the effect. Its power should work for that just as much as it would for a spell."

DL turned his head enough to look at Max. His heart was beating more normally now, and his chest was rising and falling in a more even rhythm. He seemed to be unconscious, though.

"Ekaterina!" No answer. DL was on his own against the bringer of madness and oblivion.

"Entertaining as madness would be, I must be getting back to freeing

Loki. I think paralysis will do." He touched DL—and nothing happened.

DL thought about faking paralysis, but Dubh's horrified expression told him there was no point.

"How can this be? I feel the power of the book flowing through me." He looked at the volume as if it were broken.

DL was just as surprised. All that power, and Dubh's touch had less effect on Ekaterina's body than it had the first time.

Several hunks of rock cracked loose from the ceiling and hit the ground, one on Dubh's right, one on his left, and one right in front of him. The faerie looked up and screamed.

DL took the opportunity to glance at the ceiling. Max's spell was failing fast. No sign of the magic remained in the area right over Dubh's head.

Dubh's power, amplified by Merlin's book, surged upward to prevent a cave-in. The magic prevented immediate collapse, but it crackled and flickered. Dubh strained to weave a more powerful spell.

A ray of emerald light struck Dubh from behind, and he screamed.

Max was conscious again.

With what was obviously considerable effort, Dubh fended off the ray. Max stayed on his feet but looked too shaky to mount another attack. Nor could DL, still pinned to the wall. The snakelike spell relaxed its coils just a bit, though. If DL had a minute, he could break loose again.

Dubh's eyes widened as the ceiling above him sagged, and rock splinters showered down on him. He opened a portal so fast the usual silver swirl was more like a lightning flash. The faerie gripped Merlin's book and raced through the portal, which vanished as fast as it had appeared. The ceiling collapsed—but only in the area where Dubh had been standing.

DL broke free and rushed over to check on Max.

"I'll be fine in a minute," said Max, who looked more like recovery would take weeks. His skin was ghost-white, and his voice was a raspy whisper. "I was pretty close to death, but I hung onto the staff—instinct, I guess. It pumped Yggdrasil life force into me."

"I thought it was supposed to protect you against physical harm in the first place," said DL.

"It offers some protection, but not invulnerability. Anyway, the protective runes are aimed at things like combat injuries, not surviving in a vacuum." Max raised an eyebrow. "What happened to your accent? You sound...very different."

"There's no easy way to say this. I'm DL."

"How could that have happened?"

"You'd know better than I."

Max frowned. "If I had to guess, something went wrong with my efforts to give Ekaterina enough of a boost to send her into the dragon body to help you. The situation wasn't quite as chaotic as that inverted world where we first met Dubh, but it was pretty weird. I was trying to mix power from three different sources in a highly magically-charged atmosphere—and then Dubh attacked."

"She must be in Hell right now. We have to get her back!"

"And put you back in Hell?" asked Max.

"I'm fine." Her thought came through to DL and Max with surprising clarity.

"You beat the dragon?" asked DL.

"Not exactly. I'm just used to this kind of internal battle. I have to fight bloodlust every day, remember. That experience gave me the skills I need to handle this one. The dragon persona isn't gone, but I'm suppressing it well enough for the time being.

"I'm not sensing hostile magic near you, so I take it you beat Dubh."

"Not exactly. He got away again."

"I'll start digging you out right away. The various dragon collisions collapsed almost the entire cave up to where you are."

"Can you dig straight down to us?" asked Max. *"That might be faster, and it would also be easier to refill the hole. The sealed tunnel will then serve the same purpose the spell over the cave mouth served."*

"I'll see what I can do."

"Is that wise?" asked DL. *"We just had part of the ceiling collapse just a few feet away."*

Max's lips moved slightly, as if he didn't have enough strength to smile. *"That was me trying to stop Dubh from escaping. It was easier to release the magic holding the part of the roof right above him than it would have been to attack more directly."*

"*Sneaky!*" thought DL. Max's magic was still holding the rest of the ceiling together—barely.

"*Ekaterina, it should be all right to dig carefully, DL and I will move a little farther down the tunnel, just in case.*"

Max took one shaky step. At that rate, he would get out of danger by the time he turned forty. DL picked him up despite his feeble protests and carried him to a safer spot.

"Once we get out, do we have any way of telling where Dubh is?" asked DL. "The Nine Worlds can't exactly be searched quickly."

"It could be searched much faster if I'd had time to master the seidr trance," said Max. "Luckily, I was alert enough to sense a few things when Dubh opened a portal. He went back to Helheim. He probably wants to consult with Hel to figure out a different way to start Ragnarok.

"He obviously hasn't succeeded in breaking Loki's chains, and now that we're on to him, he knows we could warn the Aesir. They could make coming back to try again very difficult for him. He's going to need a new approach if he honors his agreement with her."

The ceiling where they had been standing vibrated in rhythm with Ekaterina's digging, and rocks crashed to the ground.

"Guess it was a good thing we moved," said DL. "Anyway, making a new plan might take Dubh time."

"We have to hope that's what happens. It's a question Hel won't be anticipating, and Dubh isn't likely to be much help to her. He's not exactly a systematic thinker, and he doesn't know much about the Nine Worlds.

"He's also not as knowledgeable about magic as he'd like us to think."

"How do you know that?"

"Even with Merlin's grimoire, he wasn't having too much luck holding the ceiling together. He's far better at disrupting than he is at preserving. A well-trained sorcerer should be able to do both. Even worse, look how his touch attack failed. He already knew a lot of magic forces didn't see it as a spell—my house defenses, for example. Why would he think Merlin's grimoire would be any different? It empowers spells. Rookie mistake!"

"That's especially damning criticism—coming from a rookie," said DL, grinning.

"Hey, I'm sorry about this whole body-switch thing."

"You were trying to help Ekaterina save me under almost impossible conditions. I can't hold this against you—unless, of course, it's permanent."

"That idea would have frightened me before," said Max. "Having gotten this sorted out once before, though, I have more confidence."

"Well, kind of sorted out. My real body is still in Álfheim on supernatural life support—I hope."

"I think you'd know if your real body died," said Max, but he didn't sound too sure.

They were saved from the awkward silence by dragon claws breaking through the ceiling. In a short time, Ekaterina had created a wide enough hole for her to reach down and lift them out. She parked them on a safe spot nearby and filled the hole back in.

Max tried to contact Esras. He had no special bond with the druid, and the distance would either cause a long delay or make communication impossible.

Fortunately, Max had recently been in DL's body, and Esras was in constant contact with it now, so Max was able to use it to make a connection. That enabled him to verify that the body was still alive. It also gave him a chance to let Esras know what was happening. The druid agreed to pass on a message to the Aesir that they should set a heavy guard on Loki's prison, just in case Dubh tried to come back. That was one less thing to worry about.

By the time Max was done, so was Ekaterina. She scooped DL and him up in her claws and flew back in the direction of Helheim at top speed.

"At least in Helheim we'll have some allies, assuming Thor, Freyr and Freya are still there," said Ekaterina.

"Did you forget how we left them?" asked Max. "I don't think they were that happy with us."

"Yet Freya gave me Brisingamen. I know they wanted us to rescue the hostages first, but we did just keep Dubh from starting Ragnarok. I can't believe that won't be worth something."

"Ekaterina, I'm not feeling...thirsty at all," said DL after a while.

"I wasn't either, not since I've been on the Norse plane. The Yeouiju told me it's using some of its energy to feed me."

"You know what this means?" asked Max. "The Yeouiju is constantly adapting. Even being split among us in some bizarre way, it still manages to do things it wasn't created to do. I've never heard of a spell or magic object that was that adaptable. Even many magical beings take a long time to develop new magic."

"Are you saying the Yeouiju is alive?" asked DL.

"In a way, yes, I think it is," said Max. "It's not really autonomous. It's connected to you, even if now it can't always make the most of that connection. But there are times when it seems to make decisions on its own. Besides that, it definitely figures out how to do things unconnected with its original purpose."

"Wow!" said DL. "To think I've been ignoring it for months!"

"Its social needs must be very different from ours," said Max. "After all, we now know it could have spoken to you any time it wanted to. It just didn't. It could have spoken to Ekaterina. It could even have spoken to me."

"It was waiting," said DL. "It was waiting for me. I let it down."

He couldn't escape the feeling that if he had tried to reach out to the Yeouiju earlier, his friends could have avoided all this peril.

ONE SURPRISE AFTER ANOTHER

"I DOUBT you really let the Yeouiju down," said Ekaterina. "Certainly, it's never said so. If the idea bothers you, though, ask it when you get the chance. Right now, we should be thinking about strategy. We're going to reach Helheim sooner than you think. What will we do when we get there?"

"Reunite with Freya, Freyr, and Thor," said Max. "Then find the hostages. Then go after Dubh. Our Norse friends already have Outcast, and you know where my grandmother is, right, DL?"

"If she's still in the same place, yes. Balder might have recommended someplace else, though."

"Since the geography is continuously switching around, it won't matter where she went," said Ekaterina. "We'll need to use this dragon body's sense of smell, and my body's, at closer range. For Maeve, we can use Max's relationship with her as well. That isn't what I was worried about. We need to figure out how to respond to Hel. I doubt she's just going to let us walk in and take the hostages."

"If she relies on her dead army, you can incinerate it fairly easily for us," said Max. "I'm sure she has other resources at her disposal, but, since none of us know what else she might be capable of, we'll have to confer with Freya and the others."

That answer didn't appear to satisfy Ekaterina, who spent much of the trip in silence, her reptilian face unmoving, her eyes narrowed as if she were trying to see some way out of their dilemma. DL tried to find something reassuring to say, but how could he? They were in dangerous and unfamiliar territory. No amount of sugarcoating was going to make their situation look any better.

When the grim landscape of Helheim came into sight, Ekaterina headed to the gate where Hel had first confronted Max, Ekaterina, and the three former gods. The ground was scorched from DL's earlier attack on the undead.

"On the way down, I saw Sleipnir grazing some distance away," said Ekaterina. "That means our Norse friends haven't left. I'll try to sniff them out."

Ekaterina started coughing hard enough to blow over a tree. "Hel is cleverer than we hoped. DL, can you smell what I mean?"

"Ugh, the whole area beyond the wall reeks of rotting corpses. It wasn't like that before."

"This is bad," said Max. "We already knew she could block any kind of magical search for the hostages. Now she's made your acute sense of smell is useless, too.

"There are two other things I can think of. This staff has runes carved by Freya herself. It should have an affinity for her and for her other staff. That might be a connection Hel hasn't thought to block. Give me a few minutes, and I'll see what I can do."

Max closed his eyes and stood still as a statue for a while. The runes on the staff glowed softly, pulsing in rhythm with something.

"It isn't to Max's heartbeat," whispered DL. "I…I can tell exactly how his heart is beating. It's a little creepy."

"Vampire hearing is as acute as vampire smell," said Ekaterina. "We also have…an affinity for the human circulatory system."

"I can feel Freya's presence, but I'm not getting any sense of her exact location," said Max, eyes still closed. "I'm going to try to seek out my grandmother."

After a few more minutes, he reported failure on that as well. "I guess it makes sense. If someone could detect a close relative, then Freyr should have been able to locate Gerda on his own."

"What about sight?" asked DL. "Hel has blocked smell, but don't you and I also have really acute vision, Ekaterina? You could fly us over, and maybe we could spot someone."

"If not a person, maybe at least my house," said Max.

"Yeah, Maeve could have returned there," said DL. "Shall we give it a try?"

"We have nothing to lose," said Ekaterina, taking them gently in her claws and rising into the air.

An aerial view of the land of the dead was dizzying, to say the least. The geography shifted below them, giving the whole place a blurry look as if they were seeing it through a layer of fog. Roads shifted, and whole buildings came and went as the dead moved around.

"This is even worse than when I was walking around down there," said DL.

"You're looking at it in a different way. When you were looking around before, you must have seen only part of what was happening around you. You didn't know then how fluid the place is. Now that you do, perhaps you can see more of it. Even now, I'm not sure we're seeing all of it."

"In that case, perhaps you should let us down, and we'll explore from ground level. You can watch over us from above."

"I don't like that idea. The shifting landscape may make it difficult for me to get close enough to help if you are threatened in some way."

"On the other hand, just flying around up here doesn't seem as if it will do much good," said Max. It's too hard to get enough detail to know what's going on.

"Wait a minute! Hel is blocking magical detection of people, but, as far as we know, not of locations. I might be able to focus my eyes to pick out the copy of my house below. It's worth a try, anyway."

Max's eyes glowed for a moment, and he smiled. "I see it down there!" He pointed to a spot where DL saw only a tangle of unfamiliar buildings, but as Ekaterina descended, he could see the roof of the house as well.

"There's not much clearance right now," said Ekaterina. "I can't get close enough to the ground to let you down safely."

"I'll float us down," said Max. As soon as he got his levitation working, Ekaterina let go, and he and DL floated gently downward until their feet touched the ground.

Before anything else changed, they jogged up to the front door and knocked. Maeve answered, much to their relief.

"Come inside quickly—not that it will make much difference now."

"I thought you'd be glad to see us," said Max. "Why are you so cranky?"

"Because you're in danger in Helheim," said Maeve. "I can't tell exactly what's going on, but there's a tremendous buildup of mystic forces. Hel is plotting something—something extremely bad I'll wager."

"Dubh came here after we defeated him in Midgard," said Max.

Maeve shook her head. "This is even worse than I feared. Of course, you wouldn't have been in so much danger if you had picked a less conspicuous way to arrive. You know dragon flyovers aren't exactly an everyday occurrence here, right? The dead in general won't notice, but Hel's warriors will, Hel will, and Dubh will. And just in case any of them missed your arrival, you have DL circling in the air right above us."

"Actually, I'm DL."

Maeve's eyes widened in shock. "Another body switch? What kind of foolishness have you been up to?"

"At least I'm in a human…looking body," said DL, eyes narrowed and lips tightened in irritation. "You trapped me in a Western dragon carcass."

"So that's Ekaterina overhead? I would have credited her with better sense."

"I accept that heartfelt apology for transforming me into a monster," said DL, every word sharp with sarcasm.

"I'm sorry," she said quickly, "but I did warn you of the danger. At least your mind has returned to normal."

"No thanks to you—and not completely. The dragon persona keeps trying to reassert. Ekaterina seems better able to handle it than I can."

Maeve raised an eyebrow. "You mean you switched bodies on purpose?"

"No, it was yet another magical accident."

"Mine," said Max, looking at the floor.

"It wasn't your fault," said DL. "Anyway, we'll get it sorted out later. Right now, we need to move fast. Is Balder still with you?"

"He's upstairs resting. I'm afraid he won't be much use for power-sharing for a while. I expected him to be restored by now."

"It's all right," said Max. "We have another power source." He held up the staff for her inspection.

"This is…I don't know. *Amazing* seems an inadequate description. How did you come by it?"

"It was a gift from the duergar king—long story. There'll be time for that later. Right now, we need to figure out where the other hostages are."

"I'm afraid I have no idea," said Maeve.

"When I last saw Outcast, he was with Thor, Freya, and Freyr near one of the longhouses that surround Hel's hall," said Max. "I'm not sure we can find our way there, but as one of Hel's…guests, you can do it, right?"

"Oh, I can get you there. I'm just not sure you'll be alive by the time I do. Perhaps finding a place to hide would be more prudent."

"If only that were an option," said DL. "None of us know for sure what Dubh and Hel are up to, but they could strike any time. Right now we're burning daylight—or whatever passes for it here, anyway. Staying here longer isn't likely to make the trip any safer."

"There is wisdom in that, I suppose. Yes, I can take you. It's a fairly long trip, though. I know this place is mutable. To me, it looks like our neighborhood in Eau Claire. Hel's hall is way beyond where the city limits would be, which means it's a few-hour trek on foot. If you use me as a guide, you'll be stuck with the same limitation."

"It's not hours at the speed we could move," said Max. Ekaterina's body is naturally fast, and you and I can both use magic to speed ourselves up."

"We can," Maeve said. "That will make us more conspicuous—but I suppose I shouldn't worry about that. Hel can probably keep track of any of her subjects—and right now, that includes DL and me."

"Can you speed me up as well?" asked Balder as he came down the stairs.

"You still need your rest," said Maeve in her most maternal tone.

"I feel surprisingly renewed. Perhaps it is the break from my other-wise pointless existence here. I may not be able to contribute much, but I intend to come and aid your efforts as much as I may."

Strong-willed as Maeve was, she had no luck convincing Balder to stay behind, so she reluctantly agreed. Knowing how much punch Balder packed, DL figured it was better to have him along than leave him behind. Even a small part of his power would be better than none.

It took only a minute or so to speed everyone up and just another two or three to link everyone else to Maeve so that they could see what she was seeing. That helped everyone stay in sync as they ran through the streets of what looked like Eau Claire, though it was grayer and grimmer than the real thing. The shadow of the dragon above made the place even darker, but her presence was comforting.

"The streets are empty," said DL. "When I first walked to the house, I ran into other people."

"Because you weren't really dead," said Maeve. "The dead mostly see their own town. In that town, they see only the other dead who dwelled there when they were alive."

"So it is with me as well, though my route a longer one," said Balder. "I have to walk from the image of Breidablik, my former home, all the way out of the Helheim image of Asgard. I sometimes think Hel herself crafted the road between to make it as difficult as possible for me to come to her."

"The scenery must be better," said Max.

Balder looked in his direction, but his eyes seemed to focus on a point far beyond him, as if he gazing into the past. "I would rather be in places unlike the ones I knew in life. To be surrounded by familiar objects that are not really familiar when one looks closely is sometimes almost more than I can bear. The fact that most of the Aesir and Vanir are not dead makes the place practically empty, which is even worse. My wife, Nanna, is there, but she killed herself to be with me. I have never told her, but sometimes it pains me to look upon her."

"You almost sound as if you wish Ragnarok would happen," said Maeve. "You and Nanna would be back in the world of the living."

Balder looked horrified. "Yes, we would—at the cost of the lives of our parents, brothers, sisters. Almost everyone we know will have to die to fulfill our promised return. Who could want such a thing?"

"Plenty of people," said Max. "You are more virtuous than most."

DL wondered if Balder was really that virtuous. What if the Aesir really was trying to bring Ragnarok to pass? What if DL's transformation into a Western dragon had not been the accident Balder made it out to be? If not for Ekaterina's intervention, DL could have caused chaos all over the place. And even Ekaterina could not have saved him on her own. Freya's loan of Brisingamen, which Balder couldn't have anticipated, was the only thing that pulled them back from complete disaster.

Just as Maeve predicted, when they got to the city line, just beyond it stood Hel's hall, every bit as bleak as DL remembered it. There were dead guards, but their attention focused on the dragon. Maybe they were among the multitudes DL had incinerated earlier. Whatever caused their eyes to fix on the air above them, they made no move to stop DL and the others from entering. Getting in was almost too easy.

Hel was there as if waiting to greet them. Next to her was a bound and sleeping Outcast.

"You have wasted your time coming here," she said. Her stare, intense to begin with, was made more so by the rapid shifting between living eyes and dead ones. "If I could refuse the likes of Thor and Freya, I will certainly refuse you."

"You may have noticed there is a dragon overhead," said Maeve. DL was impressed by the way she seemed completely unintimidated by the fierce former goddess. "One signal from us, and it will burn the roof right off of this place."

"Burn the entire hall to the ground if you wish," said Hel. "I can have it rebuilt before anyone notices the difference. As for me, you can't kill me any more than the Aesir could. Thor's hammer could have crushed me even faster than the dragon could have burned me, but he held back. Temperamental as he is, even he knows the Nine Worlds could unravel if I were prevented from playing my part in the destined Ragnarok."

"Destiny does not require that you keep the hostages you have taken," said Balder. "Release them, and let these strangers be on their way."

"And are you now the ruler of this place, that you can give me orders?" asked Hel. "You are a subject here every bit as much as the lowliest dead human. Do not force me to prove it to you.

"As for the rest of you, let us step outside, and I will show you just how little hope of defeating me you have here."

Without waiting for an answer, Hel turned and moved through one of the other doors so rapidly that even a vampire couldn't have kept up. DL picked up Outcast so that the trip wouldn't be a total waste, and they all followed Hel outside. What other choice did they have?

"Look up," said the ruler of the dead.

Ekaterina circled far above them. A darker shape approached. Darker and bigger.

Another dragon at least twice the size of Ekaterina's current body was moving in fast.

"This is Nidhogg, generously taking time off from gnawing one of Yggdrasil's roots to lend me his aid. Your dragon will not stand a chance against him."

SHOWDOWN

EKATERINA WAS ALREADY TURNING to face her unexpected foe, but DL had other ideas.

"Get out of here!" He knew the Yeouiju had a hard time connecting through that Western dragon body Ekaterina was in, and he got no response.

"Yeouiju, can you reach her?"

"Not immediately."

"Max, Maeve, what can we do to help?"

"Not a thing," said Hel. In his panic, DL had forgotten she was standing right there.

Ekaterina breathed fire at Nidhogg, who responded by spraying poison at her. The two streams met in midair and destroyed each other.

"Keep looking up and pretend to be focused entirely on the dragon battle," thought Max. *"I don't think Hel has any way to hear our thoughts. Maeve, Balder, and I will see what we can do,"*

"Fast, please," said DL. Why wasn't Ekaterina just flying away? She looked as if she could fly faster than Nidhogg.

"The dragon's too far away for a direct attack with magic," said Max.

Ekaterina evaded Nidhogg, who was twice her size. Why wasn't she running?

"Nidhogg can't wander too far from Nifleheim," thought Maeve. *"Ekaterina only needs to leave the area to be safe."*

Nidhogg lunged at her and barely missed skewering her in the side with his claws.

"Yeouiju, you have to find a way to tell her to run."

"I got through," said the Yeouiju. *"She says she will not leave."*

DL shuddered at the sight of another near miss in midair.

"Why the hell not?"

"I know," thought Balder, still connected to Maeve from the earlier power sharing. *"It is not that Nidhogg cannot venture beyond Nifleheim and Helheim. It is that if he does, that might be a trigger for Ragnarok, in which he plays an important part."*

Nidhogg landed one blow, and DL could almost feel Ekaterina's dragon flesh tearing beneath his claws. Ekaterina managed to break away, but now she was wounded.

"Ekaterina traveled all over Europe," thought Max. *"She must have heard the story of Ragnarok."*

An enormous drop of blood hit the ground near them and steamed on the cold ground. Unlike Eastern dragon blood, it smelled like acid.

"I don't care how she knows it!" snapped DL. *We have to do something."*

Ekaterina was trying to circle in a wider pattern, but she was moving more slowly now, and the flapping of her wings was more erratic.

"The spear of Lugh! I bet it could reach Nidhogg and be powerful enough to pierce its hide."

"It's back in Álfheim, isn't it?" asked Max. *"It can be summoned by its last wielder—but that was you in my body. I'm not sure which of us—"*

"We're both here! Surely one of us can do it."

Nidhogg scored a quick scrape to Ekaterina's tail, but again she managed to break away. Now she had two wounds, though. Her dripping blood splashed on the ground.

"It's fast, but not instantaneous. It might not arrive in time."

"We might be able to portal it here if Max and I work together," thought Maeve. *"You'll have to keep Hel distracted, though."*

"I'm on it," thought DL, stepping toward Hel. "Stop this!"

Hel laughed in his face. "You are in no position to give me orders.

Your dragon is an intruder in my kingdom and will suffer the consequences."

DL's fist was in motion almost before he thought about it. He smashed Hel in the face, and she fell backward. He was on her with another punch before she could focus her magic on him.

He hadn't thought about her shifting back and forth between life and death, but he realized the implications when his second blow struck unfeeling bone. The momentum was still carrying Hel backward, but she recovered control, hit the ground, and rolled out of the way, thwarting his third punch.

She was up again and moving even faster than a vampire. One skeletal hand absorbed the impact from his fist while another grabbed his throat.

"It isn't so easy to defeat death," said Hel.

"It isn't easy to strangle a vampire, either," said DL. He tore her hand away with his left hand, then punched her with both. Hel stayed skeletal, so he couldn't inflict pain, but he could drive her backward.

"Dubh!" she screamed.

DL flew backward as if a gigantic invisible hand had struck him and hit the ground hard enough to leave a body-shaped impression. Where was the rogue faerie? He was lurking nearby, invisible but betrayed by the enormous surge of power as he prepared his next attack.

DL drew his sword and charged Dubh, but the magic forces wedged between them were too great to overcome. Merlin's book was once again saving the little faerie rat from getting the beating he so richly deserved.

"What do we have here?" said Dubh, looking at DL as if he were some kind of freak. "It's like those cookies mortals find so tasty. A vampire with a failed-dragon filling!" He looked up. "And above us a dragon with a vampire filling. You know, changing bodies all the time isn't going to make you any less a failure, Dumb Loser."

DL had no idea how Dubh had heard that old nickname he hated so much. Hearing it from the faerie made him crazier than he would have expected. He did manage to hold onto his sword this time, but he started slashing wildly at the magic in the air, forgetting for a moment that if it came from a spell in Merlin's book, it wasn't vulnerable to the sword's power over faerie magic. The blade hit the magic, but it bounced off without cutting through the streaming power or even changing its course.

By the time he realized he was just wasting energy. Dubh twisted the power to surround him, making even the smallest movement difficult.

"You will shortly have the honor of being confined by the very spell that conquered Merlin himself," said Dubh. "You'll be Hel's guest—by which I mean prisoner—forever."

The magic solidified around DL like concrete drying—at a thousand times normal speed. He could have called out to Max and Maeve for help, but he wasn't sure they'd gotten the spear yet. If not, he couldn't afford to draw Hel's attention to them. No, he would have to get out of this on his own.

The occasional plop of dragon blood around him reminded him of Ekaterina's suffering, but it also gave him an idea.

"Yeouiju, can you do anything with that blood?"

"Do anything? I do not understand."

"It's from my body, even though that body's changed a lot."

"It's from a much-changed copy of your body. I can't do much."

"I need you to drop some of it on Dubh. Can you try?"

"For you, I will try. A little manipulation of the wind might do what you want."

DL had no idea if the blood was as acidic as it smelled, but it might at least distract Dubh. He wasn't far away. If his concentration wavered even for a moment, that might give DL a chance at reaching him or at least breaking out of the area where the spell was gradually encasing him in what looked like glass but felt like steel.

While he was waiting for a miracle, DL glanced up. Ekaterina was still in the air, but she had sustained more wounds. Time was running out.

"Max?"

"Almost there I think."

Almost there wasn't good enough. DL thrashed around in an effort to break the hold of Dubh's spell, but it only tightened.

He felt a breeze. Was it the Yeouiju trying to aim dragon blood at Dubh, or was it just a coincidence?

He looked up and froze. Ekaterina, a wing injured, dived toward the ground with Nidhogg right behind her, moving closer by the second.

Ekaterina crash-landed on the ground nearby with enough force to cause a small earthquake. Nidhogg plunged after her, claws ready to tear her to shreds.

The ground shook hard enough to knock Dubh off his feet. The spell shuddered, and DL threw himself into a frenzy trying to break loose. The glasslike magic that bound him cracked a little.

Nidhogg roared and veered, missing Ekaterina and crashing nearby. Metal glinted between two of the dragon's side scales.

The Spear of Lugh had arrived just in time.

Nidhogg rose from the ground and shook himself so hard that the air he displaced blew like a gale in all directions. The spear shook loose, but it flew back against the wind and buried its point in the dragon's flesh.

Nidhogg shook even harder, blowing fist-sized stones off the ground and making the wind howl. The spear spun through the air so far that DL could no longer see it.

Nidhogg turned toward the motionless Ekaterina. Its eyes glowed like a sickly combination of ice and poison. DL strained with all his might, and another small crack formed in the spell around him.

Fast as a bullet, the Spear of Lugh shot from the sky and once more wedged itself between two of Nidhogg's scales. The dragon screamed and shook hard enough to create a storm capable of uprooting trees. The spear was flung even farther this time. Nidhogg watched the weapon's flight, its icy eyes green with fear.

The spear flashed back like a rocket, but this time Nidhogg was ready. It flew away so fast that even DL's draconic vision couldn't follow it. A blur, a flash like moonlight hitting a glacier, and it was gone. The spear gleamed as it turned and followed the beast, vanishing in a flash of sunlight. Its magic would compel it to seek the dragon until it was recalled.

DL looked back at Ekaterina. He could see the slight up-and-down motion of her breathing—unless he was imagining that. Otherwise, she was still as a colossal statue. DL could hardly bear to think of her all alone, lying there and bleeding. He wanted to do something, anything, but cracking the rest of Dubh's half-finished spell would take days. Even worse, the faerie pulled himself back up and smiled crookedly at DL. His hair was windblown and full of twigs and other debris he didn't seem to notice. His left cheek was bruised from where a rock had struck it. He still clutched Merlin's book so hard that his tense fingers were white against the leather binding.

He would finish the spell—and DL. His determined expression left no room for doubt.

DL could still move his head enough to look for his friends. They ran in his direction—until Hel, moving quietly as a dead leaf floating through the air, blocked their path. Power buzzed around her like zombie bees, and she had a triumphant expression on her almost face.

Maeve started to cast a protective spell, but one wave of Hel's hand froze the words on her lips.

"Have you not learned that I have absolute power over my subjects?" asked Hel, flashing Maeve a skeletal grin. Hel's grim authority held Maeve so tightly that her stillness and grayness made her seem like stone.

Balder kept moving forward as if he intended to challenge that authority. Hel raised a mistletoe-filled hand and let her magic surge through that parasitic plant. Balder came to a shuddering halt. He struggled so hard he risked the magic tearing him to pieces—but he got no closer to the ruler of the dead.

That left Max, who looked so alone DL feared for him. Hel sneered and raised her hand to blast him. Even as far away from them as he was, DL felt the power of the curse she intended to fling, a malediction so heavy it would make Max beg to join Maeve and Balder in death.

Moving with surprising smoothness, Max raised his new staff. Its amber flashed, and the resulting concentrated blast of sunlight caused Hel to stagger backward. She looked around as if she could no longer see Max.

Taking advantage of her temporary blindness, Max bathed her in emerald light—a mistake. The emerald was used to reinforce order, but here Hel *was* the order. The gemlike glow turned the sickly shade of dying vegetation as the ruler of the dead twisted it to her will. Max cut off the power just in time to keep her from using it against him.

Undaunted, the young sorcerer drew on the staff again. Its diamond flashed as he amplified a druidic spell through it. From the bright, pure glow of the diamond surged the power of life, contradicting Hel's power of death, repudiating it, negating it.

Hel's mouth widened in surprise as the combination of Norse and Celtic magic hit her. It did not take her long to push back, though.

Max had thrown some good curve balls, but as he and Hel battled, DL could see in their magics the difference in their raw power levels. The staff made Max considerably stronger than he would have been unaided, but strong enough to beat the ruler of death in her own domain? Her darkness pushed back against Max's light, and DL could see the answer in the light's nervous flickering.

DL longed to join the battle, but Dubh was putting the finishing touches on the spell, closing the tiny cracks DL had made in the process.

Trying to hold the life light on Hel as long as possible, Max surprised DL by working a lesser spell into the mix. What was he up to? Multitasking like that would Let Hel beat him even faster.

The nature of the spell was odd. It looked to DL like something to do with plants. On Hel, it should have no effect at all.

The tiny strand of dark green squirmed through the whiteness of Max's other spell, twisted through the blackness of Hel's magic, and burrowed into the mistletoe. Hel didn't seem to notice when the tiny sprig disappeared from her hand.

Max started alternating between the life light and sunlight, and Hel's countermagic twisted in confusion. For the moment, Max had her full attention.

Balder was moving again—away from Hel. That baffled DL until he realized Balder was maneuvering around his preoccupied queen, heading in a roundabout way toward DL and Dubh.

Hel's magic flowed forward, darkening both sunlight and life light until Max seemed doomed to be eclipsed—and then destroyed.

The moonstone—the sharing stone—flared on the staff, and DL felt Max inside of him. He did what he could to facilitate the enhanced connection, and Max drew what strength he could from him. No, that couldn't be right. Vampire bodies didn't produce the kind of energy power-sharing could draw upon. Max was reaching through DL to tap into the Yeouiju's power.

"Max! That's all that's keeping Ekaterina's body going."

"I know. I won't take too much. I'm drawing on that dragon-strong mind of yours as well as the Yeouiji."

Hel frowned at the young sorcerer as his power surged back toward her, sparkling like amber and diamonds raining from heaven.

"Stop that immediately!" Dubh cringed at the sound of Balder's commanding voice but recovered quickly. He smirked when he realized who Balder was.

"Who are you that I should listen to you? What power does a dead god have over me?"

"None," said Balder, smiling as if he didn't have a care in the world. "However, it is one of the world's wonderful paradoxes that you have no power over me, either."

Balder took a slow step forward, then another. Dubh looked at him as if he—and not Dubh—were the crazy one.

"I could blast you where you stand," said Dubh, not sounding quite as sure of himself. "Perhaps Hel will let you remain ashes instead of allowing your Helheim body to regenerate."

"If you wish to blast me, do it," said Balder.

Balder stepped close enough to be in spitting range, and Dubh blasted him with a lightning bolt. Balder laughed. Dubh could have done more damage by throwing confetti at him.

The faerie's jaw dropped. Strain showing in his face, he conjured a full-scale electrical storm. The ground around Balder was scarred black by lightning strikes, but Balder himself remained unmarked in an attack that would have fried anyone else four times over.

DL still felt Max draw gently but firmly on his draconic energy. The vampire body felt weaker than normal, but it was nowhere near shutting down. He glanced in the young sorcerer's direction. His magic and Hel's surged back and forth, but Hel's was inching his way closer to him. He was gripping the staff so hard that the knuckles of his right hand were white against its brown wood. The brown glow around him signaled that he was drawing the strength of Yggdrasil again.

Max raised his left arm and made a clutching motion in the air as if he were invoking something, but there was no obvious magic behind his gesture.

Dubh's electrical storm fizzled out, and Balder charged him.

DL remembered his conversation with Balder when they first met. The Aesir had known what he was talking about.

"Come back and face me like a man!" roared Balder, shaking his fist at the faerie. Dubh smirked again and sprayed magic in his direction. It looked like glass but felt like steel—the trapping spell!

The magic slid off Balder and puddled at his feet. Dubh's smirk faded, and he looked in Hel's direction. Hel was still busy with Max, but his pull on DL's energy was becoming more insistent, and the brownish glow of Yggdrasil's energy was flickering. At this rate, she would be able to help Dubh all too soon.

DL tested his muscles against his own confinement. Balder had interrupted Dubh in time to keep him from finalizing the spell, but DL was getting weaker from the power-sharing. Even had he not been, he could move so little that damaging the spell would be harder than cracking a brick with a toothpick.

Maeve twitched a little, restless under Hel's peremptory spell. DL could barely see her, but, even through all the contending magics around them, he could still feel the link she had set earlier. It made him feel as if their eyes met—two trapped souls watching helplessly as people they loved died right in front of him.

DL looked back at Ekaterina. Was she still breathing? He couldn't be sure. Nor could he feel her through the Yeoiuju.

He squinted. How much blood was there on the ground? Much of it was probably beneath her, but he could see a pool at least as wide as a house.

He stared at her and pushed against the spell, which didn't budge an inch.

His eyes wanted to stay locked on her, but a flash caught his attention, and he looked back toward Max.

The Spear of Lugh gleamed in his left hand. Without letting up on his magic, he pitched the spear in Hel's direction. She had not seen it close up before, and her feeble attempt to push it aside did not keep its implacable point from smashing through her naked skull. The momentum threw her backward. She fell to the ground, and the spear dug into the soil, pinning her in place. DL felt a surge of strength as

Max stopped drawing on him.

Dubh, looking panicked, broke off his futile attempts to find a spell that could harm Balder. Power surged from the book as he tried to levitate the spear out of Hel. The ancient weapon made a scratching noise as it twisted in Hel's skull, but it didn't move even an inch out of her. If anything, it sunk in a little deeper. A tired Dubh, even amplified by Merlin's grimoire, was no match for it.

Max sent bursts of magic crackling toward Dubh. Weak as they were, Dubh flew off as if death itself were chasing him.

"What have you done?" asked the stunned Balder. "Killing Hel will interfere with destiny. There will be dire consequences."

"Pardon me for not consulting you, my lord," said Max without a hint of fear. "But, as you can see, she isn't dead."

DL looked down at Hel. She writhed as she tried to free herself. A clean shot through the head had not been enough to end her life.

"How did you know this would happen?" asked Balder. "Even I did not know she could survive such a wound."

"I couldn't be sure," said Max. "But she is normally between states, neither living nor dead. Can something that is not truly alive truly be killed?"

"You are an exceptionally good thinker for a mere mortal," said Balder.

Hel tried to scream, but since the spear ran through her mouth, the best she could do was undecipherable gurgling.

Balder moved closer to get a better look. "That is a fine spear, rather like Odin's Gungnir."

"It can be summoned by its last wielder," said Max. "Once I was sure it had driven Nidhogg back to Nifleheim, I recalled it."

"Will it keep her the way she is now?" asked Balder, looking down at the fallen daughter of Loki with obvious satisfaction.

"It was lent to me by Esras of Tír na nÓg, to whom I must eventually return it."

"Someone needs to check on Ekaterina," said DL. "Once she hit the ground, she stopped moving, at least as far as I can tell."

"I'll go," said Maeve. "Lord Balder, will you come in case I need your strength? Max, why don't you free DL?"

Maeve and Balder hurried off, and Max moved just as quickly to stand next to the trapped DL.

"The fact that Dubh didn't finish the spell will make it much easier to remove," said Max. He looked exhausted, and it took him a little time to build enough power, but once he had it, the amber sunlight of the staff melted the spell to a glassy puddle, and DL stepped out of it.

"That's a relief," he said. "You made that look easy."

Max was shaking again. "Easy isn't how I'd describe it. If I hadn't studied Merlin's magic, I would never have been able to break the spell without using a lot more force—which I don't have right now."

Maeve and Balder returned, and DL's momentary joy faded when he saw the looks on their faces.

"What's happening?"

"She is not dead," said Balder. "Her wounds are mortal, though. Neither one of us know how to heal a dragon, and she has lost much blood."

"Max?" asked DL. "With your new staff, couldn't you—"

"I'll try," said Max, already running in the dragon's direction. DL followed. Balder and Maeve moved more slowly, as if they didn't want to witness Ekaterina's death.

Outrunning Max, DL knelt on the blood-drenched ground and tried to take the dragon's head in his arms, but it was far too big. Her eyes remained closed. He felt no warmth, saw no sign of life.

SACRIFICE

"Max! Hurry!"

His friend was by his side in a second. "She's still alive, but just barely. Maybe a healing spell, amplified by the staff, can save her."

Max put everything he had into the spell. He got paler and paler. Cold sweat dripped from his brow, and his body began to shake. The brownish glow of Yggdrasil kept his life force from sinking too low. Even that glow got fainter, a sure sign Max was reaching rock-bottom. The dragon, however, didn't stir.

"Maeve! Can you and Balder share your power with Max?"

"Power...not the issue. The healing methods I...I know weren't designed for dragons. They aren't working."

"Dragons can regenerate, though. Why isn't she?"

"Eastern dragons can regenerate," said Maeve. "Western ones have more limited powers of self-healing."

"Wait! My blood—well, the blood in my real body—can heal. Maeve, use that portal wizardry to bring Esras and my body down here."

"Your body is nearly dead. There isn't going to—"

"Just do it!" Without a word, Maeve opened a portal back to Álfheim. She couldn't go through it herself because her current body only worked in Helheim, so Max went. While he was gone, and DL pressed himself as close to Ekaterina as he could, hoping his presence might make some difference. He still couldn't feel either the blood bond or the Yeouiju bond, and the Yeouiju remained silent. Maybe the multitude of unfamiliar tasks thrust upon it had finally proved too much for it.

DL should have felt more concerned about that, but his fear for Ekaterina, like the dragon body she now inhabited, was so massive that it filled his mind. Even the few other thoughts that did somehow slip through that all-encompassing fear were hidden in its shadow.

He couldn't hug her enormous body. He clung to as much of the side as he could. The scales felt as cold as the Arctic. Whatever life remained was so slight that he felt no sign of it.

Max returned with DL's limp body and a sputtering Esras.

"DL, this body is only barely alive as it is. Drawing blood is not a good idea."

"Esras, I need you to keep my body alive," said DL as if he hadn't heard the druid. "Max, Maeve, I need you to cast a spell to increase blood production. Why are you looking at me like that? It's possible, isn't it?"

"That kind of spell is intended to replace blood lost from battle wounds," said Esras. "It's not intended to create the lake of blood you'd need—"

"Just do it! We don't have very long."

Max met DL's eyes, opened his mouth, closed it again, and went to work. Maeve and Esras reluctantly followed his example.

"I have rested enough if you need to draw on my power," said Balder. He looked at DL with eyes that had seen too much suffering. "I understand better than they do. I would do for Nanna what you are willing to do for Ekaterina—do it and not count the cost."

The others might not have understood, but they labored for a long time to give DL what he wanted. It took time, but they managed to extract twice the amount of blood his body would normally hold. Balder helped apply it to the wounds.

DL had seen dragon blood heal before. The process had always been rapid. Max had come back from a bullet wound in the chest and been pretty much his old self in minutes. However, the body Ekaterina now inhabited responded very little. It didn't die, so his blood must be doing some good, but it showed no sign of healing, either.

Western dragons should feel warm, not cold. Ekaterina still felt chilling enough to breathe ice rather than fire. Max assured him she was still breathing, but if so, she wasn't breathing enough to move a feather. He tried using the vampiric senses of his current body to pick up her heartbeat. With Esras and Max, he could hear the beat of their hearts without trying. Even the Helheim bodies of Balder and Maeve had something that sounded a little like a heartbeat. From Ekaterina, he could hear nothing. He told himself the armorlike scales made the beat impossible to hear, even for a vampire—but he knew that wasn't true.

Esras looked at DL with a doctor-about-to-give-bad-news expression. "The Western dragon body is just too different. Your blood cannot heal it effectively."

"Keep trying," said DL. "Maybe she just needs more blood."

"No," said Esras, his eyes on DL even as he continued his efforts to sustain DL's body.

"No? Are you telling me you're just going to let her die?"

"I'm telling you I won't let you die in a hopeless effort to save her."

"Maybe there's something else we can do," said Max. "I…I never learned it because I never thought I'd need it, but Merlin's grimoire has a spell that could heal a dragon."

"But Dubh's got the book," said DL. "He could be anywhere right now. Maybe he's not even in the Nine Worlds anymore. No, we have to keep doing what we're doing."

Max got up from where he had been kneeling next to DL's body. "I'm not going to let you die in a lost cause, either."

"Nor I," said Maeve.

DL resisted the temptation to draw his sword. He certainly wasn't going to use it, but he was mad enough to.

"I'd risk my life for any of you. I have risked it for you, Max. Is this all my friendship is worth to you?"

"They have done what can be done," said Balder gently. "Do not waste your anger on them. Ekaterina yet lives. Perhaps you were right to think there might be another way to save her."

DL looked down at his own body's pale face. The skin looked more like white wax than flesh. Then he looked over at Esras, Max, and Maeve. "Can you at least keep working while we try to find another solution. Another few minutes isn't going to kill me, is it, Esras?"

"I can't be sure," said the druid. "If we're very careful, we can probably keep going for a little while without too much risk."

"Then do it. Balder, you are more familiar with the Nine Worlds than any of us. Do you have any ideas?"

"Alas, no. What dragons we have here are always evil. No one would have wanted to save one. What of your people? In your world, you told me there are good dragons. Could they not help?"

"Dubh sealed the exit from this plane—unless that's changed," said Max.

"Last I heard, the elven sorcerers were still working it," said Esras. "I have no doubt we could find an answer in our world—but there's no way to get there from here right now."

DL reached out for the Yeouiju. It hadn't spoken in some time, but he could still feel its power animating the vampire body.

"Yeouiju, how about you? Can you help?"

"In my present condition, I'm not strong enough. Besides, I need part of my strength to sustain the body you now occupy."

Saving Ekaterina's temporary body at the expense of her real one wouldn't have made sense, but it did give DL an idea.

"Yeouiju says he can't help, but that reminds me of the vampire body I'm in."

"I wouldn't have thought that would be an easy thing to forget," said Maeve

"Well, I'm not used to it yet. Anyway, if Ekaterina's close to death, I could turn her," said DL. "That would buy us some time."

"DL, Ekaterina knows how to fight the bloodlust, and she said fighting that dragon persona was similar," said Max. "She can only just manage to keep one or the other in line. What would happen if she couldn't handle both at the same time?"

"We'd have an undead dragon," said Esras. "An insane undead dragon."

DL was beginning to feel like Dumb Loser again. That really had been a terrible idea.

He narrowed his eyes as if he were trying to look inside his own brain and fish out an answer. Was that a tiny spark of inspiration? In a moment it glowed like a cartoon light bulb.

"I'm an idiot!" That was exactly the kind of line Maeve would have had a field day with when he first met her. Now even she looked dumbfounded.

"I've had you putting all this effort into saving what amounts to a throwaway body. The thought of Ekaterina dying had me so turned around I forgot that we've still got two bodies to put two souls in. The dragon started out as my land-of-the-dead body, though I wasn't actually dead. It's just extra baggage.

"All we need to do is put my soul and Ekaterina's soul back in the right bodies. Then we can let the dragon die."

"Oh, is that *all* we need to do?" asked Maeve with some of her old sarcasm. "You do remember that none of us know how to do that, right? Since Hel can't interfere this time, Freya could sort you out easily—but she's not here. Lord Balder, do you have any idea where she is? She, Freyr, and Thor came to Helheim with Max, but there's no sign of any of them."

"I cannot say," said Balder. "Were they inside Hel's domain?"

"Last I saw them, they were looking for the hostages near Hel's hall," said Max. "Ekaterina and I left right after they found Outcast."

"If they were in that areas for too long, Hel could have hidden the way out from them," said Balder. "All she had to do was bury them in the memories of the various dead. They could have seen through the illusion, but if she set up a complex enough spell, each time they realized what they were seeing wasn't real, they would get hit with another unreal scene. They wouldn't be able to see their real surroundings anymore, which means they couldn't find their way out."

"They're trapped?" asked Max.

"Freya should eventually be able to break the spell, but in Helheim Hel's magic is stronger than hers, so it might be some time."

"Which means she can't help," said Esras. "Not in time, anyway."

"Yeouiju helped me out of my body when I was trying to help Maeve open a portal to rescue Max and me. He could shift me into my own body. Then all we have to do is shift Ekaterina. Her soul should have an affinity for her own body, right? All we need to do is help her along a little."

Yeouiju must have been listening because it immediately responded. *"I could put your soul back in your own body. Your other request I cannot fulfill. I helped the vampire into the dragon body, but conditions were different then. I cannot feel her now. If I cannot sense her, I cannot move her."*

Max and Maeve had heard as well, and neither looked happy. "Are there any other possibilities?"

"Odin is the only one whose mastery of seidr equals Freya's," said Balder. "He could do it, but he isn't here, and we have no way of knowing when or if he will come."

"That is so like Odin," said a grating voice behind DL. "He is never around when one needs him."

DL didn't need to turn around to know that who was behind him. The looks of horror on everyone else's faces told him all he needed to know.

MAX AGONISTES

Unfortunately, it wasn't just Hel who had suddenly appeared. A large number of undead warriors converged from all directions—without any dragon to incinerate them this time.

DL had his sword out without even thinking about it, and Max held up his staff in the same reflexive way, but Hel raised a bony hand. "Hear me out if you want the dragon to live.

"Oh, and do not flatter yourselves into thinking you can defeat me in my own realm. You did catch me by surprise with that spear, but, as you can see, even it couldn't hold me. The very ground to which it bound me is *my* ground. I was able to merge myself with it, and the spear could no longer find me."

"It could find you again now," said Max. He raised a hand, and the Spear of Lugh flew into it as if it had been patiently waiting for his summons.

"I would only escape again. Meanwhile, my army would kill those of you who still live—and you would remain here forever. Even Odin could not rescue you then."

"What do you want?" asked DL.

"To be allowed to rule here as I see fit."

"Not it if means—" DL began.

"Silence! You are not of the Nine Worlds and have no business intervening here."

"By harboring a fugitive and keeping hostages he brought you, you have involved yourself in *our* business," said Esras.

"And for that reason, I am prepared to offer you a way to obtain what you want. A way to save the dragon and leave here with any hostages from your own world—if one of you will pass my test."

"What would you have me do?" asked DL.

"The test is not for you," said Hel, eying him contemptuously. "It is for him." Her bony finger was pointing straight at Max.

"I will—" began DL.

"You will learn your place!" shouted Hel. Her undead warriors swung their swords and spears as if they were aching to use them. "Who are you to question the word of a god?" DL started to say something else but stopped himself. What was the point of arguing with her?

"What test would you have me pass?" asked Max.

"One that is suited to your ambitions, my young sorcerer. In your hand, you hold a staff of Freya. Would you master seidr? Would you wish to draw as much power from the runes as she can? All this and more you can have—as well as what I just promised—if you can prove yourself worthy."

"By doing what?" If Max was trying to conceal his impatience, he was not doing a very good job.

"When Odin wished to master the runes, he hung himself from one of Yggdrasil's branches and wounded himself with the spear Gungnir. The master of the Aesir remained thus, his wound unhealed for nine days and nine nights, staring into the depths of the well of Urd, from which the runes originated. When he had survived this trial, the runes became one with him, giving him power over destiny second only to the Norns. You will be subject to a similar trial."

"This is madness!" protested Balder. "No mortal could survive such an ordeal. Odin himself very nearly died."

"That is why I am willing to vary the details," said Hel. "This sorcerer could not hold the kind of magic Odin could, so his ordeal will be correspondingly less.

"Urd bubbles from the spot where one of the roots of Yggdrasil is buried in the earth. Another root lies much closer to us, in Nifleheim, near the spring Hvergelmir, the source of all waters. From Hvergelmir, in turn, flows the river Gioll, which borders Helheim. Few know this, but the Nifleheim root extends all the way down to a spot near Gioll. To prove his worth, the sorcerer will tie himself to that root, pierce himself with the spear he carries, and hang there for one day and one night. He will become a master of the runes in so doing, and I will swear a solemn oath to do all that I have promised if he succeeds."

"And if he fails?" asked Balder.

"All of you will be no worse off than you are now—totally at my mercy."

"What you ask nobody could do…no human, anyway," said DL.

"Ah, but the young sorcerer is not entirely human, is he? I sense a trace of faerie there, and he has handled this book of Merlin of which Dubh has told me so much. He might survive. If he refuses, he'll die for certain. If he accepts, he—and all of you—might live."

"I'll do it," said Max. He took a step toward Hel, who smiled hideously at him.

"I knew you would have the courage," said the ruler of the dead.

"No good will come of this," said Balder.

"This is like a deal with Satan," said Esras.

"Max, I forbid this," said Maeve.

"What must I do?" Max's tone was an odd combination of confidence and desperation. He stood tall as he always did when his mind was made up. He didn't even glance at the others.

Balder reached for Max's arm. "She would not be offering this deal if she could get a better result by killing all of you. She has something more to gain here—something more terrible than you can imagine."

"Silence, my dear cousin," said Hel. "This is not your choice to make. Nor is it yours," she said to everyone else. "Max alone can make it, and he has."

"Max, you can't do this," said DL.

Max turned to him, looking as sad as a little kid whose puppy had just died. "A minute ago, you were ready to die to save Ekaterina. How could I not risk death to save her, you, Esras, Maeve, the hostages?

"I don't want to do this. I don't have any choice. Hel, the dragon is going to die before the test is over."

"Nothing dies here unless I wish it," said Hel. With a wave of her hand, she sent grayish magic in Ekaterina's direction. It formed a cloud that surrounded her completely. "The dragon will live at least until the end of your trial. Satisfied?"

Max examined the great beast. "The magic is adequate to keep the dragon from dying. Now, the oath."

"*Max!*" thought DL frantically. "*You know this isn't right!*"

"*It's the only way. Have a little faith. Maybe I'll survive.*"

DL longed to take his sword and cut Hel into tiny pieces. She'd reassemble, of course, but he'd feel better—for about two seconds.

The undead warriors had gotten close enough to strike in seconds. Any move against Hel would provoke an attack.

"*Maeve, what can we do?*"

"*I can't think of a way out of this mess,*" thought Maeve.

"*Yet there may be a way—if all of you are willing to chance it, for it is fraught with peril,*" thought Balder.

"*So is anything we do at this point,*" thought DL. "*What do you have in mind?*"

"*Max can survive the trial if we use the Celtic power-sharing to channel my strength into him.*"

"*That sounds almost too good to be true,*" thought Maeve. "*Where does the peril come in?*"

"*During Odin's test, he forbade any of the Aesir or Vanir to come to his aid. I am sure Hel will propose something similar in this case. If she detects what we are doing, she will consider the trial void and kill all of you, including Max.*"

"*The Celtic method of power sharing is different from the Norse, which is rune-based,*" thought Maeve. "*Hel's not familiar with our kind of magic. We should be safe.*"

"*Max is chancing so much for us. I think we have to chance this for him,*" thought DL.

"*We will be discreet,*" said Maeve. "*If we send Max only as much power as is absolutely necessary, and if I disguise it to make it appear as if it is a manifestation of his own power and his faerie ancestry, we just might fool her."*

Formulating the oaths took an agonizingly long time. Since Max was relatively inexperienced in such matters, Esras asked to assist him, and much to everyone's surprise, Hel didn't object. Balder hovered close by as well, though Hel's disapproving glance made it clear she expected no interruption from him.

"Loki's daughter is as tricky as her father," thought Balder. *"She is inserting language into the oath that will void the test in the event of outside interference. However, there's been no discussion so far of binding us by oath not to interfere. It's almost as if she is deliberately leaving a loophole that would tempt us to help Max."*

"As long as she can't tell we're interfering, I don't see a problem," thought Maeve. *"Anyway, we still don't have a better option."*

DL didn't like the uncertain expression on Balder's face. Maeve was right, though. They had no other choice. Tough as Max was in some ways, it was hard to imagine him surviving even a ninth of Odin's ordeal on his own.

Once the provisions of the oath had been worked out, Max and Hel both swore a Norse eidr—and, at Esras's insistence—bound themselves by an Irish geas to guarantee that neither could break their pact. DL felt the magic settling around them. It was passive, soft as cotton, light as air. From what DL had been told, though, the smallest hint of violation would transform it into steel. Even Hel could not fight its compelling weight upon her if she violated her oath.

Just as Balder had predicted, though, Hel made no attempt to bind any of Max's companions in the same way. They were outside the magic circle, seemingly free to execute their plan.

"We will go now to the place of the test. Those of you with Max may come if you wish—but do not interfere, or the test will be void, and all of your lives forfeit."

As if to underscore her words, the dead warriors pressed them even more closely.

"Bring Outcast," thought Maeve. *"That cursed aura of his seems to unsettle Hel a bit. He might help distract her."*

DL was embarrassed to admit he'd forgotten all about the little guy.

The warriors did not attempt to stop him when he left. Nor did they prevent him from rejoining the group when he came running back at vampire speed with the sleeping child in his arms.

He looked at Outcast and couldn't help but be reminded of himself when he was that age—an orphan in foster care. He thought he'd had it bad. At least he hadn't been under a curse or trapped in the land of the dead.

Hel seemed to be making their march to Gioll as long as possible. He knew both she and her warriors were capable of reasonable speed, but now they all walked at typical movie-zombie speed. If they all started mumbling about brains, he would not have been surprised.

Finally, they reached the fast-flowing river that must have been Gioll. Further down, it had been the river of clashing swords, but here it was just deep, black water in which nothing cast a reflection. Nearby was a mountain tall enough that DL couldn't see the top of it. Hel used magic to push away some of the soil and rock, revealing an enormous root. Even in this place of death, it pulsed with life and vitality, just what one might have expected from one of Yggdrasil's roots.

"Lay your staff upon the ground, and give your spear to me," said Hel.

"You're not getting the spear!" said DL.

Max raised a hand. "This is covered in the oaths. She can't use it, except to wound me so that the test can begin. I...I wasn't sure I could bring myself to do it, and I couldn't ask one of you. Once the test is completed, she must return it to Esras, whether I succeed or fail." He looked directly at DL. "Trust me."

"It's her I don't trust."

Esras put a hand on DL's arm. "The oath will bind her in the way Max described."

DL hated the idea almost as much as he hated the test, but he stayed where he was. Max placed the spear in Hel's bony hands, and her skeletal grin made DL's blood run even colder than the vampiric norm.

A few of Hel's warriors tied Max to the part of the exposed root that was closest to the river. Though he had agreed to the trial, the ropes bound him so tightly they dug into his skin. They could not have been tied any more tightly if Hel had feared Max's escape.

"You must look into the depths to invoke the runes," she told him—almost as if she cared whether he mastered them or not. Loki's daughter really was as tricky as her father.

DL knew the wounding was coming, but he still winced when Hel plunged the spear into Max's stomach. That kind of wound was considered a slow death, but he'd surely bleed out in less than the twenty-four hours he had to hang from the root. Already the dripping of his blood on the ground pounded like hammer blows in DL's head. He wished he could turn off the vampire senses, but even without them, he would have seen the bright red stain spreading across the lower part of Max's shirt.

Max screamed despite himself, and his face twisted in pain. DL could feel his agony through the bond. Maeve gradually amped up the connection among them and steered their strengths—especially Balder's —into him.

"You made the wound too deep!" Esras protested. "He's going to die for sure. At least let me—"

"You do nothing if you want to preserve your life—and everyone else's. I thought I was clear about that."

A ripple passed through the warriors, and they made threatening moves in Esras's direction. The druid reluctantly backed down. If looks could kill, though—and if Hel had been alive in the first place—he would have struck her dead where she stood.

The oath didn't prevent Max from using his own magic. How much good could that do him with a hole in his gut, though? DL was desperate to monitor his progress. The connections Maeve had woven for power-sharing weren't designed for two-way communication, and their earlier magical networking didn't help much. Max wasn't broadcasting anything except pain. His eyes were locked on the river. His face had settled into a pale and expressionless mask as if he were entranced. Could he achieve any kind of trance with the ache of his torn stomach throbbing through him?

DL focused on the sound of Max's heartbeat, which was too rapid, and on his pulse, which was too weak—both signs of blood loss. So was his rapid, shallow breathing.

Reaching out through the faint Yeouiju connection and the bond forged months ago when his blood had healed Max, DL tried to figure out if the strength Maeve was helping them siphon into Max was doing any good.

He could sense the gentle trickle of magic through Max's body and wished that it could be a flood. If it were, though, it might tip off Hel, whose unwavering gaze hadn't left Max for a second since his ordeal started.

DL couldn't tell what the magic was doing, except by observing any changes in Max. True to her original idea, Maeve wasn't doing anything except giving Max more power to work with. He was channeling that power through his own magic.

Hel continued to stare. Her skeleton face provided no clues about what she was thinking, but at least she wasn't denouncing Max as a cheater.

The pain's intensity gradually faded to a dull ache. Though the wound didn't heal, the blood flow diminished, and clotting further reduced blood loss. DL let himself relax a little. The extra boost had helped Max work through the pain, moderating his condition enough to be bearable.

Esras looked surprised for a second but smoothly transitioned to a poker face. He knew Celtic power-sharing when he saw it, but he wasn't about to tip off Hel, who continued to stare at Max as if he were the only other being in the universe.

DL tensed. Max's physical pain was still dulled, but a new, magical pain, swept over him in great waves. The links were jarred by his silent screams.

"*What's happening?*" DL could hardly bear what he was feeling through the connection with Max.

"*I don't know,*" thought Maeve. "*Don't let on that you feel whatever it is, or Hel will know the truth.*"

"*Odin would know far better than I, but I think it is Max's attempt to invoke the runes,*" said Balder. "*What he is attempting was hard for Odin. Even with my Aesir power flowing through him, the ordeal has to be even harder for Max. It is most fortunate that Hel didn't insist on nine days and nights.*"

Max's expression looked as if it had been chiseled into his face, but every so often he cried out from the pain. He kept his eyes on the river, just as Hel had told him to do.

"*You must be right,*" said Maeve. "*Something is flowing into him from Yggdrasil, and there is a hint of something rising upward from the river as well.*"

"The young sorcerer endures far better than I would have expected." Hel glanced suspiciously at Max's companions. "None of you would be helping him somehow, would you? Balder?"

"How could you think that?" asked the Aesir. "Have I not been a model citizen of your realm for centuries now? Did I ever break even the smallest of rules?"

Before Hel could respond, the ground shook with a California-big-one earthquake feel. The air itself vibrated.

"Is something wrong with Max?" asked DL. His friend's eyes were still locked on the river, but tears were rolling down his cheeks. DL wished he could take his place.

"The young sorcerer is fine," said Hel, looking around rapidly. "But all is not well. Someone of great power is attempting to disrupt my realm."

She glanced back at Max. "If the ritual is interrupted before its completion, the shock will kill him."

THE UNRAVELING

THE LANDSCAPE around them looked as if it were melting. Its shapes and colors flowed, merged, and split in improbable ways that would have driven a physicist to despair. Staring at the swirling, fragmenting and fracturing chaos reminded DL of the Amadan Dubh. Even with Merlin's book, did the faerie have enough magic to tear the world apart like this? DL wouldn't put it past him, but the magic around him was as disordered as the physical world appeared to be. He could not see through all the static to tell if Dubh was there or not.

Could he be hallucinating? No, the experience was too physical. The earth shifted as if a dragon were digging its way to the surface. The vibration became intense enough to rattle every bone in DL's body. Esras and Maeve raised their hands as if to cast a spell but looked puzzled.

"What's causing this?" Maeve asked.

"I can't tell," said Esras, squinting off into the distance as if he expected the answer to be written on the horizon. "So much is going wrong all at once. Something is disrupting the balance of this world— maybe even this entire plane—but I cannot discern the origin of the chaos."

More frightening then their confusion was Hel's reaction. Her eyes darted back and forth as if she expected an attack at any moment. She didn't even glance at Max, who had been her sole focus until the fabric of reality started to ripple.

DL would have expected her dead warriors to ignore the danger—after all, they couldn't die twice. Yet they shuffled around nervously, their wide eyes staring out into at the disintegrating landscape as if it would swallow them the moment they looked away.

The young sorcerer was the only one who seemed oblivious to the change. He still stared unblinkingly into the depths of the Gioll. His psychic pain still throbbed through his connection to DL, which was otherwise dead. What he saw in those dark waters remained a mystery.

DL wanted to do something to protect Max, but what? Fighting some kind of monster would be easy. Well, perhaps not easy, but maybe doable. Fighting an earthquake or a major unraveling of reality? He didn't even know where to begin.

The distortions around them bulged inward as if to crush them. Maeve and Esras started raising what protection they could, but their magic looked pale and fragile against the ever-shifting storm that threatened it. Hel raised her hands as if to push the unhinged chunks of reality back. Her spell dribbled into the fragments which drank it up hungrily, leaving nothing behind.

The bulge exploded in a blinding flash of lightning, but because it was not sunlight, it didn't blind the vampiric eyes DL was looking through. Nor did it blind Hel, who stumbled backward and almost fell when the shock wave struck her.

So far away that DL could not have seen without his sharp, vampiric eyes, Thor, Freyr, and Freya surged out of the maelstrom. DL breathed a sigh of relief. They hadn't found the other hostages, but at least they had found some way to break out of Hel's maze. Reality, no longer tortured by the collision between the magics of the Aesir and the elaborate deceptions of Helheim, struggled back toward coherence.

Hel's troops raced in their direction. The former gods faced at least a thousand dead warriors, but that wasn't their most daunting challenge.

Hel still gripped the Spear of Lugh in her skeletal hands. The oaths she had sworn as part of her agreement with Max prevented her from attacking the young sorcerer, DL, Esras, Balder, or Maeve—but the newly arrived Aesir were not parties to that agreement.

With an easy grace that made her look as if she threw spears every day, she tossed it toward Freya. With equal ease, Freya extended a warm amber light around herself. The magic protection sagged the moment the spear struck it, but the weapon lost just enough speed to give Thor time to fling his hammer at it. Mjolnir struck the spear, driving it off course with a roar of thunder and a flash of lightning. Held by the will of its wielder, the spear struggled to resume its flight, but Mjolnir drove it relentlessly to the ground and pinned it there. The spear strained to break free, cracking the earth with its thrashing, but the hammer pressing harder, sparking as it did so.

Esras frowned. "Lugh will be displeased to hear that the spear that cannot be thwarted…has been."

Thor turned to take on Hel's warriors barehanded, and his fists hammered them relentlessly. Freyr drew the Sword of Dragon Light and hacked away, moving as if he had been born with the blade in his hand. Freya her staff to pour amber sunlight into the gray ranks of the dead, who fell back before her radiance. Reinforcements were coming from the general direction of Hel's hall, though. The battle would not be easy.

Hel glared at DL and the others. "Their interference will kill Max. You have to stop them!"

Time froze around DL—or was it he who was frozen while the world raced madly forward without him? He ached to throw himself into battle at Thor's side. However, what if Hel was telling the truth?

"I'll let the Asgardians know Max's situation," he thought to the others. *"Maeve, Esras, see if you can shield Max in some way."*

He ran toward the battle without looking back. Maeve and Esras would know what magic to use, and they had Max's new staff to help them. He had to trust that they'd keep Max safe.

The dead warriors reacted to him as a hostile presence, but he was a man—or woman, considering his current body—on a mission. He had taken them by surprise, so they had no time to coordinate a mass attack, and he had no difficulty knocking them out of the way in a series of one-on-one encounters.

He got close enough to be heard over the clash of swords. "Be careful!" he yelled. "Hel says interrupting Max's ordeal will kill him!"

"She lies," Freya shouted. The malachite on the tip of her staff spread its green, protective glow around her, deflecting the swords and spears of the dead and creating a zone of calm. DL outran the dead and stepped into her protective aura.

"What do you mean?" he asked, keeping one eye on the warriors and reinforcing Freya's protection with a few well-aimed punches.

"It is not interrupting what she does to Max that will put him in peril. It is allowing it to finish that will be his doom."

DL longed to ask why, but the dead threw themselves at her from all sides. The green protection shuddered under the impact of their sword and ax blows. She reinforced the shield, but fatigue showed in her face. How long had she wandered in Hel's maze before she managed to break free? Long enough to weaken her—and the battle against Hel's army was just beginning.

DL moved to engage the dead, but she put a hand on his shoulder.

"There are too many foes, even for a warrior as strong as you are. If you try to engage them, they will tear you to pieces."

DL scanned the mob that struck Freya's protection again and again. There were a lot of them, but they had no holy objects, no fire, no silver, no wooden stakes.

"I could take them."

Freya smiled, but it was a tense, putting-on-a-brave-face smile. "Perhaps you could. You are in some ways less than human—yet more as well." Her eyes widened. "DL? You have changed bodies again."

"That's a story for later. Let me help."

Freya's smile was fainter this time. "Only as a last resort. If you should die, Hel will have you. I have no idea whether the death of your current body will actually cause your death, but the risk is a grave one. I will not take it lightly."

Freya's staff was indeed an exact twin of Max's, just as Sindr had implied. The brown energy of Yggdrasil twined down its shaft and into Freya, who strengthened the barrier.

DL felt a little better knowing Freya had a reserve to draw on. Ekaterina's body had no power to offer her—none that she could use, anyway. Yggdrasil would help for a while. He looked around to see how Thor and Freyr were doing.

Thor wielded a sword he must have grabbed from one of his fallen opponents, but he kept frowning at it. He was used to better, but he couldn't call Mjolnir back without releasing the Spear of Lugh to race straight at Freya's heart.

The lord of thunder already had a long, bloody gash on his left arm, but he ignored it, letting tiny drops of his life splash on the ground as he hacked relentlessly at foes packed almost as tightly as the ones around Freya.

Freyr was holding his own—barely. The Sword of Dragon Light slashed through the dead with little effort, but, as before, they didn't stay down long, and new ones were coming all the time.

Preoccupied with the unsettling battle, DL flinched a little when Freya's fingers touched his temple.

He could still see the battle in front of him, but he could also see a shimmering overlay—a vision from Freya.

Two images formed in his mind, side by side: the well of Urd, on which Odin had meditated, and Gioll River, on which Max was now focused. They were both deep and magical, but the waters of Gioll were much darker. Instinctively, he knew they had been touched by death. Any knowledge of the runes that came from them would be tainted by death as well.

The images changed: a side-by-side view of a branch of Yggdrasil and the root to which Max was tied. They both looked equally powerful, but their powers were different. The branch pulsed with life. The root writhed in agony. Was that because it ran between Nifleheim and Helheim, or was there some other reason?

As if in answer to his question, DL saw Nifleheim. The root plunged into its icy soil, but just above ground level, the enormous dragon, Nidhogg, was chewing on it with swordlike fangs. He tore at the root, and his venom flowed into it, infecting it and spreading its poison clear down to Helheim.

"He'll die, won't he?" DL asked.

"Or worse," muttered Freya. "Much worse."

DL reached out to Esras, Maeve, and Balder across the battlefield. The connections among them were strained by all the magic in the air, but they still held.

"Hel misled us. Freya says she has corrupted the ritual. There's no way for

Max to succeed—or escape serious injury. Get him off that root! I'll be there as soon as I can."

"*We will do what we can,*" thought Esras. "*We are not bound by oath, but if we free Max, that voids Hel's oath. She can attack us at will.*"

"*That's a polite way of saying, 'Get your ass back here,'*" thought Maeve.

"*Right away,*" thought DL with more confidence than he felt. Even if he could fight his way through the dead horde, that could take an hour or more—assuming Freya would allow him to leave. He might not have more than a couple of minutes.

"My lady, I need to reach Max to make sure he gets free. It's last resort time."

Freya looked as if she had swallowed a mouthful of nettles, but she nodded. "I can get you away from the group that surrounds us, but I fear I cannot shield you the whole way."

"I will be grateful for whatever you can do," said DL, bowing.

Soaking up a little more of Yggdrasil's energy from the staff, Freya held onto the malachite aura of protection but launched a new spell. Amber light blazed over the dead warriors, and they backed away, covering their eyes.

They were still packed pretty tightly. DL tried to figure out how to get past them.

"Hurry!" said Freya. "They recoil from the light because it reminds them they are dead, but the effect will not last long. Go now!"

Saying a silent prayer, DL made the only move he could. He jumped high enough to land on the shoulders of one of the warriors. He jumped again before the warrior could grab him, landing in a spot where the dead were less tightly packed. A quick sprint got him clear of them—but they were far from being the only warriors around.

In the distance, he could see Hel, already striking at his friends. He was going to be too late.

No! There had to be a way.

He ripped the heads off a couple of warriors who charged him. Another lost an arm. He was no closer to his friends.

He couldn't get to Freya, whose amber light no longer held the nearby dead at bay. Thor and Freyr were just barely holding their own. If he was going to find a way to reach Max and the others in time, he had to do it on his own.

The Spear of Lugh thrashed around nearby, still held down by Thor's hammer. The dead shied away from the steady flow of sparks from Mjolnir, so that area was clear. He ran to it.

He had an idea. It might be a stupid one. It might get him killed. It was the only way that had even a chance of getting help to Max in time, though.

He grabbed the spear's shaft. Hel was its last wielder, the one to whom it responded. If he touched it, maybe he could supersede her and send the spear back to fight her.

Still struggling against Mjolnir, the spear twisted so hard in his hands that it tore the skin on his palms.

He squinted at it, struggling to interpret what he could see of its magic.

As usual, he didn't understand what he saw. He kept his hands gripping the spear shaft, making new wounds faster than the old ones could heal.

Was he sensing something from the spear or just imagining it? Vampires could sense much about their prey, but the spear wasn't animate. Still, he had the instinctive sense that the spear wasn't even aware of him. He was neither wielder nor target. He was irrelevant. Only getting free and taking the life of the target was important.

How could he not have realized that the spear wouldn't accept a new wielder in the middle of pursuing a target? His Dumb Loser days had never ended.

His blood formed an ever-growing puddle on the ground. The spear shaft was wet with it, too.

Wait! The spear did notice the blood on its shaft. It was the wrong blood, irrelevant—but the spear acknowledged its presence. The wood shifted slightly, opening tiny pores as if to drink it.

The Yeouiju prevented DL from feeling the hunger for blood, but vampires were every bit as bloodthirsty as the Spear of Lugh—not loyal to a wielder nor committed to a specific target, but like the spear in its lust for blood. They were kin in that way.

And kin were tied by blood.

The vampire body was influencing his thoughts, responding to his emotions by shifting him toward instinct rather than reason.

Vampires couldn't do magic unless they had practiced sorcery in life. Ekaterina had no magic while she lived. She could sense magic, but not manipulate it. What his instincts were driving him toward required at least some magic to work, and this body had none.

Except it wasn't an ordinary vampire body. It was animated by the energy of his poor, overused, broken Yeouiju.

And it had within it the soul of a dragon. It had a soul—a soul that had recently been in the body of a sorcerer, a soul that had felt the maddening touch of Dubh and the soothing touch of Freya.

Logically, none of that meant he had the power to bend the spear to his will—but screw logic! Instinct was his only hope.

He embraced the body. He surrendered to it.

Blood bonds. Ekaterina's body was bonded to his through the sharing of blood—the strongest tie to a vampire. The only instinctive tie. Once he let go, he could feel his own body, lying so near Hel. His body, in turn, was tied to Max's because his draconic blood had healed the young sorcerer. He could feel Max—or what was left of him—through that bond, though it felt muddied, disjointed.

He shoved those bonds at the spear, but it made only the barest acknowledgment of them. It felt them through his blood, but it didn't care.

Ekaterina's hands—his hands now—were being torn to shreds by the spear. He had to maintain his grip, though.

Esras was the druid guardian of the spear, a proxy for Lugh himself. As such, he was the prime wielder.

"I'm a friend of Esras," he said, as if the spear could understand him. Its language was only blood. Words meant nothing to it, except when a wielder commanded it.

"Maeve, can you hook me to Esras?"

She didn't reply. DL looked over in their direction and realized why. Hel had already beaten them.

Maeve was standing stiff as a statue, thwarted by her status of one of the dead. Balder and Esras lay on the ground, bleeding. That meant Max no longer had their support. Even across such a great distance, DL could hear his screams.

"Esras is wounded, maybe dying," DL told the spear. "Wounded by the last one who wielded you. She is not a true wielder."

His words fell on deaf wood. Max's screams tortured him like a stake through the heart.

Blood. Esras's blood was on the ground.

He didn't try to think his request to the Yeouiju. Instead, like the vampire body, he embraced it. He was one with the body. He was one with the Yeouiju. Together, they could do what none of them could do separately. They could forge a new connection.

Some of his blood had soaked into the shaft. Leveraging the vampiric affinity for all things bloody, DL strengthened the bond between the lost blood and that which remained in his own body. He reached out along the line of the vampire body's blood bond to his own, pulling the spear's magic into the bond.

Esras's blood was near, so near he could smell it through his body's nostrils. His mind stretched along the ground until he touched it. Carefully, he linked it into the makeshift additions he had made to the blood bond.

The blood sang in every cell of his vampiric body. He was not just linked to it. He was one with it.

"Do you feel that?" he asked the spear. *"Do you? The one who presumes to wield you has hurt your primary wielder. She is no true wielder."*

His words were drenched in blood, and the spear heard them. Esras's blood sang in his veins, and the spear heard its song.

"Thor! Call back your hammer!" yelled DL. The hammer flew back to Thor's hand, and he cried for joy as he took down five of the dead with one swing.

The spear was still in his hand, awaiting his command.

DL thought of Hel and cast the spear in her direction with all his might. It cut through the air so fast it whistled like the wind. As he followed it, the dead back away, frightened by the spear or by the blood-song in his veins. He didn't know or care which.

By the time he reached the spot of Max's torment, both Hel and the spear were gone. Near where Hel had been standing was a hole. Through his blood, he could feel the spear as it dug deeper and deeper into the earth.

Hel's absence left him free to focus on Max. Maeve's paralysis must have cut Max off from the power-sharing, but DL was still feeling the turmoil within him, still hearing his screams.

DL blinked. The magic of root and river had been subtler before. Now they were blatant, visual screams to match Max's audible ones.

The process was much further along than he had expected. What he now recognized as the unhealthy aura of the root had completely engulfed Max. DL could barely see him through the magical haze that surrounded him.

Even worse, if Freya was right, were the blood-red runes that rose from the river and flowed into Max. The runes weren't supposed to appear until near the end of the process, but here they were. One hit him, and he convulsed. Each encounter raised the volume of his scream.

DL tried to untie Max, but his wounded hands were clumsy. Even had they been healthy, strong magic held his bonds in place. DL needed something magical to counteract it.

Maeve remained frozen. Wind rustling through her hair gave her the illusion of movement, but she would be no help. Esras was still unconscious. So was Balder, and he couldn't use his own magic without help anyway. Flashes of lightning were getting closer, but Thor, Freyr, and Freya were still some distance away—probably too far to arrive before Max had been completely infected.

Outcast had claimed to know some magic. Supposedly, that's part of why he had been cursed. The story could easily have been a lie, but DL had always been inclined to trust the boy.

What good would any magic he had be at this point? The boy himself was in an enchanted sleep sustained by the binding holding his hands.

DL had just manipulated magic, but it was a small adjustment, working with preexisting magic and driven by a vampire's affinity for blood that would not help in this situation.

There was one other potential source of magic—Max's new staff. Did it work like Merlin's grimoire? Could someone without magic of his own still use it to cast spells?

Come to think of it, DL had a little magic of his own—sort of.

"Yeouiju, I need you to get Max untied."

"I feel as if I drank blood. I feel…soiled."

"It wasn't great for me, either, but I had no choice. Now—"

"The magic upon his bonds is too strong."

"I figured it would be, but can you make use of this staff?" DL picked it up. He could sense the magic, but the wood felt flat and lifeless in his hand. *"It is made from the wood of the world tree, crafted by the best duergar and with runes etched into it by Freya herself. Can you get anything from it?"*

"The nature of its power is alien to me, but I will try."

DL watched the staff for any sign of connection as the Yeouiju worked. A couple of times he thought he saw a flicker of power, but it might have been his imagination.

"Master, I have failed you. The staff has power, but I do not know how to access it."

"You did what you could," said DL.

He looked over at Max, whose eyes were staring mindlessly at the river as the runes flowed up to him.

Max knew how to use the staff.

"Yeouiju, is part of you still in Max?"

"It is, but it is a small part, like an echo. It is overwhelmed by greater forces."

"Can you get from his mind anything that might help you use the staff to free him?"

"I can try."

The Yeouiju did not sound hopeful, but DL had no choice but to wait. Freya might have found a way to come to him if he had any way of communicating with her, but he knew his shout could never carry that far, and, as far as he could tell, she hadn't kept open the channel she used to send him the vision.

The staff flared with power so suddenly that he dropped it. He scooped it up, glad no one had witnessed his fumbling.

"I know a little now. I have not mastered the staff, but aim it at the bonds, and I will try."

One rune, in particular, glowed brightly on it.

"Eihwaz." The voice sounded like Max whispering. *"The rune of journeys. One cannot journey if one is bound."*

"He is held too strongly," said the Yeouiju. *"I cannot break him free."*

"Can you break Maeve free?" asked DL. It was grasping-at-straws time.

"Her body belongs to this place, not to her. It is held in a way I cannot overcome."

"Outcast—can you break him free?"

"The one you speak of is not bound as strongly. I will try."

This was truly the last thing DL could think of. There was still a chance the Asgardians would break through, but more dead warriors kept coming as if there were an endless supply.

DL had become so used to hearing Max scream that he had almost stopped being aware of it. When Max suddenly stopped screaming, it was jarring.

The flow of runes had stopped. The glow around Max was blood-red like the runes, and it was getting brighter.

Hel had tricked them all—and there was nothing he could do about it!

Maybe, just maybe, the process wasn't completely finished.

"Yeouiju, get this done!"

"The spell is working, but I can't control the speed. At the power level I was able to draw from the staff, this is the best I can do."

The Amadan Dubh reappeared, surrounded by the stolen glow from Merlin's book.

"I really thought Hel's plan would fail," he said, smirking at DL. "I should have known Dumb Loser would guarantee its success."

More than anything else, DL longed to throw his sword so fast it would pierce the faerie's rotten heart, but he knew the bastard was fast enough to dodge a move like that and was certainly expecting it.

"By the way, Hel will be back any time now. I helped her trap that spear of yours underground. She wanted to be here in time to see the results of Max's transformation."

DL did his best to tune Dubh out. His concentration probably didn't make any difference in the Yeouiju's efforts, but it was best not to take chances.

"You're just wasting your time," said Dubh. "It's already too late to save Max—the Max you knew, anyway. Something is in that body, but it isn't him."

"If it's such a waste of time, why are you trying to distract me from it?"

Hel rose from the earth. She was back to shifting between her living appearance and her dead one, and during the times she had lips, her smile was triumphant. DL's confidence melted away.

Yeouiju kept working, though, and Outcast's bonds fell away. The little boy opened his eyes and looked into DL's.

"It's about time someone saved me!" His voice sounded the same, but there was a glow around him, getting brighter every second. Off-the-charts power surged from the little boy—who clearly wasn't a little boy at all.

Was that a good thing or a bad thing? The kid's expression offered no clue, but DL's vampiric instincts tingled.

Blood. There was something about his blood.

SPECIAL GUEST APPEARANCE

"Dubh, watch them," said Hel, waving a hand in DL and Outcast's general direction as if they were no longer enough of a threat to be worthy of her attention. She walked over to Max and stared at him as if she could see what was happening inside him.

Even though still unconscious, Max throbbed with power. It was darker than Outcast's, more subdued, but Hel was much closer to Max. It wasn't surprising her eyes would be drawn to him. Dubh, much closer to Outcast, started to snicker and then stop. In the faerie's eyes, DL could see the reflection of Outcast's glow.

"Who are you?" asked DL. The question sounded lame, even to him.

"Have you not guessed?" asked Outcast, his voice now sounding like that of a much older man. "You are a quick study in so many other ways."

Outcast's little boy form dissolved into a cloud, but not the way the landscape had earlier. The change was not chaotic or disturbed. The cloud that had been Outcast rose gently, growing as it did so. DL and Dubh were left standing in its shadow, but that didn't frighten DL, either. The emerging form was fierce, yet familiar.

Standing before him and raising a spikey white eyebrow was Yong-Wang, the dragon king himself!

"After all, I said I would be watching you. You were moving around so much, I felt the need to travel with you."

"Majesty, please, can you save my friend? He did nothing to deserve what's happening to him."

The eyebrow rose even higher. "It may be too late, but I will do what I can."

For such an enormous creature, the dragon king moved gracefully and majestically. His earth-tremoring footsteps immediately drew Hel's attention, breaking her concentration on Max.

"Who are you to intrude into my realm?" she asked, waving her own staff in his direction as if she could banish him with it.

"You have someone who does not belong to you," said Yong-Wang, using his claw to point at Max.

"He agreed to all that was done to him, and it was a great favor for which he will thank me."

"From what I can see, he will not thank you. He has suffered much, and the power within him is not exactly what he was expecting. You have deceived him about its nature. Worse, his choice was made under coercion. It grants you no rights over him."

"What gives you the authority to judge me? I am the queen here, not subject to the whims of outsiders."

"The fact that you held me and one of my subjects captive gives me the right."

DL hadn't been sure that Hel's face could convey surprise. The skeletal phase didn't, but the human one looked as if she had been slapped across the face.

"You were that boy. I knew he was dangerous! I should have killed you when I had the chance."

"I am done talking. Release your captive or face my wrath!"

At that moment, light surrounded the dragon king, darkened, and hardened into bars that formed a cage around him.

"Merlin's dragon imprisonment spell!" yelled Dubh, clapping his hands in childish delight.

He was not so gleeful a moment later, when Wong-Yang brushed aside the bars with one claw stroke.

"Which it seems only works on Western dragons," he said. "Wrath it is, then!"

His roar shook the earth far more than his footsteps had. Hel backed up a step. Dubh looked as if he wanted to flee but had forgotten how.

Though the sky had been clear only a moment ago, somehow it was raining as if rain were going out of style. DL was drenched to the skin, but his vampire body didn't feel cold.

"You...you can't—" Hel looked up at the rain, eyes wide, hands clenched on her staff. From it her power surged upward, twisting the clouds as it warred with Yong-Wang's magic.

The dragon king laughed and scooped up Hel like a rag doll. He threw her a football field from them. The bone-shattering landing wouldn't keep her out of action for very long, but it might give them time to free Max before she could interfere again.

The rain was fast morphing into a downpour of biblical proportions. DL was having a hard time keeping his footing. The much less physically sturdy Dubh was having an even harder time staying airborne. He splashed on the ground before he could get a decent protection spell going. DL would have dearly loved to rip his head off, but Esras and Balder looked as if they were in danger of drowning—not to mention DL's original body, which faced the same danger. He raced over to save them. There would be time enough for Dubh when everyone was secure.

Getting Esras and Balder conscious again was not as difficult as DL expected. However, the sight of Yong-Wang's massive form unsettled them more than he had expected.

"That's who Outcast really was," said DL. "He's here to help."

"We can use it," said Esras, though he looked uncertain. It took him little effort to shield DL's body, Balder, and the paralyzed Maeve from the incessant pounding of the rain, but he looked up at the sky, eyes narrowing in irritation.

"Perhaps your large friend could stop the rain now. It's going to be a distraction to keep the weather protection up."

"Alas, I cannot," said Yong-Wang, cheeks flushed in draconic embarrassment. "Hel lacked the time to wrest control of the weather from me, but her attempt warped the original magic enough that I cannot easily end it. It should fade naturally as Hel's innate control of this realm reasserts itself.

"Let us hope that will be soon." The druid's tone was polite but stiff —and unlike him.

Yong-Wang nodded. "I must do what I can for the young man tied to the tree root." He lumbered toward Max. Esras glanced after him, scowling.

"Are you OK?" asked DL.

"My nerves are as tight as bowstrings," said Esras. "And the rain isn't helping. Don't worry, though. I still have enough magic left to spare to make sure your body stays alive. We really need to get your situation straightened out soon, though. Even magic has its limits."

"Perhaps getting Merlin's book back from Dubh will help," said DL. Dubh was not too far away and seemed totally absorbed in a new spell. Now was the time to strike!

He dashed toward Dubh, but the ground was mud, and he kept slipping in it. Rain was slowing him down. It must have been even harder on Dubh, but the soaked faerie kept chanting for all he was worth, even though his voice was almost drowned out by the wind.

DL was almost close enough to grab Dubh when the faerie shuddered and began to grow. DL tackled him, but the spell was already complete, so Dubh kept right on growing—and changing. He threw DL off him with like a dog shaking water off.

Still lying on the ground, Dubh was morphing into a full-grown dragon. His new, dark-red scales glittered in the lightning flashes like flickering fire. His eyes burned like volcanos. His mouth was big enough to swallow DL whole. There was only one thing he could do.

"Yong-Wang! Help me!"

DL heard only the howling wind and the plop of raindrops on the muddy soil.

The transformed Dubh rose from the ground with surprising speed and roared. He looked angrily down at DL and opened his gigantic mouth. Fire burned in his throat. Tongues of flame surged hungrily toward freedom.

Dubh opened his maw even wider, but as the flames emerged, they collided with the downpour. At first, the flames won out, but they fizzled out long before they would have burned DL, leaving only a cloud of steam behind.

Roaring in frustration, Dubh swiped at DL with one of his claws. DL dodged and sprinted away as fas as the swampy ground allowed.

Dubh lumbered after him, his movements stiff as a wind-up toy's. His inexperience with the dragon shape might just keep DL alive—for another minute or two.

Where was Yong-Wang? From what DL could tell through the relentless rain, the dragon king was still trying to free Max. He hadn't heard DL's cry.

That left DL few choices. He could run toward the dragon king, but the distance was great enough that he probably wouldn't make it. Anyway, that put the dragon extremely close to his relatively defenseless friends.

DL followed the lightning. From what he'd heard, Thor could take on a dragon, particularly one whose breath weapon was neutralized by the weather. The Aesir still had his hands full with undead warriors, but DL could help out with those long enough for Thor to unleash Mjolnir against Dubh.

"Yeouiju, alert Yong-Wang that we have another dragon to deal with."

"He knows. If he leaves your friend now, there could be dire conse-quences. He has faith you will evade the dragon until he can help."

DL wasn't sure whether to smile or cry. It was great the dragon king had so much faith in him—but the thunderous thuds of Dubh's claws just behind him made him wonder if that faith was misplaced. He couldn't fault Yong-Wang for trying to save Max first, though. That was what DL wanted him to do.

The dead warriors tried to block his path, but most of them were focused on the Asgardians. He had little difficulty cutting through the lines of the few who remained, and in Dubh's rush to strike, he trampled many of the ones DL hadn't cut down on the first pass.

"Dragon!" he yelled at Thor. Of course, Thor would have to have been deaf not to have heard Dubh's earthquake-inducing footsteps by that point, but DL was responding more by instinct than by strategy at this point.

DL had expected Mjolnir to plow right through Dubh's dragon

skull, but Dubh was getting a little better at using his draconic body. He let himself fall to the ground with as much force as he could muster. Thor's hammer throw missed. Mjolnir, unlike the Spear of Lugh, didn't pursue him. Instead, it returned automatically to Thor's hand for another throw.

Dubh's colossal belly flop threw Thor off-balance, and he couldn't manage another throw right away. Freyr and Freya both fell. The only good thing was that the dead warriors had also been jolted.

Dubh jumped up with surprising speed and lunged straight at Thor. His claws struck the Aesir and knocked him aside. Thor landed with a crunch that might have been bones breaking and lay still. DL prayed he was stunned and not dead.

DL called to the Spear of Lugh. Since it drove Nidhogg away, the more amateurish Dubh would be no match for it.

The spear didn't answer his call. Hel and Dubh's magics had trapped it too well underground.

Freya and Freyr were on their feet again, but dead warriors surrounded them, hacking with their swords and axes like the killing machines they were. The green glow of malachite swirled around them and stretched over to encompass the fallen Thor. Freya's magic looked thinner and flickered more than before. Her eyes had the emptiness of someone exhausted and flying on autopilot. Freyr did not seem quite as hollow, but his sword swings were slower and cut less deeply. Thor was still out cold.

DL ran as if his life depended on it—in the opposite direction from the Aesir. They were too weak and preoccupied to stop Dubh, and there was no sense getting them killed with him.

Not needing to breathe or worry about his muscles wearing out meant he could sprint indefinitely. The flooded ground sucked at his shoes, though. He slowed to keep from stumbling, pacing himself more like a distance runner than a sprinter.

Dubh, whose strides were block-long, gained on him fast.

DL saw the enormous crack nearby, no doubt a result of the draconic shock waves. It was big enough to slide into but far too small for Dubh to follow him. That just might distract Dubh long enough for help to arrive.

Was plunging into soil responsive to Hel's will a good idea? No—but it was the only idea he had.

Dubh swung at him, and he dodged, throwing himself into the nearest crack. It was deep, but not bottomless, and his vampiric body took the crash in stride.

He jumped to his feet. Mud and rainwater poured down on him through the crack. The soil this far down was riddled with uninviting tunnels that looked as if they might flood or collapse at any moment, but Dubh was above him now, blocking out what little light there was.

Dubh dug in huge, sloppy chunks of earth, widening the crack into a pit. Mud sprayed everywhere. He reached down, but his claw fell a few feet short. He pulled it back and dug out another massive scoop.

Uninviting or not, the only way out was down one of the tunnels.

NOT QUITE HIMSELF

MAX FELT as if he was trying to crawl out of a bottomless pit. He was conscious but unconnected to the world. He was alone in darkness, with only background whispers for company.

The voice of Yggdrasil murmured to him. The runes clamored, echoing the rhythms of the Nine Worlds—and beyond.

The human mind was not designed to handle so much, and Max was having a hard time sorting it out. Yes, that was the problem. When he got used to the new forces flowing in his skull, things would be better.

But why didn't he perceive the physical world anymore? And what was that other insidious whisper, that serpentine muttering not quite covered by the racket in his brain?

Another voice spoke in his head, a new one. No, not entirely in his head. He heard it through his ears as well. It was drawing him back toward the world.

As he tried to struggle back, the rune thurisaz blazed redly in his mind. He had studied it a little with Maeve, but this was no book knowledge—the rune was carved into his mind like a physical one chiseled into stone.

The rune of Thor made his will stronger than before. The way he used to be, he might not have come back from whatever Hel did to him.

Now he knew he had the power to defend himself, to rise above her spells and schemes.

He opened his eyes. The enormous eyes of a dragon peered back at him. Once, he would have been afraid, but the wisdom of ansuz, the rune of Odin, told him it was the benevolent Yong-Wang who looked into his eyes.

"You will live," boomed the dragon king. "Live, but never again be the person you once were. That I cannot change."

"I know the runes," Max mumbled. "They are inside me now."

Yong-Wang raised a spikey eyebrow. "I fear that is not all that is inside you. However, you may have the strength to steer your own course despite the venom that nibbles at your soul. Only time will tell."

Rain fell all around them, pouring, raging, hammering the earth. It did not fall on them, however.

"Please let me feel the rain," said Max quietly.

Yong-Wang waved a claw, and the rain descended, but to Max, it was gentle, healing. Ansuz told Max that Yong-Wang's rain was normally healing, but it was not Yong-Wong who was making it soothe Max. It was the power of thurisaz that transformed it.

"Never have I seen a mortal adapt with so little effort," said Yong-Wang.

Max lifted himself off the ground and raised two arms to the sky as if welcoming the rain. He laughed like a little kid with a new toy.

"There is much to be done," said Yong-Wang. "Your friends are still in danger."

The dragon king's words changed Max's mood almost instantly. He had almost forgotten who he was, how he was connected to others. Now those memories came rushing back to him.

"Where are they?"

"Alas, still scattered. The ones called Esras, Balder, and Maeve are nearby, as is DL's body. See, they are right over there." The dragon king waved his claw, and Max could see them, even though the rain was coming down in sheets.

"Go to them. I will return, but I must deal with another dragon first."

Yong-Wang soared into the air and flew rapidly away, graceful despite his size, unhindered by the rain. Max ran to the others, equally unhindered by the rain, as if the blessing of Yong-Wang shielded him.

"Max, you're all right," said Esras. His tone hugged the boundary between statement and question.

"Never better," said Max. "The power-sharing kept me alive long enough for the ritual to complete—and for that, I thank you all."

Balder nodded, but he kept his eyes on Max as if he couldn't quite believe what he was seeing. Esras looked puzzled by the lightness of Max's tone, but he didn't comment on it. Instead, he pointed to DL. "He lives, but just barely. We've got to get the right souls in the right bodies—and soon. If we could get Freya here—"

"I think we can manage without Freya now," said Max. "The ritual worked, Esras. I now know the runes as well as any mortal can. With Freya's staff, I should be able to make everything right." He glanced over at his grandmother. "I'll free her first. That should be easier."

Balder shook his head. "As a citizen of Helheim, Maeve is in some ways in Hel's power, and it was Hel who froze her in this way. Even Freya could not probably break her loose unless she spent hours or days on it—and perhaps not even then."

"There is no harm in trying," said Max, picking up the staff. Holding it felt more natural now, but at the same time, he sensed some kind of resistance. The staff shuddered in his hand. Perhaps it no longer recognized him in his newly empowered form. If so, it would learn to know him again.

The runes answered his summons. Ansuz contributed to his wisdom and power, thurisaz raised protections around him, and eihwaz opened the mysteries of life and death to him. There was something else, too. It wasn't a rune. It was more like a force independent of the runes that slithered through and around them. Perhaps it had come from Yggdrasil, whose root had been nourished by the soil of the land of the dead. Whatever it was, it enabled him to see exactly how Maeve was held. The dark strands of magic wrapped around each muscle were as clear to him as if a diagram were painted on her skin.

He shaped the runes' power and fed it to the staff. The runes on the shaft burned red, the stones at the tip flared in a multi-colored display, and the magic flowed over Maeve, who was free in under a minute.

Released from the paralysis, Maeve teetered, then nearly fell. Max raced to her side and caught her. How had he moved so fast? Had his body been transformed in some way as well as his mind?

"How…how did you free me?" asked Maeve.

"How indeed?" asked Balder. "How could you, a mortal, undo Hel's control in her own realm?"

"I guess Hel was right—the ordeal made me the master of the runes."

"As a greater ordeal made Odin their master, but I doubt even he could have done what you just did."

"Freya warned us there was something wrong with the ritual," said Esras.

"Even if there was, I think the dragon king saved me from whatever else was supposed to happen," said Max. "All I am now is more powerful and knowledgeable than I was."

Esras and Balder were looking at him as if he had started sprouting an extra head a minute. Even Maeve looked uncertain of him.

"Look, if there was some side effect I don't know about yet, we'll deal with that later. Right now, we need to get the right souls back in the right bodies. Esras, you yourself said DL's body wouldn't last much longer, right?"

The druid nodded reluctantly. "It's already held up better than we had any right to hope."

"Ekaterina in the dragon is closest. As I recall, Hel stopped that body from dying, but she might pull the plug at any moment, so I should do something about that situation first."

"But what?" asked Esras. "We don't have her body to put her soul back into, nor do we have any other suitable receptacle."

"We have DL's body. The Yeouiju, who is familiar with both, can ease Ekaterina's transfer. Once DL is back with Ekaterina's body, we can switch them, and we're done."

"That's all well and good," said Maeve. "You don't know how to do that kind of switch, though. None of us do."

"I know now. I can use a variation of the same seidr move Freya used when she put me back in my own body."

"You have mastered seidr as well?" asked Balder.

"The runes seem to be showing me the way." Max sat down on the ground. It was muddy, more water than dirt, but he didn't care. "Watch over my body while I'm out of it. I should be back in just a minute."

Esraz opened his mouth and raised his right hand as if he wanted to object. Ignoring him, Max slid into a seidr trance as if he'd been doing it his whole life.

Eihwaz showed him how to project his mind out of his body the Norse way. Fehu protected him and facilitated his travel to the dragon body. Since fehu was linked to the primal fire of Muspellsheim, it also eased him his mind into that body as he reached for Ekaterina's soul.

She wasn't conscious. She lay in the body of the dragon like a faded image of her former self.

"Ekaterina?"

Her soul shifted uneasily as if a nightmare were whispering to her, but she didn't wake up. Could he make the switch without her conscious cooperation?

The runes revolved through his mind like planets around the sun, each traveling its path in harmony with all the others—and with Max, who was both center of their dance and apprentice to their masteries. Mannaz, rune of the self and humankind reached out and linked Ekaterina's individuality to his so that he could pull her gently toward him and guide her in her sleepwalking toward DL's body.

Knowing that Hel might try to grab her soul—or his, for that matter —he reached out to the runes for additional protection, and Algiz, the rune of shielding, answered his call, cloaking both his soul and Ekaterina's in the warmth and security of its power.

"Yeouiju, I bring Ekaterina's soul to reside temporarily in DL's body."

"Not My Master, you have…changed."

"For the better, I hope. Will you help me ease this transition? It will not be long before this soul can return to its own body, and your master will, at last, be restored to you."

"I do not know if I should."

Since his own grandmother doubted him, he shouldn't be surprised the Yeouiju did. "This is the soul of the woman whose life your master begged you to save. By accepting her into his body, you do his will. Besides, *that body cannot survive much longer without a soul. He will have no place to return to if it dies."*

Max felt the Yeouiju's power lift Ekaterina from his guidance and place her gently into DL's long-vacant body as if she belonged there.

Being nearly dead in the other body for so long had left Ekaterina exhausted, so Max put her into a regenerative sleep using the runes thurisaz and kenaz. That would be good for DL's body, too.

Max was expecting at least a little praise for getting Ekaterina out of the dragon body before it died and keeping DL's body alive, all in one neat move. Esras, Maeve, and Balder were all happy about those developments, but they were still suspicious of him.

"You learned the runes in less than a ninth the time Odin took, and you handle them like an Aesir who has known them for centuries," said Balder. "Even Odin required a little practice to use the runes so smoothly. I can't help thinking that Freya was right."

"I still can't see why Hel would make me more powerful on purpose," said Max. "It makes more sense to assume she was trying to trick me or kill me, and something went wrong with her plan.

"Esras, Maeve, you remember when Merlin told me I was supposed to have been one of his incarnations but that his imprisonment changed his destiny—and thus mine?"

Both druids nodded reluctantly.

"Well, maybe this is the universe's way of trying to set things right. I was supposed to be a powerful sorcerer—and now I am."

"Your *body* was supposed to be occupied by a powerful sorcerer," said Esras. "Had that happened, your soul—what makes you Max and not Merlin—would have been born as someone else. I don't see how making you more powerful balances things out.

"Anyway, from what I've seen and from what Morfesa's told me, you might have become a powerful sorcerer without that ritual. The process would just have taken longer."

"Speaking of Morfesa, wouldn't our time be better spent finding her, Gerda, and Adreanna?" asked Max.

"Perhaps it would be best if we joined Thor, Freyr, and Freya first," said Balder. "We don't know how Hel has the hostages imprisoned. We might need their help. The dragon king might prove invaluable as well."

"Since Yong-Wang isn't back yet, Dubh must have used a portal to escape or something. I assume the dragon king is tracking him. If so, Yong-Wang could be gone for some time." Max looked across the plain to where Thor's lightning flashed, still visible against the raging storm. "As for the Asgardians, they're still fighting the dead warriors. We could help them, but they aren't in any danger, are they? We can't say the same of the hostages."

"No one is safe," said a familiar, grating voice.

Hel had risen from beneath the ground, this time looking human more often than corpselike.

Before she had looked arrogant, angry, or grim. This was the first time Max had ever seen her look frightened.

HEL'S DUNGEON

DL RACED DOWN one of the tunnels—not an easy task, considering how uneven it was. Stumbling around was better than becoming Dubh's chew toy. At the rate the newly transformed dragon was digging, the best plan was to get as far away from him as possible and hope Thor or someone would notice him and take him out.

It was a good thing DL was in Ekaterina's body rather than Max's. As a vampire, he could see in the dark as well as in his own body, maybe even a little better. He was also better able to keep his footing than he would have in Max's body.

It didn't take long before he could no longer hear Dubh digging. Not much later, he couldn't even feel the vibration. Had he really moved that far, or had Dubh stopped digging for some reason? Either way, DL figured it was a good time to look around.

The tunnels weren't as well made as those of the dark elves or the duergar. They twisted and turned too much, as well as changing size for no apparent reason. Sometimes they widened into small caverns; at other times their height narrows so much that he had to crouch down to pass through.

Did Hel make them as she traveled through the ground? That wouldn't account for the changes in size. Besides, Hel seemed able to drop straight through solid ground, so she could probably walk through the lower layers just as easily without having to dig. That would explain how she managed to trap the Spear of Lugh in the earth.

Now that he thought of it, since he was stuck down here anyway, he might as well try to find the spear. That seemed like a good idea when he first thought of it, but his enthusiasm for it didn't last long. Part of the problem was that the vampire body could sense magic but didn't distinguish types well, and the soil around him was filled with what he assumed must be Hel's magic. He would have to get fairly close to the spear to have a chance of sensing it over the background magic—and he had no idea where it was or even what direction to go.

The one thing the presence of so much background magic confirmed was that Hel could probably trap him down here, maybe even crush him. Since there wasn't much he could do to prevent that, he tried not to think about it.

If he couldn't find the spear, maybe he should try to get back to the surface. He still had his sense of direction, so in theory, he could just start digging upward and reach the surface. That might be dangerous, though, since he wasn't sure where Dubh was, where Hel was—where anybody was, for that matter. He could use the Yeouiju to find Ekaterina or Max, but without knowing where the bad guys were, that would be risky.

Who moved through these tunnels if not Hel? Her warriors would be the most likely guess. Why would they need to move around underground?

There could be only one answer: something was kept here.

If it were just storage for magic objects, that wouldn't do him any more good than knowing the spear was down here. However, it might make a good spot for keeping the hostages or other prisoners. If they were hard to find above ground, they'd be doubly so down here—to someone without vampiric senses.

Vampires could sense warm bodies a long way away, to say nothing of smelling humans and even hearing heartbeats. Why not poke around a little, and see what he could find?

Sure enough, when he focused himself, he became aware of other living things. Some were small mammals. Maybe Hel had a gopher problem. After a few minutes, though, he sensed larger life forces. He could hear human heart beats as if the soil were throbbing in rhythm with them.

Sensing them was one thing. Finding a way to them was a whole other problem. DL didn't know how—or even if—the tunnels were organized. The one he was in might conceivably never lead directly to the spot where the hostages were imprisoned. He followed it a little further, but the heartbeats grew fainter.

He started digging. He hated using the sword for such a task, but using Ekaterina's delicate hands as tools was even more unthinkable.

He poked at one of the tunnel walls. The blade sank in slowly, and his muscles had to strain to get it even that far into the tightly packed, stony soil. It needed to be softened up before he could dig properly.

He stabbed at the wall several times as if he were fighting a giant. The unyielding soil loosened enough for him to dig at it with the sword. Bits of soil plopped on the ground—small pieces, tiny by comparison with the shovel-fulls he needed to move.

He kept digging because he had no other choice. The sword protested with loud clangs whenever it struck stone, but it didn't break or even chip. He looked at its unmarked surface, runes still glistening as if they had just been engraved. He tested its edge with his finger. It was still sharp.

He shoved the blade back into the wall, praying it would continue to take the abuse. Slowly but surely, the pile of dislodged soil grew.

DL wasn't sure how long he'd been digging when he saw light coming through the hole.

"Who's there?" He had never been so happy to hear Morfesa's voice.

"It's DL. Just a second, and I'll join you."

"You don't sound like DL," said Morfesa.

"Oh, yeah, I'm in Ekaterina's body right now. It's a long story."

"I don't doubt that. Are you alone?"

"Yeah, but only because I'm here by accident."

Like a horse that trots faster as it nears home, DL dug faster, resisting the temptation to check his sword after every few strikes. As soon as the hole was wide enough, he slid through.

Next to Morfesa was a beautiful woman who must be Freyr's wife,

Gerda. On the floor lay a college-age woman—she had to be Adreanna. She was cute, but what caught DL's eye was her skin—it was as white as Ekaterina's. She looked as if she were asleep, but if so, it was nightmare-ridden sleep. Her eyes moved frantically beneath her eyelids. She tossed and turned as if she were trying to break away from a monster. She panted like a runner. Fear twisted her face.

"What happened to her?" DL asked Morfesa.

"The same thing that would happen to most humans if faced by experiences too far beyond what they can understand. Considering what Dubh must have put her through, she's lucky to be alive."

"Is she under a spell?"

"Mine, not Dubh's. She kept becoming hysterical. I did what I could for her. This ground impedes any magic that isn't created by Hel or one of her allies. Otherwise, I might have been able to start her healing."

"You…you are dead?" asked Gerda. Like most of the inhabitants of the Nine Worlds, she had never seen a vampire, much less a good one. To her, any dead person must have seemed like a potential servant of Hel.

"I'll vouch for him," said Morfesa. "He is a friend, one of those I came with—and very much alive."

"He?" asked Gerda.

"Apparently, his soul is in the wrong body." Morfesa rolled her eyes. "Even I, who spend most of my time in Tír na nÓg, have seen many things during our stay in the Nine Worlds that I have never seen before."

"And that's without considering what's happened to us since you've been captured," said DL. He filled her in as quickly as he could.

"How fares my husband, Freyr?"

"He thinks of little besides you, my lady," said DL. "He will not be happy again until he is reunited with you."

Gerda smiled at DL for the first time, and he understood a little better how Freyr could doom himself just to be with her. Though she didn't glow the way the light elves did, that smile lit up and warmed the whole room.

"Have you a plan for getting us out of here?" asked Morfesa. "Obviously, I can't get a portal open."

"Well, I dug my way in," said DL. "I can tunnel to the surface, and then—"

"That's risky," said Morfesa. "I can't sense much through this soil, but I do feel the heavy rain above. If the ground near the surface is as soft as I think it is, your tunnel might collapse. Even if it didn't, we could drown when you broke through to the surface."

DL sighed. "I guess you're right. I hadn't thought of that. There has to be some way out of here, though."

"If only we had some duergars," said Gerda. "They could tunnel out from here easily with the right tools."

"Morfesa, you said you couldn't generate enough power for a portal. What about power sharing?"

"Adding Gerda's power didn't do it, and I don't dare try to draw from Adreanna."

"You have me now."

Morfesa looked irritated. "Don't you remember? Power sharing can't draw from a vampire. The energies are too different."

"Give me some credit. Yeah, I remember. However, this body also has the bulk of the Yeouiju in it. Most of its power is keeping the body alive, but there could be a little to spare. Could that make a difference?"

"Well, I did get close. Portals are more about skill than high power level, anyway. Gerda, are you game for another try?"

"If it gets me back to Freyr, I will wrestle the Midgard Serpent if I have to," said Gerda.

"Yeouiju, what about it? Are you able to spare some power?"

"Impeded as I am, I may not be able to supply the amount needed without allowing this body to die."

"Can you give a little if the body becomes…oh, I don't know, dormant maybe?"

"I can try, but such a thing is dangerous."

"The Yeouiju says it can do it if one of you can carry me through the portal. It may not be able to animate this body and provide enough power to get the job done at the same time."

"I shall carry you," said Gerda.

"Then I'll carry Adreanna," said Morfesa. "Distance isn't an issue, but

I'd rather try to find the rest of our group than go back to Álfheim. Once I get us above ground, I should be able to locate the others."

"That is best, anyway," said Gerda. "I would not wish to leave Helheim without Freyr. I may be needed to fight at his side."

DL raised an eyebrow.

"Did you think you were the only strong female here? My form is as misleading as yours. Though I can become human-sized, I am a Jotun—giant—and more than capable of holding my own in combat."

"Apologies, my lady," said DL. "I should know by now that women can be beautiful and strong." He was rewarded by another smile from Gerda.

It took Morfesa only a short time to establish enough connection among them to power share. That was the easy part. Opening a portal was still tough, even with a Jotun and the Yeouiju to draw on.

At last DL saw a little silver shimmer in the air and knew that Morfesa was close. Just as he noticed that, he felt much weaker and drifted toward unconsciousness.

No, more than unconsciousness. He had been close to death before. What he was feeling now felt much more like that.

The Yeouiju must be making him dormant—or so he hoped.

Maybe he should have told Morfesa about the risks.

FIRE AND ICE

"I PASSED THE TEST!" yelled Max, waving his staff. "Now you must keep your part of the bargain."

"And which part of that bargain involved bringing yet another dragon into my realm?" asked Hel. "However, I did not come to argue with you. We are all in danger. The hrimthursar—frost giants—are on their way here with murder in their hearts."

"Are they not your allies?" asked Maeve. "If they are on their way, surely you had a hand in that."

"It was not I, but the young sorcerer, who summoned them. I fear he is more powerful than even I expected him to be."

"I summoned no one," said Max.

"Not deliberately, but you used the rune fehu, did you not? Unwittingly, you drew upon the power of the primal fire in Muspellheim—so strongly that the frost giants believe the fire giants have entered Helheim. They also believe I have invited them here, in violation of our ancient agreement. Though the dead and all the giants will fight on the same side in Ragnarok, until then the forces of Nifleheim and Muspellheim are at odds with each other, and those of Nifleheim can call upon the forces of Helheim as allies. The frost giants believe I have instead allied myself with the fire giants."

"That's ridiculous," said Esras. "This is just some trick to deny us what you have promised. Surely, the frost giants cannot be as dull-witted as that."

"They are not…very reflective creatures," said Hel. "They respond more by instinct than by wit—and their instinct is telling them the fire giants have penetrated Helheim. As far as they know, such a thing could only happen with my permission."

"But if you explained—" began Maeve.

"They will listen to no explanation. They will kill everyone they can find. I will survive such an attack, but those of you who live, as well as your friends from Asgard, will not. Yet there is a way to stop them: harmonize the power of fehu with that of isa, the primal ice. It was that collision turned into harmony from which the Nine Worlds arose in the first place.

"Freya could do that, but she will not believe me any more than you druids do. Max, you can do it. You must do it."

"Why can't you do it yourself?" asked Max.

"The Norns have carved my fate into the wood of Yggdrasil itself. I am not destined for such an undertaking. But the Norns have not locked the fate of those who dwell beyond the Nine Worlds. Just as Dubh has brought disruption to those worlds, Max, you could bring hope. You could save your friends and so many others."

"That does not make sense," said Balder.

"Silence!" yelled Hel. "Do you think I don't know that Max accepted help from you and the others, Balder? Do you think I can't smell it on him? His pact with me is null and void because of you. Doing this service for me is now the only hope the hostages have."

The ground began to shake rhythmically.

"She's right about one thing," said Max. "The frost giants are coming. I can sense them. The pulse in the ground is the beat of their marching feet."

"You can stop them," Maeve said to Hel.

"I can perhaps delay them by making Gioll rise—but they will be all the angrier when they get here, and all the more certain that I am their enemy."

"What must I do?" asked Max.

"It's a trick—" began Balder.

"Silence!" yelled Hel, and Balder could no longer speak. Hel held another sprig of mistletoe. The air vibrated with the magic needed to restrain him, but it was only a whisper compared to the thundering footsteps of the frost giants, which grew more jarring by the second.

"What must I do!" asked Max, much more loudly than before.

"Let me into your mind just a little, and I will show you how to bring isa and fehu together in harmony. When the frost giants feel the effects, they will return to Nifleheim."

Maeve started to speak, but Hel silenced her as well. Esras continued to protest, but Max was focused on the horizon. By the power of thurisaz, he could see through the rain well enough to distinguish the enormous shadowy figures that had just appeared on the horizon.

Max summoned up the helm of awe, a circle from which projected eight algiz runes, each of which was crossed by three isa runes. The wisdom of ansuz told him that was one of the strongest protections known to runecraft. Having shielded himself as well as he could, he looked at the impatient Hel. "Do it."

"No!" protested Esras, but Max no longer heard him.

He felt Hel in his mind, but if she sought to harm him, the helm of awe held her back. She guided him with a gentleness he did not expect.

He was vaguely aware of Esras trying to tackle him as a way of preventing the spell from going forward, but his assault failed against the helm of awe. By the time the druid figured out how to counter that defense, it would be too late to prevent what Max was doing.

He felt the primal fire and ice face each other in his mind. Hel steered them closer together. They touched, united—and exploded with so much force that it nearly caused Max to black out.

The frost giants gave a war cry in unison and continued their advance.

"That wasn't what you said would happen!" Max expelled Hel from his mind and raised the staff. Its runes glowed with fury.

Hel laughed like stone grating against stone. "Primal fire and primal ice did come together to create the Nine Worlds—but they were not supposed to come together in that way again until Ragnarok. You have triggered the end—long before its time."

"I'll fix it." Max summoned up every ounce of runic knowledge. There had to be a way to reverse rune magic.

"No, what you will do is look inside yourself—and know the truth of who you are now!"

Despite himself, Max looked inward. A fierce image of the dragon Nidhogg stared back hungrily at him.

"You have absorbed enough of Nidhogg's venom from the corrupted root to bind you to it—and me—in a fundamental way. You are now master of the runes. I didn't lie about that. But I am your master...forever."

"That's impossible. That would break your oath," said Max, though his instincts told him it was true.

Hel gave him a blood-chilling smile. "Your companions helped you, as I knew they would. They used magic I couldn't detect, but I could sense the power of Balder within you. There is no question that they violated the agreement. My oath was void almost from the moment your test began."

Max tried to fight her growing influence upon him, but the helm of awe dissolved, rune by rune, until it was gone. He could not avert his inner gaze from the eyes of Nidhogg, which grew bigger and bigger until they blotted out his sight of everything else.

He was no longer looking at Nidhogg.

He was Nidhogg.

"There," said Hel. "That's a good dragon."

FINDING A HAYSTACK IN A NEEDLE

MORFESA STEPPED out of the portal near Hel's hall. That was a risky choice, but if all went well, she could be out of the area in a couple of minutes.

Rain pounded down on her. She raised a magic shield, but the water had already drenched her and Adreanna. Gerda carried DL through, just as he had suggested. The portal closed, but he didn't revive.

"Is she dead?" asked Gerda.

"It's hard to tell with a vampire," said Morfesa. "He'll probably revive shortly, but just in case, we should reunite with the others as soon as we can. We may need their help, and this place isn't safe."

Morfesa reached out with her mind to find Esras, whose druidic power would be easy to pick out among all the various traces of seidr. She felt him, and he was only a league or two away.

"I have just found Freyr by seidr. As I thought, he is in battle and needs me," Gerda said.

"We have two unconscious companions that we can't just throw into battle," Morfesa replied. "Let us reunite with the friends from my world, make sure Adreanna and DL are safe, and then all of us can help Freyr."

The jotun closed her eyes again. "Thor and Freya are with him, and they seem to be fending off Hel's army for now. I will do as you request."

Since Esras was at a place Morfesa had never been, she couldn't just open a portal. However, her levitation skills were good enough to simulate flight, and now that she was above ground, she had no difficulty raising the four of them on her own.

Flying made them more visible, both physically and magically, but the one virtue of the intense rain was that it gave them some cover as Morfesa maneuvered them slowly through the air. She had also done what she could quickly do to make them harder to detect, but she had no doubt that, if Hel were looking for them, she would find them. With any luck, the ruler of the dead still thought they were imprisoned underground.

As they got closer, Morfesa knew something was wrong. She had been so tightly focused on finding Esras that she hadn't noticed much else about the area, but now she could feel an enormous buildup of magical energy near him. No one in their party could possibly generate so much power. Could Hel? Perhaps Hel and Dubh with Merlin's grimoire could have managed it together.

Whoever—or whatever—was raising such forces was dangerous. Based on the location of the power, its summoner had taken Esras and the others prisoner. Morfesa slowed to a stop and did what she could to make them invisible. That would only hold if no one suspected they were near.

"What's wrong?" asked Gerda.

"I'm sensing far more magic than our party could be responsible for. You're much more familiar with this plane than I am. Can you tell me what's happening?"

Gerda went into a trance, but only for a moment. When her eyes flew open, they were filled with terror.

"Hel has found some way to tap into the runes in a manner I've never seen. Worse, an army of what you would call frost giants has arrived from Nifleheim. We could not face either one by ourselves, let alone both."

"Your instincts were better than mine to begin with," said Morfesa. "We should have sought out your kin first. Can you tell me where they are?"

"Just follow the lightning," said Gerda, gesturing toward the frequent flashes to her right. Drifting over a battlefield wouldn't have been Morfe-sa's first choice, but they needed the help of Freyr and her kin.

When they glided close enough, it was easy to spot Thor and the others, locked in combat with a horde of Hel's dead warriors. Morfesa had no idea the ruler of the dead commanded so many troops.

"They're not as skilled as the armies of Valhalla and Folkvang," said Gerda, looking down at them and sneering. "Unfortunately, they are far more numerous, and even chopping one of them to bits wouldn't keep it out of the fight for long."

"Even if we join them, I don't see any quick way to win this fight," said Morfesa.

Gerda nodded. "There isn't one. Thor isn't going to like this, but our best hope is to scoop them out of this battle. Hel's warriors can't fly, and in this rain, it will take them some time to reach the place where Hel is gathering her power. If we strike fast, we may be able to rescue your companions. Delay too long, and we may not prevail even with the help of Freyr, Freya, and Thor."

"Wise advice—but how do we go about extricating them?" Thor appeared the hardest pressed. Between his hammer and its lightning, he could devastate the dead, but they compensated by hitting him with far greater numbers. Freyr was making short work of his adversaries with a glowing sword, but he could only dispatch one at a time. Freya, enveloped in power and wielding her staff with great skill, was keeping the dead at bay, but whether or not she could break away from them was another question. She had been a goddess of love and fertility, not war.

"Leave that to me," said Gerda. She reached over to DL and unfastened Brisingamen from around his neck. "Freya will need this." She tossed the necklace in the general direction of Freya, and it floated down like a feather.

Freya grabbed it and fastened it around her own neck. The dead warriors drew back from its golden glow, uncertainty twitching through their lifeless faces.

A ray of light shot from Freya to Freyr to Gerda, binding the three. An image of a v tilted to the right filled Morfesa's mind.

"It is the rune kenaz," mumbled Gerda, her face suddenly radiant and smiling. "It is the power of fire harnessed by civilization, but it is also the bond of kinship and the burning passion of sexual love. Freya is invoking her kinship with Freyr and the love between him and me."

Glowing with fiery light, Freya and Freyr rose from the battlefield. A few spears followed them, but they burned to ashes before they could strike. The two Vanir joined Gerda and the others high above the battle. Gerda and Freyr embraced each other with more heat than the fire that formed an aura around them.

Power poured from Freya in warm, gentle waves. The energy shifted, and the image of a symbol something like a p filled her mind.

"What's happening?" the druid mumbled.

She hadn't intended to speak, but Freya glanced in her direction. "Kenaz would not have worked to bring Thor to us. What you sense now is thurisaz, a rune with a special affinity with him—and with Mjolnir, his hammer. Observe."

The rune's power arced downward like lightning. It struck Mjolnir, exploding in a blinding flash. Thor flew skyward, cursing and flailing.

"What is the meaning of this?" asked Thor. "The battle is not yet won, Freya. Why have you called this cowardly retreat?"

"Have you not yet seen?" asked Freya. "Fighting the dead is not a battle one can win. You could have stayed there until Ragnarok and never won a final victory. Let us go to where a battle can be won, or, if not, at least friends can be rescued."

"What friends?" asked Thor. He was still red-faced, but his eyes lit up.

"The very ones who accompanied us on this journey. See, the original hostages have been rescued already. All we need do is reunite our rescue party and leave this place. We can stop playing Hel's game and return to our vital roles."

"That is good," Thor said. "Her trickery has the potential to bring chaos to the Nine Worlds. Lead on!"

Morfesa's mind filled with the image of a very straight trident.

"That is algiz," Freya explained. "It provides protection, but it also has a connection to the Valkyries and can enable us to fly as they do. I could have used my cloak of falcon feathers for that, but I could not have carried the rest of you with me."

Morfesa, tiring from so much levitation, was happy to let Freya drive for a while. She could also relax her shield against the rain. With only a fraction of the effort she had been exerting, Thor caused the rain to fold around them, keeping them dry. His blessing also prevented the rain from slowing them, and they shot forward like an arrow. Clouds formed beneath them and kept pace with them, creating a magical floor to assist Freya in keeping everyone airborne.

"Gerda," said Freya as they neared Esras and the others, "take a look and see what dangers might await us."

Gerda pulled reluctantly away from Freyr, who had been embracing her since Freya had first flown him up. It did not take her long to scout using seidr.

"The frost giants have assembled."

"Ah, combat!" said Thor. "And with opponents who can actually die!"

"Not just some frost giants," said Gerda. "Most of their army, from what I can tell. Hel is also there. There is also…someone else. A great sorcerer I do not recognize."

"Would we not know anyone that great?" asked Freyr.

Freya's eyes narrowed. "She's right. I can sense the power without even going into a trance. There is…runic energy at a level beyond what anyone except Odin or me could match."

"Perhaps it is Odin," said Thor. "I would have expected him to come to our aid."

"No, it is…someone else," whispered Gerda.

"He carries a staff like mine," said Freya. "How could such a thing be?"

Morfesa reached out with her mind, but the power levels were so high that it was hard to distinguish anything specific. She tried sharpening her vision to superhuman levels—and immediately wished she hadn't.

Standing next to Hel was Morfesa's pupil, Max—but he wasn't really Max. He was somehow…possessed, but not by Merlin this time. No, not by anything half so benign as Merlin at his worst. How could this have happened?

"They know," whispered Freya. "They know we are nearby."

ENTANGLED BY ROOTS, POISONED BY BLOOD

"Nidhoggson, do you feel it?" asked Hel. "Our enemies approach."

"They will be sorry they did." Deep within him, a voice cried out that Nidhoggson was not his name, but he ignored it. He was getting better and better at doing that.

Using eihwaz to send forth his mind, he could see them floating in the air nearby. The Aesir Thor; two Vanir, Freyr and Freya; the druid Morfesa; a jotun, probably Freyr's wife, Gerda; an unconscious mortal woman, too weak to be significant; a dead body that was somehow not quite dead—and not of Hel's realm. That was a mystery he would explore once he had crushed the others.

He glanced at the captives. Hel's ground held them, all but the heads, and kept whatever magic they might have in check. They would not be able to interfere with the battle.

He paused for a second when he noticed the face of the one unconscious captives. It twitched as if he were dreaming. This one seemed more familiar than he should. Nidhoggson dismissed the thought. Hel was important. His mission was important. Nothing else could matter. Nothing else did matter.

"What is our plan of attack?"

"Counteract Freya's magic. She won't be prepared for what you can do, and by the time she realizes what she's up against, it will be too late. The frost giants will be more than enough to take care of Thor and Freyr fighting alone. As for the druid, I can get her to surrender just be threatening her colleague. The others are too weak to matter."

"They must be able to see our strength. Surely, they will run."

"Not if they can't fly. None of them can outrun the frost giants."

Nidhoggson smiled. "Shall I ground them, then?"

"You and I will do it together."

Hel willed the ground to rise beneath them, bulging into a hill and continuing to swell, thrusting toward them as a mountain. Nidhoggson probed at the energy sustaining them in the air. It was from algiz, just as he suspected. He inverted algiz in his own mind, and the strength of Freya's flight spell faded.

The Vanir's will locked with his own as she tried to counter him. They grappled like two giants wrestling. She might have won that battle, but Hel's mountain collided with her. The soil grabbed at her feet, and she struggled against its pull.

The frost giants surged forward, heading for the mountain and their prey. They could scale it in a few strides and be upon their enemies. To reinforce their attack, Nidhoggson bombarded those enemies with isa, rune of ice. The rain became hail and smashed at them like thousands of tiny hammers.

Freya countered with kenaz, rune of tamed fire. She melted the hail, but her feet sank deeper into the soil. Taking advantage of her distraction, he resumed his attack with isa.

Gerda joined the fray with kenaz. She wasn't as strong as Freya, though, and he was able to beat back her efforts.

The frost giants reached the bottom of the mountain, and their battle cry shook it. Mjolnir crushed the skull of one with a single sparkling blow. Lightning bolts took out another two, but three others were halfway up the mountain.

Nidhoggson was sure Thor alone could never hold them back, yet the thunder lord took out those three just below the summit. Their bodies fell, knocking off three more below them.

"The terrain is to their advantage," Nidhoggson told Hel.

"Not for much longer," replied Hel. The mountain sank back into the ground, carrying the Asgardians and their companions with it. Unfortunately, the frost giants were not quick-witted enough to delay their advance, and a few more fell from the mountain as it melted away.

On a level plain, the frost giants could crush them easily—or so Nidhoggson thought. As the Nifleheim warriors readied themselves to charge, Freya invoked the primal fire of fehu coupled with the protective virtue of haggalaz—mother of all runes, the cosmic egg born of the first meeting of fire and ice. Her expert working raised a wall of flames, hot but with a solid shell around it, like transparent metal. The frost giants stopped their advance, their spears bouncing off it. Behind them, Gerda inverted isa to weaken the frost giants.

"The Asgardians will wear down eventually," said Hel. "However, it would be better if they did so without killing too many more of our allies."

Nidhoggson countered Gerda with the force of isa, empowering the frost giants to even higher levels. Hel raised her own staff and blasted the enemies with ear, rune of the grave. Its dark power might give the mortal a merciful death but would doom Aesir and Vanir alike to a much slower one. Freya could counter that force, but probably not without lowering her shield, at which point the frost giants would finish them off.

With a flash of lightning, Mjolnir hurtled in Hel's direction, forcing her to cease her casting and flee into the protection of the soil. The hammer struck the ground, knocking Nidhoggson over and cracking the rocky soil for a league in all directions. Then it returned to Thor's hand as fast as it had come.

Nidhoggson looked down at the spot where Hel had vanished. He expected her to return immediately, but she did not. No matter. He would keep the enemies at bay until she reappeared.

"Max!" He barely heard the shout over the storm and the uproar of the frost giants. He wasn't sure why, but he turned in the direction of the voice.

It was one of the captives, Esras.

"Max!" he yelled again. Nidhoggson didn't understand him. The man must have gone mad from captivity. He would not allow himself to be distracted. Without Hel, he needed all his concentration to keep their foes from getting the upper hand.

Projecting isa power at the ice giants was doing no good. They didn't want to brave the fires of fehu. Instead, he inverted fehu and haggalaz and projected their combined force at the enemy shield in an effort to bring it down.

Hel stuck her head through the soil cautiously, but lightning crackled toward her, and she dived back into the ground.

It was curious Thor didn't try to smash him with the hammer. Perhaps his enemies thought him unimportant. He would have to prove them wrong.

"*Max!*" This time the voice was more emphatic and in his head. It was not from Esras this time, though. Another captive, Maeve, stared at him.

"*Max! Stop this! Fight Hel's control!*"

The old woman should not have been able to reach him. Hel had imprisoned the captives in a way that should block any magic.

Hel again rose, but the rumble of thunder as Mjolnir streaked toward her forced her back into hiding. The hammer struck the spot into which she had descended, spreading more cracks through the battered soil.

Though there was no sign of Hel, the hammer struck again in the same spot. Nidhoggson squinted at the growing fissures, some of which had reached the captives. That was why Hel's magic was losing its grip on them.

He should do something to reinforce their imprisonment. They were weak, but not necessarily helpless. However, Hel had bound them not with the runes or even with seidr, but with her own innate power over this world.

Mjolnir's next strike loosened the nearby soil enough to allow some of the captives enough movement to struggle against their earthy prison. Nidhoggson had no choice but to run over and check on them. He mustn't allow anyone to escape.

Unopposed for the moment, Gerda lashed out at the frost giants with isa inverted, but, though they did not yet advance, they held their ground. The sheer weight of their numbers made it impossible for the front line to retreat. Anyway, Gerda's magic was a minor annoyance compared to Hel's implacable spellcrafting—or his own. They could manage a couple minutes while he attended to the captives.

None of them had managed to break free, but he examined the ground around them carefully. It would hold a few more minutes, but that might not be long enough. Raidho, rune of journeys, flashed through his mind. He reversed it, and, projecting the power through the diamond on his staff to amplify it, reinforced the hold the ground had on the captives. Just to be sure, he used isa to add the strength of primal ice to the shattered soil. Hel herself could have done no better.

He started to turn away, but they began yelling at him again. He needed to silence them. He needed to avoid distraction.

He visualized uruz, rune of strength and potential. Inverting it, he started to weaken them. One of them was already sleeping a troubled sleep. It would be easy to make the other ones pass out.

"Max!" yelled Maeve. "You don't know what you're doing!"

Max must be a name. She was wrong, though. His name wasn't Max, and he knew exactly what he was doing.

Nidhoggson hesitated. A working of great power was happening nearby. He felt the magic pressing upon him like a boulder. Someone strong like Freya was invoking wunjo, rune of joy, love, and friendship to heighten her awareness of the forces binding all things together. At the same time, she was using fehu in its capacity as a pathway to transfer mind, soul, or magic from one place to another.

His eyes narrowed. It *was* Freya—and she was up to something big. He would have to stop her.

REVERSAL

"GOT HER AGAIN!" said Thor, delighted.

"That would do us more good if you could actually hit her," said Freya. "As soon as she decides there's no point in rising above the ground, she'll start casting from below. This is her soil, and we're standing on it. There is no way I can protect against the death rune and keep the frost giants back."

"Let us weave a Helm of Awe together," said Gerda. "That's the best general protection."

Freya shook her head. "Against a smaller number of adversaries, that would be an excellent plan. But against Hel and a frost giant army? They will pound us until the protection breaks. Even the two of us together can't hold back that much force indefinitely."

"We have to find some way to get through to Max," said Morfesa. "I know him. He may not look it, but he's strong. Whatever spell Hel has him under, he can break free with a little help."

"And again!" yelled Thor.

"He is poisoned by Niddhog's venom," said Freya. "Never have I seen such corruption of a mortal. An Aesir or Vanir would have a hard time overcoming it. Someone like Max? I hesitate to say anything is impossible, but if anything is, surely this must be."

"This one is disquieted," said Freyr, pointing to DL in Ekaterina's body. He no longer looked dead, and he was twitching as if having a nightmare.

"His soul is close to its own body—and knows it," said Morfesa. She looked in the general direction of the prisoners. "The vampire body is also recovering from its recent exertions. If we can get the souls into the right bodies, we have two more people who can fight on our side, one of whom is close to Max. If DL were back in his own body, he might be able to take Max by surprise."

"Getting the young sorcerer out of action would be a boon, but from this distance making the switch would be difficult. Even with Thor keeping Hel busy, we still have the frost giants to worry about, and making the switch would be difficult. I would not be able to maintain our protection if I had to perform such a complicated task at the same time."

"If Gerda and Freyr allow it, I can link them to share power," Morfesa suggested. "They could maintain the defenses while you get the souls back where they belong."

"Conditions are far from ideal, but the risk might be worth it. I will try—if Gerda and Freyr are willing."

"This Celtic power-sharing is most useful," said Freyr. "I am willing."

"As am I," said Gerda.

"Then let me know when you are all ready," said Freya. "We must all be prepared when I hand the defenses over to you. The frost giants will exploit even the slightest weakness.

It took Morfesa little time to join Freyr and Gerda for power sharing. The druid planned to lend her own power to the defenses as well, but she held back just enough to be able to follow what was happening around her.

Max was too promising a sorcerer—too promising a person—for him to be destroyed in such a way. She had to keep watching. She had to know when DL saved him.

As Gerda took over maintaining the shield around them, Morfesa felt the power flow from her smoothly. Though the Norse practiced a very different kind of power-sharing among themselves, they adapted quite easily to hers.

Freya was already in a seidr trance. Morfesa couldn't follow everything she was doing, but she did feel the depth of the Vanir's meditation. Performing such delicate magic in the middle of a battle would require no less.

Morfesa also felt the shift when Freya let her consciousness flow toward DL's body. She would make herself a bridge between it and Ekaterina's. If she managed what she was attempting, the souls of Ekaterina and DL would flow from one body to another through her. Hel would have no chance to snatch them this time—even if she wasn't dodging Thor's hammer.

Morfesa had to struggle to keep observing. Gerda was drawing on her hard enough to make her think of vampires draining her blood, despite having Freyr as a much better power source. The jotun did not seem as subtle in her use of the runes as Freya was, which could mean she needed more power to produce the same effects.

Nonetheless, the druid could sense the souls in motion. Luckily, Max hadn't recognized what was happening, and Hel was too—no, wait. Someone was trying to reverse what Freya was doing.

Ekaterina's body started writhing. The souls were caught somewhere in the middle. Neither body was inhabited—which meant both could die unless someone took quick action.

Morfesa stayed linked to Gerda and Freyr but gently eased out of the power sharing. They would have to do without her for a while.

Freya was shaking from the intensity of her concentration. Could Max be powerful enough to overcome a former goddess? Probably not— if the bodies were closer together. Because they were so far apart, and Max was standing very close to one of them, he had a shot at thwarting what the Vanir was trying to do.

Freya must have sensed Morfesa's nearness and willingness to help. "The young sorcerer can't hold me off indefinitely," she whispered. "He can block me for a while, though, and who knows what may happen in that time? Distract him somehow."

There were many ways Morfesa might distract Max, but breaking his concentration from this distance with what magic Morfesa had left? Impossible. She needed to get closer.

Morfesa cloaked herself in what she hoped was enough magic to be invisible to frost giant eyes. Then she rose into the air. She conveyed her need to Freyr and Gerda, and the barrier allowed her to slide through.

Once she was comfortably above the fray, she flew in Max's direction as fast as she could without making herself too obvious. He would be focused enough on Freya that he might not notice her—if her luck held. Luck had been in very short supply these days.

She stayed high until she was practically over Max. Then she dropped down on him with as much force as she could conjure up.

Max must not have noticed her until she slammed into him from above. Even before Hel's twisted plan, he'd had a lot of potential as a sorcerer, but he was far weaker physically than mentally. When she hit him, he was driven to his knees, and his grip on the staff loosened.

Morfesa jumped from on top of him to beside him, grabbed the staff, and tossed it away. If nothing else, the druid had disrupted Max's magic. Freya's power surged nearby. Mission accomplished, as the mortals would say.

Max was on his feet and grabbed her roughly. She looked into his eyes and screamed.

Max wasn't there at all. What looked back at her was a dragon, full of wrath and venom.

She had hoped not to sacrifice her own life to save the others. If she must, though, it was a good way to die.

FINDING MAX IN A DRAGON

DL OPENED HIS EYES. He was buried up to his neck and felt as if he had been dragged for three miles by wild horses. Even so, it only took him a few seconds to realize he was back in his own body for the first time in what seemed like forever. He wasn't completely sure how he got there—but he wasn't going to complain!

There was a fight going on nearby. Was something wrong with his vision? It looked as if Morfesa was attacking Max. That made no sense until he looked more closely at his friend.

Balder must have been right. The ritual Hel forced Max into had done something to him. The magic that DL could sense emanating from Max was several times as strong as it had been. That might have been a good thing—except that, even from a distance, DL could see an unhealthy glow in Max's eyes. A dragon of the evil Western variety was looking out through them.

Thor's hammer hit the earth with a thunderous thud somewhere nearby. Jolted, DL looked down. The soil around him was loose. The cracks and gaps spelled opportunity.

He tensed his muscles, awakened his inner dragon, and broke himself free, spraying earth in all directions. Balder and Esras were trapped nearby, but Morfesa's plight looked worse. Max—or whatever he was now—was holding her and building power faster than she was. His magic no longer looked druidic. Instead of the greenness of growing plants, it had the sickly greenness of dead and decaying vegetation, of poison—of wrongness. His power, which he had wielded to maintain balance, now worked to destroy it instead.

Racing in Max's direction, DL slammed into him with enough force to throw the young sorcerer off his feet. Max lost his grip on Morfesa and hit the ground hard. DL fell on top of him, pinning him as securely as the Spear of Lugh had pinned Hel.

"Knock him out!" yelled Morfesa. DL raised his fist, but memories of Max made him hesitate, despite the soulless fire in Max's eyes.

For a second, DL remembered Max standing up to the Collector— before the young sorcerer even realized that he had magic. He had risked himself to save DL. That wasn't the only time, either. The image of Max —the real Max, not this corrupted imitation—slowed his response.

Venom-green light burst from Max and coiled around DL like an enormous snake. His strength ebbed, and his fist trembled.

Light bright as flashing emeralds hit Max, and he screamed. Morfesa gripped Max's staff, which she had never held before, as if it might fly back into his hands. The runes glowed as her effort to overcome the sorcerer intensified.

With the staff turned against Max and DL on top of him, the sorcerer should have been an easy mark, but he pushed back against the emerald glow, turning the part nearest to him venom-dark and forcing Morfesa back a step.

"Hit him!" yelled the druid, but DL's fist was still frozen in midair as if some invisible barrier were holding it back.

Max's power surged beneath DL in a way that made his skin crawl. As if Max's muscles had quintupled in strength, he shoved DL off him with no more effort than it would have taken to push a door open. His whole body pulsed with poison-hued energy. Strange symbols blurred through the air around him, burning with the same fire DL could see in Max's eyes. The symbols became clearer. They looked like small tridents, and they formed a barrier between him and Morfesa. The light from the staff, unable to penetrate Max's defense, slid around it on both sides.

DL felt his own strength and mobility returning. Even as powerful as Max was now, he could only do so many things at the same time.

"Knock him out!"

DL lunged at Max, but he restrained himself enough to avoid breaking every bone in Max's body. That might have saved his own bones when he slammed into the barrier, physical as well as magical. The impact knocked the wind out of him and threw him backward. He hit the ground with a loud smack but held onto consciousness.

Was it DL's imagination, or had the barrier shuddered just slightly when he hit it? He jumped up and grabbed the nearest large rock. He threw it toward the barrier at full dragon strength.

The stone shattered when it hit, but Max staggered as if he felt the blow, and there was no doubt this time—the barrier rippled momentarily.

"Again!" yelled Morfesa. She redoubled her own attack, and the color of her magic shifted from emerald to gold.

DL found a rock the size of his torso and hurled, bellowing like a dragon as he did so. It struck the shield with a venomous flash, split in two, and fell to the ground. Max shuddered and grasped at his head with both hands.

As the shield rippled, Morfesa's golden light brightened to blinding intensity. "Remember!" she shouted. Max froze. For a moment, the dragon receded from his eyes, and it was Max looking out.

The barrier, shaken by the sudden absence of the mind that created it, fluttered like paper in the wind. DL could have hit Max then... should have hit him then. But at that moment, he was so clearly Max that DL halted. Would an attack now save him from turning back—or push him in that direction?

The ground opened beneath Max, and he fell, shrieking in surprise. DL DL lunged toward the crevice, but the ground snapped shut so abruptly that he couldn't follow. He fell to his knees, ready to dig, but Max's cries diminished in volume so rapidly that he knew there'd be no point.

"Hel has rescued him," said Morfesa. "Well, she's rescuing the thing he has become, anyway. Why didn't you strike when you had the chance? Oh, never mind. We need to get Esras, Balder, and Maeve free and figure out how to extricate the Asgardians from the frost giants. I think Thor is watching and will keep Hel or Max from resurfacing, but because there are two of them now, the task is more difficult. Also, I don't know how long it will be before the frost giants become frustrated and throw their combined might against the shield."

Freeing Esras and Balder didn't take long. Figuring out what to do with the frost giants was much tougher.

"There are too many of them," said Balder. "Even with the might of Thor and the magic of Freya, they don't stand a chance, and we can add too little to their power."

"Why can't they just flee?" asked Esras. "Couldn't Freya raise them out of there? The giants don't look as if they could fly."

"They can't, but there are other risks," said Balder. "An attempt to fly out could trigger a desperate frost giant attack to stop them. Not only that, but the type of shield Freya is using is hard to keep together in that kind of upward movement. It would be a vulnerable moment for those within."

DL squinted in the direction from which he could hear battle sounds. His draconic sight picked up the glimmer of Freya's shield, mostly hidden behind the ranks of giants who surrounded it.

"Is that like the one Max cast?"

"The same general idea, but much stronger," said Morfesa. "Freya has her staff—and much more experience."

"Then the protection might hold until we can get…oh, I don't know. Help from Asgard?"

"The army could be on the march even now—but it will take longer to reach us than Freya could possibly hold out," said Balder. "And it would have to smash through Hel's outer wall, no easy task."

"If the army is already on the way, why not open a portal to wherever they are?" asked Maeve. "We could shorten their trip considerably."

"We could use Balder's knowledge of Yggdrasil to open a portal," said Morfesa. "Without knowing where they are, though, we won't know where to open it."

Balder nodded. "Yggdrasil is vast and hard to map. Some say its pathways change in ways only Odin and the Norns can truly follow.

Freya has the skill to find the army through seidr trance, but I doubt she could do that from the middle of a battle."

"Nonetheless, a portal might still offer a way to save Freya and the others," said Morfesa. "I just came from there," said Morfesa. "I could open a portal back. It would be within the shield, and they could then step through to here."

Balder shook his head. "Your portal magic may harm the shield as well."

"Freya let me out without disrupting the shield," said Morfesa. "Could she let our magic in?"

"Perhaps," said Balder. "There is no obvious way to communicate with her now, though."

"Possibly through DL's blood and Yeouiju links with Ekaterina," suggested Maeve. "He could get a message through to her, and she could relay it to Freya."

"She may still be weak from the Yeouiju's contribution to the last portal," said DL. "I know she's alive, but I can't feel her right now."

"Now that I think about it, there may be a more direct way," said Balder. Druid, you hold in your hand a twin of Freya's staff, do you not? The shafts of both are made from the wood of Yggdrasil. The same runes are carved in both by Freya's own hand and painted with Freya's own blood. You could not want a stronger bond than that."

"A brilliant suggestion," said Morfesa. "However, I've never used staffs in that way,"

"We have communed from wood to wood at times," said Esras.

"And blood to blood is not hard to set up," said Maeve. "I learned how to do that from non-druidic sources."

Morfesa glared at her. "Spells involving blood are often dark."

"We need to do what works," said DL. "If the blood connection makes communication more likely, we have to use it."

Morfesa looked at him, her irritation with Maeve morphing into sorrow. "Is that how Max reasoned when he let himself by twisted by magic unknown to him? Was he, too, trying to do what would work?"

"Considering that either Hel or Max—or both—could attack again at any moment, let us prepare as best we can," said Esras. "It's not as if we are contemplating necromancy or sympathetic magic to kill someone.

Yes, blood is involved, but the use of it is about as white as any I could imagine."

Morfesa nodded reluctantly, and the three druids tried to establish communication with Freya. Balder watched what they were doing and made what suggestions he could.

That left DL to be a de facto watchman. From what he could tell, the frost giants weren't moving much, and there was no sign of Hel's undead army, of her, or of Max. DL didn't want to look the proverbial gift horse in the mouth, but the sudden calm seemed too good to be true.

Did Hel want them to communicate with Freya for some reason? Was there some flaw in their plan that the ruler of the dead could exploit? DL didn't have enough knowledge of magic to answer either question. However, there was an even worse possibility—that Hel already had everything she wanted.

She had Max and his dragon-supercharged magic. That had obviously been a key part of her plan. What if she was ignoring DL and the others because they no longer posed a threat?

If all of that were true, what chance was there that they'd ever see Max again, let alone pry him loose from Hel's clutches?

"*Yeouiju, are you still connected to Max?*"

"*I should be, but the part of me within him has not responded since a power surge some time ago. When I reach out for him, I feel…nothing.*"

DL bit his lip. There was still one other way to locate Max.

"*Can you get a message to Yong-Wang for me?*"

"*Yes, but that will take time. He is not near us. I will have to search for him.*"

"*Thanks. When you reach him, let me talk to him if you can. If not, let him know that something has happened to Max.*"

"*I will do as you request.*"

The dragon king had left to pursue the Amadan Dubh quite a while ago. Dubh must have found some way to hide from him. DL knew getting Merlin's book back and imprisoning Dubh were important, but neither one—or even both together—were as important as saving Max. If anyone could find him, it would be Yong-Wang.

"Freya understands what to do," said Morfesa loudly enough to catch DL's attention.

"DL, you, Balder and Maeve will keep an eye on the frost giants. Freya doesn't think they can sense our portal method or that they will be able to detect the Asgardians from that far away, but she urges caution."

DL had no idea what either he or Maeve could do against a charging army of frost giants, but the usually critical Morfesa spoke with so much confidence that he kept his mouth shut. If all went well, the Asgardians would be at their side before the frost giants could get to them.

"I must decline," said Balder. "I should leave before my kin arrive."

Maeve looked puzzled. "Don't you want to see them? They will certainly want to see you."

"With all my heart, I want to see them. Alas, seeing me will only remind them of their grief, for our meeting would be fleeting. I am still dead, destined not to return to the land of the living until after Ragnarok. Why would I want to rip open their old wounds?"

"There may be ways—" began Maeve.

Balder shook his head. "This body cannot exist outside the land of the dead, as you well know. Magic might be able to change that, but not without risking catastrophe throughout the Nine Worlds. It could be as dire as the premature starting of Ragnarok."

The Aesir handed Maeve a ring. "Dear lady, I hope you and your companions succeed in your quest. Victory seems near, but if you need me later on, this ring has special meaning to me. You can use it to find me in the land of the dead should you need my aid again."

Balder said quick good-byes to everyone and walked away. Once he was gone, Morfesa and Esras got to work right away.

The coordination between them and Freya was even better than DL expected. The Asgardians were stepping through a portal in less than a minute. Ekaterina carried the unconscious Adreanna through. At the same time, the shield at their old location collapsed, and the frost giants howled in frustration.

"Let us take to the air," said Freya. "They will not find us immediately, but it will not take them long." Freya and the druids working together floated them up relatively quickly. A cloudy floor formed beneath their feet. DL was thankful for anything that lessened his feeling that he might fall.

"That should be high enough," said Freya after a couple of minutes. "Hel has no flying legions, and we are so near the boundary of her realm that her magic is comparatively weak here. We should be safe here for a while. We need to plan our next move."

DL listened with one ear. As soon as Ekaterina had been able to lay Adreanna down, she had embraced him. They held each other as if they would never let go. This was the first time in a long time that had been together in the right bodies.

DL had expected to get disapproving looks, but if they got any, he didn't see them. Freyr, holding Gerda tightly himself, actually smiled at them. Even the usually all-business Morfesa seemed inclined to cut them some slack, and Maeve had used up her supply of sarcasm long ago. The Asgardians were themselves distracted at first by the realization that Balder was so nearby. They had not seen him since his death. Thor, his brother, stared out across the barren plain as if he could conjure Balder up by sheer force of will. Freya convinced him to stop, but the sparks trickling from his hammer as he passed in from hand to hand underscored the discontent in his eyes.

"If Hel is to be believed, she has already tricked Max into triggering Ragnarok," said Esras. "I heard something about bringing fehu and isa together in a certain way."

"Perhaps Hel believes that is what happened, but if that were really the case, we'd be seeing more signs of it," said Freya. "The frost giants would be making their way toward Asgard, not chasing us around the land of the dead. And where is Loki to lead the army of the dead?"

"Yet Max may have put something in motion whose effect will be apparent only later," said Freyr.

"All the more reason to get back to Asgard as quickly as possible," said Thor. "We have the hostages, whose rescue was the reason for this quest. If Hel has found a way to accelerate the pace of destiny, then our place is with our kin, readying our defenses."

DL reluctantly let go of Ekaterina. "We can't leave without Max."

Freyr frowned. "Mortals should not—"

Gerda put a hand on his arm. "This mortal helped save me, Husband. He has earned the right to speak his mind."

"It does seem as if the normal relationship between mortals and us does not apply any longer," said Freya. "All of them have fought by our side and proved themselves repeatedly. Let him have his say."

Freyr nodded. "Ladies, I bow to your wisdom. What would you have us do, then, DL? Have you a plan for his rescue?"

"Uh, no, but together I bet we can work one out."

"I respect your desire not to leave a comrade behind," said Thor. "However, if he is now a tool of Hel, how can we safely take us with him? Will he not betray us to her?"

"My grandson would never do that," said Maeve. "He may be under her influence now, but that spell can surely be broken."

"I have no wish to leave him here, either," said Esras. "But you and I both know more than a mere spell is involved. Whatever Hel did to him is part of him now."

"Freya, what say you? Your knowledge of magic is beyond any of ours," said Freyr.

"Esras and Maeve were witnesses to what befell Max," said Freya. "I must know more about what happened before I can properly judge."

Esras told Freya how Max had been forced into the ritual and what it had done to him.

"And do you agree this is what happened?" Freya asked Maeve. "Has Max been infected by Niddhog's venom?"

"I think so, but you do not know him as well as I. He is strong. He is good. He can fight the influence of Niddhog and win."

"I can attest to his character," said Morfesa. "I have been tutoring him since the time he first discovered he had magic. Even before whatever happened to him here, he was a sorcerer with much potential. Great power leads to great temptation, as we all know, yet Max has not succumbed to that temptation."

"Temptation is not quite the same thing as having a powerful alien force entwined with your mind," said Thor.

"I know a little about that, Lord Thor," said Ekaterina. "I have a bloodlust within me that constantly urges me to slaughter."

"Like a berserker?" asked Freyr.

"No, for berserkers choose their lifestyle. My life as a vampire was forced upon me. Nor do berserkers lose their reason altogether and forever. This bloodlust of which I speak breaks most people. It turns them to evil, no matter how good they were in life. Yet I have not succumbed to it either. If I can resist such a thing, so can Max."

"This bloodlust of which you speak seems mindless," said Freya. "The effect of Nidhogg's venom seems to have a mind of its own. From what Esras has said, it has not broken Max. It has replaced him with someone else—something else."

"You know something of what happened to me when I became a Western dragon," said DL. "My mind was replaced by the instincts of a dragon, and I...I couldn't overcome it. I was completely overwhelmed by it. The magic you lent Ekaterina brought me back, though."

"I sensed something of that through Brisingamen," said Freya. "It was not easy, but it could be done—through the power of love."

"Max's case is similar," said Morfesa. "Lady Freya, you see this staff I hold. It was a gift to Max from Sindr—"

"Which was not really his to give," said Freya. "Yet what is done is done. Speak on."

"When Max dropped this during battle, I was able to pick it up. Though not as skilled in its use as you would have been, I used the power of the amber—your stone—to get Max to remember himself. The effect may have been fleeting, but that proves Max's condition is not incurable."

Freya extended a hand. "Give me the staff." Morfesa quickly handed it to her. Freya closed her eyes and moved into a seidr trance, keeping a firm hold on the wood. It trembled in her hands, the runes flickered, and the gems flashed.

When Freya opened her eyes, she said, "You speak the truth, Lady Morfesa. I felt what is within Max while he held the staff, and I felt how its power touched him while it was in your hands. It is just possible that we can succeed in freeing Max to follow his own path again.

"He is infected by Niddhog, and Hel is exploiting that bond. Yet Max has within him another bond, has he not? The power of our poor dead Balder has been inside of him. I felt it."

"My brother?" asked Thor. Grief flickered in his eyes.

"He helped us much when we arrived in the land of the dead," said Maeve. "It was he who suggested that we transmit his power into Max to protect him during the rune ritual."

"He was within me, too," said DL. "He may have accidentally changed me into a Western dragon when I sought to become an Eastern one—but was it his influence that made it possible for Brisingamen to help me?"

"Perhaps," said Freya. "No one has ever been transformed into a dragon in this way. No one has ever been infected by Niddhog's venom, filtered through one of Yggdrasil's roots, either. But if there were a way to make either condition better, that Balder would somehow be involved doesn't surprise me."

"What must we do?" asked Freyr. "Undoing such dire evil is certainly not something even you can do without preparation."

"No," agreed Freya. "Allow me some time to commune again with the staff Max held. If I understand his condition better, I can decide how to counter it."

Freya closed her eyes again and settled into another trance. It seemed like a good time to see if the Yeouiju had made any progress.

"Yeouiju, are you closer to finding Yong-Wang?"

"I have found him, but he has been trapped. The one whom he pursued led him to a place of fire, and there he trapped him using the magic from the stolen book."

"I heard," said Ekaterina. "What are we going to do?"

"Rescue him," said DL with a confidence he didn't even remotely feel.

INTERLOCKING RESCUES

"The place of fire must be Muspellheim," Freya said.

"How could such a powerful being be captured by Dubh, even with the help of Merlin's book?" asked Esras.

"I know little of Eastern dragons, but from what I have seen in DL, they have an affinity with water," said Freya. "Is that not correct?"

"Yes," said DL. "That's how Yong-Wang brought that rain."

"In the Nine Worlds fire and ice are opposites, but on the plain from which the dragon king comes, ice and water are viewed as one for magical purposes, and so fire and water are opposites. That would make Muspellheim the place where he would be weakest."

"Merlin's grimoire contains a spell for imprisoning dragons, though I doubt anyone has ever used it before," said Morfesa. "Dubh tried and failed with it once, but he must have adapted it to Yong-Wang's situation. The question is what are we going to do about it? Could Max use his new power to help if we rescue him first?"

"We all share your concern about Max," said Freya. "However, it may actually be easier to rescue Yong-Wang and use his power to help Max."

"Easier to rescue him from Muspellheim?" asked Freyr, looking at his sister as if she had just suggested that he marry Hel. "We can't take on a whole army of fire giants any more easily than we could a whole army of frost giants."

"It might be interesting to try, though," said Thor, swinging his hammer just enough to underscore his words.

"We do not have the resources to storm Muspellheim, but we may not have to," said Freya, looking at Thor the way a mother in DL's world would look at a rowdy teenager who has just tried to pull off some incredibly idiotic macho stunt. "It may be possible for me to counteract the spell holding Yong-Wang from a distance. DL, will you join me in a seidr trance? The link between you and Yong-Wang through your Yeouiju will make it easier for me to find him."

"I'll do whatever you need," said DL.

"Should we back you up with power sharing?" asked Morfesa.

"An excellent idea!" said Freya. "Even if Dubh has not involved the fire giants, the stolen book makes him formidable. I would wager he would still have trouble fighting off the power of a group of Asgardians and druids."

DL lay down next to Freya, and this time she was able to bring him into a trance even more easily than last time.

He and she flew across a vast emptiness as he had when he was a dragon. Traveling mentally was even faster, though, and soon they were approaching a fiery world that looked like one continuous volcano mouth. He couldn't feel the heat, but it must be intense. No wonder the dragon king's water magic wouldn't be much use here.

He didn't even have to ask the Yeouiju to guide them to Yong-Wang. Emotionless as it sometimes was, it was eager to help.

High among flaming mountain peaks, they found what looked like a massive cage fashioned from molten rock. Within it floated the miserable looking dragon king, helpless to break free.

Around the cage, Dubh circled, still in dragon form, casting a menacing shadow over the dragon king as he guarded him like a treasure.

"*Can you distract him?*" asked Freya. "*I will need time to undo his spell, and I will not succeed if he can keep reinforcing it.*"

"*How do I do that?*" DL had experienced many things in supernatural realms, but he still wasn't that familiar with astral projection.

Freya's understanding flowed through him. *"It's safe for you to leave my side. We will remain connected. You can move about and even make yourself visible to Dubh just by willing it. As for Dubh, he cannot harm you in this form, but he may not at first realize that you are only here in spirit. Act as if you have flown your physical body here. Dodge his fiery breath and get him to chase you if you can."*

That seemed like a pretty tall order, and DL wasn't sure about Dubh not being able to harm him. After all, Hel had sucked him into the land of the dead when he was out of his body. Yong-Wang was in this world only because of him, though. He had to at least try to help.

DL willed himself to move toward Dubh. He could feel Freya looking at him, waiting for him to make his move so that she could make hers. He would have liked some time to practice moving in this form, but he didn't have that luxury.

Speeding up, he put himself right in Dubh's path. The dragon slowed, and his eyes widened.

It didn't take him long to recover from his surprise, though. He sprayed fire in DL's direction. Moving more slowly than he wanted to, DL took a full blast. The dragon's eyes widened even further.

So much for convincing Dubh he was there in body. The only thing left to do now was bluff.

"Turns out I know magic, too," he shouted at Dubh. "I can let fire pass right through me."

"How is that possible?" asked the dragon at ear-splitting volume.

"Merlin's book isn't the only powerful magic item around, you know. I came across another one. It's not from any world you know, and it gives even someone like me the power to cast incredible defensive spells."

Dubh looked at him hungrily—no, greedily. His eyes glowed with avarice. "You will give me the item!"

"Why not take it—if you can." DL smiled and gave him the finger.

Dubh roared and spat a volcano's worth of fire at DL.

"See? My magic is more powerful than yours!" To DL's relief, Dubh still hadn't figured out he was a projection—but why not?

The dragon's eyes narrowed. "You must be an illusion."

Well, close. "Do you see anyone else around who could cast an illusion of me?"

He shuddered. What if Dubh looked around and sensed Freya nearby?

To keep the dragon's attention, DL flew right at him. Dubh swatted at him with a claw, which naturally went right through him.

"See, I'm immune to all harm."

Dubh didn't look as if he were buying the I-can-now-cast-spells bluff. With the ability to create portals so easily, faeries might not need astral projection as much as the Norse did, but he had to know that such a thing was possible. DL needed another distraction.

"Yeouiju, can I change the way this astral body appears?"

DL couldn't be sure the Yeouiju could connect to his astral self, but he had nothing to lose by checking.

After an agonizing delay, the Yeouiju said, *"I do not know, but if you visualize what you want to become, I will try to give your thoughts effect."*

Dubh was fiddling with something in one of his claws. Merlin's book! He must have a spell in mind—detection of some kind probably.

Reality blurred around him for a second. When his surroundings came back into focus, he was much larger and scalier. He was the Eastern dragon he had become only once before.

"If you're not interested in bargaining for the magic I have, there is no reason for me to hang around here," he bellowed in his new dragon voice. He turned and moved away from Dubh as fast as he could—which was a heck of a lot faster than when his astral body was his human form.

So that was it! He couldn't fly as a human, so it was harder to visualize speeding around. In this form, it was much easier. Let Dubh try to catch him now!

DL had to hold back to avoid losing Dubh completely. His astral dragon form could move much faster than his physical one. It didn't take him long to adjust, and once he had, it was easy to keep Dubh almost—but not quite—out of range.

Of course, there had to be a limit to how long DL could play this game. Dubh might be insane, but he wasn't stupid. At some point, he'd have to realize that DL was a projection—and a distraction. As soon as that happened, Dubh would race back to Muspellheim and catch Freya in the act of freeing Yong-Wang.

What he needed was a way to incapacitate Dubh. He might have had a shot at that in an actual dragon body, but in astral form, he had no way to deliver a physical blow.

He might be able to lead Dubh into harm's way. The transformed faerie wasn't thinking much, or he would already have figured out DL was just a projection. He was also flying recklessly fast. DL couldn't help remembering the cartoons he'd watched when he was a kid, not to mention the many action movies later. If he led Dubh into a big enough hazard and turned away at the last minute, wouldn't Dubh crash into it and get knocked out, at the least? It was a corny idea for sure—but it just might work.

Yeah, it might work, but only if he could find the right kind of obstacle. Dubh's dragon body was huge, and crashing him into one of the Nine Worlds could cause massive destruction, much like an asteroid hitting Earth in a science fiction thriller. Everyone was always saying the balance of this plane of existence was extremely fragile. What if DL started a chain reaction worse than Ragnarok?

Only one person could help him: Freya. He was still connected with her, and she knew the Nine Worlds well enough to give him a safe place to lead Dubh.

Contacting her wasn't easy. The distance between them felt like a solar system, though DL had no idea how far apart they really were. When he finally reached her, her thoughts were like the faintest possible whispers, but he managed to make sense of them, and she did the same for his.

"There is only one place in which you can safely crash Dubh—Ginnugagap, the endless void. The cold of Nifleheim met the heat of Muspellheim there and became the source of all life on this plane. It is empty again now, and if Dubh plunges into it going fast enough, he may become lost in it. There are no points of reference by which he can navigate physically or magically. If Dubh doesn't tether himself to something before entering, he will have no way out. You, on the other hand, could find your way out through your connection to me.

"There is a problem, however. Though the place would be a fitting prison, if Dubh takes Merlin's Grimoire in with him, Max may be lost to us.

In my earlier vision, I foresaw that we will need the power of the book almost as much as we need the power of the dragon king."

"Then we're just stuck? It's only a matter of time before Dubh figures out I'm tricking him. Even if he doesn't, I have no way to get the book away from him. It's like fused to one of his claws right now. Even if it wasn't, I'm not physical."

Freya sighed. *"From what I learned from Morfesa, the book could only be used by Merlin until he passed it to someone else. He passed it to Max and Morfesa. Dubh used trickery and threats to get it passed to him, but he had not the wit to ask for Morfesa to revoke her original control. Because it was passed to her directly from Merlin, Dubh's control over it will always be secondary to hers. She can pass it to you in such a way that your command of it will override Dubh's, and if you are close enough, you should be able to draw it to you even in astral form."*

"That sounds almost too good to be true."

"You are very discerning. There is a complication. Morfesa can't pass control to you over such tenuous astral links. You will have to get closer to her. That means you will have to lead Dubh back to Helheim. I will send word ahead. Thor and the others should be able to occupy Dubh long enough for you to get what you need from Morfesa. Once you have her blessing, I will lead you to Ginnugagap.

"Much could go wrong, but this is the only plan I can see that has any hope of success at this point."

Freya implanted in DL's mind clear directions back to Helheim, and he sped on his way just slowly enough to keep Dubh pursuing him. The faerie might be crazy—but it was a single-minded kind of craziness.

From a distance, DL could see his friends still floating in their little cloudy refuge—and looking singularly vulnerable to a dragon attack. Should he veer off? He was leading Dubh right to them.

Fortunately, Thor was watching, and Dubh just missed getting knocked unconscious—or worse—by Mjolnir.

"This is a trap!" roared Dubh. He turned and flew in the opposite direction at top speed.

DL pulled up even with his floating friends and made himself visible to them. "What should I do? I'm losing Dubh."

"Get after him!" commanded Morfesa. "I've given you what you need. Get close enough, and you can get the grimoire back."

That by itself wasn't going to get Dubh trapped, but it was better than nothing. Moving at astral speed, DL had little trouble catching the faerie dragon.

"And I thought you would do what it took to earn such great power," said DL, trying to sound disdainful. "One hammer throw from Thor, and you flee like the coward you are!"

"You have no power," said Dubh. "You were just luring me in so Thor could finish me."

DL was flying close enough to overlap with Dubh. He held out his astral claws and thought, *"Come to me!"* He felt silly, but the book flew from Dubh's claws to his.

"Well, I have power now," said DL as he pulled ahead of Dubh. The faerie dragon roared as if his heart had been torn out and strained to catch up.

Freya must have been monitoring as she worked on freeing Yong-Wang. The moment Merlin's book touched DL, a route to Ginnungagap flashed into his mind. So far, so good.

As he flew far ahead of Dubh, who was roaring obscenities at him, DL allowed himself to have a certain amount of optimism. He would trap Dubh, putting an end to his mischief once and for all. Freya would get the real Max back. They would all be able to go back home, and, if they didn't live happily ever after, they would at least live happily for now.

From what Freya told him, Ginnungagap used to be between Muspellheim and Nifleheim, but as the process of creation continued, it had sunk until to came to be the lowest point in the Nine Worlds, far lower than Helheim. It was up ahead, dark, featureless, and threatening.

Dubh was still behind him. DL allowed him to get very close so that, when DL veered off, Dubh would be unable to stop himself.

It was almost time to make his move, a strange feeling crept over DL. He was losing speed. Dubh was almost upon him.

Dubh grabbed at DL's tail—and his claws scraped across it. How could he have done that?

There was only one possible answer—DL's astral body had somehow become physical.

Dubh had finally figured out what he was and used magic to even the playing field.

It was too late to veer. DL had gotten Dubh into Ginnungagap—but at the cost of plunging in first himself.

TRAPPED IN THE VOID

"GIVE ME THE BOOK!" roared Dubh. His voice sounded close, but DL couldn't see him—or anything else. Either they had traveled farther from the entrance than he thought, or Ginnungagap devoured any light that entered it.

There was another possibility. Maybe DL was blind. Dubh had generated a physical body for him but without any knowledge about what a real Eastern dragon was like. He felt queasy and weak. It was possible his eyes weren't working properly.

"Give it to me!" Dubh was nothing if not persistent.

"Come and get it!" DL tried to roar back, but the sound that came out sounded more like an asthmatic wheeze.

Dubh laughed. "You can't fight me, you know. I made your dragon form solid, but without the strength it would normally have. When I find you, I can rip you to bits in seconds."

"Yeouiju, what's wrong with me?"

"The other being who is here with us clothed your astral body in flesh of the kind you had in the land of the dead, only less skillfully."

Dubh must have picked up that trick from Hel, but knowing how he did it didn't help DL much. He had no idea how to reverse it.

Even worse, DL could no longer feel any connection to Freya and the others. Whatever part of the Yeouiju was with him remained with him, but he was otherwise completely cut off. He didn't know how to get out, nor how to rejoin the others if he somehow managed to escape.

Freya might have been right about Dubh being trapped here, but she was wrong about how DL could find his way back.

"The longer you make me search for you, the more excruciating your death will be," said Dubh, but he sounded farther away.

DL's dragon senses weren't working, but he might not have been much better off if they had been. Dubh didn't appear to be able to sense him—or even the book—any better than he could see him. Otherwise, the faerie would have found him by now.

Panic welled up inside him. He needed to stay calm. He needed to think.

He needed to do something with the resources he had: a very defective body and the Yeouiju.

"Can you fix this body? I mean, make it more like it should be."

"If I were whole. I am just a piece of myself. I lack the power."

"Can you find a way out of this place?"

"I will try, but there are no points of reference. If I had never been elsewhere, I would assume nothing existed but this place."

The panic clutched at his throat like acid reflux.

His only consolation was that Dubh sounded even more frightened. He kept yelling threats, but they sounded more and more hysterical. The faerie had no more idea how to get out than DL did, and it didn't take his feelings long to creep pretty close to terror. Come to think of it, the fact that someone with centuries of magic experience couldn't figure out how to get out wasn't all that comforting.

The only other optimism he could squeeze out of the situation was that Ginnungagap wasn't designed as a prison. From what Freya had told him, it was a natural phenomenon.

Of course, so was a volcano, but that didn't mean he could survive falling into one.

DL had no idea how long he'd been in the void, but after about the hundredth threat from Dubh, he remembered he had something else besides himself and the Yeouiju.

He had Merlin's book nestled in one of his claws. It had stayed with him when he became physical and when he plunged into the abyss.

He tried to remember everything he'd heard about it. It made a sorcerer far more powerful than normal, and it had unique spells. It might even give an ordinary person some magic.

None of that really helped. DL's knowledge of magic was limited mostly to seeing someone else do it. If he made an attempt, he'd be just as likely to blow his own head off as to break out of the void. Nor did he have magic of his own—except what he could access through his poor, broken Yeouiju.

DL remembered one of the Yeouiju's other tricks.

"Yeouiju, do you remember how you tapped into Max's magic when his soul was in my body?"

"Yes. It was hard, but I could do it to some extent."

"I have a magic book. Can you sense it?"

"Yes, Master, but its magic is unfamiliar to me."

"Can you learn how to use it?"

"Mastering such a tome would take a long time."

"I don't mean learn everything in it. I mean learn enough to get us out of here. Or maybe draw on its power to do something you know how to do."

"I will try."

The Yeouiju's trying took a lot longer than DL had hoped. After asking for a progress report a few times, he made himself stop bugging it. With his only other company being the Amadan Dubh, whose threats were becoming increasingly incoherent and increasingly farther away, he began to wonder how long it would take him to become as crazy as the faerie.

"I can draw on the book's power, Master. What would you have me do?"

"Get us out of here!" DL felt better than he had in…hours? However long he'd been trapped, anyway.

"I have no knowledge of how to navigate this void."

The momentary good feeling melted away like ice in August. DL should have known escape wouldn't be that easy.

Ice. What was it Freya had told him about Ginnungagap? The ice of Nifleheim and the fire of Muspellheim had come together in it and created a large part of the Nine Worlds. Whatever came into existence was expelled from the void.

"Yeouiju, I think large enough amounts of fire and ice coming together might get us out of this place." DL explained what little else he remembered about the beginnings of the Nine Worlds.

"Ice I can do. Fire is more difficult. I'm not sure I can create a balance that will do what you suggest."

"I know where we can get fire. To make it safe, though, you either need to give me full dragon power or make me astral again, whichever is easier."

Dubh's feeble attempt at his body melted away. The Yeouiju had decided to conserve energy rather than keep a dragon body powered up. DL should have realized that was a better idea.

"The Amadan Dubh is still a fire-breathing dragon, and he is still close enough for me to hear him. If you start creating ice, will he be aware of that?"

"I can try. It will create a reference point, so perhaps."

"Can you make the ice glow?"

"I think so." A ball of ice appeared in front of DL, glowing faintly, like a flashlight with a dying battery.

"That's good, but make it brighter." The ice flared, looking like a diamond catching the sunlight. In a completely dark void, that should have been enough, but DL didn't want to take chances.

"Make it as bright as you can."

The ice became like a small, cold sun.

"Dubh!" yelled DL, hoping his astral voice would carry. "I have mastered the power to destroy you. I will seal you up in ice."

DL had no idea whether that would really destroy a Western dragon, but if Yong-Wang was at his weakest in a realm of fire, it made sense that a fiery dragon would be at its weakest in a realm of cold.

Dubh loomed up before DL with surprising speed, his reptilian face looking especially menacing in the unearthly glow of the ice.

"Borrowed power from the book, did you?" roared Dubh, swinging his claw at DL and missing. "Did you not realize that this dragon body is empowered by the book as well? This is what I think of your ice!"

Dubh sprayed nova-hot flames into the ice. It would have steamed away instantly, but the Yeouiju kept creating more. Dubh strained to produce even more fire, but, reinforced by the book, the Yeouiju kept pace with him.

Too late the faerie realized that his epic exertions were exhausting him. Without the book to renew him, he started shrinking back into his natural form. DL lost sight of him in the clouds of rain and steam.

The clouds were all moving in one direction—and it wasn't straight up from where the ice had met the fire, as one might expect. Its path was closer to being sideways. It was being expelled from Ginnungagap. DL only needed to follow it to be free.

Dubh was screaming somewhere nearby. Gone was his draconic roar. DL could barely see him in the darkness as he struggled to catch up with the clouds that were the only way out of the abyss. He looked tiny against the endless, featureless, black void, a solitary, weary faerie gasping and reaching impotently toward those clouds that he could never hope to reach.

Having experienced just a brief slice of life in the void, DL couldn't help feeling sorry for Dubh. He hesitated a moment. Should he go back and grab the faerie while there was still time?

Dubh had been willing to kill DL and everyone he cared about. He had even been willing to provoke an apocalypse that would destroy most of the inhabitants of the Nine Worlds.

DL let himself glide outward with the clouds. He tried his best to deafen himself to Dubh's heart-wrenching screams. They echoed in his ears as he emerged from Ginnungagap, but only a little.

MAX?

ONCE FREE, DL discovered he was still connected to Freya and the others. Even better, Freya had freed Yong-Wang, who was on his way back to Helheim. She had already returned to her body. When DL realized that, he felt dangerously alone, but only for a moment. Freya sent him instructions on how to return to Helheim himself, and he was on his way.

Unfortunately, it took him longer than it had her, mostly because he had to tow Merlin's book. Every time he accelerated to full astral speed, he nearly lost it.

DL couldn't complain about the scenery. As he got more used to astral travel, he could see more and more of the Nine Worlds and the spaces between them. He could even make out Yggdrasil, its trunk looming in the distance, its branches reaching out to cradle each of the worlds.

At least half the time, he wasn't seeing his surroundings, though. He was thinking about Max. Would he ever be the same again? Would he even live through the experience?

The way his luck had been running, he half expected to open his eyes when he returned and find himself in Morfesa's body. Waking up as himself was at least some consolation. It was also a good sign that the group was standing on the ground. However, that was undercut to some extent by the way everyone was bunched together and by the subtle tingle of levitation magic all around him. Freya was ready to pull the group back into the sky at a moment's notice.

The most comforting thing was Ekaterina's chilly embrace. He was so happy to be in her arms that he only gradually noticed the grim expressions on everyone else's face.

They did perk up a little bit when DL showed them the book, which Morfesa took reverently from his hands. They were also pleased that Dubh could not intervene again.

"You shouldn't feel sad about his fate," Freyr told DL. "He would have done worse to any of us—to all of us—if it had suited his purposes."

"Why are you looking so discouraged?" asked Esras. "You have won a great victory in imprisoning Dubh, to say nothing of recovering Merlin's lost grimoire. Though it is a smaller victory, I have achieved something in your absence." The druid waved the Spear of Lugh in the air. "Despite Hel's manipulations, I managed to call it back to me."

"Unable to reach us, the frost giants withdrew," said Freya. "The dead have not tried to approach us, and even Hel seems to be waiting for something, perhaps Dubh's return. Now that we know he isn't returning, and we have Merlin's book ourselves, the balance of power has shifted decisively in our favor.

"When the dragon king arrives, we shall be at full power and ready to take on Hel. We have much to celebrate."

"I can't celebrate until Max is back to normal," said DL. The words sounded harsher than he intended.

"Everything we have accomplished has brought us that much closer to recovering Max," said Freya. "Hel will have a hard time standing against us now, even with Max's help."

DL glanced at Maeve. She returned his gaze with eyes left hollow by grief.

She knew far more about magic than he did—and she looked as if the battle was already lost.

"You don't have to humor me like this," said DL. "I can take the truth."

"Then you shall have it," said Freya. "You have earned that and far more besides.

"When I liberated Yong-Wang, he told me he had looked deeply into Max when he freed him from Yggdrasil. He saw some things even he did not fully understand, but one truth was clear to him—the venom of Niddhog has entwined itself around every part of his being. No, even more. It has become part of him. We might try to rip it out, but even if we succeeded, we would take with it much of what Max was before."

DL had an uncomfortable vision of Max reduced to a shell, going through the motions of life, but not truly living.

"There has to be something else we can do."

"There is," said an all-too-familiar voice. "You can surrender."

The Spear of Lugh and Mjolnir simultaneously hurtled in Hel's direction—and passed right through her.

"Freya is not the only one here who knows seidr and can project herself," said Hel. "I am far from here, and your petty weapons could not kill me even if I stood before you."

"We have no wish to kill you," said Freya. "Give us Max, and we will leave your domain without interfering with you any further."

Hel laughed in her usual, bone-grating way. "There is no Max. There is only Nidhoggson. He is free to go with you—if he wishes."

As if on cue, Max—DL refused to think of him as Nidhoggson—rose from the ground. He looked superficially the same, but his body language was different, subtly menacing.

His new gear was equally threatening. In his right hand, he held a staff that was both a replacement for the staff of Freya he had lost and a complete reversal of it. This new staff was fashioned from the wood of Yggdrasil—not from a branch but from the very poisoned root to which Max had been tied. Runes like the ones on Freya's staff were carved into it and painted with blood—but this time the blood resonated with the same energy DL could sense coming from Hel. Freya's staff had been crowned with a variety of stones, but the ones that tipped Max's new staff were all dark: black agate, onyx, obsidian.

The staff was nothing compared to Max's new eyes, though. There was no trace of him in those orbs that glittered with the promise of draconic fury.

DL thought he had braced himself well enough for this, but he was wrong. He froze. He couldn't have picked a worse time.

A horde of dead warriors, concealed until then by the twisted soil of Helheim, burst up from the ground almost right where DL and his friends stood.

DL moved more slowly than he should have, but the attack did get him going. The others must have anticipated something like this, for they moved as if they had been planning their strategy for hours.

Thor unleashed both the lightning and the blunt force of his hammer. Freyr swung so fast with the Sword of Dragon Light that arm and blade both blurred into a river of light. By the time the warriors had freed themselves from the soil, many of them had already been struck down. Though her sword was not as powerful, Ekaterina did more than her share of damage to those who survived the initial attack.

Protected from the dead onslaught, the spellcasters threw everything they had at Max. Freya through her staff and Morfesa through Merlin's book sent a massive burst of magic aimed at incapacitating the corrupted sorcerer. Esras, Gerda, and Maeve lent their strength, making it one of the strongest outpourings of magic DL had ever sensed. He had seen tidal waves of magic before, but this was like Noah's flood, ready to submerge anything that stood in its way.

However, Max was as ready as they were. The energy struck him hard and pushed him back, but he didn't fall. DL hadn't seen it at first, but now he could make out a shimmering defense around him that struck at the opposing magic like thousands of tiny tridents.

"It's the damnable Helm of Awe," muttered Gerda.

Freya and Morfesa amped up their attack, but Max stood his ground. Hel lent him her support, but even so, DL was amazed by his ability to withstand the combined might of Freya and the druids, especially backed up by her staff and the book of Merlin. Max resisted as if he, like Hel, had the entire power of Helheim at his fingertips.

DL fought the dead halfheartedly—Max still had most of his attention. The combination of the lightning and the competing waves of magic made the air itself crackle with excess power. He knew Freya and the others were trying to save Max, but at the rate the conflict was escalating, they might kill him without even meaning to.

Climbing up from below was slower than charging on level ground, so Thor, Freyr, and Ekaterina by themselves could contain the dead warriors. They didn't need DL, but Max did. His earlier slowness faded away. He knew what he had to do now.

He grabbed up the Spear of Lugh but didn't throw it. He didn't know if he could control it once it left his hand. Even a weak toss could send it straight through Max's heart, and the sorcerer probably couldn't fend it off and hold back Freya's magic assault. No, he needed a subtler approach.

Ekaterina was at his side as if she had anticipated his plan, and they charged Max together. They slowed to avoid slamming into the Helm of Awe's field, which would have stunned them at the very least. DL thrust at it with the Spear of Lugh. Ekaterina slashed away with her runed steel.

Neither weapon was specifically designed to disrupt runic magic, but the repeated impacts required Max to exert himself even more. He had been shaking and sweating a little even before DL and Ekaterina struck. They just might be able to get those defenses to collapse if they kept it up.

DL glanced at Max and was sorry he had. His friend was glaring at him with burning hatred. His eyes glowed with dragon venom. Even if they captured him, what the hell could they do to help him? Maybe Yong-Wang was right.

Where was Yong-Wang? DL neither saw nor sensed any sign of him. Why was it taking him so long to get back? He could have turned the tide.

Hel changed her tactics, and the ground began to grip DL's feet. He sank into the hungry soil as if it were quicksand. Ekaterina was having the same problem, as were the others.

Freya switched her attack from Max to Hel. Morfesa followed her lead. The ruler of the dead's astral body disappeared to avoid being gripped by their magic, and the soil lost its ability to suck the party down.

Max took full advantage of the respite. DL sickened as if Max were injecting poison into him. It felt like tiny snakes squirming in his blood vessels. Whatever magic he was using was so toxic that DL's draconic healing couldn't keep up with it.

Max's magic didn't affect Ekaterina at first, as if Max had forgotten she was a vampire. When he realized his mistake, he started to use the soil to bury her as Hel had been doing. Because the effect was focused only on her, it moved much faster than when the same attack had been distributed across all of them.

DL couldn't help but be disturbed by this attack. Ekaterina didn't need air—but enough soil pulling her down and keeping her down could trap her. Freeing her wouldn't be easy.

He couldn't do much to help her, though. The magical venom kept gnawing at him. The pain was so bad he had to bite his lip to keep from screaming, and his muscles were so weak that even standing up was an effort.

The Spear of Lugh twitched in his hand. He hated to take the risk, but it was the last play he had.

His vision had started to blur, but he aimed the spear as carefully as he could at Max's right arm. "Wound, but do not kill," he mumbled. "Understand?" The spear twitched again, and he tossed it weakly at Max.

DL fell to its knees, but he kept watching the spear, ready to recall it if he had to. Left to its own devices, it struck the Helm of Awe again and again, even faster than DL could have.

Freya and Morfesa turned their attention back to Max, pounding him with every ounce of magic they had left. The protective field around him looked far less bright and repelled attacks less aggressively. It seemed about to tear where the Spear of Lugh was relentlessly ripping away.

DL was at best semi-conscious, but at some point, someone must have realized he was dying. He felt healing energy surge into him, trying to push back the dark poison that burned in every cell.

With fire, Max drew a rune in the sky above them. It stank of death.

DL hadn't gotten any messages through his connection with Freya in a long time, but now she spoke inside his head. He could sense everyone else as well. *"It is cweorth, rune of the funeral pyre. If he casts the spell he's working on here, in the land of the dead, we will all burn. It will be as if we were thrown into the depths of Muspellheim. We must stop him, whatever it takes."*

DL wasn't sure why he was getting that particular message—until the poison hit him again, full force, knocking him flat on the ground.

Freya had been apologizing to him. Stopping cweorth meant abandoning her healing effort.

DL didn't want to die. His survival instinct amped up to an internal scream, but it did him no good. He had nothing at hand to save himself.

Max's rune still flamed in the sky, but DL could barely see it through the descending darkness.

LAST HOPE

DL's eyes flew open, and he struggled to orient himself. He wasn't on fire, so Freya must have succeeded, but how much time had passed? Dueling magical forces still sparked through the air, so probably not much.

His legs were rubbery, but he managed to stand shakily so that he could look around.

Thor and Freyr were still holding back the dead. Hel had returned, this time in physical form, and the spellcasters had split into two groups. Freya, Esras, and Gerda fought Hel, and Morfesa and Maeve fought Max. His eyes weren't flaring quite as brightly, but the Spear of Lugh was nowhere to be seen.

Where was Ekaterina? DL spotted hear nearby, buried almost up to the neck. Her face looked lifeless.

Despite his wobbly state, it only took him a second to reach her side. "Ekaterina!" She didn't respond to his shout. There was no way to tell whether she still lived or not.

"*Yeouiju!*" He was shouting his thoughts, something he had never done before.

"*She channeled most of what power I had to you,*" it replied. "*You would have died otherwise.*"

"How could you let her die? How could you?" DL's heart felt cold and empty.

"She was not alive to begin with. I left her enough of my energy to prevent her from ceasing to exist."

"If that's the case, revive her right now!"

"I cannot. The magic from Not My Master is still inside you. I lack the power to animate her and keep you alive at the same time."

DL looked around frantically. There were five people present who could probably break Max's spell on him, but none of them could afford to divert any of their focus from their opponents.

The Yeouiju obviously believed that Ekaterina would survive, but what if the tiny spark within her died? DL wasn't willing to take the risk, but saving her meant finding a way to heal himself or end the battle so someone else could heal him.

The Yeouiju might sometimes be cryptic, but it was always truthful. He had to believe its power was stretched as far as it could go. There would be no clever redistribution to solve the problem this time. Nor could the Yeouiju use Merlin's book. Morfesa needed its power to fight Max.

DL looked back and forth between Max and Hel. Both were hard-pressed but still holding their own. Which one looked weaker? He couldn't see any obvious difference.

"Yeouiju, why isn't the Spear of Lugh still attacking Max?"

"He was able to confuse it in some way. Its maker never anticipated souls being in different bodies. Also, when you threw it, you thought of Max, but Not My Master really is not Max anymore. He cloaked himself in the identity of Nidhoggson, and the spear became confused. It is nearby, flying in circles in a vain attempt to locate what it thinks is the intended target."

DL raised his hand and called the spear to him. That command at least was unambiguous, and the spear was back in his hand in seconds. If the Yeouiju was right, there might be one way to defeat Max and push the battle toward its end.

He ran in Max's direction, but the spell inside him scratched around a little, and he had to slow down.

Max's attention was fixed on Morfesa, who was looking pretty worn out, too. He didn't see DL coming.

"Wound—but do not kill—Nidhoggson," said DL, tossing the spear and thinking of Max's right arm. He spoke loudly enough for Max to hear him.

Max looked at him disdainfully. Was he wondering how big an idiot DL had to be to try the same strategy that had already failed? If so, DL's plan might actually work.

The Spear of Lugh kept stabbing at Max's battered shield. He diverted additional energy into it, shuddered, and the glow from his eyes disappeared.

DL looked into those eyes and saw Max looking back out. The Spear of Lugh slowed its attack, confused by Nidhoggson's momentary disappearance.

"Destroy this shield!" yelled DL before the spear could wander off again.

Max's eyes flashed as Nidhoggson returned. He glanced at DL, rage twisting his face, and morphed his shield somehow so that the spear didn't know what to do with it any longer.

"Wound Niddhogson!" yelled DL. The spear dug away at the shield again. Nidhoggson countered by switching to Max once more. As soon as the spear slowed, DL changed his orders again, forcing Max to modulate his shield and to switch personas at a faster and faster rate.

Morfesa did what she could to strengthen her own attack, and the Helm of Awe flickered from the combined attacks and from Nidhoggson's frenzied attempts to camouflage it.

"Come on, Max," whispered DL. "You can do it."

Max and Nidhoggson were now alternating so fast it was hard to tell who was looking out of those eyes at any particular moment. They blurred across his face, and his body was trembling more and more intensely.

Max's eyes unblurred. He was frantic—but he was definitely Max. The young sorcerer threw Hel's staff on the ground and let the Helm of Awe dissolve. Morfesa's attack hit with full-force, and Max hit the ground, his body shaking.

"That's Max! Stop!" yelled DL.

"We know," said Maeve. "He wouldn't have stayed that way for long."

"Attack Hel!" yelled Morfesa, and in moments they had added their strength to Freya's thrusts against the ruler of the dead. For good measure, DL sicced the spear on her as well.

Hel screamed in frustration and slid back down into the depths. The dead warriors who were still whole enough to retreat plunged back into the ground as well. In moments, the good guys had won—at least for the moment.

"We must move rapidly," said Freya. "As long as we stay here, Hel will never give up trying to change her destiny."

"My lady, can you heal me right away? I need my full strength to save Ekaterina."

"It might be best if we depart this accursed place first and then heal you," said Freya, looking around nervously. "I doubt Hel has exhausted all her tricks."

"Lady Freya, did you not see DL's clever strategy?" asked Morfesa. "It was he who stopped Nidhoggson and enabled us to win the battle."

"He fears for his lady love," said Freyr, hugging Gerda to him. "Surely, we can spare a few minutes."

"I will stand watch," said Thor. "Nothing Hel can summon up in the next few minutes could possibly get past me."

Freya looked at over at the mostly buried vampire. "If those of us who can heal all work together, I suppose it will not take long. Freyr, will you dig Lady Ekaterina out of the ground while we work? As things stand, Hel could too easily snatch her, and I fear we might never get her back."

Working as a team, Morfesa, Esras, Maeve, and Freya lifted Max's spell from DL in just a few minutes.

"It was the work of ear, rune of the grave," said Freya when they were done. "It kills slowly but surely. Lucky it is indeed that your Yeouiju was able to provide you the strength to endure until we could lift it."

DL thanked them and hurried over to Ekaterina, whom Freyr had freed and laid gently on the ground. With Max's poison out of his system, his body healed quickly.

"All right, Yeouiju, give Ekaterina the energy she needs."

She opened her eyes and looked up at DL.

"You have saved me again."

He pulled her to him. "Yeah, right after you saved me."

They embraced, oblivious to all the eyes upon them.

Max wasn't around to tell them to get a room. The thought of him made DL let go of Ekaterina.

"Max is still in trouble."

"Then we must save him," said Ekaterina as if it would be easy.

As they walked over to where Freya was conferring with the other spellcasters, DL felt as if he were stepping into a funeral somewhere in the middle of the service.

"We can't just give up on him," said Maeve. DL knew her well enough to know her diplomatic tone was a strained façade. She was angry.

"I did not suggest we do so," said Freya. "All I said was that there was no way to free him now. Perhaps after much study—"

"I beg your pardon, Lady Freya," said Morfesa, "but the longer we wait, the worse his condition will become. DL tricked Nidhoggson into bringing the Max persona to the surface often enough that Max was able to seize control, but he would have lost it again almost immediately if we hadn't overcome him. Since then, Nidhoggson has been getting stronger even though he's unconscious. A point will come—and soon—when he will be too strong to overcome. Surely, with all your wisdom, there must be something you can suggest that we could begin right away."

"I only wish it were that simple," said Freya. "Other issues must be addressed. Although Hel has not yet succeeded in triggering Ragnarok, she could already have set forces in motion of which we are as yet unaware. In such a crisis, our place is in Asgard, not here."

"Do not forget that Odin and the other Aesir could be of much help in our efforts to find a cure. Besides, anything we try to do here can be interfered with by Hel. We have driven her off for the moment, but rest assured she will return. As long as Max remains within her reach, she will stop at nothing to grab him back."

"Let her come," said DL. "We've beaten her before."

"That's the spirit!" said Thor.

Freya scowled at him. "No, it isn't. All of us together can certainly beat her if she stands alone. What if she induces the frost giants to return? Or Nidhogg itself?

"Remember, she cannot die. Nor can her troops. Even without other allies, she can keep coming at us over and over. But we *can* die. Would you have us all perish here?"

DL didn't know why he felt so strongly against leaving this awful place. He chalked the feeling up to draconic instinct. On a deep level, he just knew it was wrong.

"Aren't we expecting help?"

Freya looked at him with pity in her eyes. "Odin would never send anyone with the threat of an early Ragnarok casting its long shadow over Asgard. As for the promised faerie army, when last I checked, the entrances to this plane were still blocked by whatever Dubh did. Doubtless, I could undo his work, but the fact that it hasn't been undone by Odin suggests Dubh used some spell from Merlin's book that he has yet to figure out how to counter. Now that we have the book, I could probably use it to break the enchantment, but not necessarily rapidly. From what I observed before, the spell is intricately crafted, which suggests long planning."

"What about Yong-Wang? He must certainly be nearby." DL tried to sound confident, but he couldn't figure out why the dragon king hadn't reappeared already.

"Sadly, I have figured out why he has not returned. Hel has found a new way to use the rune of the Norns, perthro. The rune normally operates to put a caster in touch with the flow of destiny and the nature of the universe. She has inverted it in a way that forms a barrier. It makes Helheim invisible to anyone outside of it so that the dragon king could not find his way back. Even worse, she has inverted the rune of Yggdrasil, eihwaz, to block magical communication and travel, so that we cannot aid the dragon king nor anyone else. Had the spell been cast any earlier, DL, your mind could not have returned to us from Muspellheim."

"She has never been able to so potently isolate Helheim before," said Thor, looking as if he were not sure what to think.

Freya nodded. "This is yet another reason why Max must be kept out of her hands at all costs. Like Dubh, he is outside the framework of this plane and can potentially disrupt it. He is now master of the runes—and Nidhoggson has access to all that power, as well as whatever unique insight Max might have from his own plane. It must be he who developed this idea. Perhaps he even helped her cast the spell."

"Surely, you can reverse what she has done," said Freyr.

"Probably, but not here, where Hel's power is at its greatest. I would need to be outside to do it."

Freyr turned to the rest of the group. "Then I fear my sister is right. If we stay here, we risk Hel recapturing Max. We need to find Sleipnir and ride back to Asgard as fast as we can."

"I would be compelled to agree—if such a trip were possible," said Morfesa, eyes closes, forehead lined in concentration. "Alas, Hel seems to have blocked that exit as well, at least if I am seeing what I think I am seeing."

"Impossible!" said Freya, closing her own eyes. Her face froze into a mask, and she was under so long she unnerved DL. When she opened her eyes, she looked paler than before.

"The spell must not have completed its work when I first examined it," Freya admitted. "The barrier now blocks physical travel as well as magical. There is literally no way in or out."

"How can such a thing be?" asked Freyr.

"I'm afraid I know," said Maeve. "When Max was first freed after the ritual, he reversed a paralysis Hel had laid on me as ruler of the dead."

"That cannot be," said Freya. "Her rule over the dead is absolute."

"Which means she must have used the ritual to make him coruler," Maeve replied. "He did more than manipulate the runes for her. He interwove them with her innate authority over this world as well. If I'm right, that would make the spell much harder to break, would it not?"

Freya looked defeated. "He could have found a new way to bind her power to the runes, giving each greater scope than either would have individually."

She turned to DL. "For better or worse, you have your wish. We must stay here and try to free Max immediately. If we fail, then all is lost."

THE MAZE

FREYA RAISED them up into the clouds to make it more difficult for Hel to reach them. That was the easy part. The hard part was figuring out how to break Max free from Nidhoggson.

After several hours, even Morfesa and Maeve admitted they had no clue how to end the enchantment.

"It's impossible to tell where Max ends and Nidhoggson begins," conceded Maeve. "They are one being."

"But we're not giving up, right?" asked DL.

"We cannot give up," said Freya. "That doesn't mean we will succeed."

"I can't escape the feeling that we're missing something," said Morfesa. "Any spell that can be done can also be undone. It's just a question of knowing how."

"Which is exactly the problem," said Freya. "What happened to Max is without precedent."

"We do know what happened, though," said Freyr. "In that knowledge surely lies to key to reversing the process."

"That should be so," agreed Freya. "Yet we have tried what we could to undo each of the elements that went into the spell, and still it remains as intact as it was before we started."

"Nidhoggson looks as if he is getting better at resisting the sleep spell," said Thor. Max was quiet before. Now he was twisting and turning as if he were having a nightmare.

"The time will come when he can break free of it," said Freya. "Our only recourse then will be to keep knocking him unconscious."

"Balder!" yelled DL.

"Where?" asked Thor.

"No, he isn't here right now. He's the one thing we haven't considered. He was here when Max went through his ordeal, right? He was lending his strength."

"So I have been told," said Freya slowly. "Balder is a force for good, though. I cannot think his intervention had anything to do with Max becoming Nidhoggson."

"His strength changed me into a Western dragon by accident. Could it be that something he was thinking had a similar, unexpected effect on Max?"

"No," said Maeve. "I was managing the power-sharing both times. With you, I was trying to use Balder's power for something Balder didn't understand. He had a much better grasp of what was happening with Max. Looking back on them, the two experiences felt very different."

"Balder didn't cause Max to become Nidhoggson," agreed Esras. "But you channeled his power through Max's own magic to fool Hel, right? We need to stop thinking about what happened as Balder doing something directly. His power was being wielded by Max at that point. As Max became corrupted, the power he was wielding became corrupted as well."

"Yet it is true we did not consider Balder's role," said Freya. "Whether or not he was the driving force, his power was deeply involved. Perhaps we can succeed if we have his help."

Maeve held up the ring Balder had given her. "This is supposed to summon Balder if I have need of him while I remain in Helheim, but I feel no connection with him now."

"Let me see," said Freya, extending a hand. Maeve dropped the ring in it, and Freya examined the small band closely. A master jeweler could not have been more thorough or precise.

"It is as if the ring has lost whatever magic it had. I cannot feel even the faintest trace of Balder. Fear not, for I shall seek him out." Her eyes closed as she prepared herself for a seidr trance.

DL paced around their cloudy enclosure, waiting for Freya to find Balder. Ekaterina wasn't as prone to nervousness, but she paced with him to keep him company.

Freya opened her eyes. She looked as if she wanted to cry in frustration.

"I cannot find him."

"Is it that unusual rune combination again, the one that seals us in here?" asked Thor.

"No, I doubt she could work that particular magic without Nidhoggson's help. It is a variation of the approach she used to confuse us before. She is obscuring the area where the dead live with such a tangle of their memories that I cannot find Balder."

"Perhaps if you were closer, you could find him," suggested Maeve. "You found your way around Hel's distractions before."

"She was occupied with Max's transformation then," said Freya. "For all we know, she is exerting all her energy to obscure my sight now." She looked nervously over at Max. "In any case, I dare not leave Nidhoggson now that he is so close to breaking free—and I certainly cannot take him any closer to Hel."

"Perhaps I can find him," said Maeve. "I'm dead after all—Hel may not see me coming. Surely, she cannot be muddling things so much that her own dead subjects cannot find their way around."

"She knows you are with us, and she anticipated our need to find Balder," said Freya. "I doubt you will be able to get close to Balder without her knowing."

"Then perhaps I can," said Ekaterina. "I am dead, but not in the way she is used to. Her efforts to block a search for Balder may affect me differently—or not at all."

"I'm not letting you risk yourself without me," said DL. "Hel doesn't understand the power of Eastern dragons. Maybe I can see around her diversions as well."

"It might be worth a try," said Freyr.

"Or it might be handing more hostages to Hel," said Freya.

"I'll take the risk," said DL. "Max would do it for me."

"I'll take the risk as well," said Ekaterina.

"Someone needs to go who knows magic," said Maeve. "Once we find Balder, I can open a portal right back here."

Thor looked at Freya. "It sounds as if they have a chance together."

Freya studied them for a moment. "Unusual abilities and magic from another plane. Hel may not have had time to study these things, and she no longer has Dubh or Nidhoggson to help her. Yes, the plan could succeed. If you are certain this is what you want, I will lower you to the ground. Be wary, though. Hel has not yet exhausted her tricks."

"Take the Sword of Dragon Light," said Freyr, handing the glowing blade to DL. "You will need it more than I."

"May I wield it as well as you have," said DL.

Freya sailed them down on a gentle breeze until their feet touched the ground.

"Balder said there is a Helheim double of Asgard," said Maeve. "If we can avoid Hel's illusions, that should be pretty easy to find, even with the shifting geography."

They walked in the direction of the buildings they could see, mostly old Norse structures, but as they got closer, the structures dissolved into a swirling, multicolored mist that obscured everything else.

"Anybody having better luck than I am with this?" asked DL.

"No," said Ekaterina. "I was wrong to think I'd be immune."

"If I concentrate, I can catch glimpses of a more solid landscape," said Maeve. "I wasn't entirely wrong. Being one of Hel's subjects has its advantages."

Guided by Maeve, they moved forward, but cautiously, as if they were walking through a minefield.

"I'm not seeing any sign of anything that looks remotely like Asgard," said Maeve. "This place keeps pushing Eau Claire at me. That and Hel's static means it could take a long time to find Balder."

"Maybe ordinary vision isn't the best way to do this," said DL. "I know I can see some forms of energy, like heat signatures."

"That's not going to help much with the dead," said Maeve.

DL looked at her, made a silent request to the Yeouiju, and concentrated as hard as he could.

At first, he got only heat signatures. Ekaterina had little, and Maeve even less. However, dragons could sense magic, and he'd certainly seen it as well. The trick would be learning to distinguish among different kinds of magic.

After a while, he could make out the Yeouiju energy inside Ekaterina. He knew that's what it was because he could see it flickering inside himself as well. The Sword of Dragon Light had a similar, but not identical, look to it.

When he looked at Maeve, he could also see something beyond her heat signature. It was clearly magic—but just as clearly different from the magic inside DL and Ekaterina.

"You may be on to something," said Maeve after he told her what he was seeing. She looked around and squinted into the mist. "I should be able to do the same thing, but Hel's interference is feeding me too much data to sort it all out easily. If you take the lead, though, and Ekaterina and I stay close, we just might find Balder. He can't use his own magic, but it's still within him—and strong. I'd guess his signature would be more distinguishable than that of anyone here except Hel's."

"You've seen it," said DL. "Can you show me what it should look like?"

Maeve linked with him, and he saw the powerful, warming glow of Balder.

"Yeouiju, can you amplify my distance vision?"

"I'll do the best I can."

DL's draconic vision stretched farther and farther out. Could it be? Yes! Balder was a long distance away, but DL could just barely make out his glow on the horizon.

"Let's get moving!" he yelled. "I have him!"

He wanted to run at dragon speed. Ekaterina could keep up, and Maeve could fly if need be. Unfortunately, as they moved in Balder's direction, both women were hit with so much visual information that they were effectively blind. DL gave each one a hand and led them as well as he could.

Hel might not be able to dazzle DL in the same way, but she could still manipulate the geography of the place. They walked for what seemed like miles without getting any closer to Balder.

"She's playing with us," said DL, disgusted.

"The change in our environment suggests she knows we're here," said Maeve. "I should have planned for such a thing."

"If she is trying so hard to keep us from Balder, it must mean you're right, DL," said Ekaterina. "Balder must be the key."

"True," said Maeve. "I can't imagine why I ever thought you were stupid." Coming from her, that was almost a compliment. "However, knowing he is critical to us will do us little good if we can't reach him."

"Are you still linked to Balder?" asked DL.

Maeve raised an eyebrow. "If I were, don't you think I would have thought of that already?"

DL shrugged. "I guess. Can Balder see magic, too?"

"Yes, if I recall correctly, he could see it in me right from the start. How does that help us?"

"Maybe we can send him a signal," said DL, waving the Sword of Dragon Light. "I bet the Yeouiju knows how to make this thing flare like the sun."

"I do," said the Yeouiju.

With its help, DL sent a burst of sunlight straight up in the air, whitening the prevailing grayness of the place.

"There's no way he could miss that," said Maeve. "Unless, of course, he wasn't looking in this direction."

DL squinted in the direction of Balder, who seemed to be getting farther away.

"Even if he did see it, he'd probably have no better luck reaching us than we're having in reaching him," said Ekaterina. "We need a way to close that distance."

"Congratulations on stating the obvious," said Maeve. "Now, how do we do that?"

"I have an idea," said DL. "It could be dangerous."

Maeve chuckled. "More dangerous than wandering aimlessly in the land of the dead? You might as well tell us."

"Hel can control the way the land of the dead appears, right?"

"You know she can."

"And we've seen evidence that Max has been given power over the land of the dead, haven't we?"

"Nidhoggson has it, yes," said Maeve. "Even if he were here, I'm sure he wouldn't help us."

"Max and I are connected by the blood bond, and I think being in each other's bodies made that bond stronger. He's out cold right now, but I wonder if we could channel his power to bring us together with Balder."

"I spoke too soon about the stupidity thing," said Maeve.

"I'll forgive you for that dig because I know how worried you are about Max," said DL. "Do you have a better idea?"

"It would be hard to have a worse one. Channeling Max's power without his conscious cooperation would be next to impossible. Even if you could do such a thing, you might be infected by the same evil that corrupts him."

"When Max was in my body, the Yeouiju drew on his magic to try to make my body go full dragon. Max wasn't cooperating then."

Maeve hesitated a moment. "All right, I take back half the stupidity comment. Maybe the Yeouiju could channel some power from an unconscious Nidhoggson. That doesn't mean that power wouldn't infect it—or you."

"Max wasn't draconic. I am. Maybe I can resist where he failed. Regardless, do we have another choice? We need Balder. As long as Hel is playing keep-away with him, we'll never reach him, will we?"

"DL, I want to save Max, too—but not at the risk of destroying you," said Ekaterina.

He turned to her and took her hands in his. "Trust me. I know what I'm doing."

"Do you really?" asked Maeve. "Are you sure you won't destroy yourself—and fail to save Max?"

"You know what? No, I'm not," said DL angrily. "I don't have any idea whether my plan will work or not. But I know trying is the right thing to do.

"Anyway, what do you care if I sacrifice myself for Max?"

"I admit I had my doubts of your worth at first," said Maeve. "I don't any longer."

"Even though I'm stupid."

"Reckless maybe—but never stupid," said Maeve with surprising gentleness. "For someone who knows so little about magic, you have some highly original ideas. That doesn't mean they'll work."

"You can perceive the evil in Max, yes?" Ekaterina asked Maeve.

"Yes, quite clearly."

"Then can you monitor DL and help him break free if something starts to go wrong?"

"Perhaps," Maeve conceded. "If something goes wrong, it may go wrong very fast. There's no guarantee I can break the connection in time."

Ekaterina put her arm around DL. "I've seldom been so apprehensive about anything in my whole life—and you know how long that's been. If DL thinks he can do it, I believe him."

Maeve sighed. "Well, if you're determined to try this no matter what, I will do what I can to assist you. If nothing else, it will give me a great opportunity to say, "I told you so.""

DL smiled. "I'm sure you won't waste a chance like that."

"Yeouiju, I need you to connect me with Max."

"I haven't been able to feel the part of him that is connected to him since he...transformed. I will try."

DL hadn't counted on that, but he wasn't about to let that dash his optimism. "The Yeouiju is working to link us."

Ekaterina hugged him tightly, as if she feared he would be torn away from her at any moment. Maeve didn't react at all.

"I can feel him, but just barely. What would you like me to do, Master?"

DL explained the plan. The Yeouiju didn't convey emotion in the same way a person would, but DL felt nervousness from it.

"I did draw on Max's magic to power a draconic transformation, but what you are asking of me is different. Adapting power for my own purposes is different from using it in a way I could not use my own. I must consider."

"The Yeouiju is working on it," said DL.

"Why does Hel not attack us?" asked Ekaterina, looking around suspiciously.

"Because toying with us is more fun? Because she doesn't see us as a real threat?" asked Maeve. "I don't know. We may need to defend ourselves if DL succeeds."

"When DL succeeds," he said, winking at Maeve. She rolled her eyes.

"If you succeed, we will need to move rapidly. Hel is unlikely to miss what's happening if we start manipulating the environment in ways only she and Nidhoggson can."

"I am trying to transmit the necessary spell and its power from his head to yours. Prepare yourself."

"It's about to happen," said DL.

The power hit his head like a sledgehammer. He staggered and almost lost consciousness. He would have fallen if not for Ekaterina.

He got a glimpse of Max's sleeping mind. No, Nidhoggson's—he couldn't pretend it was Max anymore. The sensation was like staring across a graveyard from which zombies were slowly digging their way to the surface. The vision was tinted venom-green, and above the desolate landscape towered Nidhoggson's inner dragon. It ruled every inch of that twisted mind.

"If you're going to do something, do it!" snapped Maeve. "I don't like what I'm sensing."

"Yeouiju, I don't know how to wield this power. Guide me."

"It is alien to me, but I will try."

If DL had been a spell caster, he might have done better. As it was, he felt like an ape with a laser rifle. He might fire it by accident, but he had no idea how to fire on purpose.

The Yeouiju tried, and the world around DL shifted sickeningly.

Could this be the way the magic was supposed to work? His consciousness faded before he knew the answer.

* * *

A COLD TOUCH like drops of rain hitting Nidhoggson's face awakened him. He could sense hostile spellcasters nearby, though, so he kept his awareness deep within, where they couldn't see.

What was picking away at his mind? The sensation was simultaneously oddly familiar and totally alien. It was not Hel's touch, but it didn't seem threatening, so he ignored it at first.

He stiffened when he felt power draining, but it was only a little, and if he reacted, his enemies would notice, so he let it happen. There would be time enough later for revenge if someone were trying to hurt him.

He had a memory of tossing and turning while under the sleep spell, so he continued those movements. That strategy worked, at least as far as he could tell. No one noticed he was awake.

The fools had left his staff nearby. It was easy to roll just enough to bring it within arm's reach. Nobody noticed when he touched it.

Spellcasting while keeping his consciousness so far inside him was tricky, but not impossible. He had to work very slowly, and he knew he could not aim an aggressive spell at his enemies without alerting them. His only hope was to cast a spell upon himself.

In the air far above, he carved with ior, the rune of the serpent. He felt its touch like a gentle caress, but he held it back from beginning its work upon him until he could accumulate sufficient power to do it quickly.

When the change came, his feeble foes would be unable to stop him.

MIND WAR

DL COULD SEE a glow through his eyelids. He opened his eyes. The glow came from Balder, who was hovering over him worriedly.

"He's awake," said the Aesir, who sounded relieved.

"Get him up!" Maeve said. "Hel will be on us any time."

As Balder lifted him to his feet, DL's mind started working faster. That silver swirl was a portal.

They had Balder, and they were about to rejoin the others. The plan had worked.

He heard running footsteps—lots of them. He glanced in their direction. Hel was using one of her signature moves—a charging horde of undead warriors. They stepped through just before the wave reached them. A howl of frustration echoed in DL's mind as Balder let go of him on the other side.

Freya looked at them uncertainly. "Balder? They found you?"

"It is I," said the Aesir. "I am sorry indeed to awaken your grief again. I had hoped to spare you."

"Grief be damned," said Thor, grabbing his brother. "I can grieve again if it means seeing you again."

"Time is short." Freya explained the situation to Balder. As soon as she was done, he looked at Maeve.

"Join me to you and the others as you have before. If I can do anything to be of help, I will do it."

DL should have felt happy. They had Balder. They could get Max back. For some reason, he felt uneasy instead. Something wasn't right.

He looked down at the distant ground. If Hel was readying an attack, there was no sign of it.

He looked up. There was something forming above them, something green, squirmy and scaly, something powerful.

His mind shifted into nightmare slow-mo. Sluggishly, he looked at Freya and the other spellcasters. Why hadn't they seen? Balder's appearance and the preparation to use his power had distracted them. He wanted to yell, but the sound died in his throat.

He was seeing things through a gradually darkening green overlay.

Max! He was seeing things the way Max now saw them.

No, not Max. He had to stop thinking that way. It was Nidhoggson.

The creature's eyes were open! No one else seemed to realize.

His arms moved as if they had suddenly turned to wood, but DL managed to reach down and draw the Sword of Dragon Light. Its radiance cleared his eyes and gave him back his voice.

"Nidhoggson's awake!" he screamed. Freya started to move, but she was too late. Nidhoggson jumped to his feet. Every inch of him pulsed with power. Everyone could now see the rune above them, throbbing like the beating of a dragon heart.

Nidhoggson moved so fast that even DL was having a hard time keeping up with him. Freya lashed out at him with magic, but he used the rune elhaz to raise a shield before she could strike him. Then he used the rune uruz inverted to shoot magic downward, disrupting the cloudy floor beneath their feet. It was all Freya and the others could do to keep everyone from plummeting to their deaths.

DL didn't know anything about runes. How could he name them just from looking at what Max was doing?

DL's mind was still working sluggishly, but there was only one possible answer—he was still connected to Nidhoggson. Maybe he could use that tie to get the sorcerer back under control.

Events were moving faster than DL could manage, though. To his horror, Thor flung Mjolnir at Nidhoggson, but the sorcerer's body moved so fast it blurred, and the hammer sailed right by him. Before it could return to Thor's hand, Nidhoggson hit him with thurisaz inverted, weakening him.

"*Max!*" thought DL as loudly as he could, but Max must have been buried too far inside Nidhoggson to hear, or, if he did hear, to respond.

The throbbing rune above their heads was supercharging Nidhoggson, giving him enough power to keep pace with the other spellcasters, at least for a little while. Even worse, it was transforming him physically. Scales were forming on his skin. His fingers were growing into claws. His eyes and face were becoming more and more reptilian.

He was becoming a dragon.

DL tried to reach through the connection between them, to dig until he could find Max. Ekaterina sensed what he was doing and grabbed hold of him.

"Draw on me! Take as much of the Yeouiju energy as you need."

DL was not about to drain her back into dormancy, but he tried to gently take what he could. Nidhoggson was too busy fighting everybody else to cut him off, but DL wasn't able to penetrate very far. The parts of Nidhoggson's mind he could reach betrayed no hint of Max.

Morfesa was using the power of Merlin's book to impede Nidhoggson's transformation. Thor had shaken off thurisaz and was pressing Nidhoggson hard with hammer strikes. Freya and the others pounded relentlessly at the sorcerer's defenses. There was no way he could last long against those combined attacks. If they defeated him and rendered him unconscious again, would DL be able to break through and find Max? Probably, but Nidhoggson's frenzied defenses and counter-attacks were escalating the conflict to a level at which he might easily be killed by accident.

Nidhoggson's transformation had slowed to a crawl, but he had managed to sprout wings. They didn't look big enough to support someone his size in the air, but the sorcerer launched himself backward and flew shakily away. The dragon rune moved with him, continuing to feed him power. Thor took another shot and missed.

Once Nidhoggson had put some distance between him and Morfesa, his transformation speeded up. He was visibly larger, and his wingspan widened. He turned and sped away.

"Why aren't you following him?" DL asked Freya.

"I cannot hope to match his speed," she said. "I could let my mind follow him with the speed of thought, but he grows more powerful by the second. Keeping up with him would not be enough, and I have no sure way to defeat him."

Maeve looked frantic. "We can channel all the power we have through you. All of us together can recapture him."

Freya shook her head. "By the time we can organize that, he will be a full-fledged dragon. The only way to defeat him then will be to kill him."

"Which we will have to do," said Thor. "We cannot allow a being as powerful as Nidhogg—perhaps more powerful—to run free. He is not bound by destiny as Nidhogg is. He could destroy the equilibrium of the Nine Worlds."

"Wait!" yelled DL. "You can't kill him!"

"I know how strong your bond is with your friend," said Freya gently. "By the time Nidhoggson completes his transformation, Max will be dead for all practical purposes."

"That's just it," said DL. "I have a bond with him, a connection I made to use his power to help us find Balder. If you all lend me your strength, I can reach inside his mind and help Max regain control."

"I can bind all of you to DL in about a minute or so," said Maeve. "Some of you are bound already."

"Max is a worthy warrior," said Balder. "We should at least try to save him."

"Agreed," said Freya. "The bonds between such friends as they are strong." She closed her eyes. "The magical bond is there, just as DL said. Let us make haste, though. We have only minutes at most."

Maeve worked faster than DL had ever seen her do before, and more power surged into him than he had ever felt. Even being a full dragon had not been this much of a high. Morfesa had found a way to pull the power of Merlin's grimoire into the bond.

Nidhoggson was far away by that point, but DL had no trouble using the bond to find him. This time, though, the sorcerer didn't have to fend off other attacks. He could focus his strong will exclusively against DL's efforts to find Max.

DL would have despaired if not for the power the others were sharing with him. He was digging slowly—but he was digging. He could feel Nidhoggson's surprise.

"Get out of my mind, or I will crush you!" The words echoed like a dragon's booming voice, but DL ignored them.

A barrier that was the mental equivalent of solid stone formed in front of him. He couldn't dig through it at first, but then he remembered what Max had told him about how much magic was a question of visualization. DL pictured himself wielding Thor's hammer, and he smashed his way through the stone. Nidhoggson howled.

DL still couldn't sense Max, but he must be making progress. He could feel Nidhoggson's panic washing over him in cold, acidic waves.

Suddenly, DL was back at about age ten, being bullied by other kids at school. He felt small and alone. How could he save Max when he couldn't save himself?

Max…he had told Max about those experiences. To attack him with them, Nidhoggson had to be drawing on Max's memories. That meant his friend was still here somewhere.

DL disbelieved the scene with all his might, and it melted away. However, it was immediately replaced by another one—the day DL dropped out of high school.

His foster parents had let him. Either they'd given up on him, or they'd never believed in him in the first place. He knew what they thought. They were sure he'd never amount to anything.

They were right. He couldn't even save his friend.

Cold. It was colder than it should have been in the school office. Where was it coming from?

He remembered. He wasn't in the school office. That had happened years ago. Somewhere, miles from where his mind was, someone was hugging his body closely. Ekaterina had wrapped him in her cold arms and was anchoring him to the present.

He was no longer in the school office. He was with Max, and Max was again nagging him about getting his high school equivalency.

"You've got to get past this idea that you're not smart enough," said Max. "Intelligence isn't the problem. It's self-image."

The words were familiar, but something about the scene was wrong. Max looked so sad. He looked as if he would never see DL again.

This wasn't just a memory. Present Max was in here somehow. It was his current sorrow DL was feeling.

"Max, take my hand!" DL reached toward Memory Max, knowing Present Max was in him somewhere. Suddenly, Max was farther away, so distant he was small, almost invisible.

DL could feel Nidhoggson recovering. He had slipped for a moment, but now he was clamping down on Max, shutting him so deep inside his mind that DL could never find him.

He needed a new strategy, but what could it be?

Nidhoggson was exerting all his effort to keep DL from pulling Max out and giving him control. Could the sorcerer watch everything else in his head, though? Where could DL hit and do some damage while Nidhoggson was busy trying to lock up Max and throw away the key?

That serpent rune was fueling the transformation. DL knew it was glowing somewhere above Nidhoggson's body, but the magic that ran it was in Nidhoggson's head. That meant it was within DL's reach—if he could find it.

DL had been connected to powerful spellcasters before, even Merlin, but he had sensed mostly feelings and memories. Where in this labyrinth did the magic live?

"Freya, can you guide me to where Nidhoggson's knowledge of the runes is?"

She responded, and he let her steer. He was so used to fighting for every inch that he was surprised at how easily he slid toward his goal. Nidhoggson, caught off-guard, wasn't adjusting fast enough to his new strategy.

There it was—the serpent rune, twisting like a living thing deep within Nidhoggson's mind. Its power was immense—but so were the forces backing him.

He felt as if he were wrestling an actual serpent. It coiled around him like a giant boa constrictor and spewed venom at him.

The venom infected him, but it receded. Through him, Freya projected the serpent rune inverted, draining the power of the original.

Nidhoggson's unearthly roar of pain deafened DL, but he kept fighting the serpent, strangling it with his bare hands. Nidhoggson coun-

tered, and the serpent grew larger and stronger, shaking off the inverted
rune that had inhibited it.

"Master, you can win faster if you become the dragon."

Becoming the dragon physically required huge energy the broken-up
Yeouiju couldn't provide. Becoming a dragon in this mental world took
far less.

DL went full-dragon with a triumphant roar. The shocked serpent
rune tried to hold him, but he broke away, then rent it over and over
with his claws. As its power faded, he bit its head off.

The manifestation of the rune that had been providing dragon power
flickered and dissolved.

Nidhoggson screamed again, this time in agony. His body, almost
but not quite that of a dragon, convulsed in a desperate attempt to
complete the cycle.

Still the stubborn sorcerer held him back from Max. If DL couldn't
break through, Nidhoggson was physically far enough away from Freya
and the others to run away successfully. Sooner or later he would figure
out how to sever his bond with DL. Rescuing Max was now or never.

Were the runes all in the same headspace? DL remembered Freya's
conversation about how Hel was using perthro, rune of the Norns, to
keep Yong-Wang from finding Helheim.

If Freya was right, she had learned this new trick from Nidhoggson.
He also shared her power over the land of the dead. What she could do,
she could undo—and so could he.

Unfortunately, this time he couldn't just bash the rune with brute
force. There was no guarantee that would break the ongoing concealment spell over Helheim. What he needed was the knowledge of how to
counter it so that he could pass the details on to Freya.

Freya guided him to perthro. If ior was enormous, perthro was
cosmically vast, encompassing the destiny that flowed throughout the
Nine Worlds. It appeared to him as three old women. It wasn't the real
Norns, but it echoed them—or they echoed it. DL didn't care which. All
he cared about was getting from it what he wanted to know.

He tried to use his draconic form to intimidate the rune, but it stood
firm against him. He clawed and bit at it, but it remained implacable.

He could feel the convulsions subsiding. Nidhoggson would soon be able to devote his attention to getting rid of DL. He had to get the information he needed before that.

"Freya, help me."

The Vanir imbued his mental limbs with the essence of perthro. It could resist him, but it could not tolerate the paradox of resisting itself. It writhed, it protested—but eventually, it gave in.

DL himself couldn't understand the answer, but Freya could interpret the combination of runes and thoughts he was able to pass along to her. She lacked Hel's power over Helheim, but she could tap into Nidhoggson's power much as DL had earlier.

Nidhoggson roared, throwing everything he had into driving DL out, but it was too late. Through Freya, DL felt the barrier Hel had woven between her realm and the rest of the Nine Worlds dissolving like morning mist.

Nidhoggson roared again, and DL felt pressure all around him, as if he were being crushed.

"You should withdraw," thought Freya. *"You have done all you can."*

"Not yet. We don't have Max back yet. Yeouiju, is Yong-Wang coming?"

"He is on his way, Master."

"Freya, I must hold on until he gets here. Otherwise, Niddhoggson will make a run for it."

He felt as if he were buried under a hundred tons of concrete.

Could Nidhoggson drive him mad this way? Kill him?

He had to hold on. He let go of the dragon and visualized himself as tiny, as microscopic, as something concrete was too clumsy to crush.

Trying to keep pace with him, Nidhoggson's attack no longer felt like concrete. It morphed into mental antibiotic, killing him like an infection. He shifted his mental form again, this time mimicking one of Nidghoggson's own brain cells, so that attacking DL would be to attack himself.

That was a mistake. In his supercharged form, his mind implemented what he was seeing too literally. Suddenly, he was part of Nidhoggson's brain, and Nidhggoson's evil infected him.

Deep within the howling abyss that was Nidhoggson's mind, though, DL sensed Max for the first time since Nidhoggson had locked him away. His friend was distant, barely perceptible, but he was still there.

"You must withdraw," thought Freya. *"I can feel you fading."*

"Can you do for me what you did for Ekaterina with Brisingamen?" That spell had brought him under control when he was a Western dragon—why wouldn't the same thing work for Max?

DL could feel the pulsing of alien dragon thoughts within him. Soon they would become him, and he would become them.

"That particular spell only works between people who are romantically involved. I could craft an alternative that would work among close friends, but not in the time we have."

"Awaken Adreanna and use her as a link to Max for the spell."

"I do not even know if she loves him—"

"Just do it!" snapped DL. That probably wasn't the best way to address a former goddess, but time was short. It was getting harder to tell where he ended and Nidhoggson began.

He doubted he could pull out now even if he wanted to. He was "all in" in every sense of the phrase.

He felt a burst of Brisingamen's golden power, but it was aimed at him, not Max.

Ekaterina was with him, holding him again, pulling him back from raving savagery.

Nidhoggson tried to crush this new invasion of his mind, but the magic was too strong for him to counter in his weakened and confused condition.

DL felt another presence nearby. It was timid and confused. It was frightened.

It was Adreanna. Even with Freya doing whatever she could do to keep her calm, she felt as if she were barely clinging to sanity.

"I don't…I don't know what to do!"

"Think of Max," thought DL as loudly as he could. *"Think of Max and reach out to him."*

"I can't. I don't know how."

"You don't know how to think? Look, Max is in this mess because he wanted to rescue you." DL projected to her an image of frantic Max throwing caution to the wind to search for her. *"The least you can do is try!"*

"It is not so hard," thought Ekaterina, compensating for DL's anger

with a more soothing vibe. *"Remember what Max means to you, the good times you've had. Visualize him here with you and reach out to him."*

DL was beginning to wonder what Max saw in Adreanna. She didn't seem nearly as intelligent as he was. DL had to remind himself how much trouble he had figuring out the supernatural world when he had first been plunged into it.

Whether she really was an airhead or genius overwhelmed by the world turning suddenly upside down, she needed to get her act together. Fighting off Nidhoggson was becoming more and more difficult.

"I'll try," Adreanna thought. The power of Brisingamen increased, but it was more like an extra candle flicker than a spotlight sending its radiance toward Max.

"Let me guide you," thought Ekaterina.

"She needs to hurry the hell up!" said DL. He was still himself, but Nidhoggson was attacking with renewed strength. DL could still feel Ekaterina's psychic embrace and the power of Brisingamen, but the urge to lash out at his former friends was screaming inside his mind more and more loudly. No, it was roaring like a dragon. Like his dragon. No, not his, not yet.

DL managed to push the toxic fog of Nidhoggson's thoughts back a little, but how long could he keep that up?

Max's knowledge—Nidhoggson's knowledge—was seeping further and further into DL's mind. The experience was a little like Max's when he was tied to Yggdrasil's root. Earlier, DL had gotten enough of a glimpse to give Freya the information she needed. Now, he was experiencing the runes much more intimately, as if he could actually wield their power himself—if there were still a *himself* left.

Yong-Wang must be pretty close by now, but DL couldn't be sure he'd arrive in time. Adreanna's fumbling attempts to reach Max were proceeding with agonizing slowness. DL knew Freya was out there somewhere, but he couldn't seem to communicate with her anymore.

What about those runes? If he used them, that might pull him the rest of the way into Nidhoggson. If he didn't try, though, he might be throwing away his last chance to escape that fate.

"I have you," thought Ekaterina. *"You will not slip away completely as long as I hold you. Do what you need to do."*

DL felt her psychic arms and knew what she said was the truth. Nidhoggson was trying to fool him. He, not his poor, corrupted friend, was still the master of his own mind.

He had to act fast to prevent Nidhoggson from interfering. He knew the runes so well now that it was as if he'd spent years learning them. He grabbed the power of kenaz, which was the fire of creation but also the fire of passionate love. He also got a grip on gebo, the rune that could bind people to create a power greater than themselves—particularly a sexual pair. He tied them together with the power of wunjo, the rune that unites both people and forces.

Nidhoggson tried to stop him, but his interference came too late. DL sent the full force of that runic combination into Adreanna, transforming her in ways even he hadn't anticipated. The golden power of Brisingamen lit her up like a miniature sun, and her light tore through the darkness of Nidhoggson's mind, lighting up every corner until it found Max.

Nidhoggson screamed and did what he could to hold Max down, but the combination of Freya's power with DL's use of Nidhoggson's own power against him was too much to resist. Max tore free from his grip and became larger. Nidhoggson shrank at the same time. Max was a colossus. Nidhoggson was a microbe. With a final, whispered scream, Nidhoggson vanished.

Max took control of his own body. Freya allowed the magic of Brisingamen to dissipate, and DL, Ekaterina, and Adreanna slowly returned to their own bodies.

DL wished he had moved back faster. If he had, he might not have sensed the nightmarish truth.

Nidhoggson's controlling presence had been destroyed—for the moment. He was still there, though. DL could feel him buried deep inside Max, waiting.

THE COURSE OF TRUE LOVE NEVER DID RUN SMOOTH

DL RETURNED to his own body to find himself surrounded by a flurry of activity. Yong-Wang had belatedly arrived and urged everyone to climb onto his back as quickly as possible. No one gave him any argument. The sooner they got away from Hel and her tricks, the better they would feel.

Maeve should not have been able to leave without Hel's permission. Max, looking as worn out as if he had not slept in days, was still Hel's proxy, and freed his grandmother. Her body would dissolve as soon as she left Helheim, but her spirit would be free to return to its proper plane.

"Let us make haste before Hel countermands that order," said Freya.

DL couldn't understand why Hel didn't reverse Maeve's release immediately. Perhaps she was as stunned as Max looked.

Yong-Wang flew them back to where Sleipnir waited patiently. Freya, Freyr, Gerda, and Thor mounted him for the return trip to Álfheim. The others stayed on Yong-Wang, who slowed himself to keep pace with the horse as they traveled up Yggdrasil to the upper branch from which Alfheim was suspended.

Morfesa had no trouble using Merlin's book to lift the spell Dubh had placed on the exits. They could return any time they wanted—after they dug themselves out of all of their other complications.

Max took a lot of time thanking everyone individually. That should have been a happy time, but he looked haunted. DL knew he had reason to look that way. He hadn't been able to make himself raise the subject with Max, but the guy now had an inner dragon—one not as benign as DL's. How were they going to deal with that?

Freya surprised Max by handing him the staff Sindr had given him. "The duergar king was wiser than he knew when he bestowed this on you."

"I fear I am not worthy of it," said Max, raising his hands as if to refuse.

Freya laughed so hard she shook. Poor Max looked completely confused.

"If you are not worthy of it, I do not know who is. You have proven yourself both brave and wise."

"But...but—"

"You can feel the dragon within. Nidhoggson is not gone," said Freya. "I know that."

"I told you when I took you from the tree that you would never be the same," said Yong-Wang.

"Indeed, the change that vile ritual wrought upon you is in some ways irrevocable," said Freya. "Nidhoggson can be defeated, but he cannot be destroyed without destroying you.

"That does not mean you are unworthy. It means you will have to be ever vigilant to prevent Nidhoggson from taking control. That is why you need my staff more than I do.

"The runes have power for good in the same way they would in the hands of anyone else who knew their secrets. However, each time you use them, Nidhoggson will become that much stronger."

"Then I shouldn't use them?" asked Max. DL couldn't tell whether he was relieved or disappointed.

Freya shook her head. "They are part of you now. You *will* use them, whether you wish it or not. The trick will be using them with greater care. Channeling their power through the staff will help, for it remains uncorrupted by the ritual. You may have Nidhogg's venom in you, but when you hold the staff, you have unpolluted wood of Yggdrasil in your hand. You have my blood as well, painted into the runes, and that is no small thing. It will reinforce your already considerable willpower, and with it, you can keep Nidhogg at bay."

"You can do it," said Ekaterina. "I do it every day...with the bloodlust."

"Merlin did it every day as well," said Esras, "and he also lived for centuries. Remember he was both the son of Satan and the intended antichrist, but he chose a different path, though every step along it drove iron spikes into his feet."

"If he could do it, so can you," said Morfesa.

"I hadn't thought about that," said Max. "I remember feeling some of that struggle when he was sharing a body with me."

"There, you see," said Maeve with affected cheerfulness. "Nothing to worry about."

"I will help you all I can," said Morfesa. "Unless you think you've outgrown me as a tutor."

"Are you kidding?" asked Max. "Yeah, I know runic magic backwards and forwards, but I'm still working on Celtic magic. I can't even open a portal. Besides, I need your wisdom now more than ever."

Morfesa smiled. DL couldn't help noticing that Max made an effort to smile but didn't quite make it.

"I would make the same offer, but it is best if you do not return to the Nine Worlds," said Freya. "The power of the runes is greatest here. You will find it easier to remain balanced on your own plane of existence. Besides, we now know how dangerous someone from another plane can be here if that person has enough power. Hel and others would be bound to try to use you to disrupt destiny again."

"A shame," said Freyr. "You make an excellent comrade-in-arms. I will miss the opportunity to fight by your side again."

"As will I," said Thor.

"You will be missed as well," said Freya, looking at DL and Ekaterina. "You are both valiant and wise."

"You're giving me more praise than I deserve," said DL.

Freya laughed again, and this time even DL smiled, though Max's face remained limp. "How little you appreciate your own merits. You are a quick and clever thinker. No one without those traits could have so rapidly adapted to the trials you faced. The way you used Nidhoggson's own magic against him was brilliant."

"Maybe now you'll think about that high school equivalency test," said Max. His voice was almost emotionless, as if he were going through the motions.

"He will heal," Ekaterina whispered to DL as if she knew what he was thinking. "He has been through a great ordeal. Give him time."

"If I may, Lady Freya, I wish to say a few words," said Yong-Wang.

DL's heart skipped a beat. Was the dragon king about to pass judgment on him? On Ekaterina?

"I promised I would study your situation, and I have. I have to say that I never been so disappointed." As if he was going to enjoy destroying DL, the dragon king smiled incongruously.

DL froze. Was this the last moment of life as he knew it? How would Yong-Wang punish him?

He stood taller. Whatever happened, he would not give up Ekaterina. If that made an enemy of the dragon king, so be it.

"I am usually a better judge of character," said Yong-Wang. "I am disappointed in myself."

"What?" muttered DL.

"From the moment you accepted me in my Outcast disguise into your group, you and your friends strived to help others, even at the risk of your own lives. Time after time after time I saw it. When I could not be with you, the Yeouiju kept track of all your deeds for me.

"Even when I tested you by making you doubt your friends, you evaded my traps and found your way back to them."

"That…that was you? You made me jealous?"

Yong-Wang raised one of his spiky eyebrows. "It gives me sorrow to admit to it, but at the time I was not yet sure of you. I had to exert great power to twist you so much, yet in the end, I could not overcome your natural loyalties. That gave me another reason to appreciate your value.

"I must speak again of the Yeouiju. You have worked some kind of miracle. It is supposed to be an extension of its dragon. In breaking yours, I thought you had mutilated a part of yourself. Yet your Yeouiju did not remain a shattered remnant of its former self. Nor is it just a part of you any longer.

"It is less powerful in some respects—but in others, it is evolving in ways no Yeouiju has done before. In trying to follow your commands, it has stretched itself in new directions. It has learned how to perform tasks for which it was never intended. It has become independent.

"What good it may do remains to be seen, but it has greater potential than it did before you broke it. I have no desire to see its evolution ended. Nor do I wish you to live in my realm as I once did. You will do more good right where you are, and your friend will need you now that he, too, is in some sense a dragon."

"Thank...thank you," said DL. He bowed stiffly. He wanted to say more, but the words wouldn't come.

He had one more chance just before they were ready to leave. He felt a tap on his shoulder and turned to see a distinguished old man with a grandfatherly smile, flowing robes, a long white beard, and bushy eyebrows.

"Yong-Wang?" asked DL.

"You knew dragons always had two forms. In Korea, I am mostly thought of in my human form. I thought it was fitting you see it before I left."

"You seem...somehow familiar. I've never studied Korean culture, though, so where would I have seen you?"

"You need to study your culture," said the dragon king sternly. More lightly, he added, "You may have known someone like me once...long ago.

"You wish to remain on Earth, do you not?"

Caught off guard, DL said, "I...uh...yes. I don't mean any disrespect, but all my friends are there. The closest thing I have to family is there as well."

Yong-Wang sighed. "In truth, you belong there, though the path destiny has placed you on saddens me."

DL raised an eyebrow. "Why?"

"To answer that, I must tell you a story. Once, long ago, a great evil pursued my son and his wife. Cut off from my kingdom, they made their way to Earth, where they had a son. However, their pursuers caught up with them. The only way to keep their son safe was to flee and draw the evil ones away from their child.

"Daelun Yong, I didn't know you existed until your power awakened, and even then I was not sure who you were. I would have claimed you long ago had I known, but now it is too late."

"You're…my grandfather?" asked DL.

"I am. I thought you should know. Our worlds are far apart now. I cannot visit yours for long, and I cannot take you to mine without doing you and others a great injury. Perhaps it would have been better if I had stayed silent, but I could not bear to have you keep on thinking your parents had abandoned you. They had to leave you behind to keep you safe."

Impulsively, DL hugged the dragon king. Yong-Wang hugged him back—until he was no longer there. He just vanished. Talk about not liking long good-byes.

DL felt cheated, but a voice in his head whispered, *"I dared not stay longer. It would only have made our parting more painful or even diverted you from the path you must walk. Know that I will always be with you, though you will seldom see or even sense me."*

All choked up, DL looked in the direction of the mound portal through which the dragon king must have fled. Damn Esras for opening it so early!

He didn't realize Max had walked close enough to hear most of the conversation until Max sang, "You are the dragon prince!" He was off-key, to say the least, and that was possibly the worst parody of "I Am the Pirate King," anyone had ever heard. Gilbert and Sullivan must both have turned over in their graves.

DL forgave him, though, because, for the first time in a long time, Max was smiling. It was a little smile, but it gave him hope Max really was going to heal.

Adreanna, also willing to forgive the butchering of classic show tunes, walked up behind Max and pulled him into her arms.

To think DL had once questioned that she loved Max. There was no question now. She looked at Max the way Ekaterina looked at DL.

Max wasn't really hugging back and looked awkward in her arms. Even she noticed, though she pretended not to.

As soon as DL got the chance, he pulled Max aside. "What's up, man? You're treating Adreanna like someone you wish would go away."

Max looked into DL's eyes. "I'm not the person she fell in love with. I don't know that I can be."

DL was about to say something reassuring, but the words died on his lips.

The dragon Nidhoggson was looking out at him through Max's eyes.

That horrifying gaze only lasted a second, and then Max was back. Now DL understood, though.

Max was afraid of what Nidhoggson would do to her if he ever got out.

"We'll beat this together," he said to Max.

"Indeed, we will," said Ekaterina, walking over to them. "Is there anything in the universe we can't beat?"

DL hadn't been superstitious before, but he felt a chill run down his spine.

They had been doing amazingly well, and he prayed that their luck would hold.

The universe was a pretty big place, though. Who knew what might be lurking just around the corner?

ABOUT THE AUTHOR

As far back as he can remember, Bill Hiatt had a love for reading so intense that he eventually ended up owning over eight thousand books-- not counting e-books! He has also loved to write for almost that long. As an English teacher, he had little time to write, though he always felt there were stories within him that longed to get out, and he did manage to publish a few books near the end of his teaching career. Now that he is retired from teaching, the stories are even more anxious to get out into the world, and they will not be denied

For more information, visit
https://www.billhiatt.com

BOOKS AND BOOKLETS BY BILL HIATT

Spell Weaver Series

(Shorts set in the Spell Weaver universe are inserted where they belong in the storyline but are not numbered.)

"Echoes of My Past Lives" (0)

Living with Your Past Selves (1)

Divided against Yourselves (2)

Hidden among Yourselves (3)

"Destiny or Madness"

"Angel Feather"

Evil within Yourselves (4)

We Walk in Darkness (5)

Separated from Yourselves (6)

Different Dragons

Different Lee (1)

Soul Switch (2)

Soul Salvager Series

Haunted by the Devil (1, also includes *The Devil Hath the Power*, originally published separately)

Mythology Book (hybrid mythology text/young adult urban fantasy)

A Dream Come True: An Entertaining Way

for Students to Learn Greek Mythology

Anthologies

[The name(s) of the piece(s) by Bill Hiatt are in parentheses following the anthology name.]

Anthologies of the Heart, Book 1: Where Dreams and Visions Live

("The Sea of Dreams")

Flash Flood 2: Monster Maelstrom, A Flash Fiction Halloween Anthology

("In the Eye of the Beholder")

Flash Flood 3: Christmas in Love, A Flash Fiction Anthology

("Naughty or Nice?" and "Entertaining Unawares")

Hidden Worlds, Volume 1: Unknown, a Sci-Fi and Fantasy Anthology

("The Worm Turns" and "Abandoned")

Great Tomes Series, Book 6: The Great Tome of Magicians, Necromancers, and Mystics

("Green Wounds")

Education-related Titles

"A Parent's Guide to Parent-Teacher Communications"

"A Teacher's Survival Guide for Writing College Recommendations"

"Poisoned by Politics: What's Wrong with

Education Reform and How To Fix It"